FINAL
TRANSGRESSION

One Woman's Tragic Destiny
in War-torn France

HARRIET WELTY ROCHEFORT

Praise for
FINAL TRANSGRESSION

In this gripping, beautifully written novel about love and betrayal, Harriet Welty Rochefort vividly portrays the ambiguity and complexity of trying to survive in Nazi-occupied France, where things are never quite what they seem. The story of Séverine Sevanot, a beautiful, headstrong young woman who returns to her hometown in southwest France only to be swept up in the violent score-settling of resistance fighters there, will grab your attention and keep you thinking for a long time to come.

–Lynne Olson, *New York Times* bestselling author of
Madame Fourcade's Secret War

Harriet Welty Rochefort's historically well-grounded *Final Transgression* starts with rural tranquility and accelerates to a shocking end as a young woman's high spirits entangle her in the turmoil of Nazi-occupied France. A vigorous and compelling tale.

–Robert O. Paxton, author of *Vichy France:
Old Guard and New Order*

In her elegant and often moving book, *Final Transgression*, Harriet Welty Rochefort looks beyond the political and military headlines of World War II to probe individual lives and uncover how the German occupation of France poisoned friendships, shattered loves and forged bitter memories better forgotten.

–Alan Riding, author of *And The Show Went On:
Cultural Life in Nazi-occupied Paris*

In *Final Transgression*, Harriet Welty Rochefort has written a compelling novel of the cultural and political trials undergone by France during the first half of the 20th century. Her deep knowledge of France and intermixing of the events and the texture that defined the 1930s and 1940s—clothes, behavior, decor, everyday life in general—engage while subtly instructing the reader. *Final Transgression* succeeds admirably in edifying while moving its readers.

–Ronald C. Rosbottom, author of *When Paris Went Dark* and *Sudden Courage*

This story lays bare the ugliness of war and what people resort to in wartime, but in fleshing out her characters with sympathy for human frailty, the author enables the reader to put himself or herself in their shoes. *Final Transgression* does a wonderful job of unraveling the complicated web of local factions that clashed under the Nazi occupation of France and the hotheaded heroine seemed almost doomed from the start - there were times I wanted to chime in and steer her away from her own actions as she hurtled headlong towards her fate. A great read.

–Lilianne Milgrom, artist and author of *L'Origine*

With her deep knowledge of France and the French, Harriet Welty Rochefort gives readers a fresh tale about the endlessly fascinating period of French history, the second world war. Through a cast of characters ranging from local nobility to a family of caretakers, *Final Transgression* gives an intimate portrait of French society, with its strict codes and class resentments. Set between Paris and a small town in the southwest of France, the story draws the reader into the intrigues of the war and its devastating effects on everyone, even the many who just wanted to get through it.

The secrets that this murky time generated touch the lives of generations to come. Harriet Welty Rochefort paints this complex tableau with a fine brush and a great deal of humanity.

–Mary Fleming, author of *The Art of Regret*
and *Someone Else*

I found it easy to lose myself while reading *Final Transgression*, which begins with an apparently mundane television interview and quickly turns into an ultimate page turner. Harriet Welty Rochefort's novel explores the overpowering and often paralyzing class differences that existed in pre-war France. The vivacious heroine of the story is oblivious to the earthshaking events taking place around her. Her sparkling sense of independence and refusal to make concessions propel her towards her inevitable destiny. Harriet Welty Rochefort has spent several decades observing the intricate details of French culture and is uniquely qualified to write this story.

–William Dowell, former *Time* magazine
correspondent and bureau chief

In a taut tale of love, war and politics, Harriet Welty Rochefort's gripping novel of entangled families and deep friendships brings powerfully to life Paris and the Périgord, before and during WW2 and the Occupation.

–Martin Walker, author of the Bruno detective series

Also by Harriet Welty Rochefort

French Toast:
An American in Paris Celebrates the Maddening Mysteries of the French

French Fried:
The Culinary Capers of an American in Paris

Joie De Vivre:
Secrets of Wining, Dining, and Romancing Like the French

FINAL TRANSGRESSION

One Woman's Tragic Destiny
in War-torn France

A NOVEL

HARRIET WELTY ROCHEFORT

UNDERSTAND FRANCE, PARIS

UNDERSTAND FRANCE, PARIS, 2020

Print ISBN: 978-2-9572444-0-9

ebook ISBN: 978-2-9572444-1-6

For Philippe

PROLOGUE

Marnes-la-Coquette: June 1994

Félix Aubry pushed open the gate to his mother's house. As he strode past the pink rose bush in full bloom towards the small flight of stone stairs that led to the main door of the charming little ivy-covered cottage, a familiar mix of smells hit him. He stood still for a moment, breathing in the heady combination of the delicate Antoine Ducher roses and the sweet summer smell of apricots. His mother must be cooking; she adored stewing fresh fruit. Laced in with that seductive odor was the faint and slightly acrid scent of oils. She was working on a new painting—perhaps a still life of apricots, he thought, although she'd spent her days as a copyist in the great museums. Caroline Aubry didn't see a difference between the noble and the mundane. A bowl of apricots was as interesting to her as a portrait of a prince.

If he'd been alone, Félix might have sneaked up to the kitchen window, maybe give her a bit of a scare before bursting into the house like he used to when he was little. Caroline had loved the game then, reacting in mock horror to his scary face. Older now and more fragile, she would have been a little embarrassed to think that someone, even her own grown-up son, had been secretly observing her. Félix stopped, although he knew he could get away with just about anything as long as he showed respect. Respect, she had taught him, meant removing your hat when entering a house (he automatically took his off before getting to the front door), standing up when an adult enters the room, and other such prescriptions he had found ridiculous when young but was now happy to have acquired, especially when he saw the boorish conduct of some of his colleagues.

He turned to his companion, who had plunged his prominent nose into one of the pink roses. "Well, here we are!" he exclaimed.

"That smell—all those smells—delicious!" Kirk Morland said, laughing as he straightened up and threw his stylish linen jacket casually over one shoulder. Félix and Kirk had met a year earlier, covering events leading to the fiftieth anniversary of the D-Day landings. They had become almost inseparable despite their differences. Félix was a Frenchman of medium build, with sandy hair and blue eyes. Kirk was American, well over six feet tall, with dark eyes and hair that was almost black. He was the anchorman for a prominent U.S. television station, and Félix was a freelance cameraman who worked for a number of American news organizations. Félix admired Kirk's professionalism and his fluent, if accented, French. Kirk, for his part, admired Félix's sense of humor, his self-deprecating nature and perfect English.

When Kirk had told Félix that his network was scheduling a program about what ordinary French people had been doing on D-Day, Félix had quite unexpectedly proposed his mother as an interviewee.

"She lived through the war. She's quite elegant, and she looks very French."

Kirk had raised his eyebrows at the last comment—a lot of French people looked very French, it went with the territory. But since Félix had helped him whenever he'd needed to find out who was who in the tightly knit world of French politics, Kirk had readily agreed. Félix had gone on to tell him more about his mother: how she'd raised him alone; how she'd undertaken to teach him everything from painting to gardening to cooking and how, in spite of her age, she lived in the present, not the past.

The description he gave piqued Kirk's interest. He told Félix that he'd very much like to hear her comments, and perhaps her reflections on what it was like to live through a war and whether it had changed her life. Seeing Félix's look of discomfort, Kirk reassured him that they could always edit her interview if she went on for too long. Either way it would be fascinating material. Millions of viewers would tune in to hear real life stories from people who'd been alive during the war.

Kirk had been surprised when Félix insisted that his mother speak to him and no one else. Perhaps she was shy, or maybe too many other reporters had been pestering her. It was none of his business; he simply hoped that she'd be photogenic, and he'd get a few good anecdotes from an ordinary person who had lived through extraordinary times. He was pleased with this new angle: a novel subject, a good profile of a dignified French woman in her home, a bit of vicarious self-identification for the viewers as they wondered what they'd have done in her place. Wasn't that the business of TV news? Maybe she would tear up—cry even. Emotion, that was the ticket.

The sound of footsteps interrupted Kirk's thoughts. The lacquered green door opened, and a slightly built and slender woman stepped out into the porchway. She was perfect; her silver hair gave her a dignified air and her blue eyes sparkled with a lively intelligence. She hugged Félix and shook Kirk's hand formally after the introductions had been made. As they all stepped into the small vestibule and began making small talk, Kirk transformed automatically into reporter mode, gauging how well her low and well-modulated voice, her quintessentially French appearance and demeanor (Félix had been right about that) would play. He knew immediately that she would play very well indeed.

Even at her advanced age, Félix's mother stood straight. She smelled of an exotic perfume and was stylishly dressed in what looked to Kirk like a Chanel suit, although he employed a fashion correspondent to make observations like that. She was the kind of woman people describe as poised and elegant, Kirk mused. She'd have turned heads in her youth, and she still had that indefinable presence that would be perfect for the camera.

Kirk turned his attention away from Madame Aubry and looked around the small vestibule; every object in it seemed to have been carefully chosen. On the shelves were leather-bound copies of books by Racine, Balzac and Victor Hugo as well as a few *objets* and carefully framed photos. Madame Aubry ushered them into the main part of the house, and again Kirk was quietly impressed: it didn't correspond to his preconceptions of old lady decor. He'd imagined dinginess, musty unpleasant odors and dusty, worn antique furniture crowded into small rooms. Instead, bouquets of fresh flowers from the garden perfumed the air. The walls of the ground-floor rooms were painted a refined and restful shade of pale rose; the sofas, which faced each other in front of the fireplace, were dove gray, and the only older pieces of furniture were a marble-topped console on which a group of silver-framed photos was aligned, and at one end of the sitting room a pair of chairs he couldn't identify: Louis, probably, but which one? He'd have to ask Félix. He had the feeling Caroline was reading his mind as she indicated one of the Louis something-or-other chairs to him.

"Please do sit down, Mr. Morland. I have to apologize for my poor English," Caroline said, looking Kirk directly in the eyes, but quickly moving her gaze to Félix. "I didn't have the same opportunities as Félix—or, let us say, the war interrupted them. I wanted to go to England to practice my English and work as a governess when I was young, but you can't always choose when real life intervenes, *n'est-ce pas?*"

She's leading me right into my interview, Kirk thought. Does she know it, or is it something more instinctive? Either way, he felt himself warming towards her. Fortunately, Félix had begun filming the minute they sat down, so her first remarks weren't lost.

"When you say that real life intervenes, Caroline… May I call you Caroline?

"Please do," she replied. But she stiffened imperceptibly, a change that Félix noticed immediately because he knew her so well. Caroline was French and formal. But she was also kind, and would never want to embarrass her son's friend. She and Félix exchanged a secret look of understanding and bemusement.

Kirk plunged ahead. "Are you saying that the war was real life for you, or was it more of a parenthesis, something to get through before your real life resumed?"

"Both," Caroline affirmed, as she appraised her son's friend. These Americans were so fresh-looking, so cheerful, so optimistic! How could they begin to imagine what it was like to live in an occupied country, scrounge for food, fear that bombs might land on you? She rarely watched TV programs about the war. But when she did, she sympathized with the interviewers who attempted to capture the complexity of the times. Not many tried. Generally, they always wanted a simple answer, a black and white description. She had decided that she would be black and white for this interview. Why waste the poor man's time? Why bring up issues no one would understand?

It was only recently that Caroline had allowed herself to think or talk about the war at all. She was now, she knew, so old that she was free of her previous fears. She felt like a child at the water's edge, afraid of the ocean yet letting little waves slide over her toes, becoming more relaxed each time they did. For years she had stopped at the water's edge. She had the feeling she might soon swim out to sea, and this interview marked the beginning of the letting go.

"So, may I call you Kirk?" she asked, tilting her head and smiling. Caroline certainly knew how to charm, Félix reflected, watching her. He knew how much she hated instant familiarity, but he also knew how good she was about excusing foreigners who didn't know any better. He assumed that his colleague probably wouldn't pick up on the friendly tease, but he did, and he acknowledged it with a smile.

"Of course," Kirk replied, instantly realizing he should have addressed her more formally. Once again, he'd caught on to something in French life when it was too late. So many nuances, so many codes. Perhaps he'd have a French wife someday who would help him sort them out, he thought, his mind wandering as he took in the carefully arranged but cozy room and the view of a majestic oak tree framed in the big picture window next to the fireplace.

"Where were you when the war broke out?" he asked, bringing his attention back to the matter at hand.

"We were in Paris. I was with my parents and my sister. When we heard the Germans were almost at the city limits, we did what everyone else was doing: we packed the valuables we could transport and hid the rest under the floorboards or other places it might take the invaders too long to find. Then my mother and sister and I started walking. We slept in an abandoned farmhouse, drank water from the well and tried not to think about our few possessions, most of which were sentimental. My father had stayed behind—he wanted us to be safe and out of Paris but insisted on remaining to watch over our building, where he worked as a concierge.

"When we returned ten days later, we were astonished to see that everything was as we had left it. Nothing had been stolen, yet it would have been so easy. We resumed our lives, but everything was different—and difficult." She paused, feeling she was perhaps becoming one of those old people she so despised, telling their tales of woe.

"For example?" Kirk prodded her gently. He had a kindly face, and an encouraging expression that helped ease her self-consciousness.

"Oh, you've seen pictures of the bread lines, and I'm sure you know about the rationing," she said. "That's war—mostly it's just a terrible waste of time. You'd spend most of your day trying to get food—in fact, I think if the French are now obsessed by food, the war years may be one of the reasons. We're afraid of not having enough to eat—those of us who lived through the war, anyway.

"The younger generation," she said, looking at Félix, "was spared that. Félix is always teasing me about keeping bread that's gone stale, but I just can't throw it away."

"She can't throw away string either," Félix said, smiling fondly. "Or bicycle tires or rubber bands or broken dolls or anything she thinks can be fixed or used." He rolled his eyes as he glanced at his mother.

"And where were you on D-Day?" Kirk pursued. "At home? At work? What's your strongest image of that day?"

Caroline paused, then replied smoothly, "I don't remember all that much about D-Day. Communications weren't as good then as they are now, so we didn't get the news instantly. When we did realize that the Allies were here, people's sentiments were mixed. We were grateful and relieved that the end of the war was in sight. At the same time, though, we continued to worry about more fighting, more battles, more bombs."

7

She thought for a moment, and then added, "Actually, my strongest recollection is of the liberation of Paris in August. You've seen all those films of French women pouring into the streets and kissing the GIs. I was far too shy to kiss anyone, but I was in the crowd and remember the joy of it all. That day is more vivid in my memory than D-Day, but of course everything started with D-Day."

Kirk took a close look at one of the photos in the group on the console. There was a snapshot of what seemed to be an entire family in front of an upscale apartment building with high windows, imposing balconies and decorative carvings on its limestone façade. The men were dressed in suits and ties, and Kirk thought he recognized Caroline as a young woman. She was petite, delicate and blond, with the same fine features and clear eyes. She had her arm around the waist of an attractive, vivacious-looking woman about her age who was dark-haired, dark-eyed, and tall. Could they possibly be related?

"May I ask who is in this picture and when it was taken, Madame Aubry?" Kirk ventured. Now that he had realized his error in calling her Caroline, he decided to backtrack, be more careful.

"Of course," said Caroline. "That's why I placed it there. It's not a photo I look at often, but it's my family just before the war. Maman, Papa, me, a family friend, and my sister Séverine." Caroline paused and cleared her throat, then went on. "Other than me, they are all gone. Those were happier days, but life goes on," she declared, patting her skirt and looking directly at Kirk, not Félix.

The conversation continued for a few minutes, but Caroline seemed to have pulled up an emotional drawbridge of some sort; there were no revelations or exciting anecdotes. From years of professional experience, Kirk knew he would get no further with her; it was time to stop. Still, his audience would be treated to at least a few solid soundbites about the war and its impact from a gracious, elderly Frenchwoman in her well-furnished home. The visuals were good, he knew, but he couldn't help wishing his curiosity about the family had been more fully assuaged.

As he stood to thank her for her time, Caroline indicated a table in the adjoining dining room. It was covered with an immaculate starched white linen cloth on which a bouquet of fresh roses, precious Limoges porcelain teacups and saucers and a silver platter holding an assortment of mouthwatering tarts had been placed. All of the objects were so artfully arranged that they looked like a still life. Maybe they *were* a still life that she had laid out and painted before his arrival. He laughed inwardly at the idea of eating one of her paintings.

"And now, Kirk, won't you join us for some tea?"

Kirk accepted gratefully. Maybe during teatime she would open up, as people often did when off camera and off the record. He could always hope.

Caen: June 1994

Kirk positioned himself in front of the D-Day memorial in Caen, checking his notes and waiting for the cameramen to set up the shot. Among the many ceremonies and commemorations on this fiftieth anniversary of the D-Day landings was a formal lunch for heads of state at the Prefecture of Caen. That had inspired him to file his report from this now-thriving Norman city which had been reduced almost to rubble by Allied artillery and bombs in the summer of 1944. How fitting that a museum of history and peace had been built there on top of a German blockhouse, he thought.

He gazed at the poignant words inscribed on the memorial: "*La douleur m'a brisée, la fraternité m'a relevée, de ma blessure a jailli un fleuve de liberté.*"

Kirk had been surprised by the sudden emotion he'd felt when reading the inscription he would later point out and translate for his viewers: "Grief broke me, fraternity lifted me, from my wound gushed a river of liberty." Such noble thoughts and words. At the same time, he reflected, wars were continually breaking out all over a world in which peace might turn out to be an impossible dream.

He'd taken a tour of the museum, which was housed in a surprisingly nondescript concrete building, in the company of colleagues. Inside the entrance, a winding circular ramp led visitors down to the abyss and the hell of war in much the same way entire nations descend into war, little by little, without knowing where the path is leading. A sign on the wall announced that the Second World War had "dramatically affected the civilian population with the air raids, bombings, compulsory rationing and hard labor."

"That's putting it mildly," Kirk had thought, then checked himself.

When he saw the documents and videos attesting to the horrors of twentieth century warfare, the factual account of the Battle of Normandy and images of the suffering of soldiers and civilians, he was humbled. Like most Americans, Kirk had studied history at school, but here in the museum he began for the first time to experience the visceral sense of war in all its horror. He reconsidered the museum's location in this liberated but martyred city as an inspiring tribute to hope.

But how to sum up all he had seen and learned in a short report—the motivations, the reasons, the choices people on both sides of the conflict had made? It would take far too long, and television news wasn't meant for such intricacies. Today was a moment of memory and reconciliation, so he'd focus on D-Day and liberation and end with a message about hope for future peace.

The cameramen indicated that they were ready. Kirk

patted his hair, adjusted his tie, and stepped into position. Behind his solid, handsome American frame the memorial loomed—strangely cold, impersonal, and about as attractive as a Philadelphia office building. But within it, Kirk knew, lay messages of enormous symbolism and even optimism.

The camera rolled and Kirk began to speak: "Some fifty years ago...."

Paris: September 1994

Kirk cast a glance at the sophisticated crowd in the café and wondered about the French—especially the French women. How did they remain so pencil thin? Why did they smoke so much? How did they dress so well? Why did it look like everything they were saying was a secret? The way they almost whispered as they bent in to confide in each other... He suddenly felt very large, very American and very clumsy.

"Why so glum?" Félix asked as he entered the café and slid onto the bench across from his friend. "Has the sky fallen in on you?"

"No. Just wondering why I feel like such a klutz in your country, but I'll get over it," Kirk replied. He added, "Before I forget, thanks so much for putting me in touch with your mother. What a woman! I see what you mean—she's incredibly sharp for her age."

"Anytime, pal," Félix said with a gracious smile. "You'll owe me one someday too."

"Well, I got a nice little report out of it—which I hope you saw—and even a few kudos from back home, so what can I say? Well done, and thanks again." Kirk raised his whiskey glass in a salute. Félix was drinking wine, his favorite, a Menetou Salon. He raised his glass, and the two men drank.

"Still," Kirk continued, "I've got to say that I'm intrigued and even more stymied than I was before I started all this. Your mother, for instance. Come on, Félix—she's a veritable clam."

"Oyster," Félix replied. "In France, someone who doesn't talk is called an oyster."

"Whatever," Kirk conceded. "An oyster." He took another sip of his whisky and continued. "I know people don't like to tell their secrets to the camera. I'm used to it. But your mother..." He crumpled his napkin and placed it on the table. "There's something I can't figure out."

"Good Lord," Félix said, chuckling. "It's a miracle she even agreed to talk to you. First of all, she's reserved. And second, she has never even told me about the war, and I'm her son! Surely you didn't think she'd open up to you?"

"No, actually I didn't," Kirk admitted. He looked around the room again, gathering his thoughts. The noise level had risen as the diners and drinkers laughed and talked together, and there was a companionable, almost comforting, clinking of plates and cutlery and glassware. He leaned towards Félix once more, feeling strangely conspiratorial. "But now you can tell me what she didn't, if only to satisfy my curiosity. We're off the air, so this is just between you and me. And will you please note that I didn't ask these questions before or during the interview. Normally, I'm more hard-nosed, but your mother has a way of creating a distance and warning you off...."

"Yes, she does," said Félix flatly. "Okay, go ahead. Ask away. There's nothing so mysterious I can't tell you. It's all clear as mud to me." For a moment he looked as if he were at a loss for words. Then he continued, "We just didn't talk about the past."

"Yeah, that's what I mean. So what did your mom tell you about the war? You know—all the things she was obviously keeping to herself?"

Félix swirled the wine in his glass and looked at his friend. "You really want to know? God, I'd like to tell you she didn't tell me anything because she was a really cool, heroic member of the Resistance resistant and was too modest to reveal it. But the truth is, Kirk, my mom is like about ninety-five per cent of the French people. She and her family just survived, they just got through it as best they could. What else can you do when your army's been smashed, your country is humiliated, and you have no choice?"

"What do you mean, no choice?"

"Exactly what I said. While some people joined the Resistance became resistants and fought against the Nazis and the collaborators, most just hunkered down, kept themselves out of harm's way and tried to figure out how to eat every day."

"You're saying exactly what your mother did," Kirk said.

"Because it's true. That's all I ever heard about the war—how they were rationed so brutally, how tough it was just to survive. Ever look at the teeth of the people in that generation? They're horrible, mostly from a lack of calcium and vitamins… No wonder French people are obsessed by food—good food. My mother still can't think about bad food, stuff like a rutabaga, without wanting to vomit. And she won't buy a skinned rabbit to cook because during the war you never knew if it might be a cat." Kirk grimaced. Félix continued. "That's because the occupiers took all the good stuff—the fine wines, the caviar, the best cuts of meat, the best cheeses—for themselves, she told me. The French were left with next to nothing. Just say 'rutabaga' to any French person who lived under the Occupation and you'll get the same reaction—utter disgust!"

Kirk nodded, his brow furrowing. "Did you hear anything else—I mean, you know, political? Did she ever say she or her family were for the Vichy regime or against it?

I've asked plenty of people the same thing while I've been here, and I always run up against the usual wall of silence."

"Sure you do, and it's no wonder. It would be like asking a German if his grandparents were Nazis or not. Most people were like my mom and her family. They lived from day to day. Unless they were intensely political, heroic resisters or filthy collaborators, they just went about their business wondering how they had the bad luck to live in a time when bombs were raining down on their heads.

"Listen, I swear I never heard any interesting stories from my mom that you could have put in your report. Scout's honor," Félix said, smiling and placing his hand over his heart. "And anyway, why are you asking me now that you've finished?"

"Because I wanted to make sure I hadn't overlooked any detail that might have made a better story—even if it is too late." Kirk sighed. "So let's drop it. Here's to peace!" he said brightly, with a lightness he didn't feel.

Félix nodded, and they raised their glasses again.

As they drank, Kirk scrutinized his friend. He took in his blondness, his fair skin, his blue eyes. Something was troubling him, but he couldn't quite place it. He wondered about the family—Félix's classy, secretive mother and… his father. *Félix's father.* Who was he? Why did Félix never talk about him? And he wondered about Félix's aunt, Séverine, and why his mother's tone had altered ever so slightly when she pronounced her name.

Maybe he'd go back to it with Félix another time.

Or perhaps it would be best to let the whole subject go.

Paris: June 1948

Caroline glanced at the Jardin des Plantes through the one window in her living room, and congratulated her-self again on having landed an apartment in her favorite neighborhood in Paris. With only one bedroom it wasn't that big, but she was almost always outside, either at work or walking with four-year-old Félix. There were so many places to visit, beginning with the famous eighteenth-century menagerie inside the Jardin. Félix was thrilled by the creepy reptiles, the funny monkeys and the exotic birds, and never tired of visiting it.

She loved the idea that she was in the Latin Quarter, and that every name was linked to the past, every street steeped in history. It was called the Latin Quarter because that was the language spoken at the Sorbonne when it was founded by Robert de Sorbon in the thirteenth century. The Pantheon, with its Corinthian columns modeled after its namesake in Rome, celebrated the lives of famous French citizens from Voltaire to Victor Hugo. Caroline loved walking in this most ancient neighborhood of Paris. Depending on her mood, she would sometimes descend into the Roman ruins of the Arènes de Lutece (where she could almost visualize the gladiators if she closed her eyes) or walk up the rue Montagne-Sainte-Geneviève to pay a visit to Saint-Etienne-du-Mont, the church that contained the shrine of the patron saint of Paris. Although she was not religious, and had become even less so after the war, she would still enter the sanctuary, kneel, then light a candle. Only she knew why and to whom.

She looked down at her writing table with an expression that was close to satisfaction. She was proud of accomplishing the goal she had set for herself. For the past four years, she had put in long days at the theater, where she had worked her way up to wardrobe master, taken care of Félix, attended painting classes and written every evening after she had put her son to bed. The result of those four years of writing was now in front of her.

She picked up the manuscript as if it were a sacred object. She thumbed through it one last time, then placed it inside the black box she had bought especially for it. She had chosen black because it looked sober, almost funereal. Truth be told, she thought, this was akin to a burial, since what she had written was for her eyes only—at least for the time being. She would never show it to her parents or her friends. It would never be sent to a publisher. There was only one person in the world who would read it, some far away day in the future.

Taking a deep breath, she picked up her pen one last time to write a note to that person, which she would place on top of the manuscript before closing the lid and locking the box.

My dearest Félix, my precious son,

Before you open the document in this box, I would like to explain its origins. Shortly after the end of the war I decided to tell the tale of one calamitous, dramatic and life-changing event that occurred during those years. I did it so that I would never forget – as if I ever could. I did it to ease my sorrow, for I believe that writing is a cathartic process. I did it to set the record straight, because that is essential.

It is impossible to imagine the atmosphere of those times. That is why I start my "fictional" story with one of the worst true-life tragedies of the war: the terrible massacre in Oradour-sur-Glane that happened four days after D-Day. This bucolic little village is similar to, and not all that far from, the small town where my sister and I grew up in southwest France, a region that during the war was a seething cauldron of resistance activity and Nazi reprisals as well as fierce infighting among the French themselves.

I purposely avoided a first-person account because, although I was present at many of the events or knew about them from Séverine, of course I was neither omnipresent nor omniscient. So I somewhat daringly declared myself "an author" and let my imagination fill in the blanks.

But make no mistake: while some moments and scenes were fictionalized out of necessity, my story depicts real places, real people and real events. Most importantly, it is my truth and THE truth.

At first I wrote this only for myself. As I said, writing is cathartic. I had no words to speak, nothing to say. Not even for you. Especially not for you. I vowed not to raise a child in sadness. I needed to find a way to bring you up with a glad heart, to surround you with happiness and beauty. Yet one cannot and must not ignore the past. That is why I wrote this and why I am now putting it away for you to read. Someday. When the time is right.

With all my devotion and love,

Your mother,

Caroline Aubry, June 1948

PART ONE

PARADISE

Chapter ONE

Oradour-sur-Glane: June 10, 1944

It is a warm summer's day in Oradour-sur-Glane, a pretty little town nestled in the lush green wooded Limousin countryside. Twenty kilometers northwest of Limoges, Oradour has three schools, twelve cafés, several hotels and a variety of shops. Always lively, on this particular Saturday the village is bustling with activity. Two hundred children gather in the school hall for a scheduled medical visit, travelers linger over lunch at the Hotel Milord, anglers on the banks of the Glane cast their lines into the river, smokers line up for their tobacco allocation.

At 2 p.m. a long line of lorries and armored vehicles carrying more than one hundred soldiers of the 3rd company of the SS *Der Führer* regiment, itself part of the 2nd SS Panzer Division *Das Reich*, starts rolling into the town center. The minute the convoy stops, heavily armed soldiers leap out of the vehicles and proceed to oust the townspeople from their homes. The town crier announces the orders of the German command: all the citizens are to assemble at the *Champ de Foire* for an identity check. No one can enter or leave the village.

The inhabitants obediently head toward the *Champ de Foire*: mothers push babies in prams; schoolchildren follow their teachers; the old and the infirm get there as best they can. They are joined by people from neighboring roads and villages who have been caught in a round-up. By 3 p.m. all are present at the designated meeting place. Only one person, eight-year-old Roger Godfrin, an evacuee from Lorraine who had been brought to the village of Oradour for safety, runs for his life and escapes.

This will be no ordinary identity check. The women and children are separated from the men, who are told that the women will be led to safety outside the village. The men are then separated into six groups and led to six different enclosures; the women are not led to a place outside the village, but to the ancient village church at the heart of it.

At 4 p.m. a warning shot rings out, and the massacre begins. The Nazis aim their machine guns at the men in the barns and garages and walk across the fallen bodies, shooting anyone who is still alive at close range; they pile straw, hay and other combustibles over the bodies and set the buildings on fire. Miraculously, five men manage to escape.

At 5 p.m. the Nazis lock the doors to the church, and soldiers light the fuse to a crate of explosives they had placed in the nave an hour earlier, unleashing thick, heavy, black smoke. The women and children seek refuge in parts of the building where it is still possible to breathe. Their screams pierce the air. Soon the cries cease altogether: everyone has been asphyxiated. To make sure of it, the Germans open the doors to shoot into the smoke until they run out of ammunition. Then they set the church on fire. Only one woman, who climbs on a chair and jumps from a high window behind the altar, survives.

At the end of the sunny summer afternoon, the daily tram from Limoges enters the village. The passengers from Oradour are held at the command post where they await their fate. Two hours later they are released – to learn that the other inhabitants of the village have all been executed.

The Nazis loot and pillage all the houses before setting the town on fire. By evening, three hundred and twenty-eight of its buildings are in flames.

The once peaceful and bucolic town of Oradour-sur-Glane is now a blazing inferno.

Six hundred and forty-two townspeople, 205 of whom are children, lie dead. Only six people survive the massacre.

* * *

Why Oradour? Two days before the June 10 massacre, members of the French Resistance had blown up a railway bridge in the little town of St-Junien, ten kilometers from Oradour, to hamper the movement of German troops heading towards the Normandy front. One day later, the *Das Reich* division arrived at St-Junien and installed its command post. There, the leaders began preparations for a massacre that was designed to terrify the population and intimidate the resistance into submission.

Three months earlier, in March 1944, a beautiful young woman boards a train in Paris to return to her hometown in the southwest of France. It is a mere fifty kilometers south of Oradour in a region where the fighting between *résistants* and Nazis is at its fiercest. Hiding in the *maquis* – the dense and impenetrable forests of the area – the armed resistance fighters, or *maquisards*, relentlessly sabotage and harass the Germans.

To retaliate, the Germans root out and execute the perpetrators; they enter nearby villages and take hostages, often civilians.

As well as fighting the foreign occupying forces, the French are at war with each other, as supporters of Charles de Gaulle struggle with communists over political control of the country after the war.

The young woman has been warned not to travel to this tinderbox.

She ignores the advice.

Chapter TWO

Gare d'Austerlitz: March 1944

The young German soldier in his perfectly pressed uniform checked identity cards and stifled a yawn. He glanced with no particular interest at the people passing through his line. Most looked weary or bored. Some were in a hurry. All of them looked thin. In their rumpled, drab clothes, the passengers blended in with the oppressive cement walls of the dreary station, forming a solid mass of gray. The soldier checked his watch. Only 10 a.m. It was going to be a slow day.

Laughter and lilting voices broke into his somber thoughts. He turned in the direction of the sound and saw two stylish women in their late twenties or early thirties. Arms linked, they leaned toward each other, chattering as they moved toward him. They looked buoyant and cheerful. One was short with blond hair and blue eyes and fair, flawless skin. The other was tall with brown eyes and hair, high color in her cheeks and carefully made-up vermilion lips. Although they didn't look alike, they were dressed alike, wearing capes of brocaded royal blue velvet and matching blue berets perched jauntily on their shining locks. The capes swung open with each step they took, revealing the bright yellows and blues of their skirts.

The soldier did a double take and then, for the first and perhaps the last time in the day, smiled. Birds of paradise! Yes, that's what they were—just like the magnificent bright blue and green parrot that had perched on the branch of an apple tree in the yard of his home back in Germany one beautiful spring day when he was a boy. The bird had looked right at home, but of course it wasn't. It was totally out of place among the yard's usual callers: jet-black crows, gray sparrows, brownish thrushes and other dark or dun-colored species. For days afterwards he had wondered about the exotic creature—why it was there, where it had come from. Even after the prosaic explanation—it had escaped from its cage in a neighbor's home—he had often thought of the radiant beauty of that flamboyant bird of paradise. The unexpected visitor had given him a shot of undiluted pleasure.

He felt the same way now as he watched the vivacious young women coming closer. Surprise, wonder and delight replaced the stultifying tedium of his humdrum day. He stole another look at them. What splendid apparitions they were!

These *Parisiennes*, he mused. They were underweight, of course, because the little the Germans left to the French was rationed. Yet these two exuded vitality. They were deprived of most textiles, leather, cosmetics and just about everything else, including many kinds of food. Yet they wore makeup, extravagant hats, shoes with cork soles. What was that funny French idiom he had learned? *Avoir du chien*. It meant "to look attractive" or "have something special." Well, that they certainly did. But he still couldn't figure out the logic. Why would you say that a chic woman "had dog"? He shook his head.

When the women reached his checkpoint, the brunette flashed him a warm smile and produced a ticket. The blond, she explained, was her sister and was simply accompanying her. Of course she could go onto the platform with her to say goodbye. It was more of an affirmation than a question; he could see that she knew how to charm.

He wanted to chat with the beautiful pair, compliment them on their attire; he might have done so if the high-spirited dark-haired one with the smile had been alone. Something about the petite, curly-haired blond sister stopped him. She'd been laughing, but became silent and solemn as she passed through the line. She wasn't overtly hostile or disagreeable, but she was far from friendly and radiated her own form of resistance as she stood beside her sister at his checkpoint.

He had noticed the same attitude in other French people of her ilk. They were polite, obeyed orders, and replied to questions with minimal answers. They did not initiate or engage in small talk. Their facial expressions, or lack of, said what they couldn't or wouldn't put into words, and the message was clear: You are the occupier and we have to put up with you. But we don't have to like you and we don't have to be ingratiating.

And they weren't.

Séverine Sevanot, née Aubry. He glanced again at the gracious brunette with the expressive eyes and mouth, thinking that the softness and alliteration of her name suited her perfectly. It fitted with the sense of style she carried. He waved the sisters through and mused on the incredible self-confidence of French women, their *chien*, their *je ne sais quoi*, another expression he had picked up in France. He decided once more that he would never understand the French, the French language and especially French women, then straightened his shoulders and returned to his job. He was no longer yawning, and he no longer felt fatigued and bored. The twosome had literally brightened his day.

* * *

"Did you see how that soldier looked at our outfits? The Boches can never figure out French women; that's obvious," Caroline commented, casting a backward glance at the German. She took her younger sister's hand and squeezed it. "They can't understand that in spite of bombing our cities, sending our men away to work in Germany, depriving us of food and arresting people right and left, we'll never give up on our looks. War or no war," she added.

Séverine nodded her head in agreement. but put her finger to her lips. "Shh. He might hear you. They all know that Boche is hardly a term of affection."

"Of course it's not," Caroline retorted. "But it's a favorite nickname for them, like Fritz or Doryphore, which I'm sure they hear all the time." She grinned wickedly; "Doryphore" was the Latin name for the potato beetle, a hated pest that wreaked havoc on farmers' crops. "Personally, I prefer *Doryphore*. It's a perfect description. We used to have potato shortages because the insects destroyed them, and now we have potato shortages because the Germans steal them!"

"You're right," Séverine agreed. "But not all Germans are bad. The one back there checking identity cards couldn't have been a day over nineteen. He's just a harmless kid bored with his job." Deftly changing the topic, she ran her hand over her cape. "May I pay you a rare compliment, mademoiselle?" she asked playfully. "You're an absolute genius with fabric. Who would imagine that our gorgeous blue velvet capes were once curtains?"

Caroline executed a mock curtsey. "Thank you, Madame." Then she dropped her pose. "We're lucky I landed that job at the Théâtre de l'Odéon. I love rummaging through all that discarded material and creating outfits that make eyes pop. Even if they're German eyes," she added, making a disgusted moue.

Séverine didn't reply, her mind already elsewhere. In spite of their lighthearted banter, the sisters were troubled, each for a separate reason. Séverine was worried about catching a train—train schedules meant little in wartime—and was focused on her imminent departure. Caroline was still shocked that Séverine was leaving, a fact she had learned only two days earlier.

How like her little sister to set the stage for her dramatic announcement, Caroline thought, as she recalled Séverine's offhand invitation; would she join her for a sisterly stroll along the Seine? They had ambled eastward, arm in arm, from Caroline's place on the rue de l'Odéon, past the Ile de la Cité and the magnificent twelfth-century Notre-Dame Cathedral, and ended up at the Jardin des Plantes, one of their favorite places in Paris.

The weather was beautiful; not a cloud in the sky, and Caroline was happy to be with Séverine, whom she adored. The war permeated their lives, but at least they had food to eat, although barely enough, and clothes on their backs. And they were alive. She shuddered as she thought of a close friend who, along with six hundred others, had perished when the British had bombed the Renault plant in the Paris suburb of Boulogne-Billancourt. Exactly two years ago this month, Caroline suddenly realized. The death of her friend had brought the horror of war uncomfortably close. She didn't blame the Brits for their annihilation of a factory that had been compelled to work with the Germans, of course, but she loathed the loss of civilian lives.

Séverine nudged her, then pointed to the Gare d'Austerlitz across the street from where they were standing.

"See the station?"

"How could I not?" Caroline asked, with a slightly superior older-sister smirk.

"I'm getting on a train there and going back to our hometown. I ask only one thing—don't tell Maman and Papa until after I've gone."

Ignoring Caroline's astonished expression, Séverine turned to face the Jardin des Plantes and recited a few facts about its history. "Did you know that the garden is more than three hundred years old?" she asked. "Actually, it's three hundred and ten years old this year, and was created by Louis XIII to grow medicinal herbs. And the zoo that's on the grounds? During the Commune in 1871, famished Parisians ate most of the animals in it."

Caroline reflected, not for the first time, that Séverine should have been a teacher. Ever since she was small, she'd had such a love of learning that she often couldn't refrain from sharing knowledge, no matter the subject. Her sometimes ill-timed exposés were also a clever way of avoiding subjects she didn't want to discuss. Caroline was used to both her tactics and her unpredictability and knew it was best not to press her right now. She'd give her reasons for leaving when she was ready, and not before.

Just as those thoughts ran through her mind, Séverine's apparent bravado suddenly dissolved, and to Caroline's dismay she began to weep, giving in to the bitter tears she had been holding back, making no attempt to stop them.

"What's going on? What's the matter?" Caroline asked. She gave Séverine her handkerchief and put a comforting arm around her.

Séverine wiped her eyes and replied tonelessly, "It's Antoine. I'm leaving him. I can't give you the details. It's all too awful. When things are better I'll tell you the whole story. But in the meantime, can we agree that we won't get all teary and dramatic when you come with me to say goodbye?"

And as they always did after one of Séverine's outbursts, the two sisters had collected themselves, changed the subject and walked on together. By the time they neared the station they were even laughing and teasing each other. The blatant admiration of the German soldier checking their IDs was proof that in spite of their separate preoccupations, they had managed to appear carefree and lighthearted.

But after they had elbowed their way through the crowd to the platform where Séverine would board her train, Caroline became grave. She had always watched out for her younger sister, but she had never felt the weight of responsibility like she did now. She had so little time to speak her piece, say what was on her mind.

"Stop a moment," she gently ordered, taking Séverine's arm. "Look me in the eyes and hear me out. I don't know what's going on in your life, but whatever it is, escaping reality by fleeing to Sorignac is foolish. This is the worst time to go there." She looked at her sister closely to make sure she was listening and decided to take the risk of saying too much. "Didn't you hear what Monsieur and Madame Bernard were telling Maman and Papa about Sorignac when they visited them the other day? Unless you were wearing earplugs, you surely heard them say that our dear hometown is a hotbed of resistance activity, and that compared to the lawlessness down there Paris is a haven of peace."

Caroline sighed and continued, aware that she was treading a fine line between informing and convincing her sister and boring her. "I almost didn't believe them when they said that bands of armed resisters are pillaging and ransoming the local farmers. The Bernards say that they don't ask for a donation to their cause, they just take whatever's at hand, from jam to jewelry to money stashed under the mattress. They even robbed the local post office. Don't you find that frightening? I do!"

Seeing no visible reaction from Séverine, she plunged

on. "Even getting there is risky, since the *résistants* are sabotaging the rail lines to derail the trains. Some people have spent days instead of hours on trains from Paris to Perigueux." She paused. "Basically, what I'm trying to tell you is that it's a nightmare down there... Well, all right," she revised, as Séverine raised her eyebrows doubtfully, "maybe not a nightmare, but most certainly a high-risk zone where no one's safety can be guaranteed. And you are diving right into the heart of it! Where will you stay?"

She stopped abruptly. In spite of her best efforts, she had lost control, shown too much emotion, asked too many questions. She needed to stop the trembling of her hands and the quavering of her voice. She needed to lighten her tone.

"Why don't you come to my place? I'll even give you my bed, and I'll sleep on the floor!" She considered attempting a weak joke ("You can be just as unhappy in Paris as you'll be in Sorignac") but sensed it wasn't the moment.

Séverine, usually so voluble, remained silent. Caroline stared at her sister, hands on hips, in turn vexed, infuriated and worried. She was quite sure that Séverine had been corresponding with her mentor Gisèle, the countess of the castle in Sorignac and their parents' former employer. But regardless of her reasons for going, one thing was clear: Séverine wanted to get away from Paris as soon as possible, and hang the consequences.

It was so like Séverine to do what she wanted whenever she wanted, no matter what. It had always been that way. Why would she change just because there was a war going on, Caroline asked herself? How could anyone expect her little sister to suddenly stop being who she was—lively, active, headstrong, funny, and completely obtuse when she wanted to be? She loved Séverine and feared for her in equal measure, but knew that it was pointless to argue.

At length, Séverine finally spoke. "No need to get

worked up," she said calmly. "So what if things are happening down there? They're happening everywhere. And anyway, you know I'm not interested in politics."

Inwardly, Caroline groaned. She decided to change the subject.

"I presume you're going to see the countess," she said, trying to sound lighthearted. "Better you than me. My heavens. Remember the day of the doll?"

"Do I ever!" Séverine exclaimed. Both sisters were silent for a moment as the memories flooded back. The countess had given Séverine, who had been six years old at the time, an exquisite porcelain doll with pink cheeks, blue-gray eyes with long lashes, silk undergarments trimmed with lace and real leather shoes. Séverine, enchanted, had immediately named her Felicity and had run back home to show off her treasure—where Caroline, realizing that Séverine was and always would be the countess's pet, had retreated to her room in a fit of jealousy. When Séverine had seen the effect that the doll had on Caroline, she had quickly made amends, appointing her Chief Dressmaker and putting her in charge of designing and sewing Felicity's wardrobe.

Now Séverine laughed as she looked affectionately at her older sister. "I do believe I created your first job, and got you where you are today."

"Don't worry—I got over it," Caroline said, grinning as she reached out and tugged at a stray lock of her sister's hair.

Then she became serious again, and took Séverine gently by the shoulders. "You may not be interested in politics, but you still need to be careful," she pleaded. "We're living in perilous times. And try to eat more!" she added. "You're not slender—you're nearing scrawny!"

Séverine stuck out her tongue, then beamed as she brandished the big wooden picnic basket holding the provisions Caroline had prepared for her trip. "Perhaps I'll start by eating all this!" She lifted the cover to reveal hard-boiled eggs, several thick slices of tantalizing country ham and a ripening Camembert among the tempting array of food. "Amazing! Where did all this come from?"

"Not my ration tickets, that's for sure. A friend I work with at the theater spent the weekend at her family's farm in Normandy and brought back piles of hard-to-get goodies to share. This is your part of my part."

"And I bet you hardly took anything for yourself." Séverine wagged her finger at her older sister. "Aren't you sweet? And generous too," she exclaimed, crushing her in a hug. "I promise I'll eat everything but the basket."

Caroline kissed the top of her sister's head, then held her at arm's length, taking in the faint shadows under her eyes and the hollows in her cheeks. More than anything, she wanted to part on good terms. "Promise me something else, will you?" she asked, fighting back a smile. "Don't give the countess my regards."

Séverine made a face of mock-disapproval. "You've never forgiven her for that doll, I do swear. Come on, Caroline, have a heart," she teased.

They burst out laughing again, then winced and covered their ears as a traffic controller in a baggy uniform strutted past them, giving a loud, piercing blast on his whistle. Séverine bounded up the steps of the railway car, then turned around, touched her lips and threw a kiss to Caroline, who waved her hand and silently mouthed good-bye. She remained standing on the platform, watching the train until it was out of sight.

Chapter THREE

Inside the train, Séverine's face crumpled.

The lips that had turned up in laughter only minutes before now formed a taut line; the eyes that had sparkled with good humor now filled with tears that she hastily wiped away. She closed them briefly, then clenched her jaw, threw back her shoulders and stood staring out the smudged window as the train moved slowly from the station.

Regaining her composure, she took a sideways glance at the compartment next to her and saw that dawdling on the platform with Caroline had cost her a seat. Every single place was taken, every inch filled with passengers' belongings stuffed in the overhead racks or tucked under their feet. The corridor wasn't much better, she observed, as a young man hurried through, bumping her legs sharply with his bag. The prospect of standing there for hours, flattening herself against the corridor wall each time someone passed from one car to another, was depressing.

She fished a cigarette out of her pocket, lit it, inhaled deeply and thought about Caroline. She didn't like the role she'd had to play today, acting as if she had never heard of the risk, the danger, even the violence that threatened her both on the train and at her destination. Of course she had. But she resolutely refused to let it interfere with her departure.

She had left in a hurry, rushing out the door after she had gathered up every single one of Antoine's love letters and burned them in the bathtub. Then, still seething, she had looked around the room for something else, anything really, to hurt him the way he had hurt her. A package neatly bound by a red ribbon caught her eye: in it were the charming letters and sketches Antoine had sent his parents while he had served as a pilot in the Great War. With the passage of time, they were practically historical documents now. His parents had entrusted them to Séverine for safekeeping.

Too bad. With a cry of rage, she lit the match. She calmed down sufficiently to contain the flames, then contemplated the pile of black ashes, trying to imagine Antoine's face when he discovered the charred mess and figured out what it had been. He would be furious—and sad.

No pity, she admonished herself. He deserved this.

A rushed blur of images and thoughts surged through her mind. She couldn't control them. Like waves hitting the shore, they would come and go, come and go, ceaseless and relentless as the tides.

One image in particular, one she ardently wished she could eradicate, arose unbidden in her mind, replaying itself once again. Even now, a full week later, she found herself wondering yet again if it had been real, if she'd actually seen what she'd seen from her perch on a park bench in the Tuileries Garden. It was a fine late winter day, and she had raised her face to the clear blue sky to take in the weak rays of the sun, thinking about how lovely the gardens would be in the spring. Shivering and drawing her coat closer, she'd lowered her head and gazed into the middle distance. It was then that she glimpsed a tall man and a little boy, laughing and running down a path. For a second, an instinctive and overwhelming wave of denial flooded her mind, protecting her from shock. Nothing registered. Then everything did. The truth came like the swift stab of a sword. In a flash, it entered her very being, lodging itself in her mind and heart like a stone. The life she had led until that instant—the carefree happiness she had enjoyed, the security she had felt, her plans for a future—all vanished in seconds, leaving her wounded and bereft.

She swayed slightly as the train gained speed and rocked from side to side. Suddenly, the odors of bodies in restricted space—perfume, sweat and stale tobacco mingled with the sulfurous smell of hard-boiled eggs and garlic-laced sausage sandwiches—assailed her nostrils. She willed herself not to be sick, knowing that the reason for the queasy feeling in her stomach wasn't the stink of her surroundings. It was the shocking, unspeakable, life-changing scene she had witnessed last week that had brought her to this train, to this place, to what Caroline, ignorant of the details of what had happened, had called an escape from reality.

She stubbed out her cigarette and tried to blot out the recurring image, the despicable tableau, then focused on extracting a letter from the jumble in her purse—lipstick, comb, handkerchief, a notebook and pen plus keys to her apartment, for when and if she decided to return to Paris.

The thick cream-colored monogrammed stationery and the midnight-blue ink Gisèle always used were so familiar that Séverine almost felt the countess was there in the train with her. She envisaged her seated at the Louis XVI desk in her wood-paneled upstairs library, dressed in sensible but fashionable heels, a narrow skirt and silk blouse, her ever-present strand of cultured pearls around her graceful neck and one of her innumerable soft cashmere cardigans hanging on the back of her chair. "In case I'm suddenly needed outside," she would tell Séverine.

Since her parents had left the castle to work in Paris,

Gisèle had regularly written to Séverine, sharing her frank and sometimes amusing accounts of local news. She liked to write, and Séverine had collected a voluminous correspondence. Séverine imagined her at her desk, head bowed over pen and paper, setting down words rapidly, almost in a stream of consciousness. Yet however quickly the thoughts came, they were invariably rendered in fine and legible penmanship. That was the countess; no matter what she did, she never neglected the importance of form.

Séverine unfolded the letter now and settled against the rocking wall of the train to re-read it. The words of her beloved mentor would, she hoped, keep her mind off the discomfort of standing up and her guilt about not telling Caroline the whole story behind her flight.

Dear Séverine,

I can't tell you how happy I was to hear from you, especially with all the bad news we're getting from our friends in Paris, including the Desprès family, whose dear daughter was here recently and whom I'm prevailing upon to deliver this letter to you by hand at the next piano lesson. She says that you are a wonderful teacher, which doesn't surprise me at all—remember my little lesson about art when you were young? I made what you must have considered lofty remarks both because I meant what I was saying and because I wanted to encourage you when you were dispirited, for I knew that if you decided to give up the piano, nothing would make you change your mind, and I and all of us would have been so disappointed to see such talent go to waste.

I hope that you and your family made it through the ghastly winter cold and aren't suffering too much from the lack of food.

Our dear occupiers do indeed have a propensity to take the best for themselves. Several jeep-loads of soldiers came to the castle the other day because there were rumors that résistants ("terrorists" to the Germans) were hiding. There weren't any, of course, but I had to go through every single room with them to prove it. Before they left, our most unwelcome visitors went down to the wine cellar and helped themselves. But I guess we were lucky: if I hadn't accompanied them, and if the lieutenant hadn't been embarrassed by their behavior, the boors would have emptied the contents of the cellar. They think that everything in this country is theirs for the taking. As for "terrorists," the idea that I'd be hiding them is far-fetched. To be sure, many brave men and women are fighting for our freedom, but there are also a lot of layabouts and opportunists posing as resisters who have nothing better to do than terrorize the population. I promise not to go on and on about politics, but the present situation irks me so.

The truth is that we've got two wars on our hands. One is the war with the Germans. The other is a class war waged by the French against the French, the communists against the capitalists, the poor against the rich, the workers against the bosses. Not surprisingly, the large majority of the local rabble-rousers are communists who are finally getting their revenge on what they refer to as "the bourgeoisie." A "bourgeois," for them, it would appear, is anyone who has any commodity they want and doesn't automatically go along with their ideology or their demands. But really, my dear, is Mr. Faure, who grows his wonderful tomatoes and potatoes and green beans, a man of means, a "bourgeois"? He doesn't even own a suit! Yet only a few days ago, when he refused to hand over the bulk of his yield upon request, the leader of the group promptly had him arrested and taken away while his troop of bandits proceeded to steal not only Mr. Faure's vegetables, but the money he'd stashed in a drawer. Fortunately, his daughter wasn't there that day, for in other incidents, this group of good-for-nothings have committed unspeakable acts.

And have you heard about the kidnappings, whether for revenge or ransom? They are legion—and perhaps worse in

this communist stronghold than elsewhere. I know I shouldn't
be putting this on paper, but I cannot abide these hoodlums.
Everyone knows the war won't last forever and a reckoning
will come. How I wish it would all stop.

Now that I've got that out of my system, I can finally get
to my reason for writing. From what my friends in Paris tell
me, it sounds as if you might enjoy a break from city life and
perhaps at last accept my oft-reiterated invitation. I complain
about the lack of food, but we do have fruit and vegetables
from our land that you probably don't have in Paris, and as
you know we have plenty of space for guests, and the piano
room is and always will be yours. I know traveling is arduous
in general, and these days in particular, but if you wish to visit
us and the hometown you've been away from for so long—too
long—it would be a pleasure and a delight for us, and perhaps
a breath of fresh air for you.

Your friend Paul is here, as you probably know. You probably also know that like his father, he is a successful doctor. I'm
surprised, though, that he decided to stay in this little village
rather than set up his practice in a larger town, but of course
we're grateful he did. He and Georges have their separate consultations right there in the house. Convenient, but probably
a temporary arrangement—what do you think? Georges and
Huguette are about the same: a little older like all of us, and
dealing with the constraints the war brings. Madame Decré
still officiates over the boulangerie.

Too bad the Free Zone ended two years ago. The Germans
are in the area, and we are praying that the irresponsible
ruffians I mentioned don't harass them too much. Reprisals are
serious. But, I'll tell you about that when we see each other in
person.

Enough of this. Life goes on and I've got to tend to my work
here at the castle. As you know, I'm a terrible cook and even
worse when there's next to nothing to cook with. Fortunately,
our faithful Camille is still with us, so Amaury only has to
endure my pathetic attempts on her day off.

I do hope we'll see each other soon. We miss the sounds of your music and your bright smile!
*   With all my affection, Gisèle*

Séverine well remembered Gisèle's total lack of interest in food and culinary skills. On the rare days the countess found herself in the kitchen, smells of charred toast and burnt pans had permeated the dining area. She could barely even boil water, much less an egg. And that was before the food shortages.

She folded the letter and slipped it back into her bag. She wondered which of Gisèle's Paris friends had seen her and reported that she looked like she needed a break. Maybe none of them; maybe Gisèle had thrown that in as an argument.

She smiled to herself as she recalled Caroline's horrified description of the dire political situation in Sorignac and compared it to Gisèle's report. The difference was that Caroline had always been overprotective and had been telling Séverine what she had heard about, not what she had experienced. The countess, on the other hand, was in the thick of it all, and was irritated by, yet unafraid of, either the foreign enemy or the local communists.

Séverine's legs ached, and she was beginning to accept the fact that she would most probably spend the entire long trip standing up in the corridor. As she glanced longingly at the compartment behind her, a young dark-haired man in one of the seats caught her eye. He beckoned, unfolded his long legs, stood up with alacrity and offered her his place. He was of medium height, wore tortoise-shell glasses, and looked like a teacher.

"Please take it," he said, indicating the seat, in a tone that made the phrase more a command than an offer.

"You are very kind," Séverine replied. "But are you

sure?" The question was rhetorical. There was nothing she wanted more than to sit down and stop trying not to fall every time the train picked up speed.

"Yes, I'm sure, but you'd better hurry up." He turned his head to indicate a man determinedly advancing toward the seat he was vacating.

Normally Séverine would have refused again. Today, though, she readily accepted. "All right, then," she said gratefully, "but I want you to share my little lunch. Well, not so little. My sister packed it. You'd think I was leaving for a few years instead of a few weeks. Of course," she added, "we may be on this train for years if a bunch of idiots blow up the tracks." She sat down with a sigh.

* * *

Her benefactor was silent, but inside he was boiling. The "idiots" the young woman had so casually referred to were his comrades, communist *résistants*s risking their lives in their fight against the Nazis. He chose to ignore her remark, but filed it away in a corner of his mind.

"Where are you from?" he asked, once she had taken her place.

"Sorignac, the prettiest village in the southwest," she replied as she made herself comfortable.

"I have to admit that's true. I'm from St. Croix. How strange we never met."

"I'm sure we know some of the same people," she said, looking up at him again. "Do you know the count and countess at the château in Sorignac? That's where I grew up—not as a young countess, unfortunately, but as the daughter of the help."

"How lovely to grow up in a castle, no matter your social position." The unsolicited remark came from the overweight and unkempt woman sitting opposite the young lady, who had obviously been eavesdropping. She glanced at the two of them and then returned to her knitting.

The young lady neither answered nor looked at the woman. She simply ignored her.

The man observed the scene, half-amused, half-horrified. Only a minute earlier the young lady had frankly and humbly (at least, he had thought it was humbly) described herself as "the daughter of the help." Yet her reaction to the woman's comment showed that while she may have been born into the working class, she had quite obviously learned how to be as haughty as an aristocrat. How cutting the high-born could be without uttering a word! It was an art form in itself.

A painful memory, one he had forgotten, pierced him. When he was little, his mother's employer, who lived in a spacious, bourgeois manor, had often invited him to play and ride horses with her daughter, Marie-Laure. As he grew older, the invitations had stopped. He didn't know why. He couldn't imagine it could be a matter of social class until the day Marie-Laure walked down the street with a group of her aristocratic friends and acted as if she didn't know him. The freeze-out was done so imperceptibly that he—as she intended—was the only one to see it.

The snub was a revelation, the first time in his life he had felt not only inferior but non-existent. Was this stinging humiliation the moment he had started hating the aristocrats and the bourgeoisie? Hard to tell. As for the count and countess, he didn't know them personally, but he knew Sorignac, and anyone who knew Sorignac knew the stately château that had been in the same family for centuries. In any case, to him all aristocrats were the same. He had made up his mind on the subject a long time ago. Rich aristocrats who had more than others should not exist. Castles shouldn't exist either, but if they did they should be occupied by the people rather than the nobility.

He highly doubted that he and this young woman knew any of the same people.

She hadn't initially struck him as upper class—although she certainly was better dressed than almost all of the other people in the train. Nor had she seemed snobbish—until he witnessed the arch, imperial way she had treated her fellow passenger. Of course, if she'd grown up in the town castle, even as the daughter of the staff, it was more than likely that she had latched on to the opinions, attitudes, and even gestures of her masters—or what he was sure she referred to as her mentors. He shook his head as he contemplated the odd idea of this underling equating herself with her bosses. What a dreadful, misguided fallacy: for noble families, the only people who counted, the only ones with whom they could mix, were aristocrats like themselves who occupied the highest layers of the stratosphere and the bourgeoisie, even if they were a step down. People like her—and him—were so far down they didn't even exist.

The man never considered that his judgment might lack nuances. His opinions were black and white; he was a stranger to gray. He was for the people and against the capitalists, and that was all there was to it. Unlike this woman, who had switched sides and seemed pleased by the part she played in a restricted aristocratic universe, he had remained faithful to his class and his ideals.

In normal circumstances, he wouldn't give two minutes of his time to a woman like this one. But it would be a long train ride, and maybe he could get her to tell him a bit more about Sorignac and its inhabitants. Any information gleaned about the blue-bloods—most of whom, he suspected, were collaborators—would be useful.

The man leaned toward her with an expression of interest on his face. "Tell me a little more about Sorignac," he said. But as they talked it became apparent that she didn't know all that much. Cosseted as she was by the countess on one side and her traditional working-class parents on the other, she had led a protected life. She had little to say about people's habits or political opinions or family feuds or even their personalities, although a few people stood out. She liked Madame Decré at the bakery, but Mr. Cusset, the owner of the local grocery store, was a mystery. After years of addressing his clients with no more than a grunt, he'd suddenly lightened up and had even started to tell jokes. Some said he had taken a mistress, others speculated that he'd won the lottery. The pharmacist was so talkative she avoided him unless someone in the family desperately needed medicine. She described the doctor and his family as pillars of the community. The priest, she confided, was fine when he wasn't drinking (how he loved the excellent wines served at the countess's bountiful Sunday after-mass lunches). The principals of the girls' and boys' schools had both been there for years. Both were strict but straight as arrows, good with the children and good with the parents.

To be sure, she went on, warming to the subject, the village had its communists and even Freemasons, but they were a minority. At this, the man, who had stopped paying attention, perked up. She'd heard from Gisèle, the countess, that the communists took orders directly from Moscow. That in itself made them bad business. Gisèle had said, and she agreed, that it was their fault if there were reprisals on innocent civilians after they blew up bridges or killed Nazi officers.

"She's a parrot," the young man decided, with a certain bitter amusement. It was clear that she'd been brainwashed by her environment and that she regarded whatever this countess person said as truth. The odd thing was that she was so affirmative, so confident as she spouted off the platitudes that had obviously been put in her head. He wondered if she possessed opinions of her own and, if so, how she judged her parents and their station in life as workers.

His parents, like hers, were workers, but at least they were true to their own values and wary of their bosses. Not for a minute did they admire or seek to emulate their employers. This woman's parents, on the other hand, had become part of their employers' lives and had no desire to rebel against them.

They were deluded, as were so many of their ilk. But all that would change one day, he thought grimly. Equality for all—that was the goal. He was glad to be a member of the Party, to stand beside people who cherished the same ideas. Sure, there was a dogma and there were rules, but there was no bowing down to a god other than the god of equality. The Party offered clear-cut solutions and a path on this earth to a better world. He knew he was right and his cause was right. This young woman puzzled him, though. She seemed to have as many certitudes as he did—even if hers were wrong. Idiots indeed!

He looked more closely at her as she chattered on. She was in her early thirties, he reckoned, past the first bloom of youth, but alluring nonetheless and filled with a degree of self-possession that was startling in someone who hadn't been born into an old family or means. The manners of her mentors had obviously seeped into her soul. She was one of those people, he was sure, who never looked beyond herself or her own narrow little world. Did she even notice the Jews wearing the yellow star, having to take the last car on the *métro*? He was sure she didn't—or if she did it didn't faze her. She probably didn't have anything "against" anyone aside from the "idiots" who might ruin her train trip.

A flash of anger sent blood rushing to his face. He hated the way his emotions showed, but he liked and valued these moments of indignation. They galvanized him to action, encouraged him in his absolute belief that he and his comrades could and would change the course of history. And if people like this young lady were upset by the actions of true patriots, then that was their problem and they were the "idiots." Acts of sabotage, killings and other such tactics were the only way to rid themselves of the oppressor.

He'd heard the arguments before: if the Resistance would simply leave the invaders alone, there would be no reason for the enemy to engage in terrible reprisals. Everything would be all right if the people would listen to, place their trust in and give allegiance to Marshal Pétain, the white-haired, mustachioed, blue-eyed hero of the Great War. His followers admired his profile, so like that of a Roman statue, and overlooked his quavering voice, which they chalked up to his age—a good point because it meant experience. For them, the Marshal was imposing, reassuring, paternal, kind and benevolent.

The man was amazed that anyone could believe these fantasies. Yet far too many people did.

He wondered what this young woman would have to say about what was taking place now in the village that she'd described in such glowing, dreamy terms. Was it possible she didn't know that the nearby woods were filled with rapidly growing groups of committed Resistance fighters planning, training and preparing actions against the Germans? That Sorignac and the entire surrounding area, all the towns and villages and cities in the region, had become a prime target for the German command, infuriated and impotent in the face of the surprise attacks? Could she possibly be unaware of the political tensions between the supporters of the *résistants* and their detractors?

Almost imperceptibly, he shook his head. Perhaps she'd heard about all that, but somehow it didn't affect her. He scrutinized her once more: large, wide-set brown eyes, perfectly arched eyebrows, lustrous dark hair, a complexion that, like his, reddened as she got excited. He glanced at her white hands, her long fingers with their perfectly varnished red nails. She wore an exquisite diamond that sparkled and caught the light. Her husband, if she had one, must have paid a fortune for it.

"When was the last time you were in Sorignac?" he asked casually.

"Oh, before the war. I haven't had a chance to return until now. Maybe that's why it sounds so idyllic when I talk about it. It's probably changed with the war, but in my memory it's the stuff of dreams. For one thing," she continued, "compared to Paris, life was so easy. My sister and I attended the same school. In the morning, my mother would get us dressed and walk there with us, even though it was only a few blocks away. In the afternoon our father, still in his gardening clothes, would come to pick us up. Then he'd take us to the candy store, where he allowed us to pick out a selection of bonbons—not many, though, because he was worried they'd rot our teeth."

She cut herself off and glanced up at him, reddening. "I must be boring you," she said. "But those were lovely days. I still remember walking back to the castle with my sister, one of us on each side of our father. Now that I think about it, he was so patient with us, given that he needed to get back to work planting flowers or trimming bushes or whatever he was in the middle of doing."

By now her interlocutor had concluded that the woman to whom he had sacrificed his seat had lived in a fairytale land, unaware of class struggles. How pathetic!

"On the contrary," he said. "You're not boring me at all. Tell me more."

"Well, that's about it," she replied. "You know how small-town life is, since you're from a small town yourself.

I knew which dogs barked and which ones actually bit. I steered away from the village grouch, but loved the florist's children and would give them a treat whenever I could. When my sister and I got older we walked to and from school on our own, but by that time I generally had music scores in my head and wasn't paying attention to anyone or anything. My sister had to remind me to say *bonjour* to people I met along the way lest I be thought of as a snob. I wasn't a snob—I was absorbed in my own world."

Chapter FOUR

Séverine shifted her position and looked out at the fields of hay, the tranquil farms and the church spires that dotted the horizon as the train passed through the countryside. What she had said about Sorignac was true. She had loved her childhood days there.

But all those things she'd been rattling on about... She felt her face flush. Despite herself, she had enjoyed talking to the serious, intense-looking man. He looked to be in his late thirties, she thought. She was fairly sure he must be a schoolteacher, and felt certain that she wouldn't want to be one of his pupils—he looked so strict. Anyway, their conversation had broken up the journey. He hadn't said that much about himself—of course, she reflected, she hadn't asked. The countess's advice echoed in her ears: "Don't be such a chatterbox, Séverine! Of course you must converse to be polite, but don't carry on. Never reveal too much about yourself and your life. For one thing, you're too young for it to be interesting. For another, a little reticence will make you appear mysterious.

"No, my dear, rather than focusing on yourself, you must ask people about themselves. *That* they will find fascinating."

The countess had offered those pearls of wisdom the

first time she invited Séverine to play piano for her aristocratic friends and then take tea with them, a rare privilege. Séverine reflected that she might one day write an entire book about all the lessons the countess had given her. Others might find them self-evident or tiresome, perhaps even moralistic, but Séverine cherished these delectable nuggets of knowledge about how to comport herself in a social milieu that was far higher than the one she had been born into. With the countess, everything became material for a lesson. Even perfume.

One day, when Séverine was fifteen, she'd told Gisèle that she loved the smell of her signature scent, which was *L'Heure Bleue* by Guerlain. A few days later Gisèle casually mentioned that she had an almost-empty bottle of it. Would Séverine like it?

Scarcely able to breathe, Séverine had cupped the exquisite little bottle in her hands. Carefully removing the stopper, she had inhaled the aroma, a heady combination of woody and floral overtones that intoxicated her on the rare times she was invited to enter the countess's private quarters. Gisèle, who took her role as Séverine's educator seriously, had given her a piece of advice.

"Here's what you need to know about wearing perfume, my dear. First of all, don't put on too much. Second, spray or dab it on your clothes, not your skin. Only women of ill repute do that. Also, perfume should be worn only at night. In the daytime, one wears cologne, which is lighter and doesn't risk overpowering or offending anyone. Nights are different, of course." Here the countess had smiled at Séverine as though she were her own daughter. "They are made for romance, intimacy, magic."

Séverine was stunned. Her mother had never given and never would give her hints as to where and when to apply scent. She would never even say "women of ill repute." She never talked about romance, intimacy or magic, and

Séverine was quite sure she never would. They simply weren't part of her mother's down-to-earth world.

She had wrapped the little bottle carefully in a handkerchief, tucked it safely into her bag and rushed home to show her sister. "Look what the countess gave me!" she exclaimed gleefully. "Smell it, Caroline. Isn't it divine? And the name! Can you visualize a blue hour?" Séverine could, even at the age of fifteen. In her mind, the blue hour was at dusk, right before nightfall, when mysterious shadows gathered around the castle. She was convinced that the blue hour must be terribly romantic.

She had opened the bottle and taken a deep whiff. "The scent is so heavenly—it makes me feel like I'm in another world!" She had passed the flask to Caroline, then twirled around the tiny bedroom as her sister watched in amusement. Caroline had become accustomed to Séverine's fascination with the countess. Despite the countess's injunction, Séverine had dabbed a few of the remaining drops behind her ears, shut her eyes and dreamed of the day when she would have a bottle of her own.

Now, of course, she had several bottles of expensive perfumes for the night and colognes for the day. Her dream had come true, but with a catch...

No. She closed her mind to the dark thoughts that were threatening to invade her consciousness and rose to leave her seat. She needed some air, or at least a little exercise, and she needed to use the toilet. The train lurched, and she stumbled and fell partway into the lap of the untidy fat lady, who gave her a fierce scowl.

Her new companion swiftly reached out his hand to steady her.

"Exciting trip," she murmured, standing upright and smoothing her skirt.

"You haven't seen anything yet," he replied. "The longer they last, the worse these train journeys get. I'll keep your seat for you," he promised, making room for her to pass.

She negotiated her way carefully down the narrow aisle, which was crammed with people and their belongings—pets, children, wicker baskets, suitcases, and packages of every size and shape. Some of the people munched on whatever food they had, some conversed or quarreled. Others stood immobile at the window, gazing at the open countryside.

Séverine struggled through several cars, but to her surprise and dismay, every WC was occupied by riders using the tiny rooms as traveling compartments. She groaned inwardly. How naïve she had been to think she would immediately find a closed door and a vacant room. Not in wartime! The train lurched again, and now her need became pressing. She stopped in front of a WC occupied by an entire family—mother, father and two children—who were taking their time unpacking a lunch and who looked thoroughly at home.

"Sorry to interrupt you," she said apologetically. "But I wish to use this room for its designated purpose."

"Designated purpose! That's rich," the father responded with a leer as he stared at her lasciviously. "Odette, did you hear that? Mademoiselle wants to come into this hell hole to use it for its 'designated purpose'." He seemed to find this hysterically funny, as did his wife and children, and soon the entire family was rocking back and forth, whooping with laughter.

Séverine clenched her teeth and willed herself not to respond in kind. She longed to pry each member of this loutish family out of the WC and throw them, one by one, onto the tracks. But to get into the cubicle, she would have to get them out. She would have to be patient and polite, yet stand her ground, just as the countess had taught her to do.

As she ruminated on a plan of action, she put her hand

in her pocket and was surprised to hear a crinkling sound. It came from the individually wrapped candies Caroline had surreptitiously slipped into it as she'd boarded the train. Silently blessing her sister, Séverine fished out six pieces, which she flashed in front of the two unkempt, mischievous brats who were openly mocking her. Séverine loved children, but not these two. Still, she always had a way with little ones.

"I bet you love chocolate, don't you?" she asked sweetly. "Well, you'll have three pieces each after you and your parents have vacated the premises." She liked the sound of "vacated the premises." She could have told them all to scram, but she wanted to retain the upper hand by speaking correctly.

The parents grumbled, but seeing their children's delight at the prospect of having sweets, which were so rare, they reluctantly ceded their campground. The father, determined not to lose face, gave Séverine a disapproving look and a warning as he stamped out into the corridor. "Be quick now." Placated by the bonbons she'd just given them, the children stared at their elegant benefactress with admiration.

Shutting the door behind her, Séverine swayed with the movement of the train but managed to sit down. When she had relieved herself, she stood up, straightened her skirt and glanced at herself in the small mirror above the tiny washbasin. Despite the pounding on the door which signified that her short time was already up, she smiled as she remembered Gisèle's hand on her back each time she slouched when taking tea or practicing piano, and her admonition: "Perfect posture, my dear, perfect posture! If you don't slouch you won't act like a slouch. If you sit up straight and stand up straight, you'll elevate not only your body, but also your thoughts." At the time Séverine had thought the advice far-fetched—but now, as she took a deep breath and drew herself up to her full height, she realized it was the ideal solution to the current situation. Unlocking the door, she sailed past the irate couple like a queen before her unruly subjects, all the while giving a broad wink to the surprised children. As she did on numerous other bothersome occasions from which she had managed to extricate herself with grace, she silently thanked Gisèle for teaching her about the power of good manners.

She would tell the story to Caroline the next time she saw her. Caroline would, of course, tease her about her infatuation with the countess, but that was to be expected.

Back in her compartment, Séverine took a quick look at the fellow traveler who had vacated his seat for her, and who was once again quickly rising to relinquish his place. So polite, she reflected, but he lacked the engaging gallantry of Antoine. He looked so serious with that ironic expression on his pale face. She wondered what it would take to make him laugh. She realized that she didn't even know his name, and there was no reason to ask at this point. She hadn't given him hers either, but she didn't care; he was just someone with whom she was passing time. Now that she had returned victorious from her little adventure, she felt giddy, loquacious almost, and was happy that she had someone to talk to. The countess would advise her to be gracious, to ask questions, draw the man out of his shell. But Severine knew she would never see him again, and the intensity of her desire to reminisce outweighed any long-ago lessons in deportment.

She began to babble, telling him once again about life in the castle, how she admired the countess so much, how her father had worked tirelessly on the grounds while her mother toiled in the castle itself.

"They almost ran the place!" she exclaimed. "The countess was so sad, I'd say even desperate, when we left for Paris."

The professor, as she now thought of her new companion, nodded his head as he encouraged her to talk and listened to her words with a sort of fascination.

He clenched his fists as he reflected on how feudal it all sounded, how exploited the family had been—and how this little ninny obviously didn't even know it.

"Do you know Paul Moreau?" she suddenly asked him, referring to her childhood friend.

"I know of him, but I don't know him," he replied, suddenly alert.

His answer was only half true. He'd heard that Moreau was in the Resistance.a resistant.

Yet only a few minutes ago, she had referred to resisters as "idiots".

He looked at her with renewed interest. Did she know Paul? Maybe she didn't know Moreau after all; maybe she had only heard of him. And even if she did know him, she wouldn't necessarily know his politics.

"I presume you do, since you're asking me," he added.

He got no reply; once again, she seemed to be lost in her own strange little world.

Chapter FIVE

Saint-Jean-de-Mornac: 1919

It was the end of the day for the boys and girls in the one-room school next to the town hall of Saint-Jean-de-Mornac, population 300. Some of the children ran races; others played tag or hopscotch. Some huddled together telling stories and sharing secrets as they waited for the final bell to ring. Eight-year-old Séverine leaned against a stone wall, winded from running this way and that.

Recovering her breath, she looked across the courtyard and was surprised to see her father at the front gate. Robert Aubry rarely came to pick up his daughter from school. At this time of the day he was usually working at the manor house, where he was the gardener. Now she watched him tip his cap to the director and say a few words as they looked in her direction.

She picked up her scattered belongings—scarf, sweater and satchel—and ran to join him, already thinking of everything she'd tell him about her day at school. She didn't know why he was there, but she was happy to see him and gave him a big hug, her eyes shining with delight and pride. Of all the parents she had seen, her Papa, she was convinced, was by far the best—and certainly the best-looking.

Robert hugged her briefly and without the strength and energy of his usual embrace. He looked around the schoolyard rather than at her. He wasn't smiling, and his eyes were red. He shoved his hand into the pocket of his clean but worn trousers, extracted a large checkered hand-kerchief and blew his nose. He looked like he had caught a terrible cold.

He took her by the hand and led her away from her comrades.

"I have something to tell you," he said, as they walked. "It's about Mémée." He paused, unsure of how to continue. He was not a man of words; he was a man who communi-cated with the earth, using his instincts and his hands and his tools. Eloquence was for people with education.

But today he had a terrible message to impart. He had to find a way.

Before he could go any further, Séverine exclaimed delightedly, "Mémée! I made a drawing for her." She dug down into her book bag, took out a paper and brandished it excitedly in front of his face. "It's our goose—you know, Mr. Right at Home, the one who is always in the yard and then waddles inside the house to snoop around."

The gaily colored goose was seated on a chair at their kitchen table, a triumphant expression on his face and a white bib tied around his neck. Then Robert remembered: one recent day after shooing the invader away for what must have been the tenth time, his mother had grumbled that if the goose kept up his his bad habits, he would soon invite himself to dinner.

Séverine chuckled. "Mémée's going to love it!"

Robert gritted his teeth. This was going to be harder than he thought.

"Mémée died," he blurted out. "She's no longer here."

The little girl's joyous expression faded as doubt, denial, realization and shock succeeded each other in seconds. She burst out crying and stood, still as a statue, tears cascading down her face.

Ashamed of his gruffness, Robert bent down so his eyes were on the same level as Séverine's. He took her little hands in his, stroked her hair and explained in a gentle voice, "She went to take a nap and didn't wake up. She looked peaceful, just like she was sleeping, but she wasn't breathing."

Then he stopped. He didn't know what else to say.

But he did know that he felt especially sorry for Séverine. Of his two daughters, she was the one who had inherited his mother's wide-spaced eyes, generous mouth and infectious good spirits. Séverine followed her everywhere, even creeping into her bed at night on the pretext of needing warmth. She liked the soft, scratchy feel of her grandmother's long flannel nightgown and her smell, a mixture of the animals she had taken care of during the day, the hard soap she used and smoke from the chimney. Mostly she liked having her grandmother all to herself.

As their stone hut came into view, Robert spoke once again. "You can cry all you like. It won't bring her back." He immediately regretted his words, but it was too late. He decided to leave her with her older sister, Caroline, who was already running to them.

Caroline had taken care of Séverine from the day she was born. She combed her sister's long, dark, glossy hair and secured the undisciplined strands in barrettes to keep them from falling over her eyes. She made sure that her shoes were shined and her clothes were clean and well-matched.

Now, she intercepted them, grabbing the sketch of the goose from her sister's hands. She held the drawing away from her, then brought it closer. "This is wonderful, Séverine. All those browns and yellows and greens, and that big white apron around his neck. Plus those funny webbed feet you colored purple instead of orange. He looks so meddlesome just the way he is. We should have called him Mr. Meddle. You know what?" Her voice softened and she crouched to look into her little sister's eyes. "Mémée is looking at your drawing right now from Heaven."

She pointed up to the sky, then, straightening, took Séverine's hand and led her to a little stone ledge where they often sat to watch the cows and sheep. Looking out over the lush countryside with spring flowers pushing up through the earth, breathing in the soft air and gazing at the pale blue sky, Caroline repeated that Mémée was watching over them, that she would never leave them.

"Mémée is in Paradise now, and soon we will be too," she affirmed.

"Are we going to die?" Séverine asked. She wanted to go to where Mémée was.

"No," Caroline replied, as she gave her a reassuring hug. "But we are leaving this place. Maman and Papa have been hired to work at the castle in Sorignac. They told me today. It's just like Paradise," she added. She began describing Sorignac. The streets were lined with gold, she told her sister. The countess was a beautiful and benevolent queen, and the castle was like something straight out of one of their fairytale books. Best of all, she said, they would live in their very own cottage in a room of their own under a sloping thatched roof.

Séverine didn't believe a word about the gold-lined streets or the benevolent queen. She knew for a fact she would rather have a living, breathing Mémée than an absent Mémée looking down at them from Heaven. But she sensed that the part about the cottage was true, and she especially liked the idea of sharing a bedroom with her sister. Séverine was capable of fantasy, to be sure, but she was also logical: without Mémée, their tiny three-room house was no longer home.

Chapter SIX

Sorignac: 1919

Standing before the tall second-floor windows of her ochre-colored limestone castle, Gisèle de Roquemaurel, née Gisèle de la Boissière, gazed at the sloping red-tiled roofs of the village houses below. She tried to ignore the tempting pack of cigarettes on the Louis XVI marble-topped table next to her, but finally gave in. She took one, lit it and inhaled deeply. She limited herself to five cigarettes a week, one for each weekday with a pause on the weekend. Today was a Saturday, but she had decided to break her rule. The new gardener and his wife were coming shortly, and she wanted to receive them personally and instruct them on their duties. She treasured this moment of privacy and the view she never tired of. She couldn't imagine not having that panorama any more than she could imagine not being the lady of the castle with all the privileges and duties that lofty station entailed.

Although she knew better, she sometimes entertained the idea that feudal times had never passed, that everyone in the town below still looked up to the castle and its occupants, the de la Boissières, who had lived there since the Middle Ages. The castle, with its imposing presence, had always provided the town with a cachet it otherwise would not have had. Originally built for defense and located on a rise at the western edge of the village, it radiated a graceful solidity. Although it had undergone extensive renovations in the eighteenth century, its original form had not changed significantly since it was first built.

The entrance to the grounds was composed of a gatehouse with a narrow tower on each side. A long, wide, winding lane flanked by ancient oaks led up to the front of the castle. A terrace in back overlooked formal gardens, a fountain and topiary of carefully trimmed boxwoods. Beyond was an expanse of untamed woods.

Some parts of the interior were cold and drafty and rarely used. Other spaces were more welcoming, with blazing fires in the huge fireplaces and family silver and antiques scattered throughout. In the huge ground-floor library, book-lined shelves surrounded a massive marble fireplace, in front of which stood a group of velvet-covered chairs and silk-covered settees. With its thick Persian rugs, soft yellow silk curtains and a highly polished eighteenth-century desk strategically placed so that the person sitting at it would benefit from but not be blinded by the light, the atmosphere was formal but not forbidding. The count wanted the library to exude a masculine aura and vigorously rejected his wife's attempts to inject a woman's softer touch. The curtains reminded her of her sole victory.

Upstairs, huge gold-framed portraits of austere-looking family members lined the wood-paneled gallery that led to Gisèle's personal library, a private place where she spent as much time as she could reading, and even reciting poetry on occasion. The framed forebears that occupied the walls were mostly men of the cloth, famous generals, famous politicians, famous judges. The few women dispersed among them had only one distinction: they were the appendages of their illustrious husbands. Gisèle was intrigued by one ancestor in particular, a certain Elizabeth de la Boissière who, after dutifully producing and raising twelve children, had entered the religious order of the Carmelites and taken a vow of silence.

Gisèle's fascination with Elizabeth was due to the fact that although they had the same genes, they were completely unalike. Where the dark-haired Elizabeth looked as though time had been less than kind to her, Gisèle at thirty was blond, blue-eyed, slim and sophisticated, with perfect posture and a love of life. She couldn't imagine having even one child, never mind twelve, a stipulation upon which, thankfully, she and the count had agreed wholeheartedly. Similarly, she couldn't see herself entering a religious order, not least because she couldn't conceive of keeping silent for any protracted period of time, let alone the rest of her life. She was too fond of speech and recitation, so much so that in spite of her parents' objections she'd gone to Paris at the age of eighteen to pursue an acting career.

Over the years, she had returned to the castle frequently. After she married Amaury de Roquemaurel, the scion of an old French family, the couple had made it their permanent home. Her Paris acting days were over, of course, but she'd kept up a lively correspondence with friends in the world of the theatre and the arts, who loved nothing more than to be invited to the castle.

After her parents died, Gisèle had assumed responsibility for running the ancestral home. It was a full-time undertaking, with both pleasures and duties. Her job was to keep up the castle and grounds and to play an important part in the life of the village. She knew every family by name, participated in every town festival and was generous with what she called "her" charities. She invited the priest to Sunday lunch and the mayor as well, but depending on the political stripe of the mayor, not necessarily on the same Sunday. She had her opinions but kept them to herself. She figured that people could probably guess her politics. She was all for law and order.

Perched above the town, the castle and its occupants were at a safe remove from the quarrels that had pitted certain factions of the townspeople against each other for centuries—the haves and the have-nots, the bourgeois and the workers, the right and the left—not to mention families who continued decades or centuries-long feuds even though they could no longer remember their original causes. Everybody played out their predestined roles in this tiny universe. Workers were workers; the bourgeois were the bourgeois. And the châtelains were aristocrats, on top of them all. These different classes of townspeople had their unique ways of life, and moved in separate social circles. The Catholics couldn't bear the idea of the Freemasons, the communists couldn't bear the idea of Catholics, and the workers at the local porcelain factory couldn't bear the idea of having a boss. The Freemasons didn't mix with the Catholics, the Catholics abhorred the communists, and the bosses had nothing to do with their workers once the working day was done. This was not to say, of course, that these dislikes and disputes were out in the open. Some were, but others simmered on under a veneer of politeness.

Inhaling deeply from her cigarette once more, Gisèle hoped she would get lucky with the Aubrys, who were coming to her with top recommendations. It was becoming more and more difficult to find people willing to put in the hours needed to keep up the huge château and grounds. Just Mestre, the gardener they'd previously employed, had always done the least amount of work possible, yet never failed to beg for a raise. When tools had started disappearing, the count had let him go. It had come as no surprise to Gisèle when she heard that he'd joined up with the local leftists. What a bunch of layabouts!

She pushed thoughts of her former employee from her mind. It was time for a new start. She glanced at her watch and saw that it was time to interview the new caretakers and introduce them to their new life.

Chapter SEVEN

Sorignac didn't have streets of gold, of course, but it was indeed a kind of paradise for a little girl who had spent the first eight years of her life in a hamlet that had more barns than houses. There was a girls' school and a boys' school, solid stone mansions behind high stone walls, a market that dated back to the fourteenth century and more shops than Séverine had ever seen. There was a flower shop, a shoe repair shop, a grocery store, a bakery, a butcher shop, a store for newspapers and magazines, even a shop that sold nothing but candy. The fifteenth-century church was grand, with high, light-filled stained-glass windows that took her breath away. Séverine could already imagine herself dressed all in white for her first Communion, then later, and in white again for her wedding. And she could already imagine who she would marry—Paul, her new and now best friend in the village.

Shortly after their arrival in Sorignac, Séverine fell ill with a cold. Her mother, Germaine, had taken her at once to see Dr. Georges Moreau, the town doctor. Impeccably dressed in a starched, dark blue pinafore over a white dress with lighter blue ribbons on her braids, young Séverine had sagged in her chair, sniffling and coughing, occasionally fiddling with the toys Georges had set out for toddlers. His son Paul, who was strictly forbidden to enter the waiting room, had rushed in, peppering the new girl with questions. What was her name? Where was she from? Where did she live? Could she come back and play at his house someday?

Germaine had smiled fondly at the sweet, energetic little boy with all the questions. Séverine, enchanted, had shed her lethargy as if it were an ill-fitting coat. Soon the two were on the floor playing with a wooden train and imitating its sound.

"Chug, chug, choo choo," they mouthed at each other before breaking into silly fits of laughter.

"I'll ask Papa to get some books and games for kids our age," Paul promised her. "But I hope you won't come here only when you're feeling sick!"

Séverine knew that very day, she told him years later, that he would be a doctor. His good spirits had cured her even before she got in to see his father, the "real" doctor who had given her medicine for her cold.

From then on, Séverine became a regular visitor at the Moreau household. The new friends spent most of their time reading or inventing games in a clearing in the forest behind the house.

On one of their days in the clearing, Paul mysteriously disappeared into the woods, leaving Séverine perplexed. She was thinking of returning to the house to tell his mother, but she hesitated. Although Huguette Moreau was perfectly polite, Séverine had the feeling that she wasn't enthusiastic about her visits. She also knew that Huguette watched their antics from her post at the kitchen window, and if Paul was gone for long, she would come to find out why.

As she was deciding what to do, a dark brown, mangy creature jumped at her from behind a bush. The monster was on all fours, emitting ferocious grunts, running in zigzags from one tree to another. When it reared up on its haunches, the costume slipped off and she recognized Paul. Hands on hips, she declared matter-of-factly, "You should have glued it on. I wasn't even scared."

Paul, struggling to replace the moth-eaten fur rug he had pulled up from in front of the fireplace in the guest bedroom, growled and snarled for effect, but finally, defeated, dropped to the forest floor and crept back into the woods. Moments later, when he saw that Séverine's back was turned, he silently crept up behind her and pounced on her again. "Gotcha!" he crowed, as Séverine, taken by surprise, screamed with fear, excitement, and delight.

When they'd calmed down and were seated once again on the ground, Paul confided in her. "Mamie likes to scare me with her bedtime stories. Last night she told me about a pack of wolves that roamed the Périgord in 1766. They escaped the king's hunters and killed eighteen people. They do eat people, you know," he said, opening his eyes wide as he lunged at her and pretended to take a bite of her arm. When she glared at him instead of recoiling, Paul paid her the ultimate compliment. "For a girl, you're not afraid of anything!"

Puffed up with pride, she ordered Paul to sit down again, this time slightly out of his mother's line of sight.

"I have a surprise," she announced solemnly as she brushed blades of grass off her pink and white striped cotton dress; the pink matched the rosy blush that had risen in her cheeks. "Close your eyes."

Paul obediently shut them tight and waited until she told him he could open them again.

He saw a glimmering gold coin in the palm of her hand.

"The countess gave it to me," she said, in her self-important but shy way. "And you know what? We're going to bury it. But you have to promise to keep the secret forever," she insisted, looking at him seriously.

Paul fingered the bright, heavy coin. It would be perfect for one of his favorite games, in which he played Robin Hood, robbing the rich to give to the poor.

"Can we dig it up sometimes?" he asked.

"Yes. Whenever we come here, the first thing we'll do is make sure it's still in this very place." She placed her hand solemnly over her heart. "So now you have to repeat after me: 'I pledge to keep the treasure secret and tell no one it exists.'"

Paul placed his hand over his own heart and repeated the words. They grinned at each other. Séverine loved the treasure because the countess had given it to her. Paul loved it because he could fulfill his fantasy of giving riches to the poor. And they both loved it because it was a secret, and they loved secrets.

As Huguette called for them to stop playing and come back to the house, Paul produced a needle he had filched from his mother's sewing kit.

He held it up in the air and asked, "Are you afraid of blood?"

Of course he knew what the answer would be. "No," Séverine answered scornfully.

"Then I'll prick your finger and mine, and we'll mix our blood so that we'll be blood brothers—except you're a girl so…" His voice trailed off.

"Blood *friends*," said Séverine. "Best friends, blood friends!"

Paul punctured his own finger first, then took Séverine's hand and did the same to hers. They rubbed the two tiny spots of blood together, placed the coin in a hole in a tree as a temporary hiding place and wiped their hands on the grass before racing each other back to the house.

* * *

Now that she had Paul for a friend, Séverine was sure that everything would be all right. But she hadn't felt that way at first. During her first days in Sorignac, she had been delighted with the town—its newness and all the unusual things there were to see and do. But she missed the freedom of the country, and her beloved geese, pigs, cows, dogs and cats. She even missed the cocky goose, Mr. Right at Home.

And she didn't know what to think about the new living arrangements. To be sure, her parents had been the "help" at the manor they had worked in previously, but they hadn't lived on the grounds. Here it was different, like being part of a family that wasn't really her family.

Her parents explained that the cottage they lived in was theirs as long as they worked at the castle, but that they were replaceable. That was why Germaine and Robert never missed a day of work, never slackened their pace, they told the girls. Lessons about their social status, their precarious existence, their lowly place in the castle universe were drummed into the girls' heads constantly, especially after Germaine had heard Séverine boasting to a classmate that she lived in the town castle. She had ordered her to stop.

"People might get confused, or think we're proud," was all she said.

Séverine began to understand that as far as her family was concerned, there was something bad about being proud. She no longer told people that she lived in the castle or even in a tiny house on the estate.

Instead, she created an imaginary world in which she was the countess, living in and lording over the noble rooms of the château and the vast domain around it. She had Louis XVI furniture, ate from fine porcelain, drank only the finest champagne and ordered her maid around. But she had to be fair; in real life the countess did not issue orders to Germaine. On the contrary, she was kind to her, giving instructions clearly and never reprimanding her.

But why should she? Séverine's mother was always on time, since the cottage was a short walk away from the immense château. The count and countess had a butler, driver, cook and various other personnel, but Germaine, with her fair hair, clear blue eyes and reserved, polite manner, was seen as the person who could do almost anything, from cleaning to serving to greeting guests at the door. The count and countess came to depend on her; her husband and daughters affectionately called her the countess's "all-around lady."

Every day, Germaine washed, dried, mended and neatly arranged the count and countess's garments, dusted and polished their furniture and served—and sometimes, when the cook was off duty—prepared their meals. After finishing her duties at the castle, she took the short walk back to her family's modest cottage, where she washed and dried and mended and arranged her family's affairs, dusted and polished their furniture and prepared their meals. Germaine called it her "double day" and never complained. One set of tasks was for money, she'd say, the other for love.

Germaine kept the cottage sparkling clean, insisting that the girls pitch in and pick up after themselves. "I've spent a whole day over there," she would say to them, pointing in the direction of the castle. "I don't want to start all over again when I come home." She taught her daughters to cook, clean, iron and sew. "I hope you'll land fine positions, perhaps as teachers. But no matter what you do, you'll need these skills," she would tell them, as she showed Caroline how to hem a skirt or gently scolded Séverine for leaving wrinkles in her father's shirt.

"Daydreaming instead of ironing?" she asked one afternoon, looking fondly at her youngest child. In fact, Germaine was the one who was daydreaming: she imagined Séverine married to someone so wealthy that she herself would have a maid. The preposterous thought amused her; she gently tousled her daughter's hair and set her about her tasks again.

"You two should count your blessings," she reminded the girls regularly. "We're lucky to have this cottage all to ourselves. You're better off here than in one of those tiny servants' rooms in the castle."

Soon after they arrived, Séverine decided to see for herself. One day she slipped into the castle unnoticed through a back door, made herself as small as she could and sneaked up a back staircase to the upstairs quarters. There she saw a long hall with a toilet room at one end and many doors on each side. She knew the servants were all downstairs working, so she turned the knob of one door to peek in. The room was indeed tiny, with a washbasin, bed, chest of drawers and chair. The occupant was neat: there was a candle on a rickety table near the tightly made bed and a hairbrush on the chest of drawers. There might have been more objects to investigate, but suddenly her courage failed her: What if someone came down the hall and thought she was stealing? Suddenly frightened, she quietly tiptoed out, shut the door gently, and silently crept down the stairs. No one, or at least no one she saw, saw her.

Not long after that, her curiosity got the better of her once more. She had accompanied her mother, who was cleaning the countess's bedroom. Bored of standing still and watching Germaine mopping and dusting, Séverine slipped silently into the enormous walk-in closet, planning to pop out and startle her mother, a game she and her sister often played at home. Her mother might have forgiven her for that, but Séverine immediately became nosy. She ran her hands over the rows of gowns and shoes, and then, forgetting herself completely, opened one after the other of the ornate wooden drawers and fingered the countess's goods: ribbons, brooches, collars, gloves—a vast array of beautiful treasures.

Just as she was trying to fit a pair of sleek leather gloves on her small hands, the countess swept into the closet to look for a sweater and discovered the intruder.

"Young lady!" she boomed, her voice cold.

Séverine whirled, her heart in her mouth. She felt her face grow hot with shame as her mother rushed to her side.

"I'm so sorry, Madame," Germaine said, as she quickly pieced together what had happened. "Séverine, you must apologize to the countess and promise her you will never, ever touch her personal things again."

Séverine burst into tears and briefly took solace in her mother's arms before turning to look into Gisèle's icy blue eyes. "Please forgive me, Madame. I wanted to know what kinds of wonderful things you have because I often see you wearing lovely gloves and hats. I would never take anything from you. I only wanted to try on your gloves because... because someday I would like to be like you."

Gisèle was an actress and could spot a good performance anywhere. But she could see that the child's words were genuine. As much as Gisèle could not tolerate the daughter of a servant poking around in her affairs, she was touched by the girl's confession. Could it be true that Séverine wanted to be like her someday? Why?

Like so many of her station, Gisèle was incapable of imagining Séverine's life in the modest caretakers' house: the tiny bedroom she shared with her sister, her sparse wardrobe, the few objects that were hers and hers alone. She was incapable of imagining that Séverine could only dream of owning a pair of kid gloves, let alone several. Above all, she couldn't guess, although it was the truth, that for the child "being like Gisèle" meant having the things Gisèle had, not resembling who she was, because Séverine knew nothing about her personally.

"You may leave now," Gisèle told the child, dismissing her with as much coldness as she could muster.

She was baffled, almost amused by the child's temerity and felt the need to observe Germaine's daughter before she decided what to do about her. She wasn't like Just's son Luc, who always wore such a furtive look on his face. Séverine had rifled through her personal belongings, something she could not tolerate. But she was forthright and had defended herself courageously, appealing—however innocently—to Gisèle's vanity. It could be a subterfuge, of course, but it intrigued her. This little girl wanted "things," and without knowing it, wanted to rise above her station. She was articulate and bright—a combination that could be good or bad. Gisèle would have to find a solution before the yearning for possessions that the child could never afford to buy posed a problem.

It was a challenge, and Gisèle loved challenges.

Séverine's older sister Caroline, on the other hand, didn't pose problems. A blond replica of her mother, she was not as lively but was perfectly polite, always neatly dressed and reliable. Germaine would often bring her into the kitchen, where she would sit at one end of the large wooden table occupying herself with a project, either sewing or drawing or schoolwork. The dark-haired and vivacious Séverine, on the other hand, spent most of her time outdoors trailing her equally dark-haired father, Robert, around the property as he carried out his various chores. Gisèle often saw the little girl skipping alongside him and marveled at how his otherwise stern expression softened as he observed her antics.

She was more than satisfied with this new family. Unlike Just and his family, the Aubrys knew what to do and did their work without needing to be asked or cajoled. Robert kept the immense grounds neat. He quickly came to know every inch of land, every tree that needed cutting, every bush that needed to be trimmed, every bed of flowers that needed to be re-thought and re-planted. Gisèle soon recognized his talent and his capacity for hard work. They were employer and employee, of course, but they were also collaborators against the vagaries of nature. Inside the castle, Gisèle never had to ask Germaine to polish the silver. When the various pieces showed tarnish, Germaine made them shine. When clothes needed mending, Gisèle put them in a basket that Germaine would return to her the next day. Germaine even modified the sparse menus that the weight-conscious Gisèle planned; she increased the portions for the count, who had no need to watch his figure, and added on a dish or two especially for him. Delighted, the count began to appear in the kitchen on some pretext or other, where Germaine would press him to sample a dessert she had on hand. His refusal was stiff and abrupt at first, but before long he would simply sit at Germaine's long worktable, happy as a schoolboy, and wolf down his treat.

* * *

One day, Germaine came to ask the countess if she could invite young Paul Moreau, who was by now fast friends with Séverine, to play at the cottage.

"I appreciate your consideration," Gisèle told her, "but you don't have to ask me about whom you invite to your home. I trust my staff," she added, her coded way of saying that naturally those guests would remain on the grounds of the cottage, and that no one at the castle would see them or have anything to do with them.

"I am happy that Paul and Séverine are such good friends," she went on. "I see the doctor on his rounds, but I haven't seen his boy for quite some time." Almost as an aside, she added, "Paul's father and I were good friends at that age."

What the countess didn't say was more interesting and important than what she did. Had she continued, she would have explained that Georges had belonged to her social milieu before he abandoned the "de" in front of his name, indicating his aristocratic origins, that they had been inseparable until her parents forbade her to see him, and that her parents had warned her that any man who would abandon his social class was a dangerous influence.

"I think inviting him to play with Séverine is a delightful idea," she said, "especially because you mentioned that she is always the one going to his house." She twisted her pearl necklace slowly as she ruminated. "I have an idea but I don't want to interfere," she finally said. "I would like to invite the children over here for tea after they've played together at your home. It will be nice for them, as they'll be hungry, and it would be good for me as I'm not around youngsters that much, as you know."

The countess's "ideas" were, of course, not to be rejected. Germaine merely bowed her head in agreement and returned to her duties.

On the appointed day, Gisèle stood in the grand main entrance and watched Dr. Georges Moreau drive up the lane in his jalopy. His little boy sat in the passenger seat, dressed in a suit and tie, his dark hair neatly combed and his eyes wide with excitement. Georges' driving style reflected the man himself—careful, conscientious yet with a touch of panache. She reined in her thoughts as Georges gave Paul a quick pat on the shoulder, probably reassuring him he'd only be a minute, then jumped out of the car and glanced up at the castle. She wondered if he was thinking about the times they had shared together here before her parents declared him persona non grata. Leaping up the steps towards her, he left her no time for conjecture.

"I know it's impolite, but I asked Paul to stay in the car since we have so little time. You'll get to meet him later anyway. But I wanted to stop to thank you now because I've got a busy day and I will have no time to come later. Gisèle, this is a brilliant idea." He added in an undertone, "It's really very kind of you to have invited the two of them for tea, or whatever you're giving them, but I wonder if you realize what you're getting into. Eight-year-olds are better than two-year-olds, but they can still get rambunctious."

"Don't worry, Georges. I'm sure I can handle it."

"Don't I know it, Madame la comtesse," he murmured, not quite meeting her eye. Unspoken words hovered in the air. He lingered a minute as if he'd like to stay longer, then quickly returned to his car. Gisèle re-entered the castle, accompanied by the smell of the pipe smoke in Georges's tweed jacket, the faint fragrance of his woody cologne and the good mood he always instilled in her.

The car bounced down a narrow lane and hadn't even come to a halt in front of Séverine's house when Paul bounded out of it, barely turning to say goodbye as he slammed the door.

"So, this is where you live!" he exclaimed to Séverine. He took in the tiny downstairs room that was separated into three parts: a living/dining room, a kitchen and her parents' bedroom. A narrow flight of stairs led to the girls' room under the eaves. The entire cottage could have fit into one of the wings of his own house, but he liked the simple furnishings, the bouquet of daisies on the table and the smell of something good baking in the oven. Had it been raining he would have happily stayed inside, but the sun was shining and Séverine's mother shooed them both briskly out the door.

When they returned, Paul's crisply ironed white shirt had come out of his trousers, his tie was askew and his hands were black. Séverine's braids were undone and her hands and face were streaked with dirt. They hung their heads and sneaked looks at each other as Germaine chided them. She made them apologize for their careless behavior, then marched them into the bathroom, washed hands and faces, tucked Paul's shirt back in and re-braided Séverine's hair. On the walk to the castle, she drummed into them the need for good manners. "Don't talk too much or eat too much, and don't ask for seconds," she reminded them. "And I expect you back here in one hour sharp. You mustn't overstay your welcome."

The little party drew up at the entrance to the castle, where the countess awaited them.

"Thank you again for your kind offer, Madame," Germaine said to her. "Have a good time," she told the children. She gave them all a little wave and began the walk back home.

The children, who hadn't stopped talking since Paul arrived, fell silent, suddenly shy and overawed. The countess shepherded them in, remarking that she was glad to see Paul and how he had grown and how much he looked like his father—a carbon copy, she said—and how lovely Séverine looked in her new pink candy-striped dress. She led them into the formal dining room and sat them down opposite each other at one end of the immense, highly polished mahogany table which could seat twenty. It was laden with jam and bread and butter, exquisite little tea cakes, and two glass carafes, one filled with water and the other with fruit juice. There was also a pot of tea and teacups in case they wanted to try something more exotic.

"You must be hungry," the countess said, "although you don't look like you've run around much. Your mothers must have made you sit still all day!" She let them choose their cakes, then watched as they devoured them. Paul, she could see, was used to being with grown-ups, and quickly found his tongue again.

He began to ask her questions: Why wasn't she eating? Didn't she like to eat? He did. Did she make those delicious cakes? Did she know that he could make cakes? Next time he would bring her some *madeleines*. As he talked, he leaned towards her and told her about his school, his activities, how he wanted to be a cook but his father wanted him to be a doctor. Gisèle hoped he wouldn't talk about his mother, Huguette, and fortunately he didn't. Like Georges at the same age, he was funny, charming and endearing. She warmed to him instantly.

Séverine, although she had accompanied her mother into some of the rooms of the castle, was not used to huge dining rooms with tapestries on the wall, enormous sideboards, a majestic dining room table with huge high-backed chairs for sumptuous or semi-formal feasts. As Paul sidled up closer and closer to Gisèle, she looked around her. She was intrigued by the silk curtains, the view of the manicured grounds from the windows. She was gratified that her mother had undoubtedly polished that table, maybe even made the savory cakes on the plate in front of her, and that her father was responsible for the beautiful view.

At the same time, something new was happening, and it both excited and shamed her: she realized that when she grew up, she would prefer to be in the countess's place rather than in her parents' humble dwelling. Oh, the cottage was comfortable enough, and there were always good smells from the kitchen. Although tiny, her home was always neat and clean. But the plates they ate on weren't like these. Without thinking, she moved her fingers over the china saucer. It was so delicate, almost transparent. The plates in her house were thick and heavy. She looked at the silver, even picked up her fork to weigh it in her hands. It was heavy as well. Then she looked at the countess with unfeigned admiration. She remembered Caroline telling her about a town just like Paradise, about how there was a castle there, and a beautiful and benevolent queen. She had dismissed that fantasy at the time, knowing that Caroline was trying to find a way to console her for the loss of their grandmother and reassure her about the upcoming move to Sorignac, but now as she stared at Gisèle she realized that Caroline was right. The countess was indeed beautiful and benevolent, and Séverine had made up her mind: she wanted to be like her when she grew up.

Gisèle, who was listening to Paul, saw Séverine deep in thought, watched her fingering the china and wondered if she was bored. It occurred to her that she really didn't know what to say to children, so she decided to tell them about going to Paris when she was young. She described the crowded streets, the tall buildings, the Bois de Boulogne and the Bois de Vincennes flanking the city on each side, and the Eiffel Tower. The city was so vast, she told them, that it was divided into different neighborhoods, and some people never even left the one they lived in.

She told them about the many grand and ornate theaters, and confided that she had not only been to the theater but had acted. This made both children sit up a little bit straighter and look at her, wonderstruck. Paul volunteered that he and Séverine loved to play wolf and scare each other. Séverine giggled softly, and then confided that she loved poetry.

"Well, that settles it," Gisèle said brightly. "Would you like to see my collection of poetry books?" The children nodded enthusiastically, and the little group trooped upstairs to her library. Selecting a book of fables by the seventeenth-century poet Jean de La Fontaine, she bade Paul and Séverine sit on the sofa and read a few passages of *The Crow and the Fox*. The children, who knew the poem and never tired of it, laughed with glee at the part when the vain crow, puffed up by the fox's flattery, dropped the cheese in its beak—which the fox immediately seized. "What is the moral of the story?" she asked them.

"Flattery will get you nowhere," they chimed, almost in unison. The countess smiled and gave them each a light, affectionate pat.

"How wonderful it is that you love poetry," she exclaimed, closing the book. "Jean de La Fontaine, Rimbaud, Ronsard, Verlaine, Mallarmé—those are just a few of the greats. She plucked a small leather-bound volume from another shelf. "And don't forget the famous Occitan troubadour Bertran de Born, lord of the castle of Hautefort, which is not all that far from here. That was way back in the twelfth century. Did you know that Dante, a famous Italian poet, consigned de Born to hell for his attempt to get the sons of Henry II of England to rebel against their father?"

The children were quiet now, looking at her politely. She knew she was talking too fast, way above their heads, and perhaps should have not mentioned the word "hell." Ah well. She glanced at the mantel clock: it was time for them to leave, anyway, so she finished with a piece of advice. "Be sure to read poems out loud. If you stumble over a word you don't know, don't stop or be discouraged. Just keep reading and enjoy the rhythm and the language. You can look up the word later."

The children nodded assent.

"Your company has been a pleasure, but I promised I would send you home at five on the dot. I'll walk you to the door, and then you must go straight back to the cottage. No dawdling!"

She led the children back downstairs and along a corridor to the front entrance. "Thank you so much for coming," she told them graciously, and each child politely thanked her in return. She stood watching them as they set off together, hand in hand. Then, passing a hand over her brow, she turned and went back inside the castle, closing the door firmly behind her. She was exhausted from the excitement and the effort. How on earth, she wondered, did parents expend such energy every day?

Chapter EIGHT

"There are two things in life: the material and the immaterial. Do you know what that means?" the countess asked Séverine. The two of them were in the library, where hot tea had been served on a large silver tray.

"I don't think so, Madame," Séverine replied. She passed her hand over the soft velvet of the sofa on which she was seated, enjoying its luxurious feel. Although she had been to the castle with Paul not long ago, this was the first time she'd been invited to take tea alone with the countess. She couldn't understand why, but she knew it must be important. Perhaps she was going to be reprimanded, although she had taken care not to annoy the countess ever since that terrible day when she had been caught trying on her gloves.

She took in the brocaded curtains, the crackling fire in the enormous fireplace with its marble mantelpiece, the ancient tapestries of hunting scenes that framed it on either side and the precious antique furniture. She reached carefully for her teacup, sipped, and gazed again at the tea set. She had never seen such a thing. The pot, the sugar bowl, the pitcher for the milk—it was all silver with an intricately chiseled flower design. Séverine couldn't help thinking that her mother was the one who made that silver shine, whose cloth got black as she rubbed away at each and every delicate flower. At least she wasn't serving, she thought gratefully; she had, of course, no way of knowing that Gisèle had seen to that in order to avoid an awkward situation.

"Well, then," said Gisèle, pleased to be educating this obviously intelligent eight-year- old, "material things are ones we need to buy—clothes, food, things we need to survive. But once we have the basics, we don't have to strive to get more than what we need, or make possessions our main goal."

Séverine couldn't help thinking that it would be easy not to strive for possessions if you already had a high-ceilinged room like the one she was sitting in, with silver-framed family pictures and velvet-covered couches and a maid serving tea. But she sat up straight to show that she was listening.

"Do you mean that it's not good to desire things?" she asked.

"Well, I don't know about good or bad, but it is futile in the end. It becomes a game you can never win because you're never satisfied with what you have. You always want more!

"Now, why am I telling you this, Séverine? Because there is something else in life—the immaterial—and you can have as much of that as you want. The immaterial is not something you can buy. The immaterial is what you think, what you believe, what you feel. For example, you can buy a piano, but you can't buy the ability to play the piano or the culture needed to understand a great piece of music. That's something you have to work for, and the reward is better than anything you could ever purchase. So, you see, you can avoid a lot of frustration if you concentrate on learning, studying, trying to grasp knowledge."

The child was so well brought up, the countess mused,

observing her. She didn't fidget during the entire lecture, and although she had confessed that it was the first time she had ever tasted tea, she drank it perfectly properly, setting the cup back on the saucer without a sound. Gisèle reminded herself to compliment her parents on her upbringing.

"All this is to say that, with your parents' permission, I've engaged a piano instructor for you. You'll see him once a week and can practice on the piano whenever my husband and I are not using the room—on the condition that you practice for an hour a day. Otherwise, it would be quite useless."

Séverine, who indeed hadn't moved once during the talk, jumped up from the sofa, almost breaking the teacup, and embraced the countess. Then, without a word, she bolted from the room, clattering off down the hall and back to her cottage to share the incredible news with Caroline.

"Diamond in the rough." Gisèle murmured to herself as she stood at the window, watching the child careening down the path. "Not even a thank-you." In spite of herself, she was smiling. She would devote her next session—for she was now sure there would be a next session—to manners.

"I'll make something out of that child if it takes me forever," she heard herself saying out loud.

Chapter NINE

Sorignac: June 1928

Séverine took her place at the piano. She clasped her hands and focused her gaze on the keyboard. She hoped she didn't look as nervous as she felt. Playing for an audience was different from playing for herself. When she was alone at the castle, all was silent save the chiming of the grandfather clock, which the countess refused to remove from the music room in spite of Séverine's repeated hints. Today, in spite of her pre-recital concentration, she heard the laughing and chattering and squeaking of chairs as parents greeted each other and took their seats in the school auditorium. Maman and Papa weren't in the front row, she could see. She presumed they had found places in the middle or the back of the hall. They were like that— small of stature, unobtrusive, afraid of being showy or conspicuous. They possessed dignity but knew their place, living close to grandeur but not part of it.

She glanced at the score, then at the audience, where she briefly met the gaze of Caroline, who had taken a seat with Séverine's class in the middle rows of the auditorium. The whispering in the assembly hall stopped as Séverine straightened her back, positioned her hands on the keys and nodded to the page turner. A hush fell over the hall as she began to play. She no longer saw or heard the audience as she gave herself fully to Chopin's *Valse Brillante*.

As the music flowed through the auditorium, Germaine thought about how this evening's performance might never have happened. Over the preceding weeks, as she went about her duties in the area near the castle's music room, she had heard Séverine practicing the piece. One afternoon she had been going over the difficult parts but making so many mistakes that all sound finally ceased. Intrigued, Germaine had crept down the hall to the music room and hidden behind the half-open door. Séverine sat slumped at the piano, her hands on her lap, an expression of frustration on her face and a set to her jaw Germaine knew well.

"I can't do it!" she cried, and in a swift movement she grabbed the score with both hands and threw it to the floor.

The countess, who was standing on one side of the grand piano facing Séverine, remained calm and cool. "Séverine," she remonstrated, "please control yourself. Pick up your music and never let me see such an unfortunate display of behavior again."

Looking abashed, Séverine retrieved the scattered pages, put them back in place and apologized.

"That's better," the countess commented dryly after Séverine resumed her place on the bench. "Do you remember what I told you about the material and the immaterial? What you are doing is wonderfully immaterial. You are grappling with something larger than yourself. You are grappling with art. Even if you can't get this passage right yet, know that by studying it, by working on it, you are part of something greater than yourself. Think about Chopin when he composed this piece. Where was he? What was he thinking about? What do you know about Chopin? What was his life? What were his feelings? Go now, my child," she said, dismissing her protégée. "Read about the great composers. This is more than a technical exercise. It's an initiation into life."

Without waiting for a response, the countess left the room. Germaine scurried quietly away down the corridor. She had a lunch to cook and serve, and she especially didn't want Séverine to know that she'd witnessed the scene and overheard the countess's words.

She wasn't surprised, though, when Séverine checked out biographies of Chopin, Bach, Beethoven and other composers from the public library and immersed herself in them. She began to relax into her studies, enjoying her lessons more now that she had set the music she was playing into a broader context.

"Did you know that Chopin kept his public appearances to a minimum and played mostly in private salons?" Germaine heard Séverine ask the countess some time after the incident. She smiled to herself as she dusted nearby and strained to hear the rest of the exchange. She knew that her daughter was trying to get out of recitals by referring to the great composer's fabled aversion to them.

Unfortunately for Séverine, the countess dismissed her comment. "My, you've become a sophist," she said, not explaining what a sophist was. That was normal: it was the countess's job to furnish words and concepts, and it was Séverine's to look them up and try to understand them. "Remember, Séverine, that you're not Chopin. You're *playing* Chopin and should welcome as many opportunities as you can get to do so."

Germaine didn't know what a sophist was either, and she would never have been able to use the kind of words the countess did. Sometimes a mother wasn't enough, she reflected. Her daughter needed a mentor, someone who could bring a different experience, another point of view, and in this case, more culture and education into her life.

Her employer clearly saw something special in Séverine and was happy to hone and polish and fashion the rough material of which she was made.

She felt fortunate that the family had lived for so long in such favorable conditions. But that was now coming to an end. She had learned a week ago that Robert had accepted a job in Paris and they would soon be leaving. She was sad, but not worried about Séverine. The lessons the countess had instilled in her would serve her well, she thought, as she settled back in her chair and gave her full attention to the music.

* * *

"Séverine Aubry." The director of the school, looking distinguished in a light gray three-piece suit, articulated every syllable of her name. "First prize in history, geography and music."

As Séverine rose to accept the award on stage, she heard loud clapping coming from the middle of the auditorium. Her parents would never applaud that loudly—that would be an ostentatious public display of their joy, something they would never do no matter how proud they were of their bright, perfectionist daughter. She returned to her seat bearing three illustrated books, one on Napoleon, one on French colonies in Africa and one on the composer Hector Berlioz. The leather covers were red with gold lettering and gilt edges. She had very few books of her own and was honored to have these, marked with the name of her school, her name and "First Prize."

"Was that you?" she asked as soon as she saw her sister. "Did you clap louder than everyone else? I'm sure I heard you."

"Of course I didn't, silly," Caroline replied, looking around her to see who was listening. "It was Paul."

Séverine didn't ask which Paul. There were many boys named Paul, but there was only one who counted. As Paul's mother Huguette had accurately predicted, the two no longer spent every day together as they had when they were younger, but the link of friendship was not—as Huguette had hoped—broken.

Séverine smiled. Paul was special to her, like a brother. Sometimes she pictured him as more than a brother, but whenever she did, she would feel the blood rushing to her cheeks. She looked over Caroline's shoulder and saw the lanky young man loping toward them.

"What can I say, Séverine?" He opened his arms wide and beamed at her. "Beautiful and brilliant—it's not fair. And you've scooped up almost all the prizes! What do you think, Caroline—couldn't your little sister have been a bit more generous to her classmates?"

"Now then, Paul," said his father, who had joined the group, "you'd do well to imitate her instead of spending all your spare time trying to make the perfect soufflé."

"It's not my fault if I've got a mother and grandmother who are perfect cooks," Paul replied with assurance.

Paul's passion, from the first time he had breathed in the warm, tempting smells coming from the kitchen, was cooking. But Georges was having none of it. When he'd seen that Paul was serious about his pastime, he immediately signed him up for boxing lessons. He couldn't let Huguette make a pansy out of him. When she had told her husband that she envisaged Paul as a professional cook, he had replied tartly, "Paul will be a doctor, like me. And that's it," he'd added, closing the subject once and for all.

"Ah, Madame," Georges said now, turning to acknowledge Séverine's mother. "Paul is right. You do indeed have a beautiful and brilliant daughter. How proud you must be!"

"Séverine's a good student," Germaine acknowledged,

flattered that this man, the town doctor and their family doctor, who was so well-known and respected, had complimented her daughter. "But we hear your Paul took first prize in science and math at his school," she said, simultaneously acknowledging Paul's presence and turning the attention away from Séverine. She wanted to compliment Paul on what she had heard about his cooking skills as well, but knew from her conversations with Séverine that Georges Moreau would not approve. Instead, she smiled and kept her mouth closed; this, of course, was second nature for Germaine, a servant and the daughter of servants—which wasn't to say it was an easy task. She often found herself wanting to boast about Séverine. She would never say it, rarely indulged in thinking about it, but she was convinced that her younger daughter was special. There was something undeniably captivating about the child, a certain magnetism.

Naturally, she loved both her daughters, but she never ceased to be astounded at how different they were. Her first-born, Caroline, was a typical first child: serious, conscientious, down to earth, practical, helpful, steady, always looking out for others. And then there was Séverine, so quick to learn, so curious, so focused, creative and funny, yet impulsive, unpredictable and outspoken. From time to time, Germaine worried that the girl lived perhaps a trifle too much in her own world, that she might offend people with her outspokenness without meaning to.

Sometimes she thought that her daughters' roles had been determined before they were born. One would be larger than life with a luminous future; the other not as glittering but a devoted admirer and happy to be so. But those kinds of reflections were a waste of time, Germaine told herself. With children, you never knew.

Paul's father turned to Séverine. "We want to celebrate the end of the year. After all, my son may be good at science and math, but he's lucky to have an artistic friend like you to expand his horizons. Please come over, all of you, for a drink at our place." He looked fondly at Séverine, Caroline and their parents, who were all dressed in their best clothes. "We'll expect you for a drink Sunday a week from now at five, shall we?" He looked at Huguette, thinking she would be pleased he'd left her a week to fuss about what she would serve.

"Of course," she cooed. Her lips turned up in an expression of pleasure as she contemplated the group. But Georges saw—and hoped no one else did—that her eyes were cold.

Later that evening, as she and her husband read in the parlor after dinner, she raised the topic of the invitation. "I can understand your inviting Paul's friend to celebrate the end of the year, but her parents? Frankly, my dear, sometimes I think you don't understand the prestige of your position. What are those poor people going to do here? They'll be totally out of place! What on earth shall we talk about?" Huguette shrugged in disbelief and then gave her husband a brief hug to take the sting out of her inhospitable words.

Georges watched his wife, with her striking auburn hair and green eyes, and inevitably reflected that she'd never outgrown her own deep-rooted self-doubt. Although she had been born Huguette de Mossac, daughter of a baron, she was ashamed of the fact that her mother had been a commonplace Dupont from modest origins who had worked as a hairdresser before meeting and marrying the baron. Only Georges knew the secret of his wife's humble origins.

"You know as well as I do that Séverine and Paul are best friends, and she would probably be his girlfriend if things were different. She knows her place well, better than you think." Georges shifted in his large leather chair and glanced approvingly at the comfortable living room with its grand piano and two large, high glass doors giving on to the cobblestone patio. On the far side of the patio was the door to the annex where he held his consultations.

"And in any case," he added, "Paul and Séverine may soon part. I heard that the family will be going up to Paris, where they have some kind of connection. I hope so for them. Maybe they'll make a better living. The count and countess are perfectly agreeable, of course, but they don't pay terribly well. Surely they'll find something better in Paris."

Reassured, Huguette stooped over her husband to give him a quick kiss. "You're always so kind, Georges—sometimes even too kind. When I think of all the visits you haven't charged the Aubrys for…" Her husband opened his mouth to protest, but she raised a hand to halt him. "You can't contradict me. I manage the accounts!"

"Enough of that, Huguette," he replied. "There are many people in this town I don't bill because they can't pay, and I can't leave them ill. It's a vicious cycle—they get sick, can't get treated, can't work, and it's all downhill from there. I don't want people, especially honest people like the Aubry family, to go that way because of me. And never forget, Huguette: they have always paid me back and have no debts toward me, nor to anyone else in this community as far as I know. Upstanding people, I tell you."

He stuck his pipe in his mouth and took up the newspaper, signaling that this was the end of the conversation. He didn't want to talk about specific cases, nor did he want the discussion to turn, as it inevitably did, to the Mestre family who, in contrast to the Aubrys, did have debts they'd never pay back and were the opposite of upstanding. The father, Just, his wife Augustine, their son Luc, and assorted Mestre cousins all came to Dr. Moreau regularly for anything from the common cold to hemorrhoids, and not one of them paid.

In the beginning, Just had gone through the motions at least, but now he didn't even bother. Just's shoe repair business wasn't doing that badly, but Just was one of those people who considered that the world owed him something. He had managed to instill the same philosophy into the rest of the family and since there was no other doctor around for miles, Georges couldn't refuse their visits, although he tried to make them as short as possible. But it irritated him, and he couldn't help wishing that the entire Mestre clan were moving to Paris instead of the Aubrys.

He smiled to himself as he remembered Just's last visit, for the removal of a shotgun pellet he had received in his backside while hunting with a clumsy friend. Georges had maintained what he hoped was a detached expression as he extracted it. As usual, Just had left without paying but in an uncharacteristic show of generosity—perhaps due to the delicate nature of the procedure and in the faint hope the doctor would keep it a secret—returned an hour later holding two skinned rabbits, which Huguette had cooked in a delicious cream and mustard sauce with freshly picked chanterelles.

Celebrating the unusual occurrence, the two had raised their glasses. "To Just, who for once in his life was just!" Georges had said, laughing.

"And here's hoping it's not roadkill," Huguette added, smiling sweetly.

"Oh well, let's enjoy it," Georges replied, plunging his fork into the tender flesh and exquisite sauce.

Séverine, who was at the house playing with Paul that day, had screamed upon seeing the bloody heads and taut, furless bodies of the rabbits splayed out on the kitchen counter. Georges smiled as he remembered her shrieks, Paul ribbing her, and their high-spirited argument over the merits of cooking the animal with the head or without. Paul maintained it was good for the sauce (he'd heard his grandmother say that to his mother), while Séverine proclaimed that she'd rather die than eat anything, fish or fowl, that had been cooked with its head still on. She especially couldn't bear to look at the lifeless eyes. Paul told her she was too squeamish; she retorted that he was a savage. After a few minutes, they'd become bored and gone on to other subjects. Georges had quietly admired the way Séverine never backed down, and sometimes found himself wishing that they had had a daughter like her. He liked her show of character. Huguette, not surprisingly, found her too cheeky.

Watching Georges now, seated across the room with his book, Huguette tried to read his mind. Surely, he couldn't be smiling about the people who didn't pay him! She'd been married long enough to know that Georges wouldn't allow himself to dwell on unpleasant subjects for long and that he'd made the leap in his mind from the Mestres to something more pleasing. She pursed her lips as she fought the temptation to open her mouth. She knew Georges didn't like to discuss his patients or what she called his "charity work," and although she didn't approve, she nonetheless respected him for helping honest people when they were down and out.

She decided it was time to break the silence and sighed loudly.

"It's a pity that the Hippocratic Oath includes helping people like the Mestre family."

Georges nodded his head, not to agree or disagree, but as a sign that he was listening.

Now that she had his attention, she confided in him. "You know, my reservations about inviting the Aubry family were about the parents, not the daughters. I don't know how they will feel—or act—when they find themselves here with us. And no matter what you say, conversing is indeed a matter of social class and experience."

Georges had put down his paper and was watching her

as she plunged on, curious to know what was on her mind. Huguette rarely spoke without a purpose.

She grimaced as she prepared the justification of her bad behavior toward the family. "I remember when my mother would invite the servants for an annual reception. Each time, they outstayed their welcome—I thought they'd never leave! Of course it was up to my mother to give the departure signal, but since she never did..." She sighed and shook her head. "On the contrary, if one of them finally made a move to go, she'd rekindle the conversation. And they'd stay! Oh, well. What can you expect from people who never go out in society? They don't understand these things!"

Even as she floundered about in her self-defense, she had to admit that Séverine was bright and forthcoming and never at a loss for words. It was true, too, that her parents were acceptable guests for one evening—no more, of course. The mother, Germaine, whom she rarely saw now that Paul and Séverine were older, had a frank and open expression, not like most of the servants she knew, who were fawning and obsequious. She wore meticulously pressed clothes and had impeccable manners. The father, Robert, was short with dark good looks, pleasant enough but a man of few words. Séverine's sister Caroline, who from all appearances was the girl's constant companion and best friend, didn't have Séverine's spark, her infectious, bubbly enthusiasm, but she was at least polite and well-be-haved, and surely that counted for something.

Georges's good-humored voice broke into her cogita-tion. "Don't worry about what your mother did or didn't do and how you're going to get rid of your guests, my dear. You are a wonderful hostess. You always make everyone feel at home, and I'm sure the representatives of the lower class you have deigned to invite won't embarrass you."

"Well, I hope you're right." Huguette said, ignoring

his irony. "As long as we don't have servants for in-laws, everything's fine with me!"

* * *

"I feel like a fool," Paul raged to Séverine. After a week of hostile silence between his parents, his mother had announced to him that not only would they be hosting the end-of-the-year party for Paul and Séverine and their classmates, but that Paul would be reciting one of his original poems and Séverine would perform on the piano.

"How do you think I feel?" Séverine asked glumly.

"It's different for you. You're terrific at the piano. You could have been—could still be—a music teacher. You're used to performing. Come on, Séverine—you love it. But I'm meant to become a doctor like Papa, and poetry is something personal that I love, not something I want to stand up and recite like a kindergartner."

Séverine had rarely seen Paul so upset. She reflected for a moment, and then her eyes lit up the way they did when she was challenged, whether by a math problem or an apparently unsolvable dilemma like the one Paul was facing now.

"I have a solution," she crowed. "Don't recite one of your poems!"

"Oh, right," he retorted, rolling his eyes heavenward. "I'll go home and say, 'Maman, it's very nice of you to give a party for my entire class, and I'll do everything I can to make it a success except for the thing you want most, which is for me to recite one of my poems.' Séverine, you know my mother. Once she's got an idea into her head, nothing will take it out."

"But you don't have to take it out of her head!" Séverine said, grinning. "Leave it in! But instead of reciting something you've written, you can use a piece someone else wrote, words that mean a lot to you and that you wouldn't be embarrassed to share with others. Surely we can think of something." She shut her eyes to concentrate, then opened them and grabbed his arm as an idea formed. "Something from the English poets we studied in my class—that way no one will understand, but they'll all be impressed. How about this?" She threw her head back, closing her eyes and intoned:

"All that in this delightful garden grows
Should happy be, and have immortal bliss."

He stared at her uncomprehendingly.

"Oh Paul! You weren't listening to me when I read you that Elizabethan poetry, were you? But not to worry. It was written by Edmund Spenser, but I have plenty of others if you prefer another bard. But those lines… there's something about them." She didn't want to explain—it was the wrong time and place—that for her the delightful garden was Sorignac. Very soon she would be leaving the hometown that to her, even if it came across as over-dramatic, represented "immortal bliss."

Paul looked at her with unfeigned admiration. "You're a genius. But then, isn't your brilliant scholarly performance the reason for this party?"

Séverine smacked his arm. "Of course it is. Now let's go look at my poetry book and find something you can dazzle our friends with!"

* * *

Huguette, dressed in emerald green to match her eyes, her auburn hair swept away from her face in a chignon, offered her guests a smile. She looked perfectly at ease and ready to perform her duties as hostess.

The happy and excited crowd knew nothing of the drama that had preceded this event, of course. She and Georges had barely spoken to each other for a week. He had reiterated that inviting the Aubrys alone would not pose a problem. Huguette had refused to even consider it. She knew, however, that to break the stalemate she had to come up with a solution that would allow Georges to save face. Slowly, an idea had taken form.

They would extend the invitation to include the entire graduating class and their families. There would, of course, need to be some entertainment, and what could be more natural than having Séverine perform on the piano and Paul recite a poem? That way she would honor the guest who had been the initial inspiration for the party and also commend her son—who in spite of his scientific mind wrote poetry and recited it admirably. And of course, Séverine's parents would be able to mingle with the parents of the other children.

As she had predicted, Georges had agreed, if rather wearily—on condition that he wouldn't hear another word about it.

Huguette stood in the center of the room now, vigorously ringing a large silver bell. When she finally had everyone's attention, she invited them to partake of the buffet she and her mother and Paul had spent the week preparing: foie gras, preserved goose, various pork and rabbit pâtés, huge bowls of fresh green salads, a copious cheese plate, fruit tarts in fluted molds and several *clafoutis*, the regional flan made with cherries that was Huguette's specialty. Georges had brought magnums of champagne up from the cellar, which were resting outside on the grass in ice-filled pails. Bottles of fine wines were aligned like soldiers on the table, waiting to be opened and served.

The regular guests knew all about the bell. Its main purpose was to get them to focus on eating or mingling rather than staying put in the same place—or, worse, carrying on about controversial subjects. Huguette's mother had taught her that the best parties were ones in which serious topics and controversy were avoided—hence the bell. Huguette placed it back on the table and shepherded the gay, babbling crowd to the dining room. She shuddered as she heard the booming voice of Henri Dutreuil, the village pharmacist, who had cornered Robert Aubry. Her plans for a perfect evening were going awry.

"So we hear you're going up to Paris!" he exclaimed. Robert nodded his head in affirmation but didn't say a word. Henri, who was standing in front of the buffet holding a delicately engraved crystal glass of champagne, didn't care. On the contrary. He liked the fact that the caretaker held his tongue, a trait he found refreshing. People like Robert Aubry gave him an opportunity to hold forth on his favorite subjects—politics and religion. Just as he got started, though, he caught a glimpse of the normally discreet Georges jumping on a chair someone had dragged to the middle of the room, readying himself to make an announcement. He regretted the lost opportunity of a soliloquy.

Robert, however, welcomed the interference and sighed inwardly, relieved to have escaped one of the good pharmacist's infamous monologues. Maybe, Robert reflected, he did this at social gatherings because all day long he never got a chance to talk about anything more substantial or interesting than ear drops or suppositories. Robert knew he was only a gardener but felt lucky that his job didn't require discussing people's aches and pains.

If Robert had been less private, he would perhaps have been more talkative. He had plenty to say about the move to Paris, but he didn't feel like sharing it. He could have, though. He could have told the pharmacist about the Sorignac friend who had recommended him. "We provincials must stick together," the man had declared, explaining that the position was only for one concierge, who had best be Germaine. There would be plenty of under-the-counter work for Robert to do, he reassured him, as most of the wealthy owners knew nothing about plumbing or electricity or carpentry, and certainly nothing about Robert's specialty of gardening. He could care for their plants!

"It's a great job," he confided to Robert and Germaine. "It's true that the quarters aren't big, but they are adequate and well-heated, the co-owners are mostly pleasant, and," he noted, looking at Robert, "climbing six flights of stairs to do this or that will be nothing compared to overseeing acres of land."

That was certainly true, and while the Aubrys were sad to be leaving the castle, they both realized that even though Robert was still young, his lumbago was already making the intensive gardening and the outdoor chores he loved more difficult. He hated being cooped up indoors, but at the same time he liked the idea of being warm—and was surprised that he would even think that way. Fortunately, gardening wasn't his only skill, and from what his predecessor had told him, it sounded like he'd be more than busy doing odd jobs. That suited him, as he couldn't bear being idle.

For a brief second, Robert had actually toyed with the idea of recounting all this to the loquacious pharmacist. What a shock that would be. Fortunately, he'd been saved by Georges.

Huguette, who had been thinking all the while of the countess and envying again the unwritten protocol that ensured there was no tedium at *her* parties, had been watching Henri and wondering how to rescue Robert when a stray and fleeting memory crossed her mind. It was of a recent evening party she and Georges had attended at the castle, a splendid occasion with champagne and savory *petits fours* and men in tuxedos and women in their finest outfits and jewelry. She and Georges had been standing with the countess and the mayor and his wife in front of a huge green palm that looked like it had been transplanted from some exotic island. Generally silent and reserved, Georges had been remarkably relaxed, smiling and laughing, listening attentively and looking directly at the countess, who herself was uncharacteristically relaxed, smiling and laughing. At one point, Georges had touched her gently on her forearm and, rather than back away, she had leaned ever so slightly toward him. There was something so *familiar* about them. Huguette had turned to talk to another guest so they would be out of her line of sight and tried to put the matter out of her mind.

Now, she watched her normally discreet husband standing on the chair in the middle of the room, his arms widespread, calling for silence.

Georges lifted his glass and smiled broadly. "Please join me in a toast to our brilliant offspring, the future of France!"

"The future of France!" cried the proud parents as they raised their goblets.

Parents and children alike clinked their glasses. While the adults lifted flutes of champagne, the students raised glasses filled with orange juice. Huguette and Georges had agreed on one thing: no alcohol for the young guests.

Paul and Séverine sipped their orange juice, then Paul glanced at his watch and led her out to the terrace. "You know what? I wouldn't like to guarantee it, but it looks like we've been rescued from our pitiful performances." He inclined his head in the direction of his mother, who was taking a tour of the room, making sure that all the guests were served and that no one was standing alone. "It's astounding. I think she's actually forgotten about us!" He grinned and took another sip of his orange juice.

"Oh, too bad. I so wanted to hear your poem," Séverine grinned.

Huguette, of course, had done no such thing. From across the room, she watched them uneasily. She was relieved that Séverine was leaving town, but she could see it was too soon to let down her guard. Shaking herself out of the dark mood that was threatening her, she pasted a party hostess smile on her face as she sought out young Juliette Belmont and her parents, who were standing in a circle with Georges. An idea for a replacement for Séverine formed in her head. Juliette, whose parents were old friends, was as stable and serious as Séverine was flighty and sparkly. Paul could stand a change, she mused.

"Juliette," she mock-scolded her, "what are you doing with the old folks? Run along now. Séverine and Paul are outside. But first," she said, nodding at Juliette's parents, "I remember that you all so kindly complimented my foie gras the last time you came to dinner." She gave a little shrug, feigning modesty, as they assented. "And I also remember your saying that Juliette loves to cook. I've got an idea. We haven't seen each other for quite some time. Why don't you all come to dinner next Friday? Juliette, you can come early. That way I can share my foie gras secrets with you and you'll be able to make it yourself to impress your friends. You may not know it, but I gave Paul my recipe and he's become a master at it. We can all work together. Won't that be fun?" Without waiting for an answer, she sent Juliette on her way. She watched the girl cross the room to the terrace and prepared her next move.

"And now," Huguette announced, clapping her hands for silence, "to finish our evening, we have a special treat: a musical number from the superbly talented Séverine Aubry, followed by an original poem from our no less talented son Paul."

As the guests applauded enthusiastically, Séverine and

Paul glanced at each other. Paul sighed, looking resigned. "You know what my mother's like."

"I do indeed," Séverine graciously agreed. In spite of her irritation, she found herself almost admiring Huguette. Somehow, the woman always managed to get her way.

The two picked up their glasses and made their way inside.

* * *

In a town the size of Sorignac news travels fast, and sooner or later everyone knows what everyone else is doing, has done or will be doing. Huguette's party was no exception. Some had no opinion of it at all. Others considered it a wasteful expense, something they would never do. Most of the attendees, though, liked it so much they considered hosting a similar occasion when their own sons or daughters graduated.

Gisèle had not been invited to the festive evening. It was understood that it would be awkward for her as an employer to attend a social function with her employees.

Séverine, naturally, had rushed to tell her about it, and the countess took the opportunity to impart some words of advice. She chose her words carefully, as she had no desire to tumble off the pedestal on which the girl had placed her, and knew that her influence upon Séverine was great.

"What a wonderful way to end your high school years," Gisèle said, smiling fondly. "And how kind of Paul's parents to invite your whole family. Madame Moreau is known for being a skilled hostess." She plunged ahead. "Watch her, Séverine, to see how she orchestrates the evening. It will stand you in good stead when your turn comes, which it surely will. You'll see that she will be talking for a few minutes with each person, that her eyes will always be taking in what's going on in the room, seeing who's at ease and who's not, who's alone and who needs company. You remember what I told you when you were younger, Séverine. Everything is a lesson, so enjoy the evening but don't forget what you have learned."

Almost as an afterthought, she added, "Of course, as I said, Madame Moreau is a wonderful hostess, but she can't do everything. You'll be responsible for seeing that your sister and your parents aren't too shy to go to the buffet table, and for introducing them to any school friends of yours they don't know."

Séverine nodded in assent. She welcomed the countess's little lectures, although she would have chafed at similar advice from her mother. The countess's tone was always light, almost nonchalant. Her mother's advice consisted mainly of telling her not to get above herself, to remember her station in life. The guidance of the countess, on the contrary, was like an invisible ladder, raising her up, elevating her. When she thought about it, Séverine realized that she remembered and even cherished the countess's counsel, mainly because it came like a refreshing sip of water, not a drenching from a bucket.

Chapter TEN

In the center of the village, in a dingy and poorly lit two-room apartment above the shoe shop, Just Mestre frowned as he dipped his spoon into the bowl of vegetable soup his wife Augustine had placed before him on the table. The only sounds in the room were the crunch of bread being torn from the loaf and the muted clatter of three spoons hitting three bowls.

"I've seen almost everything," he fumed, "but now! The doctor and his stuck-up missus throw a party and invite the hoi polloi. Since when does the lowly working man find himself hob-nobbing with the bourgeoisie?" He spat out the syllables of the last word. "Are they inventing new rules for themselves?" he asked rhetorically as he bent his head and slurped his bouillon. "Wasn't like that in my day when every man knew his place, I tell you," he huffed, conveniently forgetting that he had been fired from the position Robert Aubry now held for incompetence and theft.

His wife Augustine pursed her lips and nodded. "You should have seen Séverine. There I am, passing around the *petits fours*, and she acts like she's Marie Antoinette."

When Huguette had asked her if she could help with the serving, Augustine had readily accepted, because the family needed the money. She knew that Huguette also was quite aware that their son Luc had dropped out of school, and had at least asked how he was doing; no one else had bothered.

Séverine had played the piano, and although Augustine knew nothing about music, she had been grudgingly impressed by the way the girl took control of the keyboard and created such beautiful sounds. Paul, for his part, had spoken some lines of English poetry, of which she hadn't understood a word. They obviously pleased his mother, though, which was probably the point.

So it hadn't been all bad, she admitted. But what rankled her the most was having to serve the Aubrys. Serving the servants, she thought bitterly to herself.

"Stuck on herself, I say," said Just, throwing back a glass of bad wine. "Eh, Luc?"

Luc tried to look nonchalant as he focused on his soup spoon. "Well, since I wasn't there, I don't really know," he offered, hoping to put an end to the fuss. He knew that if he hadn't dropped out of school he and his parents would have been at that party, drinking champagne and devouring *petits fours*. It shamed and depressed him to think that his former classmates were going to be huge successes in life. He even resented their parents who, unlike his, were so concerned about their futures.

But there was something else he didn't feel good about, something he would never tell his parents. It was the reason he didn't feel bad about not being invited to the party.

While his father dipped his head to his soup bowl and his mother made nervous small talk, Luc allowed his mind to wander. He was no fool: he knew perfectly well that if his father didn't drink so much and wasn't so lazy, maybe their family would still be at the castle. He himself might even have had Séverine's luck and ended up as the countess's pet project. Inwardly he shook his head: Luc had never been invited for tea with the countess. She'd never shown any interest whatsoever in him, not his studies, his manners nor anything else. And she'd certainly never encouraged him to play piano.

He remembered the day the family had moved to their quarters on the grounds of the castle. He'd been so curious and pleased, in the same way Séverine would be later when her family moved into the same house. For all those years afterwards, when she and her sister had lived in the garret he'd occupied, he'd been able to imagine them there because he knew the place so well. The cottage wasn't spacious but it had charm, and the surroundings were magical. Even if you were only the gardener and handyman, it was wonderful to live in an ivy-covered house with a thatched roof, with no one above you or under you or on the side of you, and to have as your view a fairytale castle set on an emerald-green lawn. If only his father had kept that job... But keeping jobs had never been Just Mestre's forte.

Luc had been only six years old when his family had arrived, but he remembered wanting the count and countess to like him. But for some reason he seemed to do everything wrong. He would linger by the kitchen, where the chef would take pity on the shy, carelessly dressed boy with clean but uncombed hair the same color as his copper skillets and, from time to time, let him taste one of his tantalizing concoctions. In this land of chestnuts, the little boy tested them in every form—sautéed, in purée, sugared. Luc looked forward to his kitchen excursions, and knew enough not to overstay his welcome; the cook was a busy man.

He never moved away fast enough, though, and on more than one occasion he was treated to a cold stare from the count or countess as he sampled a bite of chocolate or foie gras. Luc wanted desperately to talk to them, to describe the magical things he had tasted, but how could he, a caretaker's child, ever dare to address his elders without invitation, especially when they looked so disapproving?

He soon realized that neither the count nor the countess had any interest in him; he learned to keep his head low and avert his gaze. He reasoned that no one could criticize him if he didn't look their way, but didn't understand that it simply made him look shifty.

Soon there were no more treats from the kitchen. One afternoon when Luc stopped by the kitchen, the chef simply shook his head sadly and gently shooed the child away with a gesture that said, "I would like to, but I've got orders."

Crestfallen, the boy had slunk off into the woods by himself, as he often did when his parents had been cross with him. A naturally solitary child, he was adept at amusing himself. Deep in the forest, he pulled out his penknife and a small piece of wood he had been turning over and over in his pocket. Squatting on his heels, elbows on his knees, he began cutting into the wood, blinking away tears of shame and rage. At first his strokes were simply angry and unorganized, but after a few minutes his hand fell into a rhythm of its own. His tears dried on his cheeks and he watched in amazement as the head of a squirrel emerged from what had only a few minutes ago been simply the end of a piece of kindling.

The result of that initial effort was clumsy, but as the days and weeks wore on, he found he loved sitting in the woods among the gnarled oak trees with just his imagination for company, the feel of the sharp blade against the wood and his hands doing the work almost on their own. He carved out a deer, modeled on one he had encountered while walking down a path absorbed in his musings, his head down as usual. He had felt the strength of a gaze on him, but when he'd looked up there was only the trunk of a tree. Then, to his surprise, the trunk had suddenly moved:

the creature was exactly the same color as the forest through which it was moving. All he could see was its white tail as it bounded away, then stopped to look back as if teasing him, then leaped away once more. *It's playing with me*, he realized. He sculpted dozens of objects—animals, people, imaginary creatures—and hid them under his bed so his parents wouldn't find out what he was up to and have another excuse to call him lazy.

But as suddenly as they had begun, Luc's hours of dreaming and creating in his forest workshop came to an end. His father was fired, and the family found themselves in a dark apartment in a decrepit medieval building on a narrow street in the village, where Just set up shop as a cobbler in an empty ground-floor shop below. There was no more forest, no more animals, only dirty windows that looked out onto a crumbling building across a narrow alleyway.

Somewhat unexpectedly, Just made a successful transition from lazy gardener to competent cobbler, and began training Luc so that the minute he left school he could join him in the shop. Now, instead of holding wood in his hands while birds warbled in the treetops, Luc held the dirty, smelly shoes and boots of strangers, and the only sounds were the taps of his hammer.

When the Aubrys had moved into the cottage—*their* cottage—on the castle grounds, he had felt a pang of jealousy for Séverine—after all, she had everything that once was his. On her first day at school, he had marched up to her and pulled on her braids. But, to his astonishment, instead of running away and tattling to the teacher like all the other little girls, Séverine had whirled on him and grabbed his arm in a surprisingly strong grip. Squeezing his arm until it hurt, she had forced him to look straight into her eyes.

"Next time you do that, I WILL tell" she had told him, and flounced off.

From then on they had been, if not fast friends, at least civil to each other.

But what had marked him the most had happened a year or so later at the village fair. The little girl had sought him out, waiting until he was alone.

"Hello Luc," she greeted him.

Head down, he shifted his weight from one foot to the other, wondering if she was going to remind him about the day he'd bullied her.

"Guess what," she said as she reached into the pocket of her dress. "I found this in our bedroom. It must be yours, since it's not mine or Caroline's. It's strange—it was hidden under a plank in the floor. It's nice," she added, looking at the object as she handed it over to him. "I thought you'd want it because it might have been a present someone gave you."

Luc bent his head even lower than usual as he took the perfectly carved little cottontail rabbit. He closed his hand around it, not daring to examine it in front of her for fear of showing his emotion. The rabbit was special, the sole escapee from one of his father's fits of fury. Luc had always hidden what Just called his "fairy follies" under his bed, but one day Augustine had discovered them while cleaning. Amazed at her son's talent, she had rushed downstairs to tell Just, who, with a shout of rage, had bounded up the stairs to see things for himself. His face purple with anger, he had swept the carvings to one side and then grabbed Luc's arm and twisted it with his full force, making Luc cry out in pain. Augustine had shoved herself between Luc and his father, but the damage had been done. Luc's eyes filled as Just forced him to throw all his beloved objects into the trash.

"That's what this is—garbage!" his father spat. "Too much time on his hands," he told Augustine. "From now on, this boy is going to work. No more wasting his time dreaming."

Luc had stared at the floor, blinking back tears he dared not show his father.

The next day, he waited until his father had left the cottage, then escaped to his beloved woods to make one last carving. He chose to make a rabbit because, he reasoned, a rabbit can run. He longed to be like a rabbit, to run free, to flee his family, his surroundings and the miserable trap of his life. Falling into his familiar rhythm, turning his knife skillfully this way and that, he positioned the animal crouched on its haunches, ready to take off as fast as it could go. He had tucked the perfect little rabbit into his pocket, slipped into the cottage while his father was still at work, and hidden it under a loose floorboard. Not long after that, the family had been turned out, and Luc had not had an opportunity to prise up the board and retrieve the little carving.

And now he had it back. He was surprised by his reaction and didn't know what to say. He was overcome by Séverine's generosity.

But Séverine's kind act wasn't due to her selflessness or good heart, as Luc presumed, rather to a scolding she had received from Robert not long before.

The sisters had been playing upstairs and Séverine was showing off to get Caroline's attention. She turned her head from side to side, looked around the garret with a horrified expression and sniffed the air with a disgusted look.

"This room smells to high heaven, and I believe it's Luc, who left his body odor behind."

She and Caroline had snickered to themselves, but Robert, who was reading in the living room, had overheard. In a stern voice, he ordered them to come downstairs immediately. It was rare that their father disciplined them, and they had no idea of what he might have to say. Had they talked too loudly? Had they distracted him from his reading?

"I will not have you speak ill of other people, no matter who they are," he had told them. "Once the words are out of your mouth, you don't know where they'll go. You certainly needn't be friends with Luc," he said, softening his tone, "but you must not be mean. No talking about people behind their backs. Do you understand?"

Abashed, the girls had nodded. Smiling, Robert had patted their heads, shooed them back upstairs, and returned to the newspaper he'd been reading.

Séverine in particular had been crushed by her father's admonition. Unlike Caroline, she couldn't bear her father's disapproval. She wanted to find a concrete way to show him that she had honored and obeyed him, and to that end, she knew that sacrificing the clever little rabbit that Luc had most certainly left behind was a fitting gesture.

"Who made it?" she asked him now.

Luc opened his hand and looked at his little rabbit, but was too tongue-tied to tell her it was he. He felt his heart swell and realized he had developed a crush on her, one he hoped neither she nor anyone else could see. Some people said she was uppity because of how the count and especially the countess had made such a pet of her, but Luc didn't think she was uppity at all. In his opinion, she was the prettiest and kindest girl he had ever seen.

When Luc turned thirteen, he had quit school and begun to apprentice full time in his father's shop.

One afternoon, through the shop window, he caught sight of Séverine leaving Madame Decré's bakery shop, clutching warm loaves in her arms. Ever since she'd been a little girl at her mother's side, Séverine had come to the bakery every day after school to buy the bread for the evening meal. Cheerful, dark-haired, rosy-cheeked Madame Decré wore a pink apron with a big front pocket in which she kept treats for her favorite children, of whom Séverine was one. Luc had often watched her chatting with Madame

Decré, who would sneak her a treat when other customers weren't looking. The bakery was close to the shoe shop, but Séverine rarely passed it on her way home.

That day, though, he had seen her determinedly walking toward his shop and had turned away from the window, bending his head over a pair of shoes so he wouldn't show the delight he felt. She was probably coming to fetch the shoes she and her sister had dropped off a week ago. They had begged him to work fast.

"What's the rush?" he had asked, hoping to keep them in the store. He liked their company.

"Well, it's all my fault," Séverine said. "I was dressing up and playing around with Caroline, stomping around in our mother's only pair of heels, and I broke a strap. Since she doesn't allow us to take anything out of her wardrobe without her permission, we had to spirit these shoes out as fast as we could. And get them back before she finds they're missing!" Séverine gave him a mischievous look and confided, "You are helping us accomplish a secret mission!"

He had seen them leaning close to each other as they walked out of the shop, whispering conspiratorially and casting glances back at him, but had assumed they were simply giggling about how tongue-tied he always seemed to be around them.

The bell jangled as Séverine stepped into the store.

"Here for the high heels, are you?" said Luc, clearing his throat. "And where's your charming bodyguard?"

"Home, where I should be," she answered, hoping this would inspire him to speed up and end the conversation. Feigning interest, she politely added, "So how are things going?"

"Oh, you know, I'm just a cobbler now. I spend my days in here hammering away on people's soles while you do all that fancy studying." He spoke nonchalantly but his face was flushed. For the first time, it occurred to Séverine that leaving school had been less of a relief for him than it had been for those who stayed.

"Well," she replied, "everyone needs a cobbler. Are the high heels ready?"

"Sure they are. I may not be a scholar, but I do know how to get people's shoes fixed on time." He busied himself searching for the shoes, then set them on the countertop. "There you are, Séverine. It's on the house."

"No, Luc, I can't accept that. Tell me how much I owe you. You can't work for free."

"That's for sure," he said. Then, looking quickly around to make sure his father was nowhere nearby, he emerged from behind the counter to stand beside her. "I have something for you," he mumbled, hurriedly handing her a small, bulging envelope with her name on it. "Go on now," he said, then slipped behind the counter again. He turned and reached for a pair of pliers, purposely keeping his back to her so she couldn't see the deep blush forming on his cheeks.

Séverine had thanked him again, picked up the shoes and stepped out into the afternoon sunshine. Luc turned to watch her go, suddenly almost heady with joy. Then, just as suddenly, the feeling of elation left him and gave place to embarrassment and fear. Why had he done that? What had come over him? What if she showed the letter and his little gift to her sister, her parents, the countess, Paul and the rest of her friends? He'd be the laughingstock of the village.

As months went by and nothing happened, he felt relief. Then, as more time passed without a word from Séverine, he fell into depression and sadness, which finally gave way to bitterness. She could have said *something*, he told himself. Anything at all. But he realized now that, in her eyes, he wasn't even worthy of a reply. He was nothing to her, invisible once again.

At first, he'd been sorry when he had heard that Séverine was leaving town.

But now… her departure couldn't come soon enough.

* * *

Séverine forgot about the package Luc had given her until a few days after her excursion to the shoe shop. On her way to ride bikes with Paul she stopped and rummaged in her purse for a handkerchief. Her hand closed over the bulky little envelope, and with a guilty start, she pulled it out. Ripping it open, she saw there were two things inside: a letter in Luc's uneven handwriting and a small object wrapped in tissue paper. Curious, she undid the paper and immediately recognized the carved rabbit she had returned to Luc when they were children. Baffled, she began to read his letter, hoping there would be an explanation.

Dear Séverine,

I know you'll be surprised by this letter and the rabbit. I have been keeping it for the unlikely day you would come to the shop. I vowed that if you did, I would return the carving to you with my own hands.

I know you rarely if ever walk up this street, and I think I know why. I think your parents warned you off me, even as a friend, because of my family. I wish you hadn't taken their advice so literally—I wouldn't have bothered you and I would have been glad to have had your friendship.

When I heard rumors that your family was moving to Paris, I have to admit that I was relieved. No more waiting for the day Séverine would finally walk by this window and stop to say hello. I can't tell you how many times I sat here hoping you'd go by.

Now that you're going away, though, I want to tell you something and leave you a little souvenir. I wanted to tell you how happy you made me the day you returned the carving I left in the cottage. Not only did you return it, but you said it was nice and admired it, not even knowing that I had made it myself. That was the first time anyone ever told me that something I had done was good or nice.

I dropped out of school, as you know, and I am now a simple cobbler. Unlike you, I will probably always stay in this town. But even cobblers have dreams: if I had one, it would be to have you as a friend, and maybe even more. I have no illusions this will happen, but as a goodbye gift and a thank-you for being kind to me, I'm enclosing the carving you returned to me that day so long ago. I hope you'll enjoy having it and will think of me whenever you look at it. I just wish you could love me as I love you.

Luc

Mortified, Séverine tore the letter to bits and stashed them those and the little wooden rabbit back into her purse.

Chapter ELEVEN

"Come on, I'll beat you!" Paul yelled, turning back to look at her.

Pushing all thoughts of Luc from her mind, Séverine, who had been lagging behind, began pumping the pedals with determination.

"No, you won't!" she countered, rapidly catching up with him.

The two rode circles around each other as they headed to their destination, the nearby hamlet of Sainte-Eulalie, which was little more than a well-proportioned manor surrounded by a few low stone houses and an old cemetery next to a twelfth-century church. They had discovered it one day when venturing out of town on their bicycles, and had returned to it again and again.

Séverine and Paul loved the simple and unassuming church with its thick columns and walls, stocky rounded arches, stained-glass windows, timeworn stone floors and minimal decoration. They preferred the solidity and strength and simplicity of its architecture to the overwhelming Gothic style, with its narrow columns and soaring arches. The former inspired warmth and devotion, the other, awe, they agreed.

Paul had once visited Notre-Dame with his parents

on a trip to Paris. Although he loved the pure blues of the stained-glass windows and was moved by the rows of candles that lit up the dark sanctuary, he found that he was not taken in by the grandeur and the wealth. If there was indeed a God—and he wasn't at all sure there was—he thought He surely could present a friendlier face.

When they entered the dimly lit sanctuary, Séverine knelt at a prie-dieu, crossed herself and said a brief prayer while Paul, who preferred the architecture and styles of churches to the religion that went on inside them, looked on. He considered starting an argument about religion and decided not to. There were so many other subjects they could disagree on, and Séverine's faith was as much a part of her as his skepticism and doubt were part of him. It was one of the few subjects they had tacitly agreed not to discuss.

After their brief moment inside the sanctuary, they went back outside and strolled to a moss-covered stone bench in the nearby cemetery. Shielded by conifers and oaks, it was the place they often met when they wanted to get away from Huguette's vigilant eye and be by themselves.

Leaning back on the bench, Paul inclined his head at their bicycles, lying on their sides under a tree. "You may be better at music but, let's face it, I'm a better cyclist," he declared, grinning. "And," he continued, "I'm certainly more diplomatic."

Séverine sat up and looked at him. Clearly it was time for their habitual debate.

"And now that we've finished our school days," Paul said, warming to his topic, "I can tell you that I always wondered how you were going to get away one more time with showing the teacher how much smarter you were. You know," he said, glancing sideways at her, "some people called you pretentious. Of course, since I wasn't there, this is secondhand."

"Who said I was pretentious?" Séverine sputtered.

"Madame Dupuy for starters," he said, referring to their teacher. "I overheard her telling the principal that you corrected her when she said Kenya was in West Africa."

"Well, it's not," Séverine retorted. "It's in East Africa, and she should have known better!" She stood and faced him now, eyebrows arched and ready for battle. "And who else?" she asked.

"Luc Mestre." Paul's eyes twinkled as he waited to see how the name would strike her.

Séverine bristled. "Since when do you talk to Luc Mestre? He dropped out of school as soon as he could. So—" She closed her mouth abruptly, remembering the letter and the little wooden rabbit in her purse. Luc wasn't really all that bad, and she hoped he wouldn't end up like the rest of his good-for-nothing family, but she had no wish to discuss him further right now.

"Anyway, what are you getting at, Paul?" she said, moving the subject away from all things Mestre. "Do you mean I should keep my mouth shut because I'm the daughter of caretakers? Well, we can't all have a doctor for a father," she snapped, and instantly regretted her words. She liked Paul's father and knew of his tactful generosity in the past when her family hadn't been able to pay their bills right away. He was a good man, and Paul was right. She did open her mouth too many times when she should keep it shut. She turned her head so he couldn't see her angry tears, folded her arms and scowled at the ground.

"Slow down," Paul said, looking at her with puzzlement. With Séverine, there were always unexpected sparks, bursts of laughter or anger, unexpected and sometimes passionate reactions to mundane remarks. "I'm just telling you what I've heard. But what's this about being the daughter of caretakers? I've never heard you mention that before. Is this because you're preparing to go head-to-head with all those awful, stuck-up Parisians?"

Séverine sat back down on the bench beside him. "You know what, Paul? I don't even know any Parisians. I don't think I've ever met anyone from Paris, other than some of the countess's actor friends who come to visit her."

"Have you ever been there yourself?" His voice was gentler now. He knew the answer but wanted her to say it.

"You know perfectly well I haven't," she answered.

"Well, you'll soon see for yourself and come back to tell me all about it, won't you? I've been to Paris with my parents, but Périgord is still the best place in France, in my book." He looked around at the church, the tidy little cemetery and the lush green grass of the grounds where their bicycles were lying.

"Mine too," Séverine agreed.

He shifted on the bench so he was facing her now. "I'm sorry you're leaving, but I can't say I envy you. All that traffic, those crowded streets, so many people. Other than Paris, I've never been anywhere outside Périgord, but I've got to say I prefer it here. And you? What will you miss?"

"That's easy," she scoffed. "The forests, the oaks and the walnut trees, the cliffs where our ancestors lived, the beautiful little towns… Oh, I could go on and on!"

"You certainly could. But you forgot a few things," Paul added. "Foie gras and truffles and porcini mushrooms and chestnuts." He glanced at her slyly. "And me!"

Suddenly he jumped to his feet. "I need to stretch my legs," he said. "Let's go walk in the woods."

Séverine rose and they headed for the thick forest behind the cemetery.

"I love this place," Paul said, breathing in the smell of the earth and plucking a leaf off the low branch of a tree. "And I feel like running, don't you? Let's race each other!" He barely glanced at Séverine as he took off with all the strength of his pent-up energy. He kept running, but when he didn't hear her behind him, he looked and saw that she had disappeared. Retracing his path, he found her sitting on the ground with her back against a tree trunk, a look of misery on her face and her right leg stuck out in front of her.

"Why did you take off like that?" she demanded.

"I'm sorry. I thought you were behind me. You're always behind me," he said, trying to make a joke. She tried to laugh, and then grimaced. Concerned, Paul bent down and gently unlaced her boot. He rolled down her stocking and carefully touched her ankle, palpating the joint with the tips of his fingers.

"You're already a doctor!" she exclaimed. "With a fabulous bedside manner—or should I say, tree-side manner."

Paul stood up and looked down at her, pretending to commiserate. "I hate to tell you, Mademoiselle Aubry, but you're lucky. It's nothing. Just a bruise and a bit of swelling. You'll live, you'll breathe, you'll survive—but only by leaning on me while we walk back to the bench." He sighed.

"What's the matter?"

It was now or never, Paul decided. He took a breath. "I was hoping to spend some time with you today, here in the forest, showing you…" He paused, reddening. "…what a great doctor I'm going to be."

The two of them were silent now as they looked at each other in a new way, as if they hadn't known each other since childhood, as if they hadn't truly known each other until this moment.

Paul knew what he wanted to do. He wanted to lie down under the tree beside Séverine and take her in his arms. He wanted to touch every part of that body that was so familiar to him yet so untouched by him. He longed to kiss her, to tell her how much he loved her and how much he would miss her.

Sitting with her back against the rough bark of the tree, Séverine felt a new, powerful feeling rise up and overwhelm her pain and her anger at his running off without her. She waited, hardly daring to breathe, hoping he would sit down beside her again and embrace her. She wanted to tell him how much she would miss him, to bury her face against his chest, to connect with him in a way they had never done before. With her heart pounding, she closed her eyes and dreamed for a few delicious seconds that he had bent down and was kissing her.

When she opened them again, Paul was still standing, preoccupied with his own thoughts.

Whatever might have happened wasn't going to.

"Let's go back to the bench then," she said, and then, unable to resist, added, "I never would have fallen if we hadn't left it in the first place." She extended her arm. "Help me up and let's go."

They made their slow, halting way back to the stone bench and sat down together, side by side, as they had done since they were children. Séverine removed her boot and flexed her ankle, staring at it.

Paul's voice broke into her thoughts. "What does the countess think of your leaving?"

"She's being very countess-like," Séverine replied, rolling her eyes. "Stiff upper lip. Acts like nothing is going on, whereas I'm convinced she's unhappy. I think she hates losing Maman and Papa, who are probably the most reliable employees she's ever had. And she's been giving me all sorts of advice, almost like I'm her daughter—what to see, whom to avoid, what to say, what not to say, whom I absolutely *must* become acquainted with, even how to dress like a Parisienne—whatever that means—and, well, you name it, she's advised it!"

"You practically *are* her child," Paul remarked mildly, trying to conceal the annoyance he often felt when Séverine talked about the countess. While it was true that she was responsible for Séverine's exquisite manners, her culture, her bearing and in particular her success as a musician, sometimes he feared that the countess had had too much influence on Séverine and had turned her into a miniature and equally snobbish version of herself.

Paul was sure he wouldn't like living in Paris. He wondered how Séverine would fare, what she would become. What kind of life would she have? What kind of job? If she stayed in Sorignac, she could become the local music teacher. He could see her leading a choir of children, or teaching students how to play piano with as much grace as she did. He could see himself in the audience, watching proudly. He could see himself fetching her after the program to escort her home, putting his arm protectively around her. Somehow, he had to keep her with him, prevent her from going to Paris. He badly wanted to be with her, to love her, make love to her...

"Marry me!" Paul blurted out, spreading his arms in a dramatic gesture. "You'll be the daughter-in-law of a doctor and I'll be the husband of the smartest lady in town. And I'll teach you how to keep that charming mouth sewn up!"

Taken by surprise, Séverine's first reaction was to throw back her head and laugh with sheer delight and pleasure.

She then took a fleeting but careful look at him and bent her head so her hair would cover her face and he wouldn't see the look of distress on it. She was losing her confidant, her best friend, the little boy who had grown into such a desirable young man with his thick dark brown hair and his soulful, deep brown eyes. She loved the way those eyes lit up when he laughed—which was often. She loved the open frankness of his face, how he radiated warmth and care and kindness towards everyone. She also loved a host of other qualities he possessed, but she couldn't allow herself to think about them. Not now.

Raising her head, she managed a smile as she took his hands in hers. "Paul, I love you like a brother and you know it. You also can probably figure out in your thick head that I could love you another way without too much trouble. But guess what: daughters of servants don't pin their hopes on doctors' sons. Or, I should say, the doctor that you will be. That's the way the world is." She sighed, tucking a strand of hair behind her ear. "You know what I think? You aren't serious. You're sad, like I am, about my leaving. But you've got medical school and years of study ahead of you, and I have no idea of what I'm going to do in Paris. Plus, we'd make a horrid couple, fighting all the time. I thank you for asking me all the same, my kind sir." She got to her feet, careful not to lean on her sore ankle, and made a mock curtsey.

"You're probably right, as usual," Paul concurred. "Too bad—we would have had great-looking children." He grinned, and Séverine grinned back. Once again, the moment passed.

Inside, he felt his heart grow heavy in his chest. Séverine was right. Although his father had no concerns about social class, his mother would never allow him to marry "down." Someday, he knew, he might have to fight his mother on this issue—his father, of course, would have no desire to tangle with Huguette when and if the time came—but he had no stomach for it now. Paul could see the writing on the wall: he would make a good marriage, most likely with a girl who had the approval of both his parents.

Séverine watched Paul struggling with his emotions. She could practically read his mind, and knew that he was debating with himself about Huguette and about whom he would end up marrying. Well, that would have to be his cross to bear.

As for herself, she knew only one thing: she would have to make her own way. What way that would be she had no idea. But she wasn't worried. Gisèle had offered her more than music lessons and a cultural education. She had taught her to hold her head high, to not be satisfied with the mundane, and to have aspirations, whatever they might be. She only knew that whatever happened next wouldn't happen in the castle where she'd lived since she was a little girl. It wouldn't happen in the town she was so fond of, and it wouldn't happen with Paul, whom she loved and would miss sorely. She would go to Paris with her family. In spite of her qualms, she was ready.

The bells in the church tower began to chime the hour, and they both looked up.

"Oh dear," she teased, "they're not for our wedding." She got to her feet and held out her hand to him. "It's time we got back to town. It's getting dark and it's going to rain. Come on!"

PART TWO

THE PARIS YEARS

Chapter TWELVE

Paris: Fall 1928

Séverine sat at the table—the only table—in her parents' ground-floor lodging and frowned as she looked down at the blank sheet of paper in front of her. She needed to write to the countess, but she wasn't used to writing letters and realized she hardly knew how to begin. She couldn't dither, though. After all the countess had done to help the family get settled in Paris, she owed her a letter that was fast becoming overdue. She sat up straight—the way the countess had taught her to do when she lacked resolve— and began.

Dear Gisèle,

I have so much to tell you that I don't know where to begin. So I'll start by thanking you for finding me a job with your friends on the avenue Foch. The children don't know how lucky they are to have me as their piano teacher! (I'm joking, of course.) But, seriously, they are learning a lot, I hope. And they aren't the only ones. It seems that wherever I go in Paris I learn something new. To get to the Devères' apartment, I walk to the Place des Ternes, then up the avenue Wagram to the top of the Champs-Elysées, where I can admire the Arc de Triomphe as I continue west toward the Bois de Boulogne.

One day, on my way, I discovered an immense, ornate pink palace called the Palais Rose, which I knew nothing about. I asked around and found that it belonged to the Count Boniface de Castellane, also known as Boni, who very cleverly married the American heiress Anna Gould. Apparently, the palace is immense, with one hundred rooms, a formal garden and even a marble reproduction of the Staircase of the Ambassadors in Versailles. I walk past it every day on my way to work and dream about going inside.

Speaking of work, Caroline is doing well at the job she found, thanks to you and your Paris connections. She's gaining a reputation as the best seamstress the Théâtre de l'Odéon has ever had!

I love Paris but I miss Sorignac and the castle...."

She stopped writing as doubts assailed her. Was she giving too many details? A well-written letter should be long enough to be informative and to express her gratitude for all that Gisèle had done for her. But there were things to omit. She would not, of course, tell Gisèle that the Devère children were spoiled brats who hated the obligatory lessons. She would not tell her that her parents' quarters on the ground floor of the splendid apartment building were cramped and dark. And she wouldn't tell her that Caroline earned so little that her evening meal consisted of little more than a thick slice of bread and butter that she dipped into a huge bowl of coffee with hot milk.

She had written that she missed Sorignac and the castle, but she hadn't finished. She would tell Gisèle that she missed the music room at the end of the day, with the light from the setting sun illuminating the fleur-de-lys pattern of the wallpaper and enhancing the interwoven colors in the Persian rugs, highlighting the shine of the wood paneling her mother was always waxing, warming the interior and the velvet on the piano bench. She would tell her that she missed the grand piano and the floor-to-ceiling oak bookcases filled with tomes on music and musicians, the comfortable sofa in front of the fireplace that she would stretch out on when she was sure the countess was occupied elsewhere in the castle (on second thought, she decided to skip that detail), even the various pictures of the de Roquemaurel family that Gisèle had lined up on the mantel. She'd often pretended that the music room was her room, that the people in the photos were her family.

Picking up her pen, she finished writing the letter and signed it "Devotedly, Séverine." Then, relieved that the job was done, she rose from the table, slipped the note into an envelope and went to the post office to buy a stamp.

On the way home from her errand, Séverine hurried along the cobblestone street, deep in thought about her two bright but lazy young music students. As she stepped into the courtyard of the building where she lived with her parents, her shoe caught on the bottom metal rail of the imposing entry gate and she stumbled to the ground.

"Rats!" she muttered, fearing she had torn her skirt. It was her favorite, a knee-length, cream-colored jersey affair, the only one in her microscopic wardrobe that she deemed both comfortable and stylish.

A strong arm lifted her back to an upright position.

"Thank you," she said, brushing herself off. Thankfully, her skirt had not been torn and her knees were not scraped.

"Are you all right, Mademoiselle?"

Séverine looked up into the concerned face of a tall, well-built and well-dressed man. He was in his thirties, she estimated, older than she was by at least a decade, and possessed an unmistakable aura of assurance and command. For some reason she found herself focusing on the cuffs of his sleeves. They were remarkably white and held together by a set of solid gold cube-shaped cufflinks.

"I'm Antoine Sevanot," the man volunteered. "My parents live here on the second floor. I come to visit and generally irritate and stimulate them as often as I can." He gave Séverine a mischievous smile that showed even, white teeth. "It keeps them from getting fossilized and becoming set in their ways, I hope."

He didn't say that he'd caught a glimpse of her the first week her family had arrived and had made up his mind to meet her. Her simple misstep had been a blessing in disguise.

Séverine smoothed her skirt and held her chin high, as she always did in situations in which she was slightly unsure of herself.

"I am Séverine Aubry, and as I'm sure you probably already know, I'm the daughter of your parents' new concierge. For now, at least, I live in their quarters with them." She added, with a smile, "What a way to meet!"

Antoine was immediately drawn to her youthfulness, her lively brown eyes, translucent complexion, full lips and curvy body. He was so tired of emaciated women—they were about as alluring as sticks, really. This Séverine, in contrast, looked like someone with a good appetite, not like most of the women he knew who poked at their lettuce leaves, consistently refused dessert and looked at their wine glasses as though they contained arsenic. And she was self-possessed and outspoken, too, he noted with interest. Most of the fashionable Parisiennes he went out with were guarded, controlling their conversations as they did their calories.

He liked her voice, the way she articulated each word, the way she lifted her chin to look at him, the playful glint in her eye and her proud bearing. When she told him that she was the daughter of the concierge, she made it as a factual statement without a trace of deference to him, the son of one of the owners. He liked that as well.

"I hope your skirt is all right," he said, quietly admiring the material and the cut. "It looks like a Jean Patou."

She stared at him uncomprehendingly, then smiled. "Oh my, no. It's a Caroline Aubry original." Seeing his look of puzzlement, she said, "Caroline is my sister, and a top designer and seamstress. She can copy any model I give her. She's not yet recognized, but I'm sure she will be someday. In the meantime, I'll pass on your compliment."

Antoine, chagrined that he had dropped the name of a famous designer who catered only to the wealthy few, changed the subject. "You surely are more than the daughter of the concierge," he challenged her. "What do you do?"

"Let's see... Do you have an hour or so?" she countered. "Seriously, it's a rather long story and I don't want to bore you."

"If it's that long, may I invite you to a nearby café so that I might hear it?"

Séverine grinned. "Why not? I'll just run in to tell my parents I'm going out again." Without another word, she turned her back and hurried away from him.

Antoine watched her go, struck by her lack of artifice. He had heard that the family was from the provinces, and her behavior confirmed it. A Parisian sophisticate would have pretended she was busy, even if she had nothing to do. And she would have claimed, or at least allowed him to assume, that her skirt was indeed *haute couture*.

A short time later, they were seated at *Le Tilbury* café-restaurant. Séverine gazed around her. She liked the mix—workers downing beer at the bar, a quiet, well-dressed, gray-haired couple occupying a nearby table, a group of teenagers noisily engaged in a card game. Up to now she had only dared to look in the window, watching the café crowd from outside.

"You must think I'm rather forward, accepting your invitation when I don't even know you," she said to Antoine, "but frankly I'm happy to meet someone outside my family. Since I've been in Paris, I've barely had time to do anything but help my parents settle in and go back and forth from our place to my little job."

She told Antoine how her parents had secured positions as the caretakers of his parents' comfortable building in the 17th *arrondissement* near the Parc Monceau through a friend from her hometown who was retiring and going back home. For all the provincials, she explained, "home," whether Brittany or Auvergne or the Dordogne, was the place they had been born and raised. Paris was a place to work, to make money, before returning to the friends and family and life they'd left behind.

She took a sip of her coffee and grinned impishly at him. "And if you are wondering why the daughter of a concierge would accept coffee with her employer's son, I'll tell you all about that for another cup."

Antoine leaned back and roared with laughter, a big, resounding noise that made the waiter turn his head to look their way.

"Please go ahead. I doubt I could stop you in any case."

"You're probably right. The countess told me that I talk too much and that I should make an effort to rein myself in."

"The countess?" Antoine looked puzzled as he tried to follow.

Seeing his bewilderment, she slowed down.

"I told you it was a long story. I'll try to make it short. I grew up in the small town of Sorignac in the southwest, where my parents were lucky enough to be employed by the count and countess who live in the castle above the town. The countess—her name is Gisèle—liked me and took me under her wing. She treated me like her own daughter, and I was sad to leave her."

She realized two things as she talked to Antoine: one,

that it was the first time she had opened up to a stranger about her life back home and two, that saying she was sad to leave the countess was an understatement.

The more she confided in Antoine, the more Séverine realized that she hadn't discussed what she had seen and heard and felt with anyone, even Caroline, who had been busy with her job ever since the family had moved to Paris. She felt she was babbling now, but couldn't help herself.

"I'm learning so many things," she exclaimed. "You'll probably think what I say is stupid because you know the city, but here's what I've discovered. I much prefer being here in the west of Paris than over in the east." Without even noticing it, she drew closer to him as if preparing to offer a confidence. "I have this friend from Sorignac whose parents, like mine, came to work in Paris. They live on the rue de Ménilmontant, way across town on the east side. I went to visit her one day. Oh, it was awful! The buildings are run-down and shabby, and the streets are crowded with all kinds of odd-looking, poorly dressed types. And the odors!" She wrinkled her nose. "I could barely breathe— the whole place reeked of spices and nasty-smelling foods." She shuddered. "I know I must sound snobbish when I say this, but I'm so happy I ended up over here in the west. It's so quiet and uncluttered, the people dress in stylish clothes and the streets are wide and clean. I may only be a concierge's daughter, but I'd rather be on the bottom of the heap over here than the top of the heap over there."

She studied Antoine, awaiting his reaction. "You must think I'm a little above myself."

"I certainly don't," Antoine replied. He was charmed by her enthusiasm and sincerity and the way her words poured out in a not entirely logical jumble. "You're realistic and factual. No one would deny the enormous difference between the east and the west of Paris. They're two different worlds."

He stopped short of saying that most of the people he knew had never visited the scruffy neighborhoods she was describing and probably couldn't even locate them on the map. He was attracted to the decadent bars and cabarets wherever they were located in the city. The lively nightlife they provided was a welcome if secret break from the boredom of his wealthy bourgeois world. An image of the transgender bars in Montparnasse, which he frequented from time to time, briefly flashed into his mind, but he quashed it. He wouldn't talk about that: not now, maybe never. Séverine was so young, so pure, so virginal. He didn't even wonder if she was a virgin. It was obvious.

"But I love Paris," Séverine said, as if to reassure him. "I love wandering the side streets and exploring. Sometimes when I've finished teaching my lessons, I take the long way home to see what I can discover."

Antoine looked at her quizzically. "What do you teach?"

"Piano," she replied.

"Do you not have a piano at home?"

"No, not yet. But the conservatory in our neighborhood has practice rooms. As soon as I get more pupils and more money, I'll rent one of them. Anyway," she said, not wanting to dwell on the subject of her poverty, "now that I've given you my life story, what about you?"

Antoine laughed again, conscious that he was acting differently than he did with the women he usually invited here. Although he was always the perfect gentleman, he would sip his coffee with half-shut eyes and a bored expression, patiently enduring their prattle while he waited to bed them. Now, though, he was alert and fully engaged, his eyes wide open.

"You're going too fast for me," Antoine replied. "I'll tell you my life story if you accept a dinner invitation. And in the meantime, I'd like you to meet my parents. First of all, it's the proper thing to do. And second, I may have a solution to your piano problem."

Séverine sat still, staring at him.

"Will you come?" he asked, wondering why she had fallen silent. Was he going too fast?

When she spoke, it was to ask a pragmatic question. "Come to which? Your parents' place or dinner?"

"Both," he replied. "First to meet my parents, and then if you accept, I'd like to take you to dinner in a restaurant I think you are going to love. Actually, I don't know why I say that because I don't know what your tastes are, but it will be a good way to find out. Maybe you'll hate it," he added with an enigmatic smile.

Séverine didn't hesitate.

"I won't hate it and I'd be delighted," she answered. Today had been a first—the first time she had gone out with a Parisian, the first time she had been in a café, the first time she had spoken to someone about her old life and her new one. Her dashing, urbane companion made her feel as if she had been admitted to a secret society, the society of Parisians who lingered in cafés over strong coffee or sparkling glasses of wine, who spoke in low voices amid the hubbub.

The thought that her parents might object to her dining out with an older man briefly crossed her mind, but she'd face that obstacle when she got to it. For the moment, she was no longer alone, no longer on the outside; she was simply happy.

* * *

Antoine was already thinking about the piano in his parents' salon. He would have to use all his powers of persuasion to get them to offer the use of it to Séverine, but he was sure that could be done. They had never refused a request from their beloved only child.

In fact, his father would probably thank him. After a decorator had totally refurbished the living room of their sumptuous apartment, his mother had decided that the piano no longer fit the new décor. Its lid, a precious of art, was decorated with pink pastel cherubs sailing through pale blue clouds against a cream-colored background. His mother had decided she could not bear it, could no longer spend one more minute with the ridiculous thing in her living room, even though she was the one who had forced her husband to purchase it in an exclusive Left Bank antique shop some years before.

His father, for his part, had made it known that he would not sell the instrument he'd grown to love, but Antoine knew it would only be a matter of time before she would wage a cunning campaign to get him to part with it. Madame Sevanot could be so convincing that her husband often ended up thinking her ideas had been his own. Clever Maman, Antoine had to admit.

And now, he'd be clever as well.

A week later, Antoine ushered Séverine into Louise and Bertrand Sevanot's large, light and airy second-floor apartment. Metal and glass doors in a highly stylized geometric design separated the entry hall from the living room, where apart from the outmoded piano the ambiance was resolutely modern. Séverine, whose notion of furniture was limited to her parents' few simple possessions and the centuries-old antiques in the countess's rooms, was stunned. The room looked empty, even stark. Then she remembered one of the many lessons the countess had taught her: "You have the right not to know, but you don't have the right not to be curious. People will love it when you ask questions, as long as you are discreet and don't ask too many."

Antoine's mother told her that the style of the furniture was Art Deco, and that the pieces in the salon had been designed by Emile Jacques Ruhlmann, an Alsatian whose work was a must for those in the know. She explained that he'd broken the codes and given people—people with means and taste, she specified—a new choice of tables and chairs and other pieces with pure lines made from top-quality materials.

Séverine settled into the Ruhlmann club chair, passing her hands over the smooth mahogany arms. She had never heard of this man or the movement and didn't quite know what to think, but found that she was seated more comfortably in it than in the countess's older, stiff-backed chairs. Louise told her that Ruhlmann had used only the best, high-quality exotic woods, such as Macassar ebony and amboyna. Séverine had no idea what amboyna was, but decided she had asked enough questions and would look the word up in a dictionary later.

She liked Louise instantly, finding her as unusual and modern as her furniture. The turquoise and orange paisley shawl she had casually thrown over her shoulders was made of silk with lines of delicate golden thread running through it, and was accented by a pair of exquisite matching turquoise earrings. Her open expression and her height (she must have been almost six feet tall, Séverine calculated), the unusual blue gray of her eyes and her silver hair stylishly cut in a bob gave the impression of a woman who was supremely at ease with herself and her station in life.

Bertrand Sevanot was slightly shorter, blue-eyed and balding, well-bred and courteous, with the confident manner of a man who had always been on the right side of things. He had inherited a reputable jewelry shop on the exclusive rue de la Paix and taken Antoine into the business.

As Séverine's gaze swept the grand and luminous apartment, she couldn't help but compare it to her parents' tiny, gloomy quarters two floors down. The Sevanots' apartment was on the second floor, called the *étage noble*—Séverine had learned that the second floor was considered the best location in a building because it was easily accessible by the staircase yet high enough to be filled with light.

In her mind, she listed all the things that separated her from Antoine: upper-class people enjoyed success and prosperity and the good life. They were well-educated. They gave orders. In the lower classes, by comparison, people had little money and few possessions, and led bleak lives. They were poorly educated. They took orders. None of that, she knew, had anything to do with happiness. Her family was working class, but she had always been happy. No, it was love that was important—and that was something money couldn't buy. Her family loved her, and Gisèle loved her. In fact, it was because Gisèle had taken her into her world for so many years, grooming her, training her, explaining the arcane ways of the upper classes to her, that she didn't feel out of place in the company of people like Antoine and his parents, nor did she feel inferior to them.

As her eyes roved over her tasteful surroundings, she remembered Gisèle's lecture about the material and the immaterial. And although she knew it wasn't good to crave material goods, especially if you weren't in a position to obtain them, she couldn't help but wonder what it would be like to live among the possessions that wealthy people like Antoine's parents so casually enjoyed and took for granted.

Antoine watched Séverine and wondered, as he had wondered the first time he saw her, how she had acquired such confidence and grace. He remarked that while she was friendly, she was not overly familiar. He watched her as she asked his parents questions about the various pieces of furniture they'd chosen and why. Her interest wasn't feigned, he realized, and his admiration for her increased.

He was struggling to relate the poised and polished young woman before him to her description of herself as "daughter of his parents' concierge" when he heard Louise invite her to try out the piano. With great aplomb, Séverine rose, crossed the room and took her place on the piano bench, where she played a few measures of Chopin's *Ballade Number 1 in G minor*.

"It's in fine tune," she exclaimed, managing to satisfy both of Antoine's parents. Antoine's father was pleased because he had vowed to keep this beautiful musical instrument in tune and in the family. Antoine's mother was pleased because when the time came, and she was sure it would come soon, it would be easier to get rid of a piano that was in top condition. Both were impressed by the way she played so well, so seriously, yet with such great ease.

"Then you must come to practice on it whenever you want," Louise offered, as Antoine had predicted. "All you need to do is give us a little advance notice so we are sure not to be entertaining guests. Otherwise, we would be delighted to receive you."

Bertrand Sevanot, also as Antoine had predicted, made no objection. If Antoine's young friend came regularly, he reasoned, Louise might enjoy both her music and her company so much that she would finally stop obsessing about getting rid of the confounded piano.

As Séverine thanked the couple, her mind flashed back to the long-ago day the countess had offered her lessons in the music room of the castle. Now she had been invited to use a rare instrument in a well-appointed apartment in one of the best neighborhoods in Paris. Somehow, she wasn't surprised. She never let herself think that things could go downhill. And right now, she was simply pleased that for the moment things were looking up.

* * *

"She's a looker and a charmer, that's for sure," Bertrand remarked after Séverine and Antoine had left. Noticing the elated look on his wife's face, he issued a gentle warning. "It's very kind of you to invite this young woman to practice, Louise, but don't encourage a relationship between her and Antoine. For Antoine that is what this is all about, as I'm sure you realize. The piano is an excuse—albeit a good one."

"Fiddlesticks, Bertrand. Do you realize that our son is thirty years old and this is the first time he has ever brought a young woman to our home? I would rather have him pay court to a poised, intelligent young girl of modest origin than the floozies I fear he spends most of his time with."

Bertrand was silent, refusing to fall into the trap. His wife knew he was a ladies' man himself, and suspected Antoine of being one as well. But he was curious all the same. Why, he asked himself, had their bachelor son finally brought a young woman to their home? Was he really motivated only by kindness, helping Séverine to find a piano to practice on? Knowing Antoine, he highly doubted that was the reason.

"All right, my dear. Let's say that there's a little spark and these two continue to see each other." He stroked his mustache as he paced the room. "Now, let's go even farther and imagine that things get so serious that he proposes to her. How would we announce to our friends that our son is marrying the daughter of a concierge? Not only that, but *our* concierge!" He paused and looked fretfully at his wife as a thought struck him. "What if she's only after Antoine for his fortune—*our* fortune?"

Louise snorted. "Bertrand, you are getting ahead of yourself. It's not because Antoine has never introduced us to any of his women friends that we need to panic when he finally does. For heaven's sake, she lives downstairs. It's no more than a courtesy on our part to invite her to come up and use our piano! Second, even if they did get serious about each other, would it be such a disaster? Frankly, Antoine's not getting any younger, and neither are we. I don't know about you, but I would like to see him settle down. and I would also love the idea of having grandchildren. Wouldn't you?

"And as for our fortune and its future, the business your grandfather and father worked so diligently to make a success will go to Antoine—but if Antoine has no children, that will be the end of it. And are you really worried about what our friends might say about Antoine's associating with a woman from the lower classes? Don't be! If he continues to see her, I will tell the old cows that our beloved Antoine does what he wants—which as I'm sure you've noticed is true. If they're real friends, they won't care, and if they're not, they aren't the kind of friends we want anyway!

"Plus," she added, "I would prefer for Antoine to settle down with one woman, even very young, even a servant's daughter than to continue running around. That should not become a family tradition, if you see what I mean." Her voice trailed off, but she held her husband's gaze.

Bertrand ignored the thrust. "There's nothing to worry about. Antoine is leaving to manage our shop in Brussels soon, and he won't have time to pursue this latest interest. Believe me, he'll forget about her the minute he leaves town."

He nodded knowingly at his wife. "You, however, had better get used to hearing scales."

* * *

"I don't care if this Antoine fellow is the son of a jeweler or the president of France," Robert said when he heard about Séverine's dinner invitation. "I can say that he is polite and respectful from the few times I have seen him, but he's also thirty years old. Séverine should be going out with lads her own age." He meant one lad in particular, and didn't need to say his name. It was unfortunate that they had had to leave Sorignac, he thought. Robert felt sure that Paul and Séverine were made for each other. He was convinced that Séverine would eventually have overcome Huguette's snobbishness. He didn't doubt his daughter's ability to do anything she wanted.

"I know how you feel, Robert. But since we arrived in Paris Séverine hasn't done anything other than give piano lessons, get to know the city and spend most of her time with us. She deserves a new experience. And there's nothing to worry about. After all, Antoine's parents live in the building. It was kind of them to offer her an opportunity to practice on their piano until she makes other arrangements. What harm could come of her going out with their son for dinner?"

"Plenty. Séverine is seventeen years old. She'll come of age when she's twenty-one. Then she can do what she wants. But as long as she is underage, it is our duty to shield and protect her. She can go upstairs to practice piano all she wants as long as the parents are there—and I will check to see that they are—but I forbid her to go to a restaurant or any place else alone with the son. And that's final."

Germaine had never seen her husband in such a state. She automatically seized a broom and began sweeping the kitchen, something she often did when she needed to think. She had been reacting to the invitation in terms of Séverine's short-term happiness. But Robert was right, she admitted, as she set the broom aside and grabbed a wet mop. She swirled it around as she focused on removing every single spot and stain on the cheap linoleum floor. Robert could not know that as she silently scrubbed, she too was thinking what a pity it was that Séverine had left Sorignac, and Paul, behind.

* * *

Séverine looked around her and tapped her foot as she waited for Antoine in front of La Coupole. It was the first time she had disobeyed her parents to such an extent, and she felt frightened, guilty and excited.

"You're going to love Montparnasse," he had told Séverine, who was indeed noticing the different atmosphere. The neighborhood seemed much looser and freer than the staid, bourgeois area she lived in. Eccentrically dressed bohemians strolled by, arm in arm, laughing and talking. Some stared frankly at her, and a few of the men whispered compliments to her out of the sides of their mouths. She fixed her attention on a spot in the distance and wondered if she hadn't made a big mistake.

"Come on, don't look so terrified," Antoine teased, stepping up beside her and tipping his hat. "It's only an afternoon coffee."

"An afternoon coffee with an older man in a neighborhood I've never set foot in before, and without my parents' permission," she corrected him as they stepped inside the restaurant. But his self-confidence had already made her own nervousness disappear. She tried not to stare as they passed by older women accompanied by artistic-looking types who could be their sons or even grandsons, and fashionable young women with severely plucked eyebrows, Kohl-lined eyes, bright red lips and hair worn in short bobs. Antoine steered her to a round table for two set against the wall near the bar, where they had an all-encompassing view of the cavernous room. She was struck by the mosaic floor underneath her feet, the highly polished sleek lemonwood bar on her left, and the massive pillars, the vibrant colors—warm blues and sunny yellows and browns and greens—the geometric shapes of the light fixtures, and the huge mirrors that reflected the décor.

"Art Deco!" she exclaimed triumphantly.

"I see you've learned your lesson well," Antoine said, raising his eyebrows in surprise and appreciation. "Either my mother is a good teacher or you're a good pupil—or perhaps a little of each."

Antoine explained that although the initial plans had been to put the restaurant in a large open space, the thirty-three pillars, which plunged twelve meters under the ground and rose five meters to the ceiling, had had to be left in place to anchor the building. The solution was to make them part of the décor, so they had been covered with imitation green marble flecked with gold. The famous artists Fernand Léger, Moïse Kisling and Marie Vassilieff had created artwork for three of the pilasters; the rest of them had been painted by selected lesser-known artists. Rumor had it that the artists had been paid in drink. That may or may not have been true, but one thing was sure: with a few strokes of their brushes they had worked magic, transforming a problem into an asset.

The grand opening of the restaurant in 1927 had been attended by 2,500 guests, including Jean Cocteau, the artists Foujita, Kisling and Vlaminck, and the singer Josephine Baker. Twelve hundred bottles of Mumm champagne had been served, he told her, and even that wasn't enough. Antoine and his family had been invited, naturally.

"You could barely move, and the noise was deafening," he told her.

Séverine's eyes widened.

"Have you heard about the cockroach races?" he asked, watching for her reaction.

"The what?"

146

"One of the things the bohemians like to do, I've heard, is to go upstairs to the terrace, collect a few cockroaches, and pit them against each other. Of course everyone yells and shouts and places bets on 'their' cockroach."

"That's disgusting!" Séverine replied. "Surely you're joking!"

"Well," he conceded, "it may or may not be true, but it kind of sums up the frame of mind here—unconventional and a little bit crazy. There are all kinds of stories about things that happened here in Montparnasse—about the painters and the people in the cafés, the fights that broke out, romances that started, romances that were broken, tragic love affairs. Surely you know the most famous story of all, about the Italian painter Modigliani, who was a regular at La Coupole, and his mistress and muse Jeanne Hébuterne."

Séverine shook her head, and Antoine continued. "Jeanne was a beautiful young girl with long auburn hair from a bourgeois family who lived in the Saint-Sulpice neighborhood, not far from here. She was a budding artist and took lessons from Modigliani. They fell in love and had a child, which scandalized her parents. She was pregnant with the second one when he died from tubercular meningitis—and a life of alcohol abuse—at the age of thirty-six. That was on the twenty-fourth of January, eight years ago.

"Jeanne, whom Modigliani called Gina, was taken back to her parents' place and just one day later she committed suicide by jumping out the fifth-floor window. She and Modigliani are buried in the Père Lachaise cemetery in the east of the city."

Séverine gasped. "No, I didn't know that. Such a tragic tale. Don't forget, I was only nine years old at the time," she reminded him. "And it's not exactly the kind of story that you would tell a nine-year-old, is it? But it's so sad," she added.

"Romantic, though, don't you think?"

Séverine tilted her head as she replied without hesitation. "Romantic, perhaps, but not really. They were poor, he was an alcoholic, and she was estranged from her parents. Frankly, it sounds horrible!"

"What I like about you is that you never say what you think," Antoine kidded her. "So you don't believe in the kind of sacrificial love she felt for him?"

"I guess I don't! I'm too pragmatic. Or maybe I haven't met the man who would have that effect on me. Why would anyone run off with someone who drinks and leads a miserable life? Oh, it all sounds very romantic and tragic, and I'm sure it is, but it doesn't tempt me."

"What does tempt you?"

"Settling down someday with a good man. Being happy. Having children. I know it sounds frightfully boring and petit bourgeois. But," she added good-humoredly, "since I'm not even bourgeois, petit-bourgeois is already a step up." She folded her arms. "Anyway, I don't like labels. They don't mean anything other than to the people who assign them." She paused for breath. "Now, tell me about you. You promised you would, you know."

"Oh, yes." He cleared his throat. "Well, you can probably piece together a lot now that you have met my parents and seen the apartment I grew up in," he began. "Only child of wealthy parents, spoiled because I had no siblings to fight with, indifferent student in Catholic schools but not for long. If the war hadn't broken out, I would have finished school and gone straight into my father's business. I didn't have any particular vocation in mind. But war did break out and I ran away to fight. The battleground was the only place I wanted to be, and flying was the only thing I wanted to do, so I lied about my age. I didn't know anything about flying or airplanes, other than that I loved the idea.

"I made friends with pilots who taught me everything I

knew in record time. The rest was adrenaline and guts and pleasure. I finally got the chance to fight, and I got a kick out of being up there in the cockpit shooting down the Boches. We all did," he said. "I was a real show-off, a risk taker. I often realize how lucky I was to get out alive." He shut his eyes briefly, remembering several touch-and-go moments that were best not spoken about. "Don't worry," he reassured Séverine. "I'm not going to bore you with all my war stories."

He took a sip of his coffee, set the cup down, and resumed speaking. "You know what fascinates me about you, Séverine? Here you are, only a couple of months away from life in a small village in the middle of nowhere, and you sit in this Parisian café as if you've never known anything else. Where did you get that ease, that poise? Did it come from your countess? I love it." He sensed she was waiting for him to say more so plunged ahead. "Look, Séverine, I'll tell you anything you want to know about me, including my childhood pranks and how my mother went through a period of dressing me like Little Lord Fauntleroy. I'm not kidding—velvet suits, lace collars, long golden locks, but in my case, not curly. My father, who is generally accommodating, mercifully nipped that little initiative in the bud in no time at all. I hope he's destroyed all the incriminating photos," he said, miming mock horror.

"But that's not why I invited you here and I'm not going to beat around the bush. So please hear me out."

Almost as if to himself, he said, "Materially speaking, I have everything I need and more: affluent parents, my own big apartment overlooking the Luxembourg Gardens, a new position as head of our company's store in Brussels, a fast car that almost makes up for not having a plane. No, that's not true," he corrected himself. "Nothing could make up for not having a plane." He returned to the subject at hand. "To be frank, I've also had plenty of girlfriends, and

I have rather a reputation as a man of the world and an eternal bachelor. And that, Séverine, is my world—the world of Antoine.

"Or it was, until you came along. The minute I saw you down on your knees in the courtyard of our building, worrying about a tear in your clothes, everything changed. I don't know why, but you touched my heart. Then, when we talked, I knew you were the one. You were—you *are*—so natural and frank and engaging and real, the total opposite of any woman I have ever known, most of whom, in any case, are more interested in my money and lifestyle than in me."

He leaned toward her, his elbows on the table. "You just told me that all you want in life is to settle down and marry and have children. I don't know many women who would say that, even if that was indeed all they wanted."

He looked around the vast room and back at her. "I know what I'm going to say may be crazy, but I'll take advantage of being in a crazy place to say it anyway.

"I want to marry you. Wait—hear me out," he entreated, as Séverine blushed deeply and an expression of wariness and disbelief formed on her face. "Not now. You're too young, and I'm soon leaving to work in Brussels. But I want to go out with you every time I am in Paris. I want us to get to know each other better. I want to smooth things out with our families.

"And if you think I go around making reckless propositions like this with every woman I invite for coffee, you're wrong. My parents went into a state of shock after I showed up with you. They suspect that I'm not quite right in the head. They've never seen me like this before."

He waited. "Please say something, anything, now that I've told you what's on my mind."

"I don't know what to say," Séverine replied, truthfully. "I've never had a proposal on my first date."

Antoine looked down at his hands. "Please pardon my haste, Séverine. You were the one talking too fast the other day, talking about a countess I had never even heard of. And now I'm the one who's getting ahead of myself. I'm a pragmatic man. That's why I introduced you to my parents straight away. By the way, my mother can't wait for you to come to practice piano. It's obvious she'll enjoy your company. But it won't be easy to convince my parents, or yours. It may even take a long while. That's why I want them all to know that I am serious, that my decision is not rash, that I'll wait for you to live your life in Paris while I live mine in Brussels. But my parents should know, and you must know my plans for when I return to Paris on a permanent basis. Maybe it's not the best way forward, but I have always known what I want, and being with you is what I want. It's as simple as that—for me, at least."

Séverine avoided his eyes. She was thinking not so much about Antoine's unexpected proposal but about Paul: her first friend, and—she had to admit—the one she would always love because she knew him best. He had proposed to her as well, but that had been different. Paul was a boy with a future. Antoine was a man with a past. He had already fought in a war, had run a business, and had had scores of women. She closed her eyes slightly as she focused on the differences between the two. She and Paul were on the same wavelength, the same footing, the same ground. They'd grown up together, they knew the same people and the same places. From the day they met, they'd been inseparable.

She and Antoine, by contrast, knew each other only from the bits and pieces they had each told the other. They didn't know the same people and she had never been to the places Antoine took her. She was the student, he the guide. He had already shown her a Parisian world she knew nothing about, and she knew he would continue to widen her horizons by introducing her to museums and theater performances and different cafés and restaurants, cabarets and clubs. The color in her cheeks heightened as she thought of another world—the sensual world he would introduce to her should they marry.

She liked his confidence, his knowing what he wanted, and she was flattered, if somewhat mystified, that he wanted her. She liked being in this festive place, wearing her only fashionable outfit. She was attracted to this manly man who charmed her with his good looks and frankness and determination. She had been honest in telling him she wanted to marry and settle down. She couldn't imagine a succession of dramatic, romantic, unhappy love stories, nor being so in love she would throw herself out a window. She realized that all she really wanted was to be taken care of—and not have to give piano lessons for the rest of her life.

But, she thought uneasily, he hadn't asked her what she felt. He was putting her in his life the way you arrange a hat in a hatbox, put a handkerchief in your pocket or a key on a chain. She didn't want to be "placed" anywhere by anyone.

"Can you take me for a drive?" she asked, smoothly. "You said I should see more of Paris. We could even go to the Père Lachaise, and you can show me the gravestones of Modigliani and Jeanne Hébuterne. I'd like that."

Then she turned to him, a firm, decisive expression on her face. "And when we've done that, you'll drop me off a block from our apartment building and we'll pretend that this afternoon never happened. Things have gone too far in too short a time. I'm sorry."

The taut muscles in his face relaxed and he smiled ruefully. "You're a clever girl. I think you must have learned more from your countess than I ever could have dreamed. And, yes, I will take you for a drive and drop you off wherever you see fit. But just one more thing before we go. I respect you and your words. But don't think I'll forget either this afternoon or my proposal."

* * *

Séverine had never seen the city from the luxury of a private automobile. When the family had arrived at the station in Paris, they had taken the *métro*, the bus and the tramway. She walked to work. Now she was perched on a burgundy-tinted leather seat in a cream-colored Lorraine-Dietrich roadster for two, taking in Paris from an entirely different perspective. From Montparnasse, the couple sped to the Père Lachaise. Paris had so many monuments, Séverine reflected as they crossed the Pont de Sully over the Seine. She took in the view of Notre-Dame on the left, then in what seemed like no time at all, they passed the July Column at the Place de la Bastille. Finally, they motored up the narrow and crowded rue de la Roquette to the boulevard de Ménilmontant and the imposing main entrance of the famous Père Lachaise cemetery, whose high walls and imposing metal door delineated the border between the living and the dead.

Modigliani's grave wasn't easy to find, and Antoine thought they'd never make it before closing, so absorbed was Séverine in inspecting almost every tombstone they passed.

"Oh, I love his poetry," she exclaimed as she stood in front of Alfred de Musset's grave, reading the words carved into the stone. "Did you know it was inspired by his unhappy love affair with George Sand?"

As they turned to continue their walk, her eyes took in the full measure of the Monument to the Dead, on either side of which steps led to an upper level. Set under a mound, it was composed of a large open entrance toward which carved figures of people were heading. The central entrance clearly led to a place only the dead could go. It was eerie, and Séverine could have contemplated its strangeness for a long time, but Antoine hurried her on.

Finally, after innumerable twists and turns—one of which, to her delight, led them to her beloved Chopin's grave—Séverine noticed an unpretentious, cream-colored tomb.

"Here it is," she cried to Antoine, who had wandered away. The two read the epitaph in Italian. Séverine was touched by its description of Jeanne: "Devoted companion of Amedeo Modigliani till the moment of extreme sacrifice."

Antoine was amused to see her wipe away a tear. "I thought you didn't believe in tragic love affairs," he said in a mock accusatory tone.

She looked up at the tall trees, whose branches moved gently with the wind. "I've never been in this cemetery before. I was convinced it would be something awful, dark and dank and even smelly. But instead it's peaceful and poetic with all these chestnut trees and conifers and cats and crows and cobblestones and the different graves, from the simple ones like this to others that are bigger than the house I lived in when I was little. I think it's a perfect end of the road for star-crossed lovers."

"You're something of a poet yourself. I like your alliteration," Antoine remarked, looking at his watch; he was focused on leaving before the gates closed and was in no mood to discuss romanticism, poets, or the unhappy love affairs of famous people. She had rejected him, after all, and she was right. He was too old for her—for now, at least. He was already calculating the age at which they would be more of a likely combination, more complementary. He couldn't wait forever. In a few short years he would take over the business in Paris, and for the sake of respectability and his own ease he needed a wife by his side. With her beauty and her youth—and even her lack of sophistication, which was largely compensated for by her poise—she was the one. And he had told her that. Naturally she was, and always would be, one among the others. Marriage didn't mean death, after all.

"Watch your step," he cautioned her. "You're going to fall over the roots of your precious trees."

* * *

"Come with me," Séverine wheedled. Caroline was busy mending a costume for the evening's performance.

"Can't you see I'm overwhelmed with work?" Caroline replied, giving her sister a hug. "We'll go as soon as I've finished this hem." She made another few stitches, knotted and cut the thread, and then put the garment aside.

"Come on, let's go," said Séverine impatiently. "I've got something to tell you, but not here."

As they settled on the wobbly chairs at the café next door, Caroline said apologetically, "I'm so happy to see you, even if you did come at the worst possible time." Her affectionate smile took the edge off her words. "What's going on that's so important you'd cross town in mid-afternoon to see me instead of waiting until I get off work?"

"I'm in love," Séverine announced. She savored the puzzled look on Caroline's face.

"But you've always been in love!" Caroline exclaimed, settling back into her chair. "It's just that up until now, you've been too thick to realize it. I don't understand, though. What's changed. Have you had news from Paul?"

"I'm not talking about Paul!" Séverine replied.

The story spilled out of her in a rush. She told Caroline

about meeting Antoine, going out for coffee with him, visiting his parents, practicing the piano in their grand apartment. She confessed that he had invited her to dinner but that their father had forbidden it.

"Why would Papa do that?" Caroline asked.

Séverine marked a pause. "He thinks Antoine is too old for me."

"For heaven's sakes, how old is he?"

"Thirty."

"Oh." Caroline was silent for a moment. "But you went with him anyway?"

"Yes, and it was wonderful. First of all, we went to La Coupole. Do you know it? Such a beautiful place, and such a fascinating crowd of people. It was so noisy and gay. He told me the tragic story of Modigliani—you know, the Italian painter—and his mistress, and then we drove all the way across town to visit their grave! And that's not all." She paused for effect. "He proposed."

Caroline gaped at her.

"Of course you turned him down. Or was he joking?"

"Yes, I turned him down, but no, he wasn't joking."

A shadow passed over Caroline's face, but Séverine continued, oblivious.

"It's all happened so fast, and it's all so unlikely. Just think of it—the daughter of a concierge with a *grand* bourgeois! And somehow it seems that it was meant to be. I tripped and fell in the courtyard of our building, he picked me up and voilà! And you know what else? Antoine said he had been to see a gypsy lady who lives over near the Père Lachaise. She read his palm and told him that he would meet a sweet, simple, innocent young girl from the provinces and that he would marry her."

Caroline rolled her eyes heavenward. "Oh, please, dear Lord," she groaned. "And did she say that her name was Séverine Aubry, that she comes from a town called

Sorignac, and she has long dark hair and big brown eyes? I wonder how much he paid her." She shook her head. "You've always been gullible, but one thing is clear: gypsy or no gypsy, he's put a spell on you."

Séverine shrugged. "I'm here to ask you for a favor: not for your blessing, unless you want to give it. I'd like to ask if you will make me a trousseau."

"I suppose it's for right now?"

"No, he's going to Brussels to work for a few years and I'm going to wait for him. He doesn't know it, though. I led him to believe that I don't want to hear anything about proposals or weddings. But I'm getting ready for when he returns and comes to propose again. Because he will."

Caroline had no idea of what to do or say. Should she humor her younger sister? Mock her? Criticize her? Tell her she was being foolish? Give her the blessing she so obviously wanted? She settled on the first solution.

"All right," she conceded. "I'll make you a trousseau. But we can talk about the details later, since we may have a few years ahead of us." She checked the time on her watch, finished her coffee, then got to her feet and gave Séverine a kiss on both cheeks.

As she bade her sister goodbye and hurried back to her job, Caroline mused that any ensemble she would create for Séverine could be used for another suitor if this one didn't work out. Without even knowing Antoine, she hoped it wouldn't.

Chapter THIRTEEN

Paris: New Year's Eve 1933

Five years had passed since Séverine had sneaked out to meet Antoine at La Coupole and turned down his marriage proposal. She had, of course, no intention of running after him; he was the one who would have to do all the running if he was truly interested.

And just as she had suspected, he didn't give up. Even though he was now working in Brussels, invitations from him still came her way, although they were always cleverly disguised as social invitations from Louise and Bertrand.

"Ah, Séverine," Louise would say. "Antoine is in town. We were wondering if you would like to join us tonight for a light dinner followed by a play." Séverine almost always accepted.

Being with him and his parents felt awkward at first, as though they were two children being supervised at a family party, but rapidly the uneasiness was replaced by a delicious feeling of excitement. Being so close to and yet so far away from this worldly-wise man was frustrating and exhilarating. She could smell the citrus scent of his cologne, fix her gaze on the crinkly laughter lines around his eyes, picture the muscles underneath his perfectly fitted suit. Every once in a while, she would feel his hand on her arm as he helped her in or out of her coat. She found herself waiting for the little jolt of electricity that shot through her even if the touch was fleeting and slight. Sitting next to him at a play, she would feel her belly do flip-flops and fantasize about kissing him. She started thinking that he was far cleverer than she had given him credit for, that if this was a campaign he was waging, he was certainly winning it.

The end of Antoine's silent but effective courtship came the night he announced he would be returning permanently to Paris to head up the jewelry store on the rue de la Paix. Once again, Louise and Bertrand issued an invitation. Could Séverine join them for a performance of André Barr's *Taxpayer Follies* followed by dinner at Maxim's? Séverine didn't remember much about the play, but she was sure she would never forget her first dinner at Maxim's: the special treatment the waiters bestowed on Bertrand, who was a regular customer; the dressed oysters on the half shell; the sparkling champagne; the chirping and chattering of the superlatively coiffed and made-up ladies, dressed in ravishing beaded gowns, their expensive wraps thrown over the backs of their chairs.

What she didn't see was that with her youth and freshness, she outdid them all. Louise and Bertrand saw it though, and loved to show her off, introducing her as "Antoine's young lady friend."

Antoine, for his part, was pleased that she had remained as she was when he'd met her: spontaneous and frank, yet poised and sure of herself. She was a delicious fruit waiting to be plucked. Tonight was the time to make his intentions clear, he decided. He waited until they had all eaten their desserts, then said he had two announcements to make.

"You," he said, looking at his parents, "know the first part—I am soon returning to Paris to work in the boutique on the rue de la Paix. This dinner is to celebrate that happy occasion.

"And there's something else." He looked directly at Séverine, a tender expression on his face. "The last time I proposed to you, it was over a cup of coffee at La Coupole. You were a frightened young girl, new to Paris and the big wide world. I know—and regret—that my forwardness and bold words shocked you terribly, but you put me in my place, as you were right to do. You showed me then, and have showed me ever since, that you were worth fighting for."

He continued. "My parents know that I'm always up for a battle, and that I like to win, but that's not what this is about. You and I both see that they have welcomed you into their household, and what started as a simple offer to you of a piano to practice on has led to a true friendship. I wanted that, of course, but it might not have happened had you not been the very special and wonderful young woman that you are. I'm so glad it did. That's why I wanted us all to be together tonight. You don't have to answer me now—this isn't the time or place—but I hope that you will consider this evening as a special one, both because I am returning and because I want to ask you to be by my side, now and forever, should that be your desire."

At first no one spoke. Louise, holding her fork in mid-air, resisted the impulse to compliment her son on his eloquence. Bertrand looked at Séverine and Antoine in turn, wondering if the scene were real. Then Louise and Bertrand looked at each other with a smile of silent understanding. It was true that Séverine had become a friend and, although they wouldn't say it aloud, almost a daughter. In the beginning, she had been reserved, politely asking permission to practice the piano and leaving immediately afterward. But as time passed, she had become more natural in their company although never overly familiar. Bertrand was touched when she brought pretty bouquets of flowers she could barely afford, and Louise found herself waiting for Séverine's visits, not only to hear her play the hated instrument, but to chat with her over a cup of tea after the practice session about fashion, current events and whatever was on her mind.

Séverine, after a moment of stunned silence, finally spoke.

"Is that a proposal, Antoine? If so, I accept with all my heart."

As Antoine leaned over to kiss her, Louise looked ecstatic and Bertrand tapped on his crystal wine glass and held it high. When the general hubbub calmed down, he announced with pride that, at last, his beloved only son was marrying.

"Champagne for all," he cried.

The arrival of the precious bottles of bubbly was accompanied by thunderous clapping and hoots and hollers of good cheer and wishes for long life to the happy couple.

Chapter FOURTEEN

Paris: February 6, 1934

Antoine locked the door of his apartment near the Luxembourg Gardens and adjusted his hat and collar. He was on his way across Paris to meet with Yves and other members of the Croix de Feu, a veterans' organization known for its right-wing views. Today the group was gathering for an anti-government demonstration on the Left Bank of the Seine near the Palais Bourbon, the elegant eighteenth-century country house of the Duchess of Bourbon, which was nationalized during the Revolution and now housed the National Assembly.

The Croix de Feu was only one of the many disgruntled right-wing groups that had taken to the streets to march on the Parliament. It was joined by various right-wing and extreme-right organizations, ranging from the royalist Action Française, which wanted to restore the monarchy, to its more militant youth group, the Camelots du Roi. The one thing the disparate groups had in common was their determination to put an end to the current administration. All were protesting against the corruption of the governing center-left Radical-Socialist party and a growing series of financial and political scandals that had culminated in the notorious so-called Stavisky affair, named after the embezzler Alexandre Stavisky, who had sold hundreds of millions of worthless bonds on Bayonne's pawnshops and gotten away with it by buying off the newspapers that were trying to investigate him. His trial had conveniently been postponed for nineteen months because the public prosecutor was the brother-in-law of the prime minister, who was accused of protecting him. Stavisky's sudden death on January 8, 1934 was called a suicide, but the general opinion was that he had been assassinated by the powers-that-be to keep him from revealing secrets. But discontent had not ended with his death, which is why Antoine and his friends were demonstrating today.

As Antoine approached the Seine, he heard the roar of the crowd and saw Croix de Feu members bearing banderoles with the emblem of the cross. Among them he spotted Jean Mermoz, a well-known pilot and proud veteran.

"Mermoz," he yelled, hurrying over to him. "What are you doing with this sorry group?"

"Same as you," Mermoz yelled over the brouhaha. The two men linked arms with others to surround the Parliament with their group, but suddenly Antoine felt the itch for action.

"Let's go over there," he said, pointing toward the Right Bank. The two pushed their way across the heavily defended bridge to reach the other side.

Once there, they found themselves in the midst of a pitched battle on the Place de la Concorde, where mounted policemen were charging the rioters. Antoine loved a good fight, and was getting ready to use a sharp object he had brought along to defend himself if necessary when he was knocked down by something—perhaps a policeman or a horse, he didn't know—with enormous force. He fell hard to the cold ground, where he was trampled by the crowd and crushed into the cobblestones. *This is it*, he thought.

This is how it ends. But he couldn't give in, couldn't face the idea that the victorious fighter pilot he had once been would end up an ignominious heap on the ground.

In a burst of energy, he managed to fight against the weight of the mass above and around him and raise his body, using his hands to grab the legs of those pushing him down to hoist himself up. He didn't realize until he was finally standing on his feet that blood was running down his cheek. He ripped his shirt and pressed the fabric to his face to staunch the flow, then looked down at a man who was lying still on the ground—too still. The blow Antoine had received had been fierce, but at least he had got out with his life, unlike this fellow demonstrator.

"It's nothing," he reassured his worried comrades, who had gathered around him.

When he took a better look later on at home, he saw the wound was deep and knew that his face would be scarred for life. But he didn't care. The protest against the reviled leftist government had been worth it.

Chapter FIFTEEN

Paris: March 1934

Now that Antoine had his parents' consent to marry Séverine, the only thing that remained was for Antoine to ask Robert for his permission and blessing.

Séverine wasn't at all sure he would give it: her father, like all fathers, didn't want to lose her. He especially didn't want to lose her to an older man, he had made that much clear. But she was no longer a teenager, as she had been when she met Antoine. She had known Antoine for six years now, and she was optimistic that his charm, looks, and personality would win her father over. Added to that, and more important than anything, she thought, were the stories of Antoine's bravery as a fighter pilot in the Great War. Antoine had lived through the hell of Verdun. Not only had he survived the slaughter; he'd also emerged a decorated war hero for fearlessly pursuing and shooting down German planes. She was sure that would impress her father, who had an unassailable admiration for the young men who had survived that terrible massacre and for Marshal Pétain himself, who had also been a hero of the Verdun battlefields. But would that be enough for him?

She stood nervously with her parents, her sister and Antoine in the tiny concierge's quarters and gazed at the linoleum floor, the oilcloth on the table, the artificial flowers, the inexpensive knickknacks on the shelves and mentally compared them to the massive oak chevron parquet, the Art Deco chairs, and the expensive modern artwork on the walls of Antoine's parents' apartment. She guessed she should be ashamed or embarrassed, but she wasn't.

Robert, who should have been thinking about what was obviously going to be a request for his daughter's hand in marriage, had his mind on an article in the newspaper he had just been reading.

"Damn communist Bolsheviks—they'll be the ruin of this country," he opined, as he folded his paper and motioned for Antoine to sit in the only other comfortable chair.

"Sorry about the swearing," he said, apologizing to the ladies and Antoine. "But I was reading about a projected alliance of the socialists and communists. I wouldn't want them united in running this country."

In what was undoubtedly one of the longest speeches he had ever made in his life, he continued, "When I think that the local communists down in Sorignac had the gall to ask me to join the Party. After having to work twice as hard to compensate for Just's laziness, how could they even imagine I would want to be part of their organization? Just didn't work, he was lazy as sin, but went around with his 'comrades' agitating for more pay, more 'equality.' Why do those people think that a worker with no education and only two bare hands to make a living could possibly be on the same level as his employers?"

He paused, realizing he was getting worked up, and concluded, "I never thought I was the equal of the count and countess. Why should I ask for more? I'm a worker who works for his pay, never a day off, never sick. I don't go around demonstrating or marching in the streets or asking for more than I have. I don't believe all people should earn the same. Nonsense!"

Germaine, Séverine and Caroline stole nervous looks at each other. What was this all leading to? What must Antoine be thinking?

Antoine was, in fact, relieved by Robert's rare effusion. He and Robert never talked politics, but from what Séverine had told him, her father couldn't stand the communists. And now this sudden outburst had confirmed it. That was fine with him: he felt the same way. It occurred to him he didn't even know what Séverine's politics were. He had never asked her, and it didn't make any difference anyway, since women didn't have the vote.

Oddly, he thought, his parents and Séverine's had more in common than they knew, starting with the fact that they were each wary of finding themselves linked by marriage. Had Louise not been Louise, so totally free-thinking and avant-garde, the marriage proposal would never have come about. But since Bertrand would do anything for Louise, and both he and his wife would do anything for Antoine, it had.

Antoine looked Robert straight in the eye as a hush fell over the room. "I love Séverine and want to take her as my wife. I loved her the day I met her and my feelings haven't changed. I know that when a man and woman marry, they marry not only each other but bind their respective families together, and I understand what you are saying to me. You didn't ask me about my age or my prospects because you know I'm older and you can see that my prospects are solid. So you've gone straight to the heart of the next important matter. Some people say politics aren't important. I disagree."

He slowly pulled out his handmade Dunhill chestnut pipe with its smooth polished finish. "Do you mind? No?" He caressed the fine, dark wood Cumberland stem, which bore the company's emblematic and minuscule white spot, and filled the bowl with tobacco. "Let me say one more thing. When I was seventeen, the age Séverine was when I met her, I ran away from home to go to war. Defending my country was the only thing I wanted to do. It was my mission. I was honored to fly those planes and launch bombs on the Germans. We pilots were literally above it all. But on the ground… I saw atrocities that re-appear in my dreams still today. I witnessed slaughters and smelled the stench of the dead bodies piled all around. One day you'd be playing cards or fooling around with a comrade; the next day he'd be gone. I often wonder how I got out alive when tens of thousands in my generation were killed. I can't accept that so many gave their lives for this country, and we now find ourselves dealing with those damned communist Bolsheviks." He turned toward Robert and gave him a complicit nod.

He broke off, then started again. "Those are my last words on the subject of war. I live in the present, not the past. But we should talk about the present as well. See this mark?" He ran his finger over a short but deep line parallel to his jaw. "On February sixth I was out in the streets with other members of the Croix de Feu protesting against this government. You read the papers, so you know all about the riots and about the Croix de Feu, which was founded for war veterans by Count François de la Roque. If the count had given the order, we could have taken over Parliament, but he didn't. I was glad to be among all those veterans, and I wear this scar on my face as a trophy. I was only one among the thousands injured as we marched against a government filled with crooks. Lucky I wasn't killed. Fifteen people were. But enough of politics."

He smiled. "Back to the subject at hand," he continued, still focusing on Robert, who was listening attentively. "Yes, I'm older than your daughter—thirteen years older. You surely would have liked a younger man to ask for her hand, but I can assure you that with the experience I have in life and with my means, I can both protect her and provide for her. She'll be safe with me—and loved. And isn't it fine that you and I will never argue about politics?" he added, as he winked at Séverine.

Caroline had to admit that she had never heard such an eloquent speech in her life. It was so perfect, so romantic. It flowed. She wondered about Antoine, though, and chalked her doubts up partly to jealousy and partly to politics. Her heart was on the Left, and inside she was reeling from what he had said. Her father, she knew, was adamant about his hatred of communists. But what did he think of having a future son-in-law who calmly explained he was on the extreme right? She reminded herself never to discuss her future brother-in-law's political inclinations with her friends.

She would miss Séverine, and hoped that her funny, spontaneous and impetuous little sister wouldn't find herself either too much in Antoine's shadow or too pampered by him. No, she corrected herself: pampered was a possibility, given Antoine's glamorous lifestyle, but no one could overshadow Séverine. She couldn't see Séverine ever relinquishing her opinions or toning down her spontaneity.

She hoped that she and Séverine would remain as close as they had always been, and tried to chase away her gnawing suspicions about Antoine. Did anyone else in the room have any? She glanced at her mother whose eyes shone with the beginning of tears. Then she glanced at her father who looked transformed. Robert may not have liked the difference in age between his daughter and her fiancé, but Antoine had won him over in every other way, not least with his well-crafted speech. No, she told herself, the rest would take care of itself. For now, there was a wedding to plan.

Chapter SIXTEEN

Paris to Sorignac: September 1935

"Hey, you're not in the cockpit now!" Yves exclaimed, as Antoine pushed his brand-new gleaming red Citroën Traction convertible to top speed. "Keep that up and we'll be in the hospital instead of at your wedding!"

"This car has more elegance than power," Antoine declared. He glanced over at Yves, a fellow fighter pilot in the Great War and soon-to-be best man at his wedding. "I never knew you to be so cautious."

"And I never dreamed you'd get married, old fellow," Yves replied. "Antoine of the wandering eye, Antoine the war hero, Antoine with a different girl every night. Tell me the truth—am I dreaming? Did this Séverine put a spell on you?"

Antoine let up on the pedal as he reflected on the question. "A spell? Well, perhaps you could call it that. Or maybe I'm getting older and wiser."

A typical Antoine response, Yves thought. Men like Antoine didn't deal in analysis. Why had he even asked? If he and Antoine had remained friends after the war, it was probably in part because he rarely questioned Antoine about anything personal. Many of their fellow fighter pilots, men with whom they'd gone on daring missions in the skies, had returned to civilian life and not kept in touch. Most of them, he was sure, felt that their lives on the ground were commonplace and dull compared to their heady existence up there in the freezing cold air shooting down German planes. The men below in the muddy fields had looked up to them as heroes. The girls, impressed by their uniforms, couldn't wait to drink and dance with them. The entire nation hailed them as saviors. Confiding their state of mind was not the way of these men of action—not then, not now.

The pilots loved speed, in the air and on the ground. They'd clamber out of their one-seater planes into expensive sports cars and drive at breakneck speed straight from the battlegrounds to the Paris bars and brothels. After a night of drinking and sex, they'd rush right back to base, sleepless, sometimes still in their tuxedos, sometimes still with a girl, change into their uniforms and be up in the air within minutes. It was part of the war hero's life. Some of the men came from wealthy, privileged backgrounds, so luxury and adventure weren't strange to them. Others, direct from the farm or from ordinary lives in hamlets or villages, had no trouble transforming themselves into knights of the air by day and playboys by night.

The pilots knew they might never return alive, which accounted for the intensity of their living while on the ground. The bars, the drinking, the sports cars, the luxurious quarters, the girls—they were all part of war. The risks had to have rewards. There had to be some fun in it all, and there was. Even when they lost a man, or several men, they didn't—couldn't—dwell on it. There would be a minute of silence and then someone would tell a joke or make an inappropriate remark or gesture and they would all get back to business. It wasn't that they feared death or refused to acknowledge it; it was with them every second. And that was all the more reason to ignore it, to thumb one's nose at it. No one ever talked about being scared. There was no time to be scared. If fear crossed your mind, you were a sitting duck.

And yet they didn't deny death. Flying ace Charles Nungesser, for example, had painted a huge black heart filled with a coffin, candles, and a skull and crossbones on the fuselage of his Nieuport, inviting death as a guest on his missions. He was fearless—diving deep and shooting up the German bombers from below. During the battle of Verdun, the daredevil had so many injuries he had to be bodily lifted in and out of his aircraft.

Some of the more notorious pilots had bounties on their heads. Where that would have filled a normal person with terror, these sky fighters were thrilled by the challenge of reward for capture. Upon learning he had been singled out, one ace had gleefully painted his craft red to be better spotted by the enemy.

All that, of course, was in the past. Nungesser had vanished in 1927, along with his fellow pilot François Coli, on a nonstop flight to New York in a plane called the White Bird. The dashing, daring, brave pilots who had survived were now leading uneventful lives that could never equal what they had done in the sky. And most of them, Yves was sure, were bored.

He stole a sidewise glance at Antoine. Unlike the others, he would never be bored. First of all, he had all that family money to spend and a glamorous line of work in the jewelry business. On top of that, he had those movie-star looks, which turned the heads of men and women alike. Some women walk down the street and every single man ogles them. Not many men get that kind of attention, but Antoine was one of them. He was incredibly handsome, Yves had to admit. And as if his good looks and great build, sandy hair and blue eyes and tall stature were not enough, there was something else, something indefinable in his allure. When he was in a crowd, Antoine needed to do no more than simply stand to have every head turn towards him. He made no special effort to be affable, but he didn't need to. He was charismatic. Women were drawn to him, attracted by his masculinity, his imposing presence. He looked reassuring, which was odd for someone no woman could hope to count on. He spoke with authority, and with such ease that people listened. Even when the war was over, he carried himself with the poise, self-confidence and cool composure of the fighter pilot for whom careless mistakes and miscalculations invariably meant death.

His self-assurance, his ease in his own skin, was an asset to his job selling jewelry at his father's flagship store in Paris. Dressed in perfectly tailored custom-made suits, Antoine was serious and reserved and professional, but any woman who looked twice could easily detect the ladies' man underneath the smooth surface. Husbands, however, instinctively trusted him; they didn't seem to notice how thrilled their wives were when Antoine gently lifted their hands to place an exquisite ring on a finger or, with infinite care, wrapped a diamond-studded bracelet around their wrists.

Even more exciting was when he stood behind a waiting customer and graciously enquired "May I?" before delicately placing a sparkling ruby or emerald or diamond necklace around a lady's throat. Invariably, the lady watched her reflection, and him, in the mirror as she turned this way and that. If she was an older woman, there was no electricity—at least not for him. If she was younger, something unspoken occasionally passed between the jeweler and his client, and often they would discreetly meet up later. Antoine took that as part of his perks, the pleasurable side of his job.

Antoine had related these little indiscretions to Yves on countless occasions. How the husbands or lovers remained oblivious to the undercurrents was a mystery to Yves. He hoped for Séverine that Antoine had changed. He hoped that she was the one. Only time would tell. And tonight, of course, didn't count.

* * *

Antoine thought about Yves's question. Why indeed was he marrying, settling down? He was a man of action, not a thinker; he didn't spend time pondering motives, the reasons why he did things. But if he had answered Yves—which he had chosen not to—he might have explained that even he, a serial womanizer, had feelings; that of all the women he had been with, and there were hundreds, Séverine was the one who stirred him, invigorated him, warmed his heart. She was so sincere and so uncomplicated, so different from the women in his social milieu. Added to that was the fact that he liked to do the opposite of what most people did, and the very idea of marrying the daughter of his parents' concierge—and the reaction he knew it would provoke—amused rather than cowed him.

She was young and beautiful of course, and in his business those were not negligible qualities. It was important to have a young wife, buy her the right clothes, shower her with jewelry, even form her tastes. She was pliant; he could scarcely see her becoming a nag. That he would not tolerate. What else? Marriage gave him an aura of respectability that bachelorhood at his age no longer did. People would get off his back, stop arranging dinner parties at which there was always a single woman conveniently placed next to him. The women were invariably boring. The institution of marriage struck him as boring as well, but all in all, it was probably not that bad. And now was a good time in his life to take the plunge.

In any case, he had no intention of changing his habits. He would continue to amuse himself with any woman who took his fancy. He would simply have to arrange matters a little more discreetly.

"Here we are," Yves said, tapping Antoine on the elbow. "Slow down." Antoine turned off the main road into a bumpy, narrow tree-lined lane leading to an ivy-covered half-timbered inn hidden deep inside the forest.

"This is it," Yves announced triumphantly. "Right on time for drinks. Remember, our duty tonight is to bury the bachelor!"

Antoine crowed with delight as he scrambled out of the car, then reached back inside to grab a leather overnight bag and slammed the door.

"You said it, my man. I am here and on duty to accomplish this sacred task." He gave a mock salute, then said, *sotto voce*, "Tell me later how you engineered all this. Can't be bothered now."

The reception area was lit by a single lamp that cast a dim glow on the red walls and gilded mirrors. Yves savored the moment, then, winking at Antoine, called, "Irma, come hither. We know you're here."

A buxom blond with an impish look in her large blue eyes framed by thick black eyelashes emerged from behind a huge potted fern, her scantily clothed body covered by a huge palm leaf that was almost bigger than she was. Antoine devoured her divine body with his eyes, clapping Yves on the back as she sinuously advanced.

"Is this my soldier boy?" she purred.

"Looks like we won't have time for drinks, old chap. I wish you a most happy burial of your bachelor life. See you in the morning," said Yves, pleased by the success of his well-chosen wedding present.

But Antoine didn't hear. He was already following Irma up the stairs.

Chapter SEVENTEEN

Sorignac: September 2, 1935

They dubbed it the wedding train—an entire compartment of a coach that was decorated in white and reserved for Séverine's little wedding party. They were to depart from Paris's Gare d'Austerlitz on September 2, bound for Sorignac.

"Look for the car with white bouquets hanging on the windows," Séverine told everyone. "Or," she revised, more sensibly, "in the event the railway authorities don't go for the idea, just look for Caroline and me."

At first, Séverine had asked the women guests to bring a white dress for the ceremony, an odd request, she knew, but a sensible one to her way of thinking. "It's still summer," she proclaimed to Caroline, "and there's no reason the bride has to be the only one to wear white."

That was so like Séverine, Caroline thought: impulsive, sometimes a little off-center. She had had to convince her sister that the season for white was over, that buying anything white, even if it could be found, would be terribly expensive, and that white clothes would get dirty in the train. Caroline's pragmatism finally prevailed, with Séverine agreeing to a "white something" for each person. Caroline suggested that white handkerchiefs for the men would do the trick; as maid of honor, she would wear a white rose pinned to her dress, as would their mother. The girlfriends could do as they pleased. Séverine stubbornly insisted that she would wear an ivory Jean Patou wedding dress, which she deemed much more stylish and which she was quite sure she could wear again.

Séverine was excited to be returning with her family to Sorignac. Naturally she had invited the count and countess to the ceremony at the church. Not only had they accepted, but the countess had written a reply saying that she would love to offer a late-afternoon reception at the château for the family.

"Maman, can you believe it?" Séverine had asked, showing her the letter. "Whoever would have thought?"

"Yes, whoever would have thought indeed?" Germaine replied, surveying Séverine with the look of a mother who couldn't quite fathom what she's created. Séverine looked so much like her father but, unlike him, she was chatty and exuberant. When Caroline walked into a room, nothing changed other than the fact that she was there, a comfortable, reassuring and quiet presence. But when Séverine walked into a room, everything lit up. There was a brightness, a tension, even a longing about her. Germaine always had the feeling that whenever Séverine was in a place, even one she liked, she envisaged herself elsewhere. It wasn't that she was unhappy, not at all, but she gave the impression that there was always something more out there. Germaine prayed that her war hero soon-to-be husband would be up to the fireworks. Séverine was so impulsive and at the same time such a perfectionist.

She remembered hearing her practice her scales in the music room of the château, not once or twice, but repeatedly, until she had mastered them perfectly. She would do the same with a new piece she was learning, tackling it section by section relentlessly until the entire piece came together, flowed. No wonder the countess had invited them for an after-wedding celebration. When she had offered Séverine piano lessons all those years ago, they had been at first simply an opportunity for the little girl to have something new in her life. But Séverine had taken them seriously and gone far beyond any expectations the countess may have had. The countess admired Séverine, Germaine knew, not only for her talent, but for her quest for perfectionism and her perseverance.

And now, even though her protégée was in Paris and her parents were no longer working for her, the countess was inviting the entire family to celebrate Séverine's wedding on the grounds of the castle. Indeed, Germaine repeated to herself. Whoever would have thought?

* * *

Seated in the train with Caroline and her friends, Séverine sighed with relief. The transformation from one life to another begins here, she thought. She was delighted by the idea of returning to her hometown and watching the ugly, industrial suburbs of Paris give way to the peaceful green fields and the church spires of the picturesque villages rolling past one by one. The young women chattered and sang and ate box lunches they'd packed for the occasion, and the seven-hour journey passed quickly, or at least it seemed so to the excited Séverine. Before they knew it, they had passed Limoges and were gathering up their things, handing down their luggage and stepping out into the warm, fresh air of Sorignac.

As they made their way down the platform, Séverine turned to Caroline.

"Do you realize that I left Sorignac when I was seventeen and now I'm twenty-four and returning for my wedding? It's unbelievable."

"It is indeed," Caroline assented. She turned her head so Séverine couldn't see her expression. She wished she didn't have to believe it.

Chapter EIGHTEEN

Sorignac: September 7, 1935

A maid of honor shouldn't have such negative thoughts, Caroline mused as she stood at the front of the church listening to the strains of organ music swelling, rolling out and spilling into the surrounding streets where a few villagers had gathered here and there, hoping for a glimpse of the bride and groom. She decided to put her doubts about Antoine aside and enjoy the day as she watched Séverine and Robert standing in the narthex. Neither spoke in the solemn moment before the elegant bride took her father's arm and he led her down the aisle to give her away. The guests rose to admire Séverine as she gracefully glided down the aisle in the ivory-colored gown and long veil of lace and pearls that Caroline had designed for her.

Séverine looked right and left, smiling at family and friends, but the closer she got to the altar, the more she focused on Antoine, who hadn't taken his eyes off her since she had started her slow walk toward him. He looked like he couldn't wait until the day was over and they could both get out of their clothes and into a bed. She felt the same way. If she could have spoken to him, she would have said "Wait! In only a few minutes we'll be husband and wife." She chased away an unbidden thought: had it been Paul, they would have read each other's minds.

Luc slipped into the church by a side door to watch the beginning of the ceremony from behind a pillar where no one could see him. It would be the first time he had seen Séverine since she had left town all those years ago. He didn't want her to see him, though—it might remind her of his embarrassing letter. He watched her as she floated down the aisle and although he could only see her from the side and from far away, he thought that she had grown even more enchanting. He looked at the virile older man waiting for her at the altar, then spied the countess and Georges and Huguette among the guests from out of town, and decided he had seen enough. He receded into the shadows and left the church as silently as he had entered.

* * *

After the ceremony, Robert watched from the corner of his eye as the countess, her arm draped lightly around Séverine, talked animatedly to Antoine. He was listening politely to what was probably a tale about Séverine as a girl in the château. Robert's full attention, however, was on the count, who was discoursing on various problems with tractors and the difficulties of building a new stable for the horses.

The advantage of having a reputation as being taciturn worked in Robert's favor, he knew. No one ever expected him to talk. He was, however, expected to listen and was quite good at pretending to do so. Bending his head so he could purportedly better hear the count, he surveyed his former workplace, admiring the well-cut lawn and grounds and admitting to himself that he was relieved someone else was doing the job now. The count and countess had found a gardener whose specialty was pruning the hundreds of box trees. For the wedding reception, the man had trimmed several of them into the shape of hearts. They formed a bower that shaded a long table covered by a simple but refined white linen tablecloth and plenty of wicker chairs for the guests to sit on. With the contrasting pinks and purples and blues and yellows in the flower beds and the varying colors of the guests' outfits, the soft green of the lawn looked like a patchwork quilt. Robert was a man of integrity, a man of few words and no frills, and a man who had no illusions about his place in society. But now, watching the happy, colorfully dressed crowd gathered on the very grounds where he had worked as the employee of the count and countess, he couldn't help but feel a strange emotion, partly disbelief, and partly something like pride.

Georges and Huguette Moreau stood together near one of the heart-shaped bushes and communicated in the non-verbal way of couples who've been long married. Huguette, who prided herself on reading Georges's mind, knew that he was silently comparing Paul and Juliette's simple wedding reception in the lovely well-tended little garden of Juliette's parents to this grand and worldly champagne reception on the vast grounds surrounding the castle. Georges, she reflected thankfully, was kind enough not to state the obvious: Huguette had wanted Paul to marry someone on his own level, not someone below it, and now the very person she'd excluded had invited them to her own wedding at the château.

"Life is strange," Georges had mused to her the night before, and she had had the good grace to agree.

"Yes, life is indeed strange," she'd conceded. "Séverine has certainly come up in the world, even if it's meant marrying a man so much older than she is. Be that as it may, for a daughter-in-law, I would rather have Juliette and her stability than Séverine and her sparks." The words were tossed off lightly, but inwardly she was raging at the unintended comeuppance.

Now, as Georges and Huguette stood side by side at the wedding party, they caught a glimpse of their son Paul hurrying across the lawn. Outfitted in his best black suit, white shirt and an incongruous floppy purple bowtie, he rushed excitedly toward Séverine, then slowed down and paced himself as he suddenly remembered they were married grown-ups and no longer youngsters who told each other everything and spent most of their days together.

He made an effort to conceal the feelings of exhilaration and curiosity that were undoubtedly written on his face. He was thrilled to see Séverine after a seven-year separation, and curious to know what she thought of him. She would probably find him changed, and he hoped it would be for the better. He couldn't keep his eyes off of her as he approached. She had retained her curvaceous figure, which was now accentuated by the wedding gown she had insisted on leaving on after the church ceremony. The sleeves were flowing but the dress was fitted just enough to outline and emphasize the perfection of her lithe body. Her glossy dark hair, which he had seen in every style from pigtails and ponytails to braids to loose and tumbling over her shoulders, was pulled back from her face in a sophisticated but not too strict chignon. She still had that high color in her cheeks she got when she was excited or moved—and what, after all, could be more exciting or moving than her wedding day? A long time ago she had declared that red was the only color for her, and he saw that today she wore bright red lipstick on her full lips, complementing the blush in her cheeks. Séverine had always made him think of a rose—sweet-smelling, sometimes secretive, silky but thorny too. Today she reminded him of a full-blown tulip with all its generosity and joy and openness.

"Séverine, you are as ravishing as ever," Paul exclaimed as he arrived at her side.

Being too far away, his parents heard nothing, but even

at a distance they couldn't help but notice what a striking pair the two made. Paul was slightly taller, but both were slim, moved gracefully and wore warm smiles that lit up their faces and made other people feel special.

"They look more like twins than friends," Georges commented.

Huguette nodded her head in exasperation. She was glad the two were out of each other's lives. For one thing, had they married, which in her mind would never, ever have been allowed to happen, she would have had to put up with Georges's constant compliments and unmitigated admiration of Séverine. How painful that would have been. She congratulated herself on having engineered Paul's marriage to Juliette, who had turned out to be a highly satisfactory daughter-in-law. Even Georges liked her well enough.

* * *

Séverine blushed and smiled at Paul. "Ravishing" was the only word she had heard. Since when had Paul had such a vocabulary? Was this his wife's influence? He had, as predicted, married Juliette, who was a few feet away from them now, holding in her arms and kissing a little boy who looked very much like Paul.

"How you go on!" she replied. "If I'm ravishing, you're…" She searched for a word and couldn't find one, not because of a lack of vocabulary but because she and Paul had always had a secret language that was non-verbal. They didn't need words to understand each other. He looked at her expectantly, and at the same time they both burst out laughing.

"I'll never know what I am, I guess," Paul said, faking a disappointed grimace. For a second, they were eight-year-olds playing in the forest again.

Seeing the two of them standing there as if they were alone in the world, Gisèle took over.

"Juliette, come over here. Have you met Antoine?" the countess asked, turning to Paul's wife. Gisèle had always sensed that even if Paul and Séverine weren't aware of it, there was something strong between them, an exclusivity that shut other people out when they were together. Gisèle didn't want other people shut out, certainly not on Séverine's wedding day. But how striking Paul was, with his tall, slim build and the caring expression in his soft brown eyes. His patients, especially the ladies, must love him, she thought, glancing at Antoine, his physical opposite.

Gisèle wondered about Antoine and about Séverine marrying an older man. She knew why Séverine had married him—it was obvious she was infatuated—but she had asked herself, as Yves had, why Antoine, the very personification of the playboy bachelor, had chosen to settle down. He didn't look like the marrying type. No matter, she told herself briskly. Séverine was her protégée and she'd tried to instill in her things her parents couldn't—a love of art, a love of beauty, certain aspirations. But she couldn't tell her whom to love or whom to marry, although she most certainly would have if Séverine had been her daughter.

Joining the group, Juliette looked at Paul and Séverine chuckling and chatting together in a tête-à-tête as if they'd never been separated. Like Gisèle, she had always sensed their special relationship, a strong platonic friendship that she'd always feared would grow into something else. Now that Séverine had found a husband, however, and such a dashing and handsome one at that, she would at last be able to put an end to that worry.

"He's adorable. What's the little one's name?" Séverine asked, as she made baby faces at the miniature version of Paul whom Juliette was cradling in her arms. The infant mimicked her expressions, and she laughed at his innocent, adorable face, but a cloud passed, obscuring her happiness. It lasted only a second: she'd feel better when she had a child of her own, she told herself.

"He's called Julien Lucien Georges," Juliette answered. "Lucien and Georges for the two grandfathers, and Julien because we liked it." Quietly, she sized up Séverine, who indeed was as ravishing as Paul had said. She'd overheard the compliment from where she was standing and the word had struck her as it had Séverine, but not for the same reason. Paul had never told Juliette that she herself was ravishing. And truth be told, he had never looked at her the way he had looked at Séverine a few moments ago. There was no doubt about their complicity, and no doubt about the chemistry between them.

Juliette increased her hold on Julien, reveling in his clean, powdery baby smell. Babies. That at least was something she had and Séverine didn't—at least, not yet.

* * *

Paul had been stunned and appalled at the sight of Séverine; stunned because she was indeed just as ravishing as he had told her she was, but appalled to see her with his antithesis, a tall, light-haired older man with military bearing, who radiated self-confidence and social ease. He had already heard that Antoine had been a flying ace in the Great War, and he certainly looked the part. All that was missing was the leather flight jacket. But he had also heard about Antoine's rightist political leanings, and that filled him with unease. And as if that weren't enough, he was discovering at this very moment something else about Antoine Sevanot that he didn't like.

Antoine was, quite clearly, a skirt chaser. Not only that, but the present target of his roving eye happened to be the hostess of the wedding reception: Gisèle, of all people! Paul had never taken a close look at Gisèle before, but now he did. He had to admit that she was in fine form for a woman heading towards fifty. With her light hair and clear blue eyes, her pale, clear skin, perfect posture and her reserved and confident manner she was in fact quite beautiful, he realized. She was, given her station, an object of both fascination and even fear to those who didn't know her, and let only a few people into her exclusive inner circle—which, of course, had included Séverine for many years. Scrutinizing her now, it struck Paul that if he put Antoine and Gisèle side by side, they would make an attractive couple, both of them tall, both blond and blue eyed.

He clenched his fists as he watched Antoine lavishing his gallantry on Gisèle, guffawing appreciatively and a little too loudly at any comment she made, no matter how banal, gently propelling her by the elbow or lightly touching her back whenever the occasion gave him an excuse to do so. The fact that she didn't ostensibly move away, Paul was sure, was not because the countess liked the grotesque, inappropriate attention but rather that she didn't want to attract attention to it.

He struggled to fit his vision of Séverine with her new husband. How had these totally different people gotten together? Séverine—or at least the Séverine he had known since they were children—was smart, funny, energetic. She'd never craved money or even independence. She was happy with her circle of intimates—her parents, Caroline, the countess, and him.

Or maybe not him, he mused. She hadn't returned to the village until now. Why? How difficult was it to get a train ticket and come with Caroline for a short visit? Of course, he himself had not written to her, or invited her. In his heart of hearts, he realized that he had been afraid that if she lived in Paris she would become a sophisticated city girl. And even without that, how had he managed to ignore the fact that she was a good catch for any man, especially a manly, worldly one like Antoine? Had he really thought that carrying her in his heart could change reality?

He had, in fact, acknowledged long ago that he had totally, completely and irrevocably missed his chance to spend his life with Séverine. He had let her go. In spite of that, in spite of the fact that he had married Juliette, he had always felt that he and Séverine were a pair, joined somehow. The illusions he had lived with!

Only now, standing on the lawn at her wedding reception, did he realize that he, the doctor, the scientist, had been a dreamer, living in a fantasy world.

Still, his need to speak to her, to exchange something more than superficial remarks with her, suddenly felt urgent. How do I get Séverine alone? he asked himself. He craned his head around, wondering where she was. Suddenly, she approached him from behind and lightly tapped him on the shoulder.

"Paul, we're running out of champagne and Gisèle needs someone to go to the cellar to bring up some bottles. I volunteered you. Is that all right?"

His heart leaped as he turned to her. Were his thoughts showing on his face? Could she have suspected his feelings? How could she? No, it was an innocent move. She was a radiant bride, completely in love with this other man who was as unlike him as could be, and she had pushed Paul to the far corners of her mind a long time ago. Still, it didn't hurt to seize the occasion.

"Absolutely. I'll just take off this suit jacket and I'll be right there," he responded. "But I don't know this castle inside out like you do so if you would be kind enough to show me where to go…"

"With pleasure," she answered, keeping her voice cheerfully neutral as she searched his face. Paul had filled out, he was more of a man now, but he still had that dimple in his chin and the crooked grin she'd always loved. Lowering her voice, she confided, "I'll be glad to get away from social chitchat for a while. Come on!" She hastened her pace and added, "We can't be gone long, so let's hurry."

In the enormous dark cellar, which was almost frigid compared to the pervasive heat outside, dozens of bottles of the finest vintage champagne rested in buckets of cool water.

"Ah, so there is some left," Paul observed wryly. "I was worried that with all we've imbibed so far the supply would have dwindled."

"Paul, you know the countess. If there's one thing she's not, it's stingy." Séverine straightened up from her inspection of the bottles and looked at him, clearly pleased by what she saw. "One can't say a man looks ravishing, but if one could, I would. You look like life is treating you well, Paul. And your little Julien… How lucky you are!"

"Lucky? Oh yes, yes. I guess I am."

There was an awkward silence as he busied himself arranging bottles of bubbly in a wicker basket to take up to the party. Séverine moved toward him; he could feel her body heat and smell her perfume. Instinctively, he moved slightly away from her. She was married. He was married. Regret cut into him. He had missed the moment, let her get away, and now it was too late.

"Here, let me help you take that up," she said, sensing a change. She seized a handle of the basket.

"No, you don't," he said, grabbing the handle and placing his hand over hers. "This is mine to carry; it's far too heavy for you, and anyway, whoever saw a bride walking across a lawn with bottles of booze?"

His hand felt warm and dry and reassuring. She wanted him to leave it there. Slowly, he removed it, then took both of her hands in his, raised them to his lips and kissed them tenderly. In the semi-darkness, they drew closer and looked into each other's eyes. They stayed that way a long moment before Paul reluctantly released his hold.

He bent down and reached into the basket of chilled bottles, took one out, held it up and inspected it.

"I'm sure the countess won't miss it. We'll keep this one just for us to drink together someday," he said. "I don't know when and I don't know where, but I know that day will come. And now, let's go, beautiful bride. Don't forget. Until then," he whispered into her ear.

He offered her his right arm and took the heavy basket in his left hand, and they clung together as they made their slow way up the ancient stone steps, out of the cool underground and into the light and chatter and festivities on the castle lawn. As they parted at the top of the stairs, Séverine gave his arm a brief and intimate squeeze before she put on a public smile for the assembled guests.

"Until then," she repeated softly, so that only Paul could hear.

The warmth she felt above ground had nothing to do with the outside temperature.

* * *

From his vantage point behind a bush at the edge of the lawn, Luc watched the party breaking up. The last to go were the bride and groom in their red Citroën. Yesterday he had watched in amazement as the convertible, with its cream-colored leather seats, cruised down the narrow streets of the village. He had never seen such a luxurious car and had stopped on the sidewalk to admire it. The driver looked like a Parisian playboy with his carefully combed hair, casual but obviously expensive clothes and air of self-assurance. Luc knew he was the groom. He had heard all about Séverine's beau and her upcoming wedding and reception. Everyone was talking about it, including his father, who had concluded long ago that Séverine was a snob and accused her of demanding the "highfalutin'" wedding reception. Luc knew otherwise: Séverine had always been Gisèle's pet, and he wasn't in the least surprised that the countess had offered to give her a party.

As he stood watching all the upper-class women in their extravagant headwear and the suave men in suits he could never afford taking their leave in their costly, highly polished vehicles, he was overtaken with a stab of unaccustomed jealousy. It was a thoroughly useless waste of energy, he told himself, but that didn't stop the mounting waves of envy.

He drew back further into the shrubs as the chauffeur-driven bridal car slowly approached the spot where he was hiding. In the backseat, the groom was immersed in a tête-à-tête with a young, svelte, dark-haired woman. He knew, of course, that it was Séverine—Séverine, the bride he had glimpsed at the church earlier in the day; Séverine, the young woman who had never told anyone about the letter he had sent her; Séverine, to whom he had given one of his animal carvings—the only one, in fact, that he had kept. She'd probably thrown it out long ago. But now that he saw her close up this was not the Séverine he remembered. The Séverine of his youth had had pigtails and was natural, always running this way and that, full of energy and enthusiasm and generally giggling or being silly. This lady looked sophisticated, like a model in those fancy women's magazines. She was wearing tasteful, expensive clothes, clothes he had never seen on any woman in the village. Her silky hair was swept up in a chignon. She wore red lipstick that accentuated the bow of her mouth. He caught a glimpse of the huge diamond on her left hand. It caught the light as she gesticulated, and for some reason the sparkle left him feeling empty and sad.

Were you supposed to feel happy for people who had met such success, he wondered? Were you supposed to emulate them so that you, too, could someday ride into town in triumph? Perhaps, but all he could feel now was discouraged and unhappy. That wasn't new to him, but today in particular he felt the weight of the low status that he had inherited and from which he, unlike Séverine, would never escape. He couldn't stand having his inferiority rubbed in his face, even though he was the one who had chosen to attend the proceedings—albeit from afar. No, "attend" wasn't the word, he told himself bitterly. How can you attend if you're not invited? And he had never been invited.

He tugged on his cap, pulling it down so his face would be in shadow, abruptly stepped out from behind the bushes and walked down the street in the opposite direction.

Chapter NINETEEN

Paris: June 1940

Séverine, Caroline and Germaine marched down a dusty road on a hot and gloriously sunny June day, heading they knew not where other than away from the rapidly emptying capital.

They were three among the millions of the distraught and distressed. The roads around Paris were filled with refugees fleeing from Belgium, Holland and Luxembourg as well as the city itself. The young, the old, the rich, the poor; people who would probably never mix in ordinary circumstances, all found themselves side by side. Some pushed baby buggies heaped with possessions or wheelbarrows occupied by an invalid grandparent. Others walked beside old horses or rode in farm carts, perched high on mattresses or piles of belongings. Some were in cars, but although they had the advantage of being seated, they made little progress. Many were on bicycles. Some carried every valuable they owned, right down to their silver spoons; others had nothing but the clothes on their backs. Some worried about what they'd left behind, others about what lay ahead. But they had one thing in common: they were all running from the enemy.

One day it had been life as usual, the next had brought an upheaval of monumental proportions. The people of Paris had no clear idea of what was going on. They only knew that the Germans were invading France for the third time in seventy years. In 1870 they had annexed Alsace and Lorraine. In 1914, only 26 years ago, they had invaded France, waging a bloody and atrocious world war everyone had thought and hoped would be the war to end all wars. Now they were here again. How could this be happening one more time?

Rumors abounded, The Germans cut off heads and ate babies; they raped and pillaged. And then came sobering news that wasn't a rumor: the government had fled Paris, leaving the civilian population unprotected in the face of an enemy who would soon be upon them. That was enough; general panic had ensued, and Parisians had begun to swarm out of Paris *en masse*.

Séverine had been visiting with Caroline and her parents in the concierge's lodging when the news had broken.

"You three must leave immediately," Robert told them.

Germaine began frantically gathering up her precious copies of *Modes et Travaux* to store in the cellar.

"Germaine," he said to her, "I assure you, the Germans will not be in the least bit interested in women's stuff. Jewels, money, wine and spirits, yes, but not magazines about knitting and cooking."

"But Papa, what will we do without you? Where will we go?" Séverine asked, as if she were a little girl and not a twenty-nine-year-old married woman. "And Antoine?" She glanced around the room as if she could magically produce him.

"Antoine's upstairs helping his parents pack the silver and valuables, as I'm sure you know since you were just up there," Germaine chimed in. "They told me they had offered you a ride in their car but that you had refused."

Séverine blushed as she thought about her in-laws' incomprehension and their disappointment with her decision. She shrugged her shoulders. "You know I'd never leave you two. Can you see me rolling down some road waving at you from the comfort of my in-laws' car? Never!"

"Now, listen to me carefully," Robert said. "You three are going to walk straight out of here and keep going until you are far away from Paris. When things settle down, you'll come back. That's it." From his firm tone, it was clear that he would brook no opposition.

"All right, then, if we've got to go, let's do it fast. I'm ready, but I need to get Felicity." Séverine turned to her sister.

At first the name didn't register, and when it did, Caroline was outraged. "Are you out of your mind? Good heavens, Séverine. We're not little girls anymore. You haven't looked at that doll for years! We're fleeing Paris and you want to take her along?"

"Just in case anything happens here," Séverine replied, her eyes frantically taking in the cozy little room one last time, "we'll have saved her, at least."

"Right, and let's take the wardrobe I made for her as well," Caroline added, not even trying to moderate the sarcasm in her voice. Then she put her arm around her sister and spoke to her gently. "I understand your fear, but everything will be all right with Papa and Antoine taking care of things. Why, they can hide Felicity in a box in the cellar if you want."

The absurdity of the situation snapped Séverine out of her shocked state and she laughed so hard she got hiccups. "Isn't this ridiculous? Here's the whole of Paris waiting for the enemy to invade, and I'm dithering about saving a toy." She paused, then tried to explain. "It's because she reminds me of when we were little in the good old days, and we were safe." She looked down at her hands, then regained her composure. "You're right. Let's go. But I want to stop at our place on the way," she said, referring to the apartment she shared with Antoine. "There is something I do want to take—a good luck charm." Realizing how futile it sounded, she insisted, "We all need good luck, don't we? And we're heading south, so our apartment is on the way out of town. Plus, Caroline won't have time to return to her place to get her belongings, so I'll find something in my wardrobe for both of us to wear. Who knows how long we'll be gone?"

Now that she had regained her good humor, she gave her sister a quick once-over and added, "Fortunately, in the circumstances we're in, no one will notice we're nowhere near the same size."

In spite of the detour, Caroline and her mother readily agreed. Placating Séverine was generally preferable to arguing with her, and she had proposed a practical solution.

Germaine quickly gathered together a few changes of clothing, along with some provisions they could eat on the road. They tried to hide their apprehension as they kissed Robert goodbye and left the little flat for what they hoped would not be the last time.

In the brief time Séverine spent in her apartment, she paused in front of the floor-to-ceiling windows overlooking the Luxembourg Gardens, wondering how long it would be before she would once again enjoy this view and be reunited with Antoine, the man she loved so much. Then she remembered her mother and sister waiting in the street below and sped to the bedroom and her dark red jewel box. She picked it up and ran her fingers over the soft and supple Moroccan leather. It had been one of Antoine's first gifts to her, and had contained a single jewel, an exquisite gold brooch in the form of a butterfly—a butterfly, because she reminded him of one, he had told her. She unlocked the box now and contemplated the gold and silver treasures it contained. Antoine hadn't had time to stash the contents in the safe at the bank. How long would it be before he did? It would be better to take them, she reasoned. She slid her rings onto her fingers and attached layers of necklaces around her neck. *I'll look like a gypsy*, she thought, and reached for a huge silk scarf to hide them.

Having made that decision, she finally picked up the object she had come to retrieve. Wrapped in tissue paper, it was at the very bottom of the jewel box. She unfolded the paper and placed Luc's perfectly carved wooden rabbit in the palm of her hand, then folded her fingers around it. The wood was warm, solid and reassuring.

Maybe she was fooling herself. Maybe the desire for the rabbit was as strange as her desire for the doll, but she was convinced that it might be a good luck charm, that it would somehow give her a sense of security as she and her family fled. She pushed the rabbit deep into her pocket, shut the lid of her jewelry box, and then stepped out of the apartment, carefully closing the door behind her.

* * *

It's not fair, she thought, as she trudged down the dusty tree-lined road with hundreds of other grim, eerily silent refugees. In this lovely weather, we should be sitting on a park bench or strolling along the Seine. She shut her eyes for a minute and envisioned herself with Caroline at a table on the crowded terrace of an outdoor café in Paris, where they would pretend to ignore the appreciative looks of admirers. Séverine delighted in countering Caroline's serious nature; Caroline, for her part, always relaxed with her lighthearted sister. Every time they were together, whether walking, standing or seated, they were besieged by hopeful suitors that Séverine would flippantly ward off.

"I'm married and she's taken," she would say, indicating

her alluring blond sister. It wasn't true, but it always put them in a good mood—and the better their mood, the more desirable they became. Séverine had always day-dreamed that Caroline would marry a rich count, but she knew that would remain a daydream: her sister was utterly unattracted by wealth and not at all impressed by the aristocracy.

"Not like you," Caroline would say. Time and time again Séverine would explain that it wasn't the aristocracy *per se* that attracted her. She admired Gisèle because of her personality, not because she happened to be a countess. But Caroline remained skeptical, and the two had agreed to disagree on the subject.

Regardless of that, everyone remarked on how close they were. Shortly after their marriage, Antoine had said to Germaine, only half-jokingly, "When those two are together, no one else exists."

Germaine had nodded. "It's always been that way, Antoine. Better get used to it. They don't suffer competi-tion, even if it's you!"

Now the two sisters walked, one on each side of their mother, each in her own world.

"Look at this," Caroline said at length. "Have you ever seen so many different contraptions on people's heads? Even on this blasted road to nowhere, you can tell who belongs to what social class—who's Parisian, who's provincial, who has means and who doesn't." She pinched Séverine, forcing her to look at a well-dressed older woman in a glamorous black straw picnic hat walking next to a wizened peasant whose gray hair was covered with a simple red and white checked kerchief. "This is amazing!" Caroline observed. "Shawls, turbans, designer hats, knit caps—or no hats at all."

"Little do these poor innocent people know that you are shamelessly using them to design your first hat collection. I can already see your name in lights!" Séverine teased.

Germaine listened fondly to her daughters' banter and tried to hide her anxiety. She was worried about Robert. She had never left him before, and wondered how long it would be before they saw each other again. Robert and Antoine had remained in Paris, as they jokingly said, "to hold down the fort." The fort was, of course, the building they had in common, with Robert as the indispensable handyman and Antoine as heir to and guardian of his parents' apartment.

Louise and Bertrand hadn't wanted to leave, but in the end they had fled the city in their Hotchkiss, distraught with worries about dust and damage and the lack of gas but reassured that Antoine was taking care of their home and the business.

Robert didn't like the idea of his wife and daughters leaving, but he thought it was the best and safest option for them. Unlike Antoine and his family, he didn't have much to protect. His worldly belongings consisted of a silver tea set that the countess had given the family before their departure and some meager savings hidden under his and Germaine's mattress. He did, however, feel responsible for the almost-empty building now that the great majority of the owners were on the run—and for who knew how long. It had taken some time, but he had slowly weaned himself away from the outdoor life and his hands in the soil. Now he was accustomed to climbing stairs to fix leaks and change light bulbs. The adults in the building liked and trusted him, appreciated his efficiency and silence, and the children loved the silent, gentle man who always had a bonbon and a kind word for them.

* * *

The three women walked on, each preoccupied with her own thoughts. Séverine dreamed of being anywhere else but on the road; Caroline designed hats in her head; Germaine wondered how Robert was faring without her.

A sudden loud drone above their heads stopped them in their tracks. In seconds the drone became a roar, and the sea of refugees momentarily stilled as everyone stood and craned their necks to look up at the sky. One moment it was bright, blue and cloudless. The next, it darkened with what at first looked like swarms of geese and then became wave after wave of the deadly German Ju 87 Stuka dive bombers. Their screaming sirens filled the air and then, without warning, the flock flew low over the road and a volley of bullets strafed the crowd, sending frightened horses into the field and terrified men, women and children running for cover wherever they could find it.

Caroline threw her arms around their mother and dragged her down an embankment. Then she pulled on the shocked Séverine's arm, forcing her to go down with them. The short silence was soon punctuated by screams and cries and wails. They lay there breathing heavily and shaking with terror.

The attack seemed to last for hours, and the three women cowered against the dirt embankment, listening to the roar of the engines as they circled and returned, the chatter of the machine guns, the screams of the injured and dying. Finally, the drone of the planes receded into the distance, and Séverine cautiously raised her head to look around her. She saw a car with its dead driver slumped over the wheel, shocked survivors helping each other up, broken and shattered belongings scattered like litter. Among them was a baby carriage lying on its side. Next to it on the ground lay a tiny body. It looked just like a sleeping doll— apart from the blood. Séverine crossed herself, wept for the innocent child, and cursed the sky. There was nothing she could do. The worst had been done.

Sickened, Séverine turned to her mother and Caroline to make sure they were all right and then instinctively glanced back at the horizon to see if any more planes were coming. *So this is war*, she thought grimly.

Antoine had never talked much about his war, the first one, other than to say he hoped to God there would never be another. Séverine had never asked for details, and he had never volunteered any. The Great War, the war to end all wars, was a mixed memory of duty and bragging, alcohol and girls and heroics for him, and nothing particular for her.

As they climbed from the ditch, Séverine saw a small boy with blue eyes and light brown curly hair crying loudly for his mother. He was too warmly dressed for the heat in his short navy-blue wool coat.

"Where's your Maman?" she asked him softly. The child kept crying, his thin little shoulders moving up and down with each sob. She bent and took him by the hand, lightly but firmly. "Don't you worry, little fellow, we'll find your Maman. She can't be far. Now tell me, what's your name? What's your Maman's name? What does she look like?"

Perhaps because she was the baby of the family herself, with no one to coddle, order around, indulge or care for, Séverine had always loved little children. Her greatest desire now that she was a wife was to have not one child but several. She had a way of relating to children that made them feel safe and special. The little boy stopped crying long enough to give his name, and Séverine quickly invented a game to occupy him. He was, she instructed him, to tell her every time he saw someone dressed in white. That, she knew, would keep him busy for quite some time—the heavy film of road dust would have changed a white shirt or dress to gray in seconds.

A few minutes later, the boy's face suddenly lit up.

"Maman, Maman!" he yelled at the back of a tall, slim

young woman in a long black coat. The woman wheeled around at the sound of his voice; her eyes widened with recognition and she ran as fast as she could to sweep him up in her arms.

"Bless you, bless you," she exclaimed over and over to Séverine as she cradled the youngster in her arms. She'd had time to see that Séverine had him firmly in hand, was speaking to him with care. "Say goodbye to this nice lady," she told the little boy, who without being asked, leaned out of her arms and planted a big kiss on Séverine's cheek. Séverine tousled his thick hair and stroked his smooth cheek.

Watching the scene, Caroline and her mother entertained the same doubt, one they dared not put in words. Antoine was now forty-two, Séverine twenty-nine. They had been married five years, but there were no children, and no talk of children. Neither dared ask her why, but both knew it was not because of Séverine, who had always been perfectly clear about her ardent desire to have a family. If either of them had been unable to have children, Séverine would have told them. She hadn't. They sensed she was unhappy, but even Caroline, who was so close to her, didn't want to broach the subject for fear of encroaching upon Séverine's privacy. The discussion about children, about having them or not, was for the couple, not the sisters.

Séverine waved at the reunited mother and child and walked back to where Germaine and Caroline were waiting. "A happy ending," she told them, with a last longing look at the child that her sister and mother couldn't help but notice.

* * *

Exhausted, hungry and dirty, the three women returned to Paris a week later. At first they were happy and relieved to get back home, but those emotions quickly gave way to surprise and distress. They had left a French city and returned to a German one. In every part of the capital, signs in German dotted the streets. German flags, with their trademark black swastikas, hung from the Senate and the Chamber of Deputies and the four hundred hotels the Germans had requisitioned. As if all these changes weren't enough, the French clocks were now on Berlin time.

Parisians soon grew accustomed to the sight of impeccably uniformed German soldiers strolling down the avenues, occupying the terraces of cafés, and taking pictures of each other in front of the Eiffel Tower and the Arc de Triomphe. They even made music. Every Sunday a military band played on the steps of the Paris Opera, and other regiments gave regular outdoor concerts in the city parks. The Germans were at ease, it seemed, and why not? Wasn't Paris the most beautiful city in the world, there for their pleasure?

Germaine kept her head down and went straight back to her work as a concierge; when she wasn't working, she spent her time queuing for food. Séverine decided she hated war but not the Germans; after all, she reasoned, if France was in this predicament it was because, as Marshal Pétain had affirmed in his wobbly old man's voice in a speech to the nation, the country deserved it.

Caroline was the only member of the family who was truly incensed by the presence of the Germans; she loathed their uniforms, their faces, their gestures, their words, the way they talked, the way they laughed, the way they frowned, the way they marched, the way they walked into stores and got whatever they wanted. She was furious when she overheard some of her compatriots saying that the Germans weren't nearly as bad as they had feared, that on the whole they were pleasant, polite, and especially, well-mannered. Often, when she passed a German soldier, her heart was filled with vile words she knew better than to pronounce.

She was almost relieved to be the sister who felt so deeply the humiliation and the shame of living in an occupied land. She didn't know how brave she'd be if the opportunity came to fight for France, but she did know that she possessed the qualities of good planning, foresight, and prudence that Séverine, for all her supposed worldliness, sorely lacked. Caroline knew her fiery little sister would be more than capable of mouthing off to a pushy German soldier or spitting on a uniform, but it was obvious that Séverine wasn't put off by the occupiers in the same way Caroline was.

In fact, she and Antoine were going out on the town even more than they had before the Occupation. When it wasn't the races at Longchamps, it was a night at the cinema, the theater or the opera followed by dinner at Maxim's, where celebrities like the famous actress Arletty and the actor Sacha Guitry rubbed shoulders and drank champagne with the Germans. Restaurants like Lapérouse, Drouant and the Tour d'Argent offered delicious food and good times as well. Intellectual life flourished: Jean-Paul Sartre hunched over his notebook or held earnest parleys with Simone de Beauvoir at the Café de Flore, which provided a place to write but also a place of warmth to counter the chill of an unusually harsh winter with next to no heat in the private apartments. Despite the Aryanization of the theaters, more than fifty had remained open, and the Parisians, eager for distraction and entertainment, flocked to them. It was good for Antoine's business to be seen out and about with his alluring young wife, and he considered his presence at the cabarets and dance halls and theaters filled with German soldiers an asset rather than a concern.

Thanks to his wealth, connections and political activities, Antoine wined and dined Séverine in the finest restaurants of Paris, which always served splendid dishes and played host to gay and carefree people who were oblivious to the war and those affected by it. When settled at the table and out of sight of the fawning waiters, Séverine would occasionally swipe a piece of fruit or a few of the sweets served with coffee to bring back to Robert and Germaine and Caroline for a treat.

Séverine realized how little her parents and sister had to eat with their pitiful rations: 180 grams of meat a week was insufficient protein. Sometimes she would stand in line for rationed food with Germaine, who had none of Antoine's connections or privileges and didn't want them. As they waited in the long lines on sidewalks in front of food shops, mother and daughter would reminisce about former meals. Visions of juicy, tender steaks with Béarnaise sauce, fresh green beans and Germaine's light, tasty *pommes dauphines* floated in their heads. Daydreaming took their minds off what they were going to get when they finally arrived at the counter: the leaden bread, the disgusting butter that wasn't butter, the sugar that wasn't sugar. In the beginning, their imaginations enabled them to transform the repellent rutabaga into an exotic vegetable, but that period ended quickly.

Séverine couldn't help but think of her wedding banquet before the war: the fine wines and champagne, the lovely pink and white menu listing the thirteen different dishes the guests feasted on, among them pike, squab with olives and an enormous, perfectly presented cheese plate. Dessert came later, at the castle. Séverine could scarcely bear to remember the late-afternoon wedding party Gisèle had offered them—the fairytale setting, the heart-shaped box trees, the linen-covered tables laden with mountains of sweets. The seven-tiered wedding cake and all those other round, oval, square or rectangular pastries with their evocative names—*les puits d'amour, les tulipes, les tuiles, le Saint-Honoré*—were a distant memory to her now. How could they have known that war would destroy the pleasures of life that everyone had taken for granted?

But that was then, she reasoned. She had to adjust to now, with her parents and sister who made do with whatever supplies they could get and with Antoine who always managed to acquire whatever he wanted. She also had to accept socializing with German soldiers. It wasn't as hard as she had imagined. Most of them were perfectly polite.

"How can you stand it? I couldn't bear to be so close!" Caroline asked after Séverine had excitedly told her about a recent evening at Les Folies Bergère, where sexy, half-clothed French beauties dancing the cancan had entertained a full house of occupiers and occupied alike.

"Come on, Caroline," Séverine retorted. "They won the war. Those soldiers are a fact of life, for the moment at least, and I for one am not going to refuse to go to a play or the opera or out to dinner simply because some German soldier in uniform is seated next to me. They aren't that bad, you know." She eyed Caroline, her eyes twinkling. "Some of them are actually rather attractive," she added.

But inside, Séverine was troubled. She thought back to a recent evening when Antoine had emerged from the bedroom dressed in a light blue shirt, dark tie and dark blue trousers. He sported a black beret on his head and a band around his arm.

"What's the get-up?" she had joked. "Let me see," she said, walking slowly around him. "A funeral? A costume party?"

Her mirth faded as she saw the humorless expression on his face.

"This, my dear, is the uniform of the French Popular Party, of which I am now a member." He straightened his tie, not meeting her eye.

"I've never heard of it," she remarked. "What is it? Why the uniform?"

She and Antoine rarely discussed politics—indeed, she reflected, they rarely discussed anything of substance. All she knew was that, like her father, he was furious at the French generals who, through their catastrophic miscalculations, were responsible for France's defeat. They had placed troops along the Maginot Line, hundreds of solid cement fortifications erected on the Franco-German border in the 1930s to stave off invasion by Germany—and had totally neglected the allegedly impenetrable northern route through the Ardennes.

"Unbelievably stupid," he had exploded when he'd read the news. "One million German soldiers and fifteen hundred German tanks simply plowed their way right through it!"

For Antoine, it was clear that the Germans deserved their victory. He admired Marshal Pétain, and wholeheartedly supported collaboration with Germany.

Now, as he admired his slim, muscular silhouette in the full-length mirror and tweaked his beret to get the correct angle, he addressed Séverine's question. "It's really quite simple: we are for a strong nation and against all the elements that weaken it—Freemasons, Bolsheviks, Jews. Our uniform, of course, shows people who we are and what we stand for. But don't worry your pretty little head about all this. It's a man's thing."

Séverine stared at him and tried to hide her consternation. Never mind that her husband was actually "talking politics" with her for the first time in her married life, she could scarcely believe his paternalistic tone or the self-assured vitriol in his words. How could he be so full of contempt for all of the groups he had mentioned? For example, Georges, Paul's father, was a Freemason—a fact he now had to keep to himself more than ever—and he was the best doctor she knew, and had been like a second father to her. She also knew the Mestre family were "Bolsheviks," but she couldn't imagine them weakening anything in society. They were simply too lazy. As for Jews, she didn't know any personally, but couldn't see why they should be a target of hate.

"Why does everyone have to start taking sides and singling out certain parts of our society?" she asked him now. "Don't you think people should just live their lives, keep their opinions to themselves and wait for this horrid war to end?"

Antoine patted her arm. "This is what I get for talking politics at home," he said, smiling affectionately at her. "Not a good idea. We won't get into this again. But since we're on the topic, you may not be seeing much of me for the next little while. The German officers have plenty of money to spend on jewels for their wives, and of course there are my Party meetings. I know you will miss me, my darling, but you must be strong." He ran his hands almost proprietarily over her body and kissed the top of her head.

"I don't see all that much of you as it is," Séverine answered as she embraced him fiercely. "In fact, I never see you as much as I'd like to." She tried to keep the sullenness out of her voice. Although his announcement had made her profoundly unsettled, Séverine decided it was pointless to discuss the matter further. If Caroline asked about Antoine's politics, which she might, she would pretend not to know. She would let him lead his life. In any case, she didn't have much choice.

She liked the life she led. She liked being the wife of one of the city's most prominent jewelers. She liked the exquisite jewels and haute couture clothes Antoine offered her. She liked going out on the town with him and seeing people stare at the striking couple they made. She loved Antoine: his looks, his smell, his presence, even his authoritarianism.

She realized she didn't care what Antoine did as long as he took care of her and they started a family.

That was her top priority, war or no war.

Chapter TWENTY

Paris: May 1942

Caroline sat in an ugly but serviceable armchair near the window of her sixth-floor maid's room near the Odéon, diligently sewing a yellow star with a black border and black letters spelling out "JUIF" onto the left side of her light spring vest. It had to be perfectly attached; otherwise the police could arrest the wearer. She drew the thread through the cloth carefully, concentrating on the task. Six points to fasten, securely. It wouldn't take long.

Hearing a knock on the door, she carefully placed the vest on the back of the chair and rose to answer it.

"Séverine!" she cried, putting a hand to her chest in surprise. "What are you doing here?"

"I dropped by to see if my favorite sister wanted to go shopping with me. I've got some extra money and I want to get her a treat!" Séverine announced, sweeping into the room and smiling radiantly at Caroline.

Her expression changed from joy to perplexity as she saw the green vest and its bright yellow star. "What on earth is that? Do you have a Jewish friend? Are you taking in piecework now?"

"No, that's my vest. Don't you recognize it? The star is

for me," Caroline told her calmly. "My friend Fanny—you know, the one I told you about who works with me at the theater—has to wear one, so I decided I would as well. Out of solidarity," she added, watching Séverine's astonished expression.

"Oh, what a wonderful idea!" Séverine said. "That way you can get arrested too, and they'll put you in jail or on a train and send you off somewhere," she exclaimed. She shook her head impatiently, then faced her sister, puzzled and furious. "When I think that of the two of us you've always been the one with common sense and forethought... Are you crazy? Don't you know that this is no time for pranks? If you are detained, even when they see you're not Jewish, they won't appreciate your sympathy for those who are, believe me."

"It's not only sympathy," Caroline protested. "The Germans are wrong to arrest the Jews, to force them to wear this ridiculous star. And the French police, at least the ones I've seen, are as despicable as the Germans." She scrutinized her sister, but Séverine's face was unreadable. "Well, don't you hate the whole thing too?" she demanded. She'd never figured out Séverine's politics, although she knew Antoine's all too well. Like their parents, he was for Pétain. Unlike their parents, however, who were passive supporters, he was active. Very active. She shivered slightly as she thought about the cold January day she'd happened by the boulevard des Italiens, where a huge poster advertising an exposition at the Palais Berlitz called *The Jew and France* had caught her eye. She'd figured it would be ignominious, and it was. Inside the hall, she had stood in front of a rendition of the head of a "typical Jew" with, she read on the descriptive label, his "charnal open mouth, thick lips, large, massive, and protruding ears..." Filled with anger, revulsion and shame, she had elbowed her way through the congested crowd, stopping only once to take in a delegation of important-looking people listening raptly to their well-dressed and knowledgeable guide: Antoine. She had never told Séverine about that day.

But she didn't feel like talking about Antoine. "Fanny," she resumed, "told me that in the beginning she was going to defy the order for all Jews to wear a yellow star on their clothing. She simply wasn't going to do it. Then, when she saw others complying, she changed her mind. She doesn't say much, only that it is so humiliating, especially when she has to go to the last car in the *métro*, the only one where Jews are allowed. All she wants is to be normal, not set apart.

"The more I thought about it, the more I decided that I couldn't be her friend, a real friend, if I didn't get a taste of what she's going through. That's all," she concluded in her practical, matter-of-fact way.

Séverine shook her head in disbelief as a wave of anger and fear overtook her—and, she had to admit, a new appreciation of her older sister. Caroline had always been the one who admired Séverine—her piano playing, the social graces she'd acquired, the way she grabbed life with both hands, the way she never backed down—but today the tables had turned. Suddenly, Séverine was seeing her sister in a very different light.

"Caroline, promise me one thing. I know that you sympathize with your friend; I sympathize with her too. Who wouldn't? But please don't go through with this. It's far too dangerous."

"And certainly not in the family tradition, right?" Caroline said, looking pointedly at her sister.

Séverine shrugged her shoulders. "Each to his own. Antoine is for the Marshal, as are a lot of other people in this country, including our parents."

"Including you?" Caroline asked, not wavering.

"Including me," Séverine replied firmly.

"So, if you approve of Pétain, you approve of this!" She tapped the yellow star.

"Things aren't that simple, Caroline. It's not that I approve or disapprove. Frankly, I don't see any particular sense in it, if you want to know. But there's nothing I can do about it, and I'm for the Marshal, so that's all there is to it."

The sisters faced each other, unblinking, for a few moments.

"All right," Caroline said at last. She reached over and picked up the vest, then carefully snipped the threads holding the yellow star in place. "But this isn't the last you'll hear on the subject."

The sisters were silent for a moment, each regarding the other as though seeing her for the first time.

Finally, Caroline broke the silence.

"What are you reading?" she asked, nodding at the book sticking out of Séverine's bag.

Séverine brightened. "*Gone with the Wind*. It's set in America during the Civil War, and the main character—"

Caroline interrupted her. "Don't tell me. I read it. The main character is Scarlett O'Hara, who has one goal in life, which is to wrest Ashley Wilkes away from his goody-goody cousin Melanie."

To her relief, Séverine burst out laughing. "Well, you're right about Melanie, and I have no idea why Scarlett would even bother with a drip like Ashley. Frankly, I think she's totally deluded."

"Absolutely," Caroline assented, glad they had found something they could agree on. "Now," she said, "didn't you say something about taking your favorite sister on a shopping trip? I can't go at the moment"—she nodded at a pile of mending on a side table— "but let's do it later this afternoon."

"That's fine. I'll come by again after lunch," said Séverine, gathering her hat and coat. The two sisters embraced and Séverine let herself back out into the dim hallway and closed the door behind her.

Caroline stood for a moment, deep in thought. It struck her that her impetuous, lively and stubborn sister was a lot like Scarlett O'Hara: passionate, single-minded, and filled with life—and its illusions. For Scarlett the illusion was that she would someday land Ashley, for Séverine the illusion was that Antoine would someday give in and make her a baby. No wonder she couldn't think straight about politics, Caroline thought. Her mind was totally occupied with the sole idea of convincing Antoine to become a father. But how could she live with such an anti-Semite? Had her handsome husband kept her in the dark about his activities? Or did she, like Scarlett O'Hara, see only what she wanted to see?

She had never lied to Séverine—not about anything important, at least. She had agreed to remove the yellow star from her vest, but she hadn't agreed to change her thinking on the subject. On the contrary, her encounter with Séverine had served to highlight the injustices around her, and had strengthened her resolve.

Caroline turned away from the door and walked over to her dresser. "You can come out now," she said softly. She pulled the heavy piece of furniture away from the wall to reveal a small door leading to an adjacent low-ceilinged storage room, and stood back as her friend Fanny stepped into the room, stretching out a crick in her neck.

"Well, you heard it," said Caroline. "Now you know what my family's like."

"Your family's like most of the people in this country," Fanny replied with equanimity. "They want to keep out of trouble. And it's obvious that your sister loves you very much." She strode over to the pile of mending and picked up a piece on the top. "Tell me more about this new turban," she said briskly. "How do you want to proceed?"

The two women had met at the theater, where Caroline worked as a designer and Fanny as a seamstress. They had hit it off at once, and were soon calling themselves "the mutual admiration society." Fanny admired Caroline's talent for fashioning costumes, dresses, skirts, and pants out of old tablecloths, curtains, sheets or just about any material she found. Caroline, for her part, admired Fanny's ability to prompt actors who had flubbed their lines while calmly and methodically ripping out hems and mending tears on costumes. When Caroline told her colleague that she was an amateur milliner, Fanny had asked to see her work. Dazzled by Caroline's creativity and talent, she had immediately offered to help.

Caroline had readily agreed; her reputation as one of the city's best seamstresses meant that her workload was getting too much to handle alone. "I can't pay you," she'd said, "but your reward will be sharing my sumptuous dinner of a buttered baguette, if we can find any butter, and coffee made with chicory and acorns and who knows what other awful things." The two grimaced; ersatz coffee was one of the less appealing aspects of the war, in the eyes of many Parisians. "Plus," Caroline added, plopping one of her most outlandish creations on Fanny's head, "a cut on any business I might pick up in the future."

They had shaken hands on it and settled into a comfortable partnership. Caroline designed and Fanny applied her expert cutting and sewing techniques as well as serving as an occasional model. With her long auburn hair, large brown eyes, high cheekbones and wide mouth, she had, Caroline told her, a perfect face for a hat. It was still too early to know whether they could make a business of it, or if their ingenious creations would remain a hobby. But at the very least, they agreed, they would try to earn enough money for themselves and their families to keep warm during the winter and be stylish at all times.

Their latest creation was an elegant but easy to wear turban for women who lacked time or shampoo, or both. Helping Parisian women with the arduous but pleasant task of remaining feminine and fashionable in wartime was an important part of Caroline's project. And in this, she was lucky. The Germans had seized the leather and the textile industries for their own needs, so the French were suffering badly when it came to shoes and clothes.

Hats, however, could be made from almost anything, and were literally the crowning glory of every Parisian woman's outfit. A hat was no mere head covering: it was a political statement, a message to the enemy: you may be here and we may lack many things—food, soap, supplies—but we'll crown our heads with the fanciest, most colorful, most outrageous, most artistic and ornamental tops and turbans, and you can't stop us!

* * *

By the time Séverine knocked on the door for the second time that day, Caroline had made up her mind. No more secrets. She would tell Séverine about her hat-making with Fanny, and invite her on a special and important trip across Paris, one that Fanny, for obvious reasons, couldn't make.

She knew she was good at hat-making, and she knew she wanted to make a go of it. But she also knew that she had neither Séverine's connections nor Séverine's exuberance and ability to convince anyone of anything when she wanted to. She was sure Séverine would go along with her idea of presenting her work to the various hatmakers in the city, and she was right.

During their shopping trip, she broached the idea, and confessed her secret about Fanny. The outcome was even better than she had hoped: Séverine enthusiastically warmed to the idea. One warm afternoon a few days later the two of them set out on their mission, treading all over Paris in their wooden-soled high heels to knock at the doors of the city's best milliners. They had chosen their outfits carefully. Séverine had picked out an "all business" outfit for Caroline, a simple navy-blue suit and a stunning red hat, one of Caroline's own creations. She chose a red ensemble for herself.

"It's my color and it draws attention, which is what we want," she said. Not only that, but the bold color gave her the confidence she needed to get into the shops of the milliners, not all of whom were anxious to receive two strangers toting a portfolio of designs.

The Occupation, however, had taken its toll on the city's businesses, and the pair found door after door politely but firmly closed in their faces. Disheartened, they approached the last shop on their list. It was an upscale boutique on the boulevard Victor Hugo in the fashionable 16th arrondissement, founded by the city's best-known and most celebrated hat designer, whose creations were the talk of the town and featured in all the women's fashion magazines.

"Worth a try," Séverine said with a weary smile, making a thumbs-up gesture to her dejected sister.

As they neared the door, however, they saw a yellow sign affixed on the window designating the shop as a Jewish business. Caroline recoiled, thinking of her friend Fanny and her yellow star. Séverine, on the other hand, squared her shoulders, walked purposely to the door and rang the bell. She loved nothing better than a challenge, and here was a real one: Jewish business or not, she needed to know if they would be allowed into this exalted establishment.

Séverine went straight to the point. "We would like to see the owner," she announced to the person answering the door. The bluntness of her approach was softened by the amiability of her expression and her gracious manner.

"May I ask who you are and why you are here?" the salesperson responded, glancing at the attractive brunette garbed in red and the petite, fair-haired, blue-eyed woman in the navy suit and striking hat.

"Please tell her that my name is Séverine Sevanot and this is my sister, Caroline Aubry. She designs dresses and jackets, but her passion is hats. I'll leave it to her to explain why we are paying a visit to your shop." Suddenly inspired, she pointed to the shop's window display. "As for me, I would love to try on one or more of these wonderful creations. They are quite breath-taking."

"Very well," the young woman replied solemnly. "I'll check to see if Madame Hertzberg is available." She beckoned them in, shut the door carefully behind them, and then with a quick backward glance at the sisters, disappeared behind a thick green velvet curtain into the back room, leaving them alone.

"Going to make her report," Séverine whispered. "Oh, look at that black velvet number with the ostrich feather—I simply must try it on!"

"You're so relaxed!" Caroline replied, almost accusingly. "The strain may kill me."

"Buck up!" Séverine advised, as she did a mental check on which hats would suit her, and which would not.

Suddenly the green velvet curtain parted again, and a woman stepped out onto the shop floor. "You wished to speak with me?" Madame Hertzberg asked. A certain air of gravitas followed her into the room. She was tall and svelte with dark eyes and hair and a no-nonsense look.

Caroline stared at her, tongue-tied. She wanted to say, "I'm so sorry. I saw the sign on the door and I abhor it," but was suddenly paralyzed with shyness and indecision.

Thankfully, Séverine spoke first, filling the room with her confidence and energy.

"You are probably wondering who we are and why we're

here. As I told your assistant, I am Séverine Sevanot and this is my younger sister, Caroline. She is perfectly capable of introducing herself and also of coming here alone, but when she told me about presenting her designs to the foremost milliner of Paris, I talked her into letting me come along. I must admit that my interest was selfish, but I'm so glad that I came. This is a real treasure trove," she exclaimed, spreading her arms to take in the entire room.

Before Mrs. Hertzberg could utter a word, Caroline found her tongue. "First of all, thank you for receiving us. We appreciate your time more than you can know." She paused as she searched for the right words. "You may think that I'm either overreaching or impertinent or both, but I want to tell you first of all that I venerate your work. I could never measure up to it. My only hope is that you can give *me* hope. My passion, as my sister mentioned, is hats, but I'm a beginner. I would like to have your professional opinion of my work, if you would be so kind, and perhaps some advice as to how I can improve."

Madame Hertzberg took the sheaf of designs Caroline proffered and placed them on the highly polished wooden counter. She lifted the pair of spectacles that were hanging from a chain on her neck, put them on and, without a word, pored over Caroline's work. Turbans, cloches, toques. Hats with huge brims, hats in rabbit fur, hats to wear to the market, hats to wear to the races, hats to wear to the opera. Caroline's collection boasted *chapeaux* of every shape, made of every available wartime material. The hats, Madame Hertzberg noted approvingly, made the outfits, not the opposite. One sketch in particular, a hat in bright red felt with a long, bright red and orange printed silk scarf trailing down the back, caught her attention.

After a few minutes, she looked up from the portfolio to face the tense young woman who was trying not to show her anxiety. "As you know, I create and sell my own work, and as I'm sure you can imagine, in spite of that I'm always getting requests from designers to look at and eventually sell their work. I don't do it," she said, firmly. "Or rather, I rarely do it, because when their work is bad, it's bad and when it's good, it's not as good as mine."

She cast another look at Caroline's portfolio on the counter.

"You have talent, that's for sure. Is that what you wanted to hear? Or was there something else?"

Séverine, who was busily engaged in trying on hats and acting as if she were ignoring the conversation, waited for Caroline's answer.

Caroline was mystified. Madame Hertzberg, the *crème de la crème* of Parisian hatmakers, had told her in almost the same sentence that no one was as good as she herself was, but also that she, Caroline, had talent. Was that the end of it? It couldn't be. After all, Madame Hertzberg had left the door open by asking her what she wanted. At least there was a chance.

"Thank you, Madame," she said, trying to keep her voice from shaking. "I am honored to hear you say I have talent. And yes, there is something else." She hesitated, not knowing whether she dared continue. "I would like to know if there is even one hat in my collection that you would consider taking for your store." She faced her interlocutor silently, not moving as she waited for the verdict.

Séverine froze with the hat she was trying on halfway to her head, no longer pretending not to be listening.

Madame Hertzberg appraised the dignified young woman standing in front of her. She had obviously worked up her courage to come to her shop and ask to see her in person, and to Madame's considerable surprise, her collection showed great promise. In fact, although she'd never say it, some of her hats would sell immediately.

"There is one." She turned again to the book of sketches

and pointed at the joyful red hat with the red and orange scarf. "There may be more." She looked directly into Caroline's expectant blue eyes. "Come back and we'll talk business."

As she parted the green curtains to return to the back of the store, she added, "One more thing before you leave, young lady. You used the word 'venerate' to describe your opinion of my work. I am gratified, but would prefer a simpler word like 'admire.' As you know, designing is a matter of choice, of selecting the color, shape and form that best expresses what you are trying to do. It's the same thing for words. You have to choose the right one, the one that expresses exactly what you mean. For example, I admire you—both of you," she said, turning to acknowledge Séverine, "for coming here today." And with that unexpected and to their minds undeserved compliment, she left the room before Séverine could tell her what she had decided to buy. That was all right—they would return together another time soon. They left the shop with happy hearts.

Paris: June 1942

Every Sunday, the Aubry family followed an immutable tradition, gathering in Robert and Germaine's minuscule quarters for their traditional after-mass lunch. Séverine remembered the simple, plentiful, delicious meals her mother had made before the war, and reproached herself for having taken them for granted. They had never had a lot of money, but between Robert's hunting and Germaine's talent for canning and cooking plus the extras the countess had sometimes given them to "improve the ordinary," the table had always been bounteous.

But that was in the provinces, where food was easy to grow and easy to get, and this was wartime Paris, where you had to stand in line with ration tickets for items that were often long gone before your turn came. Shopkeepers could get you what you wanted for a price, of course, but Robert refused to dabble in the black market.

"If there's one thing I can't stand, it's dishonesty," he would say, making a face as he helped himself to a spoonful of Germaine's watery rutabaga soup.

Antoine's parents, in contrast, had good things to eat—sausages, Camembert and other luxuries they brought back from their country estate in Normandy. One day, in a spontaneous but rash gesture, Louise proposed that the two families join each other on Sundays for lunch upstairs and coffee downstairs. Germaine and Robert were horrified by the idea of lunch in the grand apartment of their employers and in-laws. Bertrand—even though the idea had come from his wife—couldn't really see himself sipping coffee with Séverine's family in their modest quarters.

"Your mother's offer is so kind," Germaine had told Antoine. "But she mustn't go to such trouble."

Antoine read between the lines, transmitted the message, and everyone was relieved to be off the hook. Even so, it had been a close call. "You really should turn your tongue ten times in your mouth before speaking," Bertrand admonished Louise.

In the end, Antoine lunched with his in-laws downstairs, after which he and Séverine went back upstairs for coffee. His parents were happy with the arrangement, and also happy that Antoine had finally settled down and that the delightful Séverine was the one who had managed that supposedly impossible feat by capturing his heart. They liked their impeccably dressed and well-mannered daughter-in-law so much, in fact, that Antoine had to implore Louise not to show her off. He could see the wicked pleasure she would get in inviting her snobbish friends, having Séverine perform on the piano, letting them witness her beauty, grace and intelligence, then shaking them up with a few casual words–"Séverine's parents live in the concierge's quarters on the ground floor, you know. So convenient. Her mother's the concierge, and her father is our building's most precious handyman. I don't know how we got along before they came!"

Her words, he knew, would be motivated by a desire to set herself apart from the rigidity of her social set and display her open-mindedness, but they would be hurtful to Séverine. He had no desire to put his wife in that kind of position.

Although the two families didn't dine together, Antoine's parents did from time to time manage to press upon Séverine's parents special treats in the form of food or wine. Germaine and Robert accepted their offerings in the name of keeping peace in the extended family—and after one particularly exceptional Camembert they decided not to let guilt be a visitor at their table.

It was a perfectly ripened Camembert, not too young, not too old. Its soft white rind bore a few red-brown streaks, and the inside was neither distressingly chalky nor dreadfully runny. Sometimes Camemberts smelled like unwashed socks or cabbage, but this one was redolent of the raw milk provided by big, lazy, brown-spotted cows grazing in the green pastures of Normandy, and the aroma was divine. They accompanied the cheese with a bottle of vintage wine that Antoine's parents had presented at the same time and agreed that while the black market wasn't for them, profiting from the generosity of Séverine's in-laws from time to time would at least give them something extraordinary to remember when the war was over. After all, it couldn't go on forever.

Robert and Germaine sat at each end of the oval table with Séverine and Caroline on one side and Antoine on the other.

"I can't stay long," Antoine said, glancing at his Rolex. "My father and I are doing our genealogy. The government demands that owners of businesses go back three to five generations to prove they have no Jewish ancestors. If we can't furnish the baptismal certificates, they'll either shut the store down or replace the owner with an Aryan administrator. Of course, in our case that's not going to happen, but talk about a waste of time. I've got to help him sort this out."

Caroline and Séverine exchanged a look as they both thought of Madame Hertzberg. They had returned to see her at the appointed time; Caroline had been excited to present more of her collection, and Séverine had been looking forward to buying a chic turban and a glamorous picnic hat she'd spied earlier.

But the shop had been boarded up and Madame Hertzberg had vanished.

Seeing their distress, a neighboring shopkeeper took them aside. He told them what they already knew: that being Jewish, Madame Hertzberg had been forced to turn her boutique over to an Aryan administrator, who would sell or rent it. At first, he said, she'd been allowed to remain in the shop because she was indispensable to its success, but now she was gone. The shopkeeper knew nothing else. No one did. And it was too bad, he said. He had had a cordial relationship with Madame Hertzberg and liked her. He couldn't say more.

"Caroline, you're not eating. Have some of this delicious Camembert," Antoine urged her.

She looked across the table at Antoine, then at Séverine. An image of Antoine shepherding a delegation through the exhibition about "The Jew and France" flashed through her mind. Not for the first time, Caroline wondered what Séverine knew about her handsome, anti-Semitic husband.

"No, thanks. I'm not hungry."

Chapter TWENTY-ONE

Paris: May 1943

From where she was standing in the living room, Séverine watched Antoine. Even sitting still in a chair, his posture was perfect—relaxed, not rigid. At the same time, like a lazy lion, he was in a resting position, ready to spring. Always ready for action—except when it came to making babies. He obviously didn't comprehend why it was so important to her. She'd have to try again.

She approached the chair from behind and slowly massaged his neck. He dropped the paper he was reading, put his long arms behind him and caressed the hands that were kneading his flesh.

"Trying to distract me, eh?" he asked, standing up to face her and feeling her breasts through the thin material of her dress as he drew her into his embrace.

"Oh, I know that's not hard to do," she answered, gently pushing him away. The temptation to end the discussion in bed was overwhelming, but she felt it was time to hold her ground, confront him with the one question whose answer frightened her the most and to which she now wanted—and inwardly feared—a true answer.

It wasn't as if this were the first time she had brought the matter up. She had done so in various ways since the war began, often talking about the nation's new motto, which had changed from "Liberty, Equality, Fraternity" to "Work, Family, Fatherland." Much as in medieval times when the churches featured graphic images of good and evil in the form of paintings or gargoyles because people couldn't read, the Vichy government used brightly colored posters as an eye-catching technique to get its message across to the people. Posters featuring ordinary scenes or ordinary men and women were a way of showing what the National Revolution was all about.

Séverine had seen one that suited her purpose. It featured two houses, one in fine shape, the other crumbling. The roof of the proper, upright yellow house was held up by four pillars, each featuring an important aspect of the new France under Vichy: education, the crafts industry, the peasantry, and the Legion, which referred to the Legion of French Volunteers against Bolshevism. In case people still didn't understand, the words "Discipline, Order, Work, Family and Fatherland" were written on the structure.

The other house, representing the old France, was built on foundations of laziness, demagoguery and international-alism. It was dilapidated and sat askew, brought down by the evils of the Popular Front, which had governed between 1936 and 1938: those evils were the Freemasons, Jews, greed, the Parliament, and even pastis, a popular lic-orice-flavored anise aperitif. A large Star of David loomed above the old house.

Séverine particularly liked the mention of family on the new house—which, she rationalized, made the pros-pect of motherhood not only a pleasure but a duty to be carried out for the country. Almost every day, she brought the subject up with Antoine who, despite his support for the Marshal, wasn't particularly interested in the "family" part of the new motto. Every time she raised the issue, he laughed her off. But she persisted, refusing to believe him when he said he didn't want any children, that it would always be the two of them. This wasn't something Séverine had envisaged when they'd married. In fact, she'd imagined quite the opposite, so much so that she had ignored his comments, and had even taken them as a joke.

"I love it when you tease me," she'd told him during one of their recent discussions on the matter. She'd nuzzled up close to him, sniffing the familiar light, spicy, nutty aroma of the expensive black-market tobacco that had permeated his corduroy jacket and the soft, bespoke white poplin Charvet shirt he wore beneath it. Every season he would order dozens of made-to-measure shirts, plus pajamas and ties, from the prestigious shop on the Place Vendôme. The clothes, made of the finest material, were part of his image. So was the Dunhill pipe. Antoine would never be a cigarette smoker; he was too calm, too thoughtful.

He had not replied. Instead, he had enfolded her in a warm embrace. Being there like that, with those strong arms around her, made her feel protected and strong. But it didn't solve her problem.

Today she decided to try again, with fresh ammunition. "You know, Antoine, I saw this poster on a wall the other day as I was walking home—in fact, two posters in different places. The first one said: 'If you want to rebuild France, first give her children.' The second one said: 'A household without a child, a couple adrift.'" She didn't tell him how powerfully the second poster had struck her as she stood transfixed, contemplating the young couple perched on a raft in a rough sea with high winds that had shredded the mast. She had drawn closer and stared at it so intensely that the couple had seemed to transform into herself and Antoine before her eyes. She felt as if Marshal Pétain was speaking directly to her. What kind of patriot was she in wartime if she didn't have a family? And patriotism aside, what kind of life would she have without children in it?

Why didn't Antoine understand this? Why was she the only one of the two who wanted a child?

She tried to sound casual as she continued. "I've been thinking about the Vichy motto 'Work, Family, Fatherland' that replaced 'Liberty, Equality, Fraternity'. You're pretty good at work and fatherland," she remarked, and it was the truth: his jewelry business and his political activities ate up most of his time. She wanted to blurt out how unhappy she was, tell him everything, beg him to start a family this very minute, but felt she mustn't go too far. Torn between speaking her mind and the fear of being a nag, she fell silent.

"So," said Antoine, "I'm lacking when it comes to the family part, and to please Marshal Pétain, you want to make babies, is that right?" he asked, as he looked down at her indulgently. "Don't you enjoy being alone with me? Two's company, three's a crowd, no matter what Marshal Pétain says, and you know that I think he's right on most things, don't you?"

"Why wouldn't he be right about this?" Séverine replied sharply, not even bothering to conceal her growing irritation. "And come on, Antoine—you know as well as I do that this isn't about the Marshal; it's about us. Neither of us is getting any younger, and we have had a wonderful time since we got married but…" She broke off again.

"But what, Séverine?" Antoine asked. His voice took on a tinge of exasperation. "When you married me, you knew you were with an older man. I never promised you children, but you think and act as if the plan has changed. You're becoming obsessed by it. Why don't you find more pupils for piano lessons, take up a hobby? There are plenty of other things to do in life than raise squalling babies." Almost as an afterthought, he added, "By the way, it's easy for Pétain to encourage the French to have families. He's a well-known womanizer and has no children. He may project the image of a friendly grandfather, but he's actually icily formal, even with people in his own social class."

Séverine felt as if he had slapped her in the face. In previous discussions—and they had been numerous—he had always changed the subject or given her the idea that he would take her wishes into consideration. Now he wasn't pretending. This was real. He was telling her in no uncertain terms that she would never have a child. Not with him, at least.

Inwardly, she shook her head and refused to believe it. It was only a matter of wearing him down. He would like children, she was convinced. She would have to humor him, find a way. He'd mentioned her taking up a hobby. Unbeknownst to him, he'd given her a truly excellent idea for a pastime: getting him to capitulate and make her a baby. She had to win this battle.

In a lighthearted tone, as if he had said nothing of great importance, she acquiesced. "You're right, my dear. I definitely must get more pupils and a hobby. I'll start working on that right now."

Antoine suppressed a sigh as he returned to his easy chair and his newspaper. Children, he ruminated crossly. No more children.

Paris: June 1943

Antoine stretched out on his bed, propped himself up on his elbow, and contemplated the naked red-headed beauty sleeping next to him. His gaze traveled across the large, square room, with its valuable, colorful oriental rugs, to the high windows from which he could see the tops of the trees in the Luxembourg Gardens across the street. But he quickly returned to feasting his eyes on the splendid creature lying on Séverine's favorite pale pink satin sheets. He had seen a lot of women in his time, but never one like this. She was positively lascivious.

When she and her husband had walked into the shop, he had had to force himself to look the other way. The husband was an older man, quite a lot older, but that was nothing new. Many of Antoine's clients were very rich old men whose fortunes attracted a certain type of very rapacious young women. It was a fair deal. The woman got fine clothes and fine jewels and, if she played her cards right, a grand apartment or manor where she could live out the rest of her days once her provider had graciously departed for another world, with or without her help. In turn the man used the woman as a statement to the world, one that announced that he might be old but still had the power and the money to avail himself of firm, unwrinkled and tender young flesh.

Dressed in a perfect-fitting navy-blue three-piece suit, the tall, courtly, silver-haired gentleman had looked like a senator or the head of a major company. With the in-disputable authority of the decision-maker, he had guided his wife—Francine, he called her—straight to Antoine and reminded him of the appointment he had made to look over a selection of diamond bracelets. Francine was of medium height, slim, with a head of long curly red hair, white skin and the sexiest half-closed violet-blue eyes Antoine had ever seen. For a brief moment, he had re-gretted they weren't looking for necklaces. He would have loved to touch the incredibly white skin on her neck. But a bracelet would do. In fact, he found that barely touching a woman's arm was exciting, electric and erotic.

His usual practice was to speak directly to the man, who, after all, had the money and was buying the merchandise. He generally allowed himself only a couple of cursory looks at the woman. The first was a quick glance, one that showed respect and courtesy. Nothing more. The second, if he found her worth his time, lasted longer and was more direct as he tried to determine whether she was looking at him as well, whether she was responding to his signals.

His first glance at Francine told him all he needed to know: she was obviously used to the effect she had on men. Her return glance at him was brief but direct, and the message in her magnetic violet-blue eyes had been clear. The rest was easy: writing up the bill (the diamond and ruby bracelet was the price of a nice-sized apartment), then slipping a tiny note with a time and an address into the purse that had been slightly opened to receive it.

And now, he was in his bed in his flat with her. It was the first time he had ever brought a woman to his home, and he had had a few qualms of guilt. He knew Séverine was out in some suburb giving a piano lesson and wouldn't be back until late. He had plenty of time, but he decided that in future it would be better to go to his bachelor quarters instead.

Francine awakened slowly. "What are you looking at, my darling?" she asked, putting her leg over his.

"What do you think I'm looking at? You, of course. You are gorgeous with clothes on but sensational with them off. I knew that the moment you walked into the shop."

"I saw your interest right away," she said, mischievously pinching him. "Fortunately, my husband didn't. Will we see each other again, or is this a one-afternoon stand?" she asked, caressing his erect penis.

"What a question, my dear. We'll see each other over and over again. But not here. It's too..." He trailed off.

"Too what? Too full of your wife? You men! You think it's so daring to have a woman in your wife's bed, and then once she's in it you decide that maybe it wasn't such a good idea." She breathed in the jasmine and musk scent of the Chanel No. 5 perfume that permeated the sheets and appraised the precious antique dressing table with its cheerful jumble of powder puffs and creams and lipsticks and porcelain jars. Further away, in the adjoining dressing room, she could make out Séverine's delicate low-cut pale pink silk nightgown hanging on a hook. "From what I can see, my rival might not appreciate the competition." She raised her eyebrows and offered an observation. "I think you dare not tell me that she is erotic and exotic. I bet she's dark-haired and devilish, a real fury in bed. I don't know why I say that. It's just an impression, a feeling I get while lolling in these satin sheets. What luxury," she sighed, stretching herself voluptuously.

"You're right about her dark hair, but the rest is none of your business." Antoine made an effort to soften his tone, but he was firm. These whores were always getting above themselves. "You and I will meet in a place where there's no competition, as you say. And," he warned, "you will never speak of my wife again. Deal?"

Francine agreed, smiling to herself. He had hoped to wound her, put her in her place. After all, she wasn't much better than a prostitute. He hadn't hurt her, though. His remarks only reinforced her opinion that all men were little boys once you scratched the surface. But what did she care? She had a wealthy, elderly husband who would adore her for the few years he had left, and a new lover who was strong and exciting, young, rich and well-connected. Neither man could get enough of her long, red curly hair and sleek body, but while one repelled and revolted her, the other captivated and charmed her, setting her on fire. She was sure she'd be seeing a lot of this Antoine.

In a final glance around the exquisite room, she took in Antoine's wife's perfumes and powders, her pink nightgown and pink sheets once more. Then she put the vision of the room's rightful occupant out of her mind and focused solely on Antoine.

Chapter TWENTY-TWO

Paris: March 1944

Séverine sat on a bench in the Tuileries Garden, where she had walked to get some fresh air. The day was sunny and perfect, with blue skies and huge, puffy white clouds. She had brought with her the cherished leather-bound copy of Keats' *Endymion*, a gift from Caroline, who knew that she loved reading in English. Before diving into it, she surveyed the plants and trees and the landscaping and reflected that the Tuileries were an illustration of Keats's oft-quoted line, "A thing of beauty is a joy forever."

She pulled her coat tighter against the slight chill and was getting ready to read when her gaze landed on a man who looked like Antoine strolling down a lane with a young boy. The child was about ten years old, she wagered, and had Antoine's eyes, Antoine's bold features, Antoine's sandy hair and even his confident way of carrying himself. The resemblance between the man and the boy was striking. Séverine anticipated telling Antoine about the two over their evening meal. She would even tease him. "So, in spite of saying you want no children, you've got a hidden one?"

The boy took off running, and the man who looked like Antoine chased him slowly, on purpose. He obviously wanted to let the lad win his race.

"Papa, Papa," the little fellow yelled. "You're out of breath! I beat you!"

The child turned to face his father, an expression of triumph and joy lighting up his face, and the man threw back his head and laughed. The two of them linked hands and strolled on. Séverine felt her entire body go numb.

She stared at the place they'd been, hoping it had been a bad dream, that her eyesight had gone off, that she was hallucinating, and that it wasn't Antoine but someone who looked uncannily like him. Was she dreaming? She looked around to see if anything else around her had changed. The tall, stately chestnut trees stood like sentries, still bereft of their leaves. The warmly dressed mothers chatting with each other as they watched their youngsters play hadn't budged from their benches. No, all was as it should be.

A couple of tall, good-looking German officers ambled toward her on the path now, talking in low voices about who knew what? Goethe? She couldn't understand a word of German, but the two looked erudite, cultured. Séverine agreed with her father and mother and Antoine that the Germans had brought something good to France—a sense of order. "Pétain's not wrong," they all agreed. "We French need one thing the Germans have and we don't—law and order."

As if they were reading her mind, the German officers looked over at her as they passed by. "Bonjour, Mam'selle," they greeted her with a nod, appraising her petite French frame, her highly colored cheeks, her big brown eyes and her fashionable attire.

She quickly bowed her head over the book she'd brought with her. The conquerors returned to their conversation and strolled on.

The man and boy were out of her sight now, so she began to think that perhaps she'd not seen them at all, that she'd not seen her husband holding the hand of this sandy-haired, blue-eyed boy child who looked like him and called him "Papa," that she'd not seen her husband holding back and yet pretending to pant with effort as he pursued his son down the tree-lined lane.

Why, when, where, how? How could she have been so ignorant? How could Antoine have a ten-year-old son? She made a rapid calculation: if it were true, it meant that in the very beginning of their marriage, when he had clearly indicated that he didn't want a baby, it was because he already *had* a baby. He didn't want to be a father because he already *was* a father.

Stunned, stupefied, and shamed, she chose to say nothing to Antoine until she had proof of her suspicion. Over the next weeks she returned to the Tuileries at the same time on the same day, where she forced herself to observe the two of them over and over again. There was no mistake. The resemblance was striking, as was the complicity. From her perch on a bench underneath the shade of a chestnut tree, she reluctantly but relentlessly spied on them. She saw how comfortable they were with each other, how the boy looked up to the father with respect and love and how the father looked at his son with pride and indulgence. She saw a tender, paternal side of Antoine that pierced her heart.

One day she followed them out of the Tuileries and down a nearby street to the door of a well-appointed building on the rue du Mont Thabor. The doorman greeted them as if it were a matter of course—which it clearly was. He gave a play salute to the little boy, then fished in his pockets to find a bonbon. Antoine smiled indulgently and reminded the little one—his son—to say thank you. She could imagine the rest: his mistress welcoming them warmly, the little boy pleading with Antoine not to leave, the mistress telling him not to worry, that Papa always came back, didn't he?

The echoes of his words— "no children" and "aren't the

two of us enough?"—resounded in her head, over and over. The scope of his lie, the realization that she had stubbornly believed that she could bring him round to her point of view, that in her blindness she had wasted so many of her childbearing years, was impossible to comprehend. It felt like someone had punched her in the stomach, leaving her gasping for air. She could barely breathe.

It was then that Séverine decided to stop following Antoine. She had seen enough, didn't want to know any-more, and had made a decision.

The rest was a rush. She sent word to Gisèle that she would at last accept her kind invitation to visit, then impatiently waited for her response. As soon as it came, she packed her suitcase and asked Caroline to accompany her to the station.

She left a note for Antoine. It contained only one word. *Adieu.*

PART THREE

PARADISE LOST

Chapter TWENTY-THREE

Sorignac: March 1944

The day before Séverine's arrival, Gisèle was searching for some sheet music in the piano bench when she heard a loud steady buzz, like a giant swarm of angry bees. Running to one of the west windows, she saw a long line of German vehicles – almost a hundred of them, she guessed. They were camouflaged against the brown and green of the trees along the route and moving rapidly toward the village. She hoped it was a mirage and squinted to get a better look. If it was a mirage or hallucination, it was a frightening one. What could they be doing here? Surely they must be passing through the town on their way to another place. But where? She rapidly made the sign of the cross and went to question the servants, who always seemed to know more than she did.

Minutes later, Madame Decré, who was bustling around in her bakery, heard and then saw the first of the jeeps roll past. She closed the metal shutters quickly. Her instinct told her to hide, but she didn't know where to go. It wasn't that she was guilty of anything other than her opinions: she loathed the Occupation and the occupiers. Would they be able to read her mind if they stopped to interrogate her? Like Gisèle, she wondered if Sorignac was

239

their destination or if, as she hoped and prayed, they were going elsewhere.

At the shoe shop, Luc heard voices in the street outside yelling "The Boches are here!" His customer didn't even wait for a receipt as he plunked the pair of boots he had brought for repair down on the counter and dashed from the shop. Outside, people were scurrying home, and most of the shopkeepers were locking their doors and closing for the day. Luc stayed put. He pretended nothing out of the ordinary was happening and applied himself to repairing a run-down heel. He knew the name of the man who had left his boots and scribbled it on a note that he stuck in them. He continued to work as he waited for orders from Pierre, his cell leader.

Dressed in his white lab coat, Paul was examining a patient when he noticed that the normal soft murmur of sound in the adjacent waiting room had turned into a concert of loud voices accompanied by hurried footsteps, slamming doors and the sound of gravel crunching in the courtyard. Two patients knocked on his door to inform him that a convoy of Germans was heading toward the town hall, but Paul had seen or heard nothing to substantiate the rumor. Still, considering the increased level of resistance activity in which he and his father were involved, he wouldn't have been surprised if it were true. Only a couple of days before, they had fetched arms, explosives and other supplies by the light of the moon from a nearby drop site where a British Lysander had touched down. This might be a day of reckoning, Paul thought as he calmly returned to examine his waiting patients. He hoped he was mistaken.

Unless they were resisters, Jews or communists, most of the apprehensive townspeople tried to reassure themselves that if the Germans were there, it wasn't for them. One more ordeal, they grumbled, as the soldiers sealed off all the entrances to the town and marched into the town hall.

In a loud, firm voice, Kommandant Kurt Walnitz barked orders to the mayor. "All townspeople are to gather at the town hall with their identity cards. In the meantime, you will provide a list of all the communists and Jews in this town. *Schnell*," he added, examining the inscrutable face of the mayor.

The mayor wouldn't help him, so the Kommandant ordered a soldier to arrest him and search the city records, as they had done in countless other towns before this one; it was an easy way to identify Jews in any given area, since they were all registered.

"Jacob Solomon, Regine Horowitz and Maurice Gold," a soldier read out loud.

The mayor kept his face blank, hoping that those three and the others had fled to safe hiding places. As for the communists, he reasoned, it would take even the mighty Gestapo some time to track them down in this area of dense woods and forests.

The Kommandant was pleased at this good start. His troops had been sent to the region expressly because the Jews here were too dispersed and therefore difficult to find and apprehend. Something had to be done, and the goal was clear: hunting for Jews and arresting them was a primary objective. But the assignment also included ferreting out and neutralizing the largest possible number of *résistants*. Their orders were to arrest all men between the ages of 18 and 40 who had refused to be sent to the Reich to perform forced labor, and to intimidate the civilian population and bring them to heel so they would quit helping the Resistance.

To carry out the task, they needed to be swift and efficient. Headquarters was right—a week in the area should be sufficient, the Kommandant estimated. He looked forward to a good week's work, after which every *résistant*, every communist, every Jew his troops could find would be dead or deported, and every person who had ever aided and abetted them would think twice before doing so again.

Kommandant Walnitz had seen tough places in his career, but this region in the southwest of France was among the toughest. Guerrilla warfare, carried out by volatile groups of courageous men and women who had little training, scant organization and few arms, was skillfully slowing down the occupiers. Some of the men had fled to the *maquis*, uninhabited and isolated rural areas where they could hide in the thick underbrush, either to escape the compulsory work service in Nazi Germany, or simply because they craved action. Some were young and inexperienced at waging war; others were hardened veterans of the Spanish Civil War. These *résistants* may not have had much in the way of ammunition, but they had something better—they knew the terrain, benefited from the aid of the locals, and were filled with purpose and determination.

In light of this activity, the German command had declared Sorignac and the entire area off limits. No one could enter or leave without a pass; villagers had a 5 PM curfew, roundly resented because it kept farmers from working full days in the fields and the locals from tending to their gardens after work or even taking a stroll around the village's little streets. In spite of those measures, acts of resistance ranging from graffiti to sabotage and guerrilla warfare not only continued but increased. Nothing would stop the rural revolt of these freedom fighters, who were always on the move and semi-organized, even though they sometimes lacked discipline. But tragedies such as the one in which an entire group of thirty-three *maquisards* had been wiped out by the Germans had brought home a hard lesson: you could never be careful enough. Informers were everywhere: talking could and did kill.

The Germans were helped in their battle against the French Resistance by the French collaborators who had joined the Milice, a paramilitary group founded by the Vichy regime with German aid. Some signed up because of regular pay, better rations and an exemption from forced labor in Germany, others because they had families or friends who had perished in Allied bombing raids. Some criminals, told that their sentences would be commuted, joined as well. Whatever their diverse backgrounds and motives, all had one thing in common: they relished rounding up, torturing and killing Jews *and résistants*. Decked out in their wide blue berets and uniforms of blue jackets and trousers and brown shirts, the members of the Milice roamed the countryside, where they had the advantage of speaking the language and knowing the people and the terrain.

The Kommandant, however, scorned the Milice troops despite their loyalty to his cause, dismissing them as brutal apes. It was one thing—a normal thing—to be against the enemy; quite another to apply excess zeal in their support. The French were so divided, he mused. Even the Resistance was split into several groups based on different political beliefs and modes of action.

Not for the first time, the Kommandant wondered about the French. What a puzzling country this was, he mused, with its long history, fabulous food and drink, formidable monuments, varied scenery and alluring women. The French didn't deserve such beauty. They were too unpredictable, flighty, quarrelsome and quick to anger. And yet, he had to admit, it was this contradictory combination of quirkiness, creativity, cold rationality and hot blood that made the country special.

As a soldier, he admired an enemy who could put up a good fight, and the resistance in this part of the country was fierce. The *résistants* could never win the war, though, if only because they were so disorganized and could never agree on anything.

Now Kommandant Walnitz drew himself up to his full height and spoke sternly to the mayor. "It is in your best interests to give us what we ask for—the faster the better, if you want to escape severe reprisals." His eyes were flat as he looked out the window at the crowd of men, women and children gathered in the square, guarded by so many armed soldiers they couldn't have made a run for it even if they tried. "I presume you want to protect your citizens," he added. The mayor nodded uneasily. "Then order everyone to remain here until all identity cards are checked." With that, he strutted off to oversee the soldiers going through the records, hunting for the Jews.

* * *

Séverine knew none of this when she arrived in the little town a couple of days later. At first sight Sorignac was the same as ever. The castle dominated—or protected, depending on who was doing the describing—the little village below, with its bevy of small shops clustered together, its town hall, police station, marketplace, church and schools.

But as she looked around, she was shocked to see that it wasn't the same at all. The German flag flew over the town hall and the police station. German soldiers milled around on foot or patrolled in jeeps. They went in and out of shops, they sat on the café terraces. While they went about their duties, townspeople formed long lines in front of the bakeries and butcher stores. The lines were composed mainly of women—many of the men were in the *maquis* or prisoners of war. Cars were scarce but bicycles were everywhere. Séverine vowed to get one for herself so she could get around more easily.

She knew she should hurry to the castle, where Gisèle would be waiting, but she wanted some time to reacquaint herself with the town. Plus, she wanted to pay a visit to Madame Decré. As she joined the queue in front of the bakery, she reflected that bread had taken on an importance it had not had when it was abundant and fetching it had just been one of the day's chores. The customers in the long queue clutched their ration cards; hers was somewhere else. It didn't matter. She wasn't there for the bread.

As the queue inched forward, she turned her head to see if she knew anyone. No one, not a soul. Strange, she reflected. Heading toward the bakery on a blue bicycle, though, was a tall, good-looking man she recognized immediately.

"Paul!" she cried out, causing people in the queue to turn and stare. She shrank slightly as the shabbily dressed villagers took in her brocaded blue velvet cape and matching blue beret and then turned resolutely back to the business at hand.

Paul braked his bike, leaned it against a wall and rushed to her.

"What are you doing here?" he cried breathlessly. "When did you come?" Aware of listening ears and inquiring eyes, he didn't ask her why she had returned to the little village at this particular time. And he didn't ask the obvious question: what was she doing alone?

"You know that Maman and Papa and Juliette and Julien would love to see you," he went on, his words tumbling out one after the other. "Do you have wheels? Can you come see us or should I come get you? Where are you staying?"

Séverine was reassured to see that although years had passed, Paul was the same as ever, always wanting to know everything right away but not in any particular order. "I don't have wheels yet," she said, smiling, "but of course I'll come see you. It's not that long a walk."

She didn't tell him she was staying in the castle. The

words her mother had uttered long ago echoed in her head: *Don't mention the castle. No one needs to know where you live*—the same words she had used to warn Séverine from the time she was old enough to travel the streets of Sorignac alone. She knew her mother meant well and wanted to protect her daughter from the villagers' jealousy, but following Germaine's advice had ultimately made things worse for Séverine, whose silence had been mistaken so often for snobbery.

But all that belonged to the past. What could it matter to anyone now, she asked herself? In wartime, the villagers, especially the women here today, had plenty of other things to think about—getting food, standing in long lines, raising children alone.

Still, Sorignac was a small place and although the people in line didn't know her and she didn't know them, the entire town would soon be aware that the woman who had grown up in the castle, gone to Paris to live, but returned to Sorignac for a wedding reception thrown by the countess had returned. Ah, the might of the Sorignac grapevine. How the news had traveled when the townspeople learned of her marriage at the castle to Antoine! Antoine… She knew she would have to face questions about what her illustrious husband was doing and why he hadn't come with her. She'd already decided to announce that he was ill and would join her later.

Grinning widely, Paul said, "I'll hold you to that." Then, telling her he needed to see a patient, he bade her farewell, dashed back to his bicycle and continued on up the road.

"See you soon, then!" Séverine called after him, waving. She turned her attention back to the queue but found herself suddenly ill at ease. The other women, she knew, had all heard her exchange with Paul. Now, one weary-looking young woman holding a baby and shifting her weight back and forth on her heels openly stared at her Parisian finery. She poked the arm of a friend, who turned to give Séverine a once-over. A wave of exhaustion washed over her. Although she had moved up several places in the line, she didn't want to be part of it any longer. She wanted more than anything to put some distance between herself and these envious, inquisitive harpies. She could see Madame Decré another time.

Now, she had another decision to make: which road should she take to the castle? When she was young, her parents had advised her not to take the street where Luc worked in his father's shoe shop. But of course she had, once or twice, and for doing so, had ended up with that annoying letter from Luc and the beautiful carving.

But why should she avoid that street now? She was a married woman, and her involvement with Luc ended long ago. She wanted to bury the past, emancipate herself from her little-girl life. Maybe Luc didn't even work in the shop any longer. And what could he do to her, anyway?

As she approached the street where Just's shop stood, she saw that the building was still decrepit but that the outside walls of the ground floor had been painted and a bright new sign had replaced the rusty old one. The window, featuring the tools of the trade and polished and repaired shoes and boots and bags, was so clean it was almost transparent.

She had counted on the window being as she remembered it—dirty, with cobwebs, making it impossible to see what was inside. Now, out of the corner of her eyes and without turning her head in his direction, she clearly saw Luc, standing at the counter chatting with a customer. She saw his copper hair, his blue jacket and corduroy trousers. She noted that he looked more relaxed, more clean-cut than he had on the long-ago day when she had been inside the shop and he had pressed the package with the little carving into her hands.

She passed the store quickly and let out a breath she hadn't realized she'd been holding. He wasn't the bogeyman. If she'd gone in, they'd have exchanged greetings and that would have been it. But there was no reason to do so.

In the brief moment she passed in front of the store, Luc saw her too. Like her, he didn't turn his head. He remained focused on his customer, but in his peripheral vision he had seen that the finely dressed woman who walked quickly and looked straight ahead was Séverine. He wondered what she was doing in town.

He blushed as he remembered the package, the letter and the carving. His expression hardened as he recalled the humiliation of her lack of response to his youthful declaration of love and his gift of the rabbit he had so carefully carved. He also remembered spying on her when she had returned to Sorignac for her wedding. He hadn't been invited, of course.

And now she had sailed past his shop without a word, a wave, a sign, or a hello.

He thought of his parents and glowered at the irony. They were poor and ignorant and jealous, and he had never wanted to believe a word they said about anything. But Just had been right about Séverine: "Too big for her britches."

* * *

As she walked up the road towards the castle, its solidity, its stateliness and grandeur struck her as it always had, even when she had lived there. In Paris, her dreams were filled with memories of its rooms, its smells, its atmosphere, its views, the way it had looked on her wedding day when she'd returned for the reception on the grounds. It had been and still was her home, and she couldn't wait to see Gisèle.

As she drew nearer, she played a favorite childhood game. She switched to the opposite sidewalk, then settled herself comfortably on a little stone ledge warmed by the sun, closed her eyes tightly, then opened them and looked straight ahead at the massive stone walls and the huge entry gate flanked by two towers. Her gaze traveled up to a high second-floor window. She could make out the curtains tied back on either side, and although that was all she could see from the street, she clearly envisioned the grand piano, the velvet-covered piano stool, the Louis XV chair on which Mr. Burgos would nervously shift back and forth while giving her piano lessons. She winced as she remembered the way he kept time by patting her on the back. She remembered the way the room looked at the end of the day with the sunlight pouring in through the western windows and the scent of the fresh red roses Gisèle arranged in vases around the room. She wondered if Gisèle had changed the furniture or rugs, and found herself hoping she had not.

Gisèle stood at the window of the music room, watching the young woman looking up at the castle. It had been nine years since Séverine had been married there, nine years in which they had corresponded but had not seen each other. Yet, even if Gisèle had not been able to make out her face, she would have known by her bearing that the young woman staring intently up at the castle was Séverine. Her protégée had always been proud, and it showed in the way she carried herself. Gisèle smiled to herself as she remembered how often she had ordered Séverine to straighten up.

No time for reminiscing, she admonished herself as she slid away from the window and descended the marble stairs to the ground floor.

"I am so happy you are here at last, Séverine!" she exclaimed, embracing her. "When I think that the last time I saw you was at your wedding!" She held Séverine at arm's length and immediately wished she could take back her remark: there were dark circles under Séverine's eyes, and the fact that Antoine was nowhere to be seen told her he was most likely the reason for her sadness, perhaps even for her return.

Gisèle hastily changed the subject. "Ah, but that was all so long ago. You must be tired, my dear. Those trains are ghastly. A friend of mine told me it took her twenty-four hours to get to Paris from here. Unbelievable! It's like traveling to China." She adjusted a button on her cashmere sweater, then launched into a soliloquy on the difficulty of getting food, the interminable lines at the local grocery store, the cheese shop, the butcher's and the bakery, and the merits of her own vegetable garden, which she and the count relied on.

Glancing around the vast foyer as she led Séverine to the library, Gisèle spoke so softly that Séverine could hardly hear her. "The Germans are here—and I do mean *here*." She threw a look full of meaning at Séverine, who waited for further explanation. "You're not my only guest," she explained, putting a finger to her lips. She grimaced, then threw up her hands in a gesture of resignation. "You know that we have no choice in such matters. A wing of the castle was requisitioned for the Kommandant. Officers get the best; the soldiers are staying in hotels in the town."

Once in the library with the door shut, Séverine also spoke in a low voice. "I saw the Germans in town," she replied. "But why are they here? Did something happen?"

"Well, if you ask them, they will say they are in the area to maintain law and order. But they are, of course, looking for Jews, communists and resisters. Around here, that adds up to a lot of people. In answer to your question, yes, a lot has happened. Many young and even not so young men—and a few women—have taken to the nearby forests to organize and train for actions against the occupiers. They're underequipped, but they know the terrain and

have been very successful at harassing the enemy by blowing up bridges, destroying munition factories, gathering
intelligence. The Germans have come here specifically to
put a stop to it."

She paused, looking troubled. "So, we've got the
maquisards against the Germans and the Milice, and the
Germans and the Milice against the *maquisards*. That's
one thing, and of course it's rather obvious. What's less
obvious is that given the general disorder, you don't know
who's killing whom." She glanced nervously at the library
door, as if she feared that her German guest might be on
the other side of it, listening. "A couple of weeks ago, a
man was executed, and his body was hung in the public
square. No one knows whose side he was on. And this sort
of thing happens a lot more than you would think."

She looked as if she were going to continue. Instead,
she said, "It's all very distressing. War is war. But you can't
begin to imagine the score settling going on. The war
seems to have given everyone a perfect pretext for dealing
once and for all with old feuds and personal vendettas that
have nothing to do with the Germans."

From the vantage point of her favorite, and in her opinion, only comfortable chair in the library, Séverine saw that
Gisèle had aged, but well. Dressed in her usual at-home
attire, a straight skirt and silk blouse with a cashmere
sweater thrown over her shoulders, she looked thinner
than usual, but with rationing, wasn't everyone? She must
wear gloves for gardening, Séverine reflected, looking at
her perfectly manicured smooth hands. Gloves... She
remembered their first encounter so many years ago, when
the countess had caught her in her dressing room snooping
in her drawers and inspecting, with great fascination, her
many pairs of gloves. At that time Séverine couldn't conceive of anyone having even one pair of leather gloves, let
alone dozens. And now, she herself had lots of them. And
a cheating, lying husband.

As the countess continued to talk, Séverine remembered the first time she'd been invited to tea with her. Then, as now, the countess had led and Séverine followed, mentor to student.

"I swear, Séverine, sometimes I think you were born into the wrong family," Caroline would tease her as she handed her a broom. "Don't forget to return to earth—it's your turn to sweep the floor."

Séverine snapped out of her reverie in time to pick up the end of Gisèle's sentence. "... infuriating and incredible. These *résistants* going around blowing up railroad tracks to stop the Germans from progressing—they're putting us all at risk. After the last episode, a bunch of Germans roared up the lane in their jeeps and barged right into the castle. They actually dared to push me aside, and then set about exploring every nook and cranny, convinced that we were harboring terrorists. The commander actually slapped me—*slapped* me, hard. It was a horrible experience." She shut her eyes briefly as though willing the memory away. "Oh, they were terrible. Rude and brutal. They opened all the cupboards upstairs to see what they might loot, then 'inspected' the cellar, where they had the nerve to open and swill some of our best bottles of wine. They would have hauled off the entire contents of the cellar if their leader hadn't put an end to their party.

"After that episode, I never wanted to see another German soldier on this property again. Now, though..." She crossed the room and turned up the volume on the radio. The soothing sound of chamber music filled the room. "You should see the things that go on in this village," Gisèle continued, warming to the subject. "In the name of fighting the Germans, some of the people in the Resistance have employed unusual methods, to say the least. Do you remember the Lafaure family, who have a big farm near town? They got a visit from a bunch of ruffians who forced them at gunpoint to 'contribute' an entire lamb and other provisions to the cause. This particular group was led by Luc Mestre, who's obviously found himself a new occupation. When he's not working in the shoe shop, he and his friends are busy requisitioning, or should I say holding up the villagers for money to fill the coffers for the cause of liberty. They do need money for arms and food, but they could get it another way, I'm sure. Luc even looks like he's prospering from the war. He's better dressed, more confident, and leads his troop of bandits with authority. At least the war has given him something to do. Fortunately, there are upright people like Paul…" Her voice trailed off.

She bent closer to Séverine and asked, "Do you know what I mean? I'm not supposed to know what anyone is doing, but I know that Georges and Paul are both engaged in the Resistance." Séverine gave her a questioning look, to which she replied, "Oh, I have no details, and I don't really want to know. Anyway, you don't hear about what people like Paul and Georges are doing because they keep a lower profile than Luc and his bullies, who roam the countryside forcing innocent citizens to hand over supplies and money.

"Anyway," she concluded, sitting back in her chair, "I've said enough, and we won't discuss this subject again. It's all so fatiguing and, I have to admit, rather frightening. I've made up my mind, though. If Luc's men come and use force to get food or supplies, they'll get nothing. *I'll* resist them and their odious techniques!"

She clapped her hands as if to force herself to finish and poured the now lukewarm tea. "What a way to welcome you," she said, shaking her head. "Enough of this. I shouldn't get so worked up. It's bad for my heart." She cleared her throat. "And you, my dear, no problems getting here?"

"Yes and no. In the beginning I didn't have a seat on the train, but this nice fellow who turned out to be from around here gave me his, so that was fine. I feared delays, accidents, or attacks, but the train got through and here I am!"

"And your parents. Are they well?"

"Maman and Papa and Caroline are well," Séverine said, puzzled that the countess hadn't asked about her sister. She added, "Thanks to you, Caroline is busily carving out a career as a hatmaker when she's not working on costumes at the theater. And Antoine," she continued brightly, avoiding Gisèle's gaze, "generally runs circles around me, but he's come down with something; I don't know what, some kind of stomach problem. He didn't want to travel in his condition, which is why I'm alone."

Gisèle acknowledged her fib with a nod and a word of sympathy. She was sure there was more to the story than that, but would never pry. Séverine would tell her what was wrong with Antoine when she felt like it.

The conversation was interrupted by a light rap on the door. Gisèle turned down the volume on the radio, then walked to the door, opened it and raised her voice.

"Séverine, let me introduce you to Kommandant Walnitz. He is staying in the west wing, not far from the music room which you know so well."

Gisèle employed the tone she used when wanting to dismiss someone while remaining courteous, and the officer picked up on it. He bowed slightly.

"Madame, I will not bother you with frequent requests, but speaking of music, I was wondering if you would mind my playing the piano—of course, at a time that would not inconvenience anyone."

"Please feel free, Kommandant. I would be delighted, as would my guest," Gisèle said. Briefly, she explained that Séverine had grown up in the castle and taken piano lessons for years.

Séverine found herself staring at the Nazi officer who,

with his military bearing, blue eyes and charisma, reminded her of Antoine. He looked so proper, but then so did
Antoine. She shuddered involuntarily. She wasn't sure, but
she had the impression the Kommandant actually clicked
his heels as he bowed his way out. She bit back a smirk.
As soon as the officer had left the room, Gisèle closed the
door, turned back to Séverine and quite naturally fell back
into her position as mentor. "Be careful, my dear. I saw the
expression on your face. We can't get rid of these people, so
no trouble, please. And don't fret about the piano. He's got
no time to play it."

* * *

The Kommandant's analysis of the French penchant for
disorganization—especially compared to his countrymen,
who were the masters of organization—was correct. As the
war continued, the Resistance grew, branching out into a
number of factions and movements as varied as the people
themselves. Paul and his father had joined the Secret Army,
a clandestine coalition led by the provisional government
in exile created in London in 1942 by Charles de Gaulle.
Secret Army actions were dangerous and secretive; neither
Paul nor his father ever spoke of them to anyone.

Another main Resistance group was the communists.
Both communist and non-communist *résistants* had the
same ultimate goal, which was to liberate the country from
the German occupiers. However, their ultimate goals for a
liberated, postwar France were totally opposed. The communists foresaw a "people's government" after the war, with
strong ties to Russia. The Gaullists foresaw a government
led by their hero, Charles de Gaulle, who would work with
the Allies to construct an independent France.

Luc had joined the communist resistance. He had

become a Party member mainly because his father had been one. Before the war broke out he had been ambiguous, wondering about believers in general and about the belief and faith of his cell boss, Pierre, in particular. He was amazed by the man's stalwart convictions and his strict adherence to the Party line. Luc himself, on the other hand, felt he was a communist in the same way he imagined some people were Catholic: they went to church and participated in all the rituals, more out of tradition than anything else. He attended cell meetings and participated in discussions, but for the most part his heart wasn't in it.

For one thing, he didn't buy into that credo about the dictatorship of the proletariat. His thoughts about money and property and owners were certainly not communist. He liked making money. He liked buying nice things. He would have loved to own a house and a fine car, one like the convertible that Séverine's husband had driven into Sorignac. He even liked the idea of moving up the social scale. His dream was to have a chain of shoe repair stores someday, with many employees, of whom he of course would be the boss.

Pierre had warned him more than once about turning into a bourgeois capitalist, but he didn't really have to worry. Luc would, it was true, spin off into a dream world in which he was a rich boss—and then plunge back into reality. He was the underdog and always would be. You couldn't belong to the Mestre family and escape the family fate. He knew he would have to move far away to shake off the reputation of his father, who was lazy and uneducated and never paid his bills if he could help it. He would fantasize about living elsewhere and making up a past in which he came from a grand family, a family with famous ancestors and fine manners and money. In that scenario, he would also have had a good education, which wasn't the case. But that make-believe had nothing to do with real life.

Luc vacillated between his working-class condition and his bourgeois aspirations until the day Pierre decided to take him in hand. He made him study the strikes of 1936 when, for the first time, French workers had occupied factories all over the country. Pierre figured that when Luc learned about their struggles, their enthusiasm, their force and fight and strength of conviction, he would see he was part of something larger than himself.

"It's true that you're alone in your shop," Pierre told the young man. "But even so, you need to know about these movements, to be inspired by them. You need to see that the working class can and did arise and demand its rights. Thanks to the Popular Front, we now have paid vacations and a forty-hour work week. We can no longer be exploited. You must never be ashamed of being a worker, and you must always think and act in solidarity with the working class."

Luc, who rarely talked, was so inspired by Pierre's confidence in him that he offered a confession in the form of a question.

"What if you're a working-class man and you're attracted to, even in love with, a bourgeoise?"

"That's impossible," Pierre retorted. "You would betray the ideals of your class." He squinted at Luc. "That worker wouldn't be you, would it?"

From the rigidity of Pierre's pose and the stern tone of his voice, Luc knew the answer he had to give. "No," he stated firmly, "It was an idea I had, that's all."

"Don't get too many ideas," Pierre warned him.

When the war broke out, he took Luc aside once again, almost as if he were confiding a secret. "You know, Luc, that the ultimate goal of the Party is to take the reins after the liberation of France."

Luc liked the idea of being in power, as Pierre well knew. And he liked the attention he got from Pierre. At last, he reflected, someone believed in him! He wondered why, what he had done to deserve his attention and support, but didn't ask. Instead, he strove to satisfy, even gratify, his mentor.

Pierre, for his part, was pleased by the converted Luc, who no longer entertained doubts about his faith in the Party. He observed that Luc was adept at requisitioning money, supplies and other goods "for the cause" no matter the method—and looked the other way.

Luc occasionally wondered if his strong-arm tactics might eventually harm his business after the war, but time after time, he brushed his doubts aside; all was fair, he told himself, if it was in the service of the Party—and himself.

* * *

As Luc caught a glimpse of Paul Moreau opening the door of a bar in the center of town, he crossed the street and followed him in. He bought himself a beer and then strolled casually over to Paul, feigning surprise as he greeted him. The two men quickly sized each other up. As usual, Luc was struck by Paul's unassuming nature and self-confidence. He looked reassuring. No wonder he had so many patients, he told himself. He thought of how his family had always taken Georges, then Paul, for granted. But what could he say to him? "Sorry that I grew up in a roguish, shifty family. It's not my fault." Well, it wasn't, he kept telling himself.

Paul looked up as Luc approached and remarked to himself that Luc looked more self-assured than he had when he was younger; then, he could never look anyone in the eyes, never mind speak to them. He had heard about Luc's involvement in his communist cell, and had heard outraged citizens complain of being harassed for a "contribution" to the group's resistance efforts. Paul disapproved, but being a doctor had taught him tolerance for most kinds of human behavior—aside, of course, from that of the hated and hateful Vichy Milice. At least Luc was on the right side.

In any case, he figured he knew as much about Luc's resistance activities as Luc knew about his, which was nothing. Clandestine activities were exactly that—clandestine. Paul and his father had joined the Secret Army shortly after Georges had been dismissed from his duties at a nearby hospital because he was a Freemason and hence on Vichy's list of undesirables. The loss of income "wasn't good," Georges had told Paul in an understatement, but it reinforced his conviction that the country needed to get rid of the poisonous ideology and brutality of the Nazis and Vichy. Both he and Paul were now more determined than ever to do whatever they could to vanquish the hated enemy.

"So, how's your war effort going?" Luc asked Paul who was sipping his beer.

Paul pretended not to understand. "Well, you know that as doctors, we treat any and all wounded, so if I were told to bandage the entire German Army, I'd have to do it. Hippocratic Oath, you know." He took another sip of the beer, but Luc reflected that he drank like a doctor: he knew that one beer would be Paul's limit. "That doesn't mean I'd like it."

"And you? How's business?" Paul hoped his question would get them off the subject of the war and the Resistance and the elephant in the room, which was that the Germans had arrived in town in force.

Luc took a long draw of his drink and plunked the glass down on the counter. He sensed Paul didn't want to talk. "Oh, I'm doing all right. I repair the occasional shoe, sell a shoelace from time to time." Paul reached into his pocket for some change to pay the bill, but Luc waved him away. "It's on me today," he said, ignoring the look of astonishment on Paul's face.

Luc stared at Paul's back as he exited the bar. Some people had it all—looks, money, talent. The two weren't of the same world. Yet Paul treated Luc with equanimity. There was no familiarity, no fake friendliness, but there was also no condescension. From the time he was a boy, Luc had loved to pretend he had a father like Paul's—a calm guide, a moral compass. How different his life would have been. Well, Pierre at least believed in him. He shrugged his shoulders and ordered another beer.

Chapter TWENTY-FOUR

Huguette embraced Séverine, then drew back a few steps to get a good look at her.

"What a sophisticated Parisienne you've become," she remarked, taking in Séverine's city clothes, a purple and white striped blouse and purple skirt, completed by a shocking pink turban and heels. Purple and pink. Only Séverine could carry that off, she mused.

"If I'm a sophisticated Parisienne, it's entirely due to Caroline, who gets the least expensive and most fabulous material from various places in Paris—don't ask me where—and then goes to work on them. She made this hat, you know, and even wants to make a business out of her hobby. I'm glad someone in our family has artistic talent. As for my heels, they are Wartime Specials, as you see, concocted from the finest cork available!" Smiling, she extended a foot to show Huguette.

"Well, you may look like a worldly Parisienne, but you haven't lost your sense of humor," Huguette proclaimed. "Georges will be so happy to see you." She turned as Georges hurried into the room. "Look, Georges, at what a city girl Séverine has become." She re-examined Séverine's outfit, comparing it to the plainer clothes of her daughter-in-law Juliette. Juliette couldn't measure up to this finery, and that was too bad, but Juliette was sweet and respectful, and a good mother. Séverine was not always sweet, nor was she always respectful, Huguette mused, and who knew what kind of mother she would be. All she knew was that if given a choice between the two young women, she would rather have Juliette as her daughter-in-law than Séverine. She was glad she had done everything in her power to make that happen.

"My dear girl." Georges embraced her warmly. "You can't know how happy we are to see you and have you back with us a while. Are you staying long? And where?"

"I'm staying for as long as I can," Séverine replied. "And for the moment at least, I'm at the castle but I don't want to wear out my welcome so ..." Her voice trailed off. "We'll see."

"How is the countess?" Huguette asked. "We hardly ever see her."

"The countess is still the countess," Séverine replied equably, suspecting that Huguette was jealous. Knowing how much the woman would love to know about what was going on in the castle, she added, enigmatically, "Rather regal." She smiled. Huguette would have to settle for that.

"I can see why you wouldn't want to impose on her for too long, and I am sure you wouldn't want to stay away from that striking husband of yours for too great a spell either," Huguette replied. "I do believe he turned the heads of every woman in this village. They're still talking about what a suave pair you made at your wedding." She added, as if it were an afterthought, "No children yet? I'm sure your parents ask you that regularly. Grandchildren are such a blessing." She fiddled with her pearl necklace and awaited the response.

"They must be," Séverine replied, wondering, once again, how Huguette could spring for the jugular so artfully. She had always had a second sense of what would hurt her opponents the most, but to her credit she would drop the subject once she'd seen the arrow hit its target.

"Well, let's sit down and catch up," said Huguette. "Georges, do get us some drinks and try to see where Paul is."

"He's here," Paul said, as he walked into the room. "For heaven's sakes, Séverine, when I said you should come see us, I didn't mean the next day!"

Georges and Huguette watched as the two immediately began to chatter as though they'd never been apart. Georges loved seeing them together this way and had to admit that while Paul and Juliette were compatible, it was nothing like this. Huguette's face darkened momentarily, and then brightened suddenly as Julien, who looked uncannily like a miniature version of Paul, entered the salon with his mother.

Shaking Séverine's hand politely, Julien took a seat near Georges, who was now comfortably ensconced in "his" chair beside a low table on which sat a puzzle he and Julien had been completing. Juliette remained near the door, watching the lively exchange between Séverine and Paul—an exchange that died down as soon as she entered the room.

Séverine turned to look at her and noticed not what Juliette and Paul did, but what they didn't—they didn't move close to each other, they didn't make eye contact, they didn't joke with each other.

Juliette spoke in a soft, almost inaudible voice. "How are you, Séverine? Are you back here for long? You look like such a city lady now. Not like us country folks." Her eyes were half-closed as if she were drowsy and needed a nap; there was an odd timbre to her speech.

Huguette sped to the rescue. "Now Juliette, you know you and your girlfriends here always look fine, as fine as women can look when a war is on and we are deprived of so many goods."

Juliette looked at her placidly, nodded her head, and sat down on the sofa, where she reached into a basket and pulled out a boy-size navy-blue sweater she was knitting. On the other side of the room, Georges and Paul were engaged in an earnest conversation with Julien. Huguette sat by herself, admiring her family. For a moment Séverine felt like an outsider who had invaded private territory. She wondered again about the change in Juliette, whom she'd always seen as a sweet and simple girl, utterly devoted to Paul. She didn't look devoted now. She looked uninterested and sleepy. In fact, she looked like part of the furniture.

Huguette glanced at her watch, stood up and briskly signaled the end of their visit. "Séverine, now that you're back in town, you must come see us more often. We'll make sure that we all get together. Like old times, isn't that right, Juliette?"

Juliette barely looked up from her knitting. "Yes, *Mère*," she repeated mechanically. "Like old times."

As Séverine rose to leave, Julien detached himself from his father and grandfather and planted himself solemnly before her.

"You're a pretty lady."

"And you," Séverine replied, as she contemplated his engaging expression and soft brown eyes, which were so much like Paul's, "are a world-class charmer." Like your father, she thought, and wondered if anyone in the room was reading her mind.

* * *

"How did you get out of your mother's clutches? I swear, she still acts as if I'm going to snatch you away!" Séverine called out as she pedaled uphill beside Paul on the bike she'd borrowed from Gisèle. For the moment, she could still carry on a conversation because they were close enough to hear each other, but it wouldn't be long before he left her behind. In their younger days, they were always racing, and she had even managed to beat him a few times. She realized now, though, that while she might be good at running up and down the steps of the *métro*, Paul was used to bicycling all around the village and beyond to see patients. He wasn't even out of breath.

"My mother's clutches! Séverine, you know I've never been in her clutches even though she is—let's say—ever-present. Hey, my dear Parisian friend, if you come back to the village and start insulting me right away, I won't be your bike partner anymore," he teased. "And it looks like you're going to need me to push you up these dinky hills!"

"'Ever-present.' I love it! How is she with Juliette, by the way?"

"Oh," he replied breezily, "they get along famously. Juliette loves learning about how to run a household. My mother loves to teach her everything she knows—how to fold clothes, throw a dinner party, make a cherry pie, keep the men in the family in line..." He raised his eyebrows as high as they would go, wiggling them to make her react, and was surprised when she didn't.

They pedaled in silence for a few more minutes until they reached Sainte-Eulalie, the hamlet they had always ridden to as children, where they dismounted and parked their bikes against the wall of the little stone church.

"You know, this must be the hundredth time we've done this," he remarked.

"The hundredth? Are you kidding? We came here on average at least twice a week for ten years. That probably makes it closer to a thousand."

"I didn't know you'd acquired such rapid calculating skills. You've improved a lot." Paul started to rib her, then stopped as he watched Séverine turn her back to the church and walk in the opposite direction to the cemetery across the road.

"You're not going inside?" he asked, surprised.

"No, God and I are on rather shaky terms these days."

"You know I don't care much about religion, but isn't that even more of a reason to get down on your knees, pay your respects, talk things out, ask something of a saint, or whatever it is you do in there?" he inquired.

"Maybe someday, maybe even soon, but right now I'd rather talk to you." She made her way to the bench they used to share against the back wall of the graveyard. They loved that particular spot because it was hidden behind a row of tall cypress trees that acted as a shield, allowing them to see without being seen. "It's been too long. I've missed your horrible jokes and your impertinent questions. I'm dying to sit here and talk to you like we always used to do. I think we must have discussed every subject in the world."

"I think we did. Of course you gabbed so much I can't even remember what we discussed. But I did miss your chatter," Paul joked. Then his expression grew serious. "You can cut your act out now—carefree, happy, up in the air. I'm a doctor, remember, and have been trained to look at what's troubling people. I ask them where they hurt and how much and how long and since when. What's ailing you, Séverine? You come here all by yourself at one of the worst times since the war began and tell us that your dashing jeweler husband has a stomachache. Surely you can do better than that."

When she remained silent, he persisted. "You don't go back on childhood promises, do you? We vowed to always tell each other the truth, so you owe it to me." He took her hand and, in a gentler voice, he asked, "Don't you think so?"

She nodded her head in agreement. "Remember when you asked me to marry you all those years ago? I can't decide if it's a good thing you were kidding or a bad one. It looks like I might not be the marrying kind." A tinge of irritation entered her voice as she added, "By the way, if I had known this was going to be one of our truth sessions, I wouldn't have come."

She was quiet for a moment, and Paul waited patiently. Then, in spite of her declaration, she continued, "I know nothing escapes you, Paul, and was planning to tell you about why I'm here. As you probably have already surmised, things aren't going well with Antoine. I'll spare you the details. Let's say that I'm here because I need time to think things over, away from my life in Paris." She pulled on a blade of grass and contemplated it. "Nothing's perfect, right? Is your life perfect?"

Paul lit a cigarette and inhaled deeply as he pondered her question. Séverine was the only one who put him on the spot. In his family he was the adored son, husband and father. In the village he was the young and personable doctor who had a kind word for all. Those people respected him, admired him, even loved him, but Séverine had always been the only one who wanted to know more about him and his feelings, to explore beneath the surface. She had always put blunt questions to him and refused to accept a false-sounding or tossed-off answer. She made him think.

Most assuredly nothing was perfect. The war, for example. It would be perfect if this war were over. He could do without it. But who had a choice? He thought about the various ways in which his compatriots reacted to being overrun by the German occupiers, who had taken the best of everything for themselves, leaving only the crumbs for everyone else to squabble over. Some—though admittedly not that many—had immediately found the situation untenable and entered into resistance and defiance. They printed anti-German flyers on hidden presses, gave the Germans false information, even if it was only false directions, observed a rule of silence and refused to converse with them. Others wholeheartedly embraced Vichy and the occupiers, joining collaborationist political parties and embracing the new national motto of "Work, Family, Fatherland." There were extremes at both ends of the spectrum. The *résistants* ranged from ordinary people performing simple acts in their daily lives to those performing dangerous, risky missions. The collaborationists ranged from those who verbally supported the Vichy regime and its ideas to those who took on some form of military engagement.

In between those citizens were the vast majority, who dealt with the travails of the war on a daily basis but didn't take a stand. That was impossible for Paul and Georges. From the beginning, they had quite naturally gravitated towards doing everything they could to counter Pétain. That included, but was by no means restricted to, risky night missions to help British planes land in designated fields outside the village, finding hiding places for the British soldiers and treating their wounds.

And now the Nazis were in Sorignac itself, engaging in roundups and making arrests. The only thing to do was to continue working, keep a low profile, and offer help when needed.

As far as his family went, he and Juliette got along in spite of what was euphemistically referred to as "her problem", and he adored their son. He had never been unfaithful to his wife. They were by all accounts a good couple. But was that enough? Being here once again with Séverine, he found himself lightening up in a way he never could with Juliette. Maybe it was old habit: he and Séverine could read each other's minds, had the same sense of humor and laughed over things only they found funny—Paul's imitation of a cow or her cruel mimics of certain pretentious village characters.

He studied Séverine. Today she wore no makeup, had let her long hair down and was wearing some kind of odd skirt that she informed him was actually a pair of trousers. She looked so natural, as good as or even better than the last time he had seen her in what must have been an extremely costly wedding dress, her face made up and her hair pulled back in a chic chignon.

Why had he been obsessing about her ever since she arrived, he asked himself? If only she'd stayed away… Unbidden, an image of the two of them as young children unfolded in his mind. As if it were a scene in a movie, he watched the two eight-year-olds sitting in the woods pricking each other's fingers with a needle until blood came. They had vowed to be blood friends forever.

He wanted to freeze that moment in time, keep it with him always. He also wanted to stay in the cemetery behind the cypress trees with her forever; it was ridiculous, a wild dream of course, but that was the effect Séverine had on him. At this very moment he wanted nothing more than to take her in his arms. That was also on the order of fantasy: they had been friends for years and he had never even kissed her. Only once—on her wedding day, ironically—had he physically communicated his interest in her. It wasn't a kiss on her lips—how inappropriate that would have been! No, he had taken her hands in his so ardently that he had felt it as the prelude to a different relationship. He was certain she had felt it too, but there had been no time to ask…

Short of a kiss, he wanted to comfort her now, to tell her that indeed nothing is perfect. He wanted to joke about her not taking him up on his offer of marriage all those years ago, an offer he himself had known was impossible, first of all because he'd been too young and hadn't finished his studies, and secondly, because Huguette would have put up too many obstacles to their happiness. At the time, he had blurted out his proposal without thinking. Now he was thinking too much.

As usual, Séverine read his mind. "You're not answering my question because the answer is complicated, right? Why don't we leave it there and enjoy ourselves? And by the way, your mother can relax, Paul. You and I have always been and will always be best friends." She crossed her index and middle fingers and held them up to him. "We're as close as this, and nothing Huguette can do or say will change that. But we *are* both married, and I think we'd better get out of here. Someone might see us and start talking—not that I care, but you should. The incredibly handsome married village doctor with the sophisticated married lady from Paris…Can you see how tongues would wag?"

Reluctantly, Paul stood and pulled her up from the bench. He wanted to hold her close, run his fingers through her thick dark hair, lift her face to his and kiss her. Why had he never done it before? Instead, he mounted his bike and waited for her to get on hers.

"People gossip no matter what you do in this village," he acquiesced, turning to take a look at the face he knew so well. He loved everything about it: the full, sensuous lips, the porcelain complexion that would redden so suddenly, the expressive brown eyes that were a constant thermometer of her emotions.

"Damn it!" he exclaimed, dismounting his bike and pulling her away from hers.

"What?" Séverine asked. "What are you doing?"

"Here's what I'm doing." He drew her close to him, kissed her tenderly, then stood back. "That's something I should have done years ago."

"We," Séverine corrected him. "That's something *we* should have done years ago."

"Then," he said, lifting up her chin and looking at her expectantly, "shall we make up for all that lost time and give those tongues something to wag about?"

* * *

"Do you think we'll go to hell?" Séverine asked rhetorically, lying back in the grass and fiddling with the buttons on her blouse. She raised her head slightly and looked around the silent, empty graveyard. "I mean, isn't there something sacrilegious about making love in a cemetery?"

"Not if you don't get caught. Thank God there was no funeral today. You are so beautiful, Séverine." Paul helped her with a recalcitrant button, then stroked her cheeks and kissed her eyes. "I never dreamed this would happen. I guess I wouldn't allow myself to. You said nothing's perfect, but this was. Don't you agree?"

"Pure perfection, even on this hard ground. And you're right. It's a good thing we didn't get caught." She stretched her arms lazily above her head. "We are totally immoral, and I loved every second of it and want more and more."

"You can't know how long I've wanted to hold you in my arms."

"How long? And tell me, if that's true, why didn't you?"

"You can figure that one out, can't you, Séverine? When you left town, I don't know why, but I was convinced you were coming back. But you didn't, and time went by and we both got married—and there you are. By the way, did I tell you how much I wanted to punch your daredevil husband's face at your wedding reception?" He thought for a moment. "Maybe I should have."

"We had such a tender moment in the cellar before we got interrupted. I never dreamed there could be so much love in a simple kiss of the hand." Paul drew in a breath—so she had felt it, too. "I could have stayed down there with you forever. But I was distracted, thinking about other things, such as, for example, why my husband of only a few hours was paying so much attention to every woman but me."

"I wondered about that as well. Is that why you're here? You don't have to tell me if you don't want to, but I kind of suspect that he's not the easiest man to live with, unless you can turn a blind eye to his womanizing."

Séverine was silent.

"Have I said too much?" he said. "I'm sorry, but we're both adults, so we might as well talk things out, not hide things from each other."

Séverine moved closer to him, put her hand on his arm. "We have so much to catch up on. I told you I'd spare you the details, but I've changed my mind. You and I have to tell each other everything. I want to hear about you and Juliette as well. It's not easy for either of us."

She reached across him to grab a cigarette, but he quickly stopped her. "No, you don't. I know everyone smokes, including me, but I think it makes women look tough. And you're not."

"You're right. I probably smoke too much anyway. You know, I light up when I'm upset—and these days that's almost constantly—but also when I'm relaxed, which is right now. Anyway, I don't need a cigarette. I need to be with you."

She looked at Paul's expectant face, took a deep breath and began. "Well, here's my story. I can't keep this from you, of all people, and I don't want to. I was quite young when I met Antoine. It was right after I had left Sorignac and you and everything I loved. What can I say? He was engaging and exciting. He took me everywhere, gave me a whirlwind introduction to a milieu where everyone is glamorous and the only concern is for having fun. Oh, sure, I grew up in the castle and was coddled by the countess, but her world was not at all like his. I guess you would call his world *nouveau riche*, whereas the countess believes it's vulgar to show off or to talk about money. She has her charities, of course, and people rely on her for help, but she doesn't talk about it. But in Antoine's circle of friends I saw nothing like that.

"I have to admit that in spite of the class difference between our families, he was always good to mine. But to get to the point, what happened was that the more I was with him, the more I realized that I had no overwhelming ambition other than to settle down and have a family. All I wanted was a child of my own—you have one, so you know how precious that is. But he kept stalling until one day he said outright that it wasn't going to happen. I persisted in believing that he'd change, and that I'd make it happen; I couldn't accept life without a child. I became so focused on my goal that I overlooked a lot of signs—like unfamiliar perfume on his shirts, and one day a long strand of red hair in my own bed."

Her eyes flashed with indignation. "Then, recently, I saw Antoine at the park with a boy about Julien's age who looked exactly like him, and I mean *exactly* like him. The child called him 'Papa'. And that's why I'm here. You see, he already had his child."

Paul's eyes were wide, and he was silent for a moment. "For God's sake, Séverine. What a liar. What a cad. And here I had you pegged as being up there in Paris living the good life. I'm so, so sorry." He pulled her closer to him. "Babies," he murmured. "I'd love to people this world with little Séverines and little Pauls."

"It wouldn't be possible. They'd be too perfect, too smart, too good-looking," she retorted before changing the subject. "Now it's your turn. Tell me about Juliette. By the way, I even forgave you for marrying her instead of me, but then who was I to defy your indomitable *mère*?" she added, watching for his reaction. "You know as well as I do that I am capable of standing up to Huguette, going against her will. But I wasn't going to fight for you if you weren't going to fight for me. And you didn't. Anyway, at the time we were both too young and didn't know much about anything, did we?"

Paul listened carefully. What she said about being so young and about his inability to take a stand, to fight for her, was on the mark. He gently pulled Séverine up and brushed the leaves and blades of grass off her clothes and hair.

"I'm serious, so listen to me, Séverine. We'll talk about my mother whenever you want. We'll talk about the past whenever you want. I think we'll end up agreeing with your conclusion: that we were both so young, too young. But for the moment I'm going to tell you something you should know. I guess when you were at our house yesterday you could see the problem with Juliette."

"I saw she was in a strange state. Is she expecting?" Séverine asked.

"No," he said, emphatically. "Most certainly not. I don't want a baby with all the problems that go with an alcoholic mother." He saw the look of surprise on her face, then plowed doggedly on. "She's fine some days, but on others she can barely take care of Julien." He lit a cigarette now and took a long drag. "Juliette started to drink when Julien was a baby. I don't know. Maybe it was my fault. I was away during the week at medical school and not at home to help her when she was tired, although she had my mother. Apparently, that wasn't enough. Or, now that I think about it, perhaps it was too much. She told me I was the one she wanted to help her, that she felt like she was imprisoned, that she didn't have a life. She doesn't seem to understand that between consultations in the office and house visits, I can't be with her all the time the way she wants.

"But let's not waste our time together with that." He looked at his watch. "I've got to go. Same time, same place tomorrow?" Séverine nodded in agreement. "But let's come separately. People might start wondering." They kissed, not

timidly or cautiously as they had the first time, but ardently and avidly. They teetered as they stood, locked in each
other's arms, until they separated and cycled reluctantly
back to town.

* * *

Paul whistled all the way home. It was the first time since
Séverine had left for Paris that he had felt such energy,
love, desire and good humor. How barren, how empty, his
life had been. Julien had been his sole source of happiness
until Séverine had turned up, and he hadn't even realized
it.

He was wondering how to conceal his obvious joy and
sexual exaltation, something he had never felt with Juliette,
when he wheeled into the courtyard and saw his mother
step out the front door. She looked distraught, as if she
were looking for someone. Him.

"Juliette's not well," she announced. "Not well" was the
family euphemism for very drunk. "You'd better go see her
right away." But he didn't need to, for Juliette had appeared
behind Huguette, sloppily dressed with her blouse hanging
outside her skirt, her hair disheveled, a leer on her face.

She no longer showed the lethargy that Séverine had
noted. On the contrary, she flew at Paul in a rage, yelling
insults, kicking and even biting him as he strong-armed
her in an attempt to get control.

"Been with the bitch, eh?" she slurred, freeing herself
from his hold. "Couldn't wait until I had my back turned.
Think I didn't see the way you two looked at each other?
Inviting that slut into a respectable home," she sneered.
"You couldn't wait to get out of this house and be alone.
It was written all over your lustful faces. D'you think that
'cause I'm a lush I don't see?" She let out a string of chilling,

hysterical shrieks that quickly descended into a volley of sobs interspersed with hiccups.

Julien, alarmed by the commotion, ran up beside her now, and she grabbed him, placing him like a shield in front of her. "Go with her, if that's what you want. You've always neglected me, so your absence wouldn't make much difference. But I won't make you a gift of a divorce. Oh no! No divorce—and Julien will stay with me and never see you again." As if to accentuate her words, she clutched the little boy tightly, making him cry out.

Paul's heart sank as he watched his son realize that whatever his mother was doing, it wasn't a game. The child looked bewildered and frightened and when she stopped rocking back and forth and almost fell, releasing him inadvertently, he rushed to the safety of his father's arms.

"Papa, what's the matter with Maman? Why is she making those funny noises? Why is she shouting?"

"Maman's overtired, *mon petit*. She needs to rest. Be a good fellow and go with your grandmother. If you ask her nicely, I bet she'll make you her special hot chocolate with the foam."

The doctor part of him took over now as he put his arm around Juliette, who had slumped to the ground. He dragged her to her room and tucked her into bed, then stood back and watched her as she began to snore, a deep, throaty sound like an animal suffering. Perhaps he should send her to an institution to dry out, he thought unhappily. He was amazed he hadn't had the idea before, despite being a doctor, but then Séverine hadn't been here to give him a new perspective on a life he no longer wanted.

* * *

As Séverine made her way back through town towards the castle, she wondered how she would mask the ecstasy and boundless happiness she felt. She knew she was wearing a huge smile on her face; she couldn't help it. It must be so evident that she had made love only a short time ago. In a way, she didn't care. She wanted the world to know.

She stopped at the florists to buy a bouquet of spring flowers for Gisèle. She knew Gisèle would be embarrassed, that the countess continued to think of her as the daughter of her former employees, which was true, and poor, which was not. Séverine wondered if she would say "No, you shouldn't have," which, she had told Séverine, was impolite to utter when receiving a gift. We'll see if she remembers her own advice, Séverine thought.

Her next stop was the bookstore; she wanted to give a book to Julien, who reminded her so much of Paul at the same age. She considered a recipe book. After all, he surely must have been in the kitchen watching or helping his father with his hobby. On the other hand, he might not be interested in cooking at all, in which case the book would be useless. In addition, she couldn't sign it "To dear Julien from Séverine" as she would like, because she wouldn't want Juliette or Huguette to know it was a present from her.

As she was contemplating other possibilities, she came across a book of recipes for chocolate desserts, only chocolate desserts. She knew that the boy loved chocolate—she'd seen him dip into a box when she was at the house—and was sure that if he himself didn't make the recipes, Paul or Huguette would. She was wickedly delighted at the idea of Huguette using a recipe book that had come from her. In any case, the point was not the gift; it was the idea behind it. She loved the father; she loved the son. She would give Julien's present to Paul tomorrow.

Gisèle saw Séverine skipping up the steps to the

entrance of the castle and hurried to greet her. "I haven't seen you so lighthearted since you were a child," she remarked, looking at Séverine curiously.

Séverine thrust the bouquet of flowers into her hands. She waited for the countess to break her rule and say "Oh, you shouldn't have," but of course she didn't. True to form, she thanked Séverine graciously and said the blossoms were exactly what she needed for the dining room.

They walked together to the ground-floor library, where a servant had set up a linen-covered table with the silver tea set that Séverine had always admired. She caught herself thinking it was so good to be back home, and realized that this was indeed her home. Paul, the countess, the castle—what more did she need?

"That's a dreamy look on your face, my dear," the countess remarked. "Are you that happy to be here?"

"Oh, I am. You can't imagine. I think I'll even go up to the music room and play the piano later on, if you don't mind."

"Mind? That's your room and your piano. I'd be delighted and honored. And perhaps, but only if it's not too presumptuous of me to ask, you might perform at a party I'm planning in a few days?"

"Certainly. I would be happy to," Séverine promptly answered, as she smiled to herself. Nothing had changed. Gisèle's last sentence with the "perhaps" was not a question, but an order: Séverine was to perform at her party. But Séverine didn't mind. She loved the countess and understood her way of speaking in codes—the artful way she had of getting you to do what she wanted you to do without overtly asking. Were there jobs available for people who could translate countess-language into ordinary language, she wondered? After growing up in the castle, she was sure she would be the perfect candidate.

"May I borrow your bicycle again tomorrow?" Séverine

asked, remembering that she needed wheels so she could meet Paul again.

"Why do you ask?" Gisèle countered. "The bicycle is yours for as long as you are here, and I hope that will be a good, long time."

"So do I," Séverine murmured. "So do I."

* * *

Séverine pedaled effortlessly up the hill, thinking of Paul. The prospect of seeing, feeling, hearing, smelling, touching and tasting him made her feel airy, buoyant and light, almost heady.

At the church, she flung her bike up against the wall, marveling at her energy, and ran to their meeting place.

He wasn't there. She looked at her watch. She was on time, and he was always a little late. Nothing to worry about. She imagined herself as he would see her, dressed in red, her hair in a loose chignon waiting to be undone. She stretched her arms above her toward the towering pine trees and the sky. She felt happy and peaceful.

Paul appeared from somewhere behind her, dressed not in casual clothes but a suit. The way he approached her—slowly, almost woodenly—and his downturned lips and somber eyes frightened her.

"What's wrong? What's the matter? Has something happened?" She instantly thought of Julien. Perhaps there had been an accident?

She started to take off the lightweight shawl she had thrown over her shoulders, but he stopped her.

"Keep your wrap on. I'm not staying." His voice was hoarse, different. "I… I thought about yesterday. I was wrong. I have to stay with my family. I'm not free to love you, and I can't ask you to wait for me."

Séverine stood totally still and silent, as if paralyzed.

Paul moved closer but didn't touch her. She could see his eyes, immense with sorrow.

"I am so, so sorry, Séverine," he said softly. "You'll never know how sorry I am."

And then he went away.

* * *

First there had been Antoine in the Tuileries, in a race with a son she did not know he had. She had watched him and the boy, all the time thinking it was an illusion, a hallucination, a fantasy.

Now it was Paul. She tried to remember his words: *I'm not free to love you, and I can't ask you to wait for me.* What did that mean? Why had he said that? What had changed? Was she dreaming once again?

She felt herself go cold. She sank down heavily on the bench, contemplated the ground where they would have made love once again, then got up and mechanically headed back to her bicycle. She supposed she'd go home to the castle. But she suddenly realized that without Paul, Sorignac was no longer home.

As she cycled back to town, partially blinded by the afternoon sun, she became angrier and angrier—with herself, with Antoine, with Paul, with life itself. She rode furiously, her eyes fixed on the handlebars. When she finally looked up, she saw a huge column of black smoke hanging over the valley below. Some farmer was burning his fields, she supposed, or maybe a barn had caught on fire. But she wasn't that curious. She had too much on her mind.

She slowed down as she realized she had no place to go that was hers, no one to go home to. She looked at her existence in a way she never had before. The only person she could count on in the village was Gisèle. But she was no longer a child, and while she loved and looked up to her, Gisèle couldn't solve her adult problems. Antoine had betrayed her; Paul had failed her. She recoiled at the irony of it all: Antoine had no sense of responsibility. Paul had too much.

She stepped off the bicycle and stood there, shaking with chagrin and fury, sorrow and pain. She wheeled it off the roadway, then knelt down on a patch of grass in the cool shade of a tree, wiped the sweat off her brow, and wept over Antoine's cold-blooded betrayal, Paul's startling, incomprehensible rejection, the wasted years, her child-lessness and the utter emptiness of her life.

After a while her sobs subsided, and she straightened up and wiped her cheeks dry. No, she vowed, she would never trust or depend on a man again. She needed to act, to make a plan. She would return to the castle, pack her bags and leave for Paris, where Caroline would take her in while she tried to sort things out. But how do you sort things out when you've been fooled by the two most important men in your life? How do you have what you most want in life—a child—when there's no one to have it with? The thought of Antoine, his hypocrisy, his treachery, made her blood boil once more, made her heart beat faster. As for Paul, it was too early to sort out her feelings. She was confused, disappointed, too thunderstruck by his sudden turnaround.

She got back on the bicycle and was soon on the main street of the town. Where could she go now? She saw the sign for the Hotel du Périgord on her left, remembered dining in its restaurant with her parents on special occa-sions. She had never even considered entering it on her own for a drink at the bar. That was something nice girls didn't do. But it looked warm and inviting, and in spite of the fact that she wasn't a drinker, she wanted a drink. Maybe I'll turn into a Juliette, she thought. Wouldn't that be ironic?

No more nice girl, she decided as she opened the door. She heard an explosion of laughter and turned to see a boisterous group of German soldiers drinking, shouting, joking and clapping each other on the back. Some stood at the highly polished zinc bar, while others sat at little tables that had been set up next to a tiny dance floor. Only then did she remember Gisèle telling her that the hotel served as the Germans' informal headquarters. A few other women were there as well, some of them clearly professionals plying their trade, others … Suddenly she felt weary. She didn't want to know who they were and why they were there. She decided to order one drink and leave.

Things looked up after the first drink. The world looked different, better. Maybe she could indeed resurrect her life from the ashes. She groaned inwardly. How could things have come to this point? Preferring not to analyze her situation or dwell on her misery, she ordered a second drink, and then, finishing it quickly, a third. She got up to dance, alone, but was soon joined by a short, fat German who stank of too much beer. She didn't care. It was fun to dance, forget her troubles.

"Mademoiselle… *très jolie*," he murmured, ogling her lasciviously and pressing himself against her. He smelled of sweat and beer breath and held her far too closely, but never mind, she told herself. She was here to have fun, and if it meant dancing with a nasty little German, then so be it.

As the afternoon wore on, it seemed to her that others broke in to dance with her, and that she laughed a lot and suddenly thought of herself as witty, clever and brilliant. At the same time, she knew something was wrong. She felt herself stumble, then someone picked her up and led her to a chair, making sure she didn't slip off of it. The kind face of the German—did Germans have kind faces, she asked herself? —the one she'd met in the castle, some name that started with a "W", loomed in front of hers. The officer, who knew what could happen when an entrancing young woman had too much to drink, seemed to take responsibility for her. A good thing, she thought dimly; she, like many other women, had heard the stories of what happened to women when soldiers lost control of themselves.

The Kommandant bent down to her now and said firmly, in a low voice. "Let's be discreet, Mademoiselle. You've had too much to drink. I will escort you back to the castle." He took her arm gently and pulled her to a standing position.

Across the room, Luc, who had entered the bar to deliver a pair of boots to the Kommandant, tried to conceal his alarm upon seeing Séverine. Behind his confident exterior, though, he was trembling. When he had told Pierre about the Kommandant's aide depositing a pair of the officer's boots at the shop for fast repair, his leader had immediately seen it as an opportunity.

"Get word that you'll deliver his boots to the hotel," Pierre had told him. "Make up some story about wanting the soldiers to see what good work you do. While you're there, take a look around, see who's there, try to pick up any information you can about their moves."

Séverine had spoiled it all.

He didn't have time to speculate on why Séverine was there, sitting in the officer's lap no less, but he knew one thing: he wanted her out. What if she identified him as a communist? But it was too late to leave—the German had spotted him and was signaling him to come to his table.

Luc strode across the room, shook hands with the Kommandant, delivered the highly polished boots and cast a glance at the inebriated Séverine as if she were a problem rather than a person.

"I know her, I have since we were children. I can take care of this," he informed the German with what he hoped was the right mixture of respect and self-confidence. Turning to Séverine, he announced, "Time to leave, my dear. You've had far too much to drink." He gave the Kommandant one of those man-to-man looks that said 'These women! We've got to protect them when they go too far, like this one obviously has.' He helped Séverine to her feet. "Come on now. I'll take you home." He didn't say where home was, but he had heard she was staying at the castle and couldn't imagine her anywhere else. He gently pulled on Séverine's arm.

The Kommandant tightened his grip around Séverine's waist.

With two different men making demands on her, Séverine briefly regained lucidity. In a resurgence of energy, she slapped Luc's hand away. "Don't touch me," she slurred. "Good old Luc to the rescue. I don't need you. I'm not your dear. I'm *this* guy's dear," she said, leering at the German and leaning against his chest.

"Come on, Séverine," Luc said in exasperation. "You're pickled. Be a nice girl and come with me. You know you have nothing to fear. I'll take you home, you'll sober up, and we'll all be happy things didn't get any worse, I can assure you."

She scowled at him. "I don't want you, Luc. I may be pickled—rhymes with tickled, ha ha—but know what I want. And it isn't you." She turned pointedly back to the German Kommandant, patting his face and enjoying his embarrassment.

Luc threw up his hands in a gesture of resignation. There was no point pursuing this any further, he knew; if he pushed Séverine, who knew what she would blurt out at him? He felt ready to punch the Kommandant, but he knew he would be killed on the spot if the Germans found out who he was.

He looked at Séverine one more time. She had always possessed the bearing of a queen, but now she was slumped across the Kommandant's lap. She had always spoken so articulately. Now she slurred her words. He looked at her wedding ring, in the form of a daisy with small diamond petals encircling a large diamond in the center. Every time she moved her hands, the precious stones emitted small shafts of bright light. He could imagine the ring sparkling as Séverine held a glass of champagne and conversed with the country's wealthiest men and women in tastefully decorated reception rooms; he imagined the huge gilded mirrors, the gleaming parquets and floor-to-ceiling windows. He had never been invited to such receptions, of course, and would never be able to afford a piece of jewelry like the one on Séverine's delicate finger.

"Well, I tried," he said to the Kommandant, giving what he hoped was a casual shrug. "She's all yours. I wish you luck."

The German officer departed with Séverine, and the music and the noise and the drinking carried on. Luc watched them go. He was going to leave the place very soon himself. He realized he was no longer worried about Séverine informing on him; no one would be able to understand her garbled words. As for the Germans, they were pigs when they drank, imbibing too much too quickly. These drunkards weren't going to provide any worthwhile information—they could barely stand up, let alone formulate a coherent sentence.

Today, they were in a particularly festive mood, opening an unusually large number of bottles they retrieved from a large number of cases, perhaps from a cellar they had looted. That, at least, he could tell Pierre.

He sniffed the air. It smelled of stale liquor and body odor. He couldn't bear to be around them one more minute.

On his way out, he glanced at the crates on the floor.

They had been filled with bottles of vintage wine when he entered. Now they were almost empty. He wondered once again about the sheer number of bottles; he wondered what they had been celebrating.

* * *

Gisèle rearranged a bouquet of flowers while trying to decide whether to change into more relaxing evening wear for a recap of the day with Séverine. Her thoughts were interrupted by a loud knock on the door. She opened it to find her houseguest, the Kommandant, with a disheveled and decidedly tipsy Séverine looking foolish as she leaned on his arm. The officer could barely conceal his irritation and disgust.

In a flash, Gisèle summed up the situation and reacted accordingly. She managed to look both upset and indulgent as she gave the sorry-looking Séverine a once-over. Then, with a sign and a shrug, she said to the Kommandant, "Ah, my little protégée. She has obviously misjudged her capacity for alcohol. Thank you for escorting her home. Now, if you'll excuse me, I'll take over and we won't say another word about this regrettable incident."

She wasn't sure how good the officer's French was—his accent sounded very good indeed—but she counted on the slightly imperious and firm tone of her voice to get the idea across. He was being dismissed. Still wearing a distinct look of displeasure, he bowed formally and left to spend another night in the west wing.

Her heart beating fast, Gisèle bolted the door. She pushed and pulled at a giggly Séverine and managed to propel her to her bedroom. With a physical strength she didn't even know she had, she hauled her onto the four-poster bed and left her on top of it, fully clothed.

"Tomorrow's another day," she told herself. She dreaded it.

* * *

Gisèle sat in a wing chair in the library, her hands folded, her legs crossed at the ankles, as she waited for Séverine. Before sunrise—she couldn't sleep after dismissing the Kommandant and getting Séverine to bed—she'd slid a note under her door. It said simply "10 o'clock. Breakfast in the library." Séverine would be surprised, she knew: Gisèle rarely ate breakfast and when she did, it was early and in the dining room. Séverine would know that the summons was not for breakfast, but for a "talking-to".

Gisèle had spent the night pacing anxiously back and forth in her bedroom. She hadn't allowed herself to go to the library, the place she read, wrote and conducted serious talks like the one she planned to have this morning, until she had calmed down. She knew that once she was in it, facing Séverine, she would need to project an image of authority and self-assurance, just as she had when she had let Just go all those years ago. Before she confronted him she had been in her bedroom, frantically rehearsing what she would say. Once in the library, though, she had stood perfectly straight, her clear blue eyes looking frankly into his, to deliver the simple message: he was fired. The fact that she hadn't liked or respected Just hadn't made her job any easier. She simply had never liked dismissing workers. It reflected poorly on her; it meant she wasn't a good judge of character. She had always tried to be, but today, once again she wasn't so sure.

* * *

At 10:15 Séverine, her eyes filled with sleep, let herself quietly into the library.

"I am so sorry," she apologized, looking at her watch and smiling sheepishly at Gisèle. "It was a late night."

"Sit down, Séverine." Gisèle pointed to the sofa, where the eight-year-old Séverine had drunk her first cup of tea. An image of the captivating child flashed through her mind, but she shut it out. She mustn't let nostalgia get in her way.

"I know about last night," Gisèle said brusquely. "The entire village knows about last night."

"What do you mean?" Séverine asked.

"Please." Gisèle made a silencing motion and held up a small package.

Séverine frowned. "What is that?"

"It's for you. Delivered to the door anonymously early this morning." Gisèle handed her the package. "Open it."

Séverine turned it over in her hands, puzzled, then ripped off the crude brown paper wrapping, which bore her name in block letters. Inside was a black wooden coffin the size of her hand. "What's this all about?" she said, looking at the countess in bewilderment.

"What this is all about is your unpardonable conduct last night," Gisèle said, fighting to keep the anger and disappointment from her voice. "What got into you, Séverine? In all the years I have known you, I have seen you act in many different ways—funny, flippant, enthusiastic, frustrated, angry. But I have never seen you, until now, do something quite so imbecilic, something that has put you—and perhaps the rest of us—in danger."

Séverine's eyes flashed and she opened her mouth to protest.

"Please hear me out," the countess cut in. "You're a grown woman, Séverine, and I'm no longer your mentor. When you were growing up, I tried to open you up to the world, teach you the manners that would make it easy for you to move around in a society you weren't born into. I hosted your wedding reception, and if you're here now, it's because I wanted you to have a place of refuge to get away from a marriage that seems to be going badly, even though I don't know the details. You have always had a spark I admired. You've always been spontaneous, even unbridled, and until now, I've found those qualities attractive in you."

She picked up her teacup, sipped, and replaced the cup carefully in its saucer. "I know you, Séverine, and my guess is that you let yourself go last night because of recent disappointments in your personal life. But look at the facts from an outsider's viewpoint, by people who don't know you like I do. A married woman, alone in a bar that the German soldiers stationed in this village have adopted as their watering hole, gets drunk and is escorted home by the officer staying in this castle. You tell me: what does that look like?"

Séverine sat motionless as Gisèle answered her own question. "I'll tell you: it looks like you consorted with the enemy." Her voice faltered briefly. "Your irresponsible conduct has compromised everything I've tried to do." Then, in the angriest tone she had ever used with Séverine, she said, "I don't know what set you off last night, but you would have been better off coming back here to cry on my shoulder than prancing into a bar alone and making a fool of yourself with the Kommandant."

Indignant, Séverine broke her silence. "You can't talk to me like that. You can't order me around the way you always have. If I want to drink in a bar and dance with German soldiers, so what? I can do whatever I want without your approval or disapproval. All men are liars and cheaters anyway, so what's the difference?" She eyed the countess boldly. "And *you* certainly talk to German officers."

"I talk to them when I am obliged to. I don't socialize or

drink with them," Gisèle said in a flat voice. "I have managed to create a working relationship with the Germans billeted in this town. The castle has been searched. A wing was requisitioned for the officer who brought you home last night. I have to put up with that, but I don't like it. So far, with the exception of the search I told you about, the Germans have kept their distance and I want to keep it that way. I am polite to them because I have to be, but there has never been and there will never be any familiarity. Do you understand?

"And do you also understand that I cannot have a person who has transgressed the rules as a guest, even if those rules are unwritten? Your behavior is jeopardizing everything I've tried to do. You're a danger to me now, Séverine, but I'll take care of myself and the castle. I always have. But most of all you are a danger to yourself. Don't you see what's going on? Don't you see what's going to happen when the Germans lose the war and people suspected of collaborating get their due? Do I have to draw a picture? There are a lot of people around here who have scores to settle, and are doing so even as I speak. I don't want to see you on anyone's list of suspected collaborators, so I'm going to 'order you around', as you say, one last time.

"While you were sleeping off your hangover, I called Georges, who said that Paul will take care of this. He'll be here soon to help you get out of town. You must do everything he tells you." She raised her hand in a silencing gesture as Séverine started to protest once again.

"I don't know what went on with you and Paul. All I know is that you visited his family the day before yesterday, that you were euphoric yesterday and that I didn't see you until last night, when you were escorted to the door in a terrible state by the German officer who is staying in this castle." She paused. "Whatever happened between you and Paul the last two days is not my business, but as long as you are in my home and with me, you and your reputation are my concern. There is only one solution for you, and that is to leave this village as fast as you can. You're lucky Georges and Paul love you so much and will take such risks for you."

She stood, signaling the end of the talk. "There's nothing more to say. The situation is clear: you've been seen fraternizing with the enemy; you've received a coffin. It's a serious warning. If you don't accept help, your life is in danger. I can't keep you here any longer."

She walked toward the door, then stopped a minute to regain control over her trembling voice and turned back to look at Séverine. "Do you know what the Germans were celebrating in the bar last night? Yesterday afternoon, a group of soldiers surrounded the mayor's house, shot him at point blank range, then looted his cellar before burning his barn and house to the ground. He was an honorable man who had impeccable taste and loved good food and drink. He was a frequent guest at the castle." She paused again and pressed her lips together, her face deathly pale. "But I'm getting off track. The wines that the soldiers—and you—were imbibing at the hotel were his. They were booty, the spoils of war if you will."

Séverine blanched. The smoke she had seen as she cycled back to the town. All those crates on the floor of the bar filled with bottles of fine wines the German soldiers kept taking out and opening. They had been celebrating. A wave of nausea seized her.

Gisèle stared at Séverine, willing herself not to rush over and comfort this naïve young woman who so clearly still needed her.

But it was too late now. She couldn't undo what had been done. This time Séverine had gone too far.

With a last glance at her protégée, she turned, stepped out into the hallway, and closed the heavy wooden door behind her.

* * *

Shortly after Gisèle had called on the pretense of needing a doctor at the castle, Georges shut the door to his office and stood facing Paul. Neither man spoke as they each took their respective places, Georges in his old leather chair behind his sturdy oak desk, Paul in front of the desk seated on one of the utilitarian chairs for the patients. Fitting, Paul thought glumly; right now he felt he did indeed need a consultation.

Georges searched his son's face. He couldn't say he was surprised by what Paul had told him—that he loved Séverine and was planning to leave Juliette for her—yet he would have preferred not to hear it. At the same time, he was touched that Paul would come to him for advice.

"Paul, my son," he said gravely. "Let's deal with first things first. The countess has asked me to enlist your help in getting Séverine out of town." He told Paul briefly of the events Gisèle had recounted to him. "Séverine has been impulsive and irresponsible, and now her life is in danger. You and I know that Séverine has never been interested in politics—but others don't. Appearances count, and her being in that bar with the Germans looks bad, very bad. As far as the rest of what you have told me is concerned, we'll discuss it later." He took out his pipe, filled it from the gray cubic package of *le petit gris* Caporal Superior tobacco on his desk and gently tamped the tobacco down with his finger. He lit it, took a satisfying puff, and turned his attention back to Paul.

"I know how you feel about Séverine, and how close you two have always been. From what I have observed, your bond with Séverine has strengthened rather than weakened, despite your being apart, and it's led to the situation you are describing to me now. You've got a major problem

292

on your hands with this, Paul. I wouldn't want to be in your place. If you choose Séverine, you'll be a pariah. She was already branded as a social climber, even though she's always been loyal to her family and never denied her social station. If you pursue things with her, she'll be branded as a home-wrecker, even though she most certainly is not. And her actions last night have marked her as a collaborator, even though we both know that she isn't, and that her only mistake was to get drunk and act foolishly."

He leaned back in his chair and took another draw on his pipe. "What you do regarding your personal situation with Séverine is your decision, but one you will need time to think out carefully. I'm not for breaking up families. I never believed in passion or a passionate act as the basis of a marriage. Only you know what, in good conscience, you can or cannot do." He hesitated, then added, "Since we are talking about honesty, Paul, I'll be honest. They say you only have one soulmate in life. Séverine is clearly yours. But they don't say that when you find your soulmate, you should automatically drop everything to be with her. You make your choices and accept the consequences.

"Take your responsibility, but don't lose out on true love. Don't live a life of regrets."

"Would you be talking about Gisèle?" Paul asked hesitatingly, aware that this was the first and most likely the last talk they would have on the subject.

"Oh, I have no regrets. Your mother is a fine woman. And Gisèle and I were like you and Séverine, close as two fingers on a hand. As you know, we are still great friends. She would do anything for me and I for her. Her calling you to come rescue Séverine is an example. But as for marriage—no, I didn't want to live my life as the doctor who lives in the castle. But as I said, I know what a soulmate is, and Gisèle is mine." He closed his eyes a few seconds, then rallied. "For the moment, however, let's focus on removing Séverine from immediate danger. Do you have a plan?"

"I'm going to the castle to speak with Séverine. She's so furious with me that she may not want to listen, but I'm certain she'll do what the countess tells her to do. I'll have a friend drive her to Sainte-Eulalie, where she'll wait for me to come later in the day to drive her to the train station in Limoges. From there, she'll take a train to Paris. She's safer there with her family than here. She's safer anywhere than here."

Georges nodded his head as Paul moved toward the door. "Godspeed," he said sadly.

Outside the study door, Huguette stepped away and moved back towards the kitchen. *Soulmate*. She wasn't surprised that Georges had described Gisèle as his soulmate; that had always been painfully obvious to Huguette, but hearing it cut her to the quick. The sting of her husband's words was quickly replaced by anger at Paul and Georges and Séverine and Gisèle, pity for Juliette and Julien, and an urgent need for action. The rest of them could waffle around and discuss their contemptible sentiments, but, she resolved, none of this was going to happen. Paul would not desert Juliette, nor would he run away with Séverine. It was all so preposterous. For a brief moment, she saw her family as a flimsy house of cards falling apart in front of her eyes, each member going his or her separate way. Setting her jaw, she disappeared into another part of the house.

Chapter TWENTY-FIVE

Luc drummed his fingers on the counter as he waited for Pierre and the other cell members to turn up. Why had they chosen his shop right in the heart of the town, he wondered? Suspicions might be aroused, even though they'd taken precautions. Everyone had been told to bring a pair of shoes or a satchel or boots, supposedly for repair. Still, Luc preferred that their meetings take place in the woods out of town. There, at least, it was safer.

Pierre came first, dangling a pair of well-worn boots in his hand and shoving them roughly across the counter. "You've worn these out, I see," Luc mumbled dutifully.

"I can't think of a finer repairman to take them to," Pierre replied, unsmiling. "Everything all right here?"

"Yes. I'll be closing the store soon. Go on up to the kitchen." He nodded his head to the wooden stairs leading up to his tiny quarters.

As the three others arrived, Luc busied himself with all the end-of-the-day activities. Soon he took out the Closed sign, fixed it on the door, turned off the ground floor lights and headed upstairs to where the four men were already seated at a rectangular wooden table. He acknowledged them with a nod and closed the curtains.

"I wish the war was over, if only to get some real coffee

instead of this ersatz stuff," Luc said with a grimace as he filled their cups.

"It will be over sooner than you think if we keep up the pressure," Pierre replied. He adjusted his horn-rimmed glasses, glanced briefly at his colleagues around the table and started the meeting.

"I don't have to tell you about the danger we're currently in. You've seen it for yourselves, with the arrival of the Boche troops right here in the village." His eyes showed a glimmer of satisfaction in spite of his ever-present self-control. "We've done such a good job of harassing the enemy that Wehrmacht troops have been sent here with a specific goal: to wipe us out and intimidate the population. That's their job. Ours is to intimidate the collaborators and make examples of traitors so that people see the cost of being on the wrong side."

One man raised his hand. "How can you know for sure who is a collaborator? Is a woman smiling at a German soldier a collaborator? Is someone whose job forced him or her to trade with the Germans a collaborator? That would mean most of the population," he remarked.

Pierre's eyes narrowed as he gave his comrade a dismissive look. He looked pointedly around the table, eyeing the men one by one. "This is no time for doubts. Never forget who we are fighting and why. We are fighting to defeat Fascism and establish a socialist government in France with the help of Comrade Stalin, and thanks to the heroic efforts of the Red Army. We cannot achieve our goals if we lose sight of them. We must be tough, unbending, efficient."

He proceeded to read out a list of villagers who had engaged in activities that had put them on the side of the enemy. The accusations ranged from refusing to give to the cause when asked—whether the request was for vegetables, meat or money—to "consorting with the enemy". For women, that meant anything from flirting to sleeping with a German.

Hélène Martin, he read. *Gestapo*.

Jean Gaucher. *Gestapo*.

Bruno Laurent. *Gestapo*

Robert Luchaire. *Gestapo*.

The man who had asked the question about collaborators stared at a spot on the tablecloth. *Gestapo*? That was a serious charge, one without proof. How could Pierre be sure of what he was saying? What were his sources? And didn't these people, no matter what they'd done, or were said to have done, deserve to plead their case, be put on trial? He knew two of the people on the list and couldn't bring himself to suspect either of working for the enemy. Yet he didn't dare protest. He, like everyone else, was afraid of Pierre.

The last name on the list was Séverine Sevanot. Pierre found particular satisfaction in rolling her name off his tongue. His suspicions, starting with their conversation in that ride down on the train from Paris, had been confirmed. The drunken incident with the Germans was in line with all she'd told him about her aristocratic life up there in the castle and her pro-Vichy sentiments. And finally, her behavior in the hotel bar clearly demonstrated whose side she was on. She'd betrayed her class, and now she'd betrayed her country.

Luc felt a cold shiver run through him. He should have known that Séverine's name would be on a list—after all, he was the one who had reported back on the evening at the bar—but now he was shocked and startled to hear her name out loud. He struggled to keep his hands from shaking and averted his eyes so as not to meet Pierre's gaze.

Once again, he imagined Séverine as a young girl, shy and polite, kind to him and witty. He remembered Séverine admiring his carvings, exclaiming over the perfect little wooden rabbit, tucking into her pocket the package with the love letter he'd written her and never mentioning it again. Séverine had always had everything he wanted, but he had never quite been able to work up the resentment or jealousy his parents and other villagers had towards her. Despite everything, despite himself, he'd had a soft spot when it came to her. He couldn't help it.

But those images were quickly replaced by others: Séverine, back in the village for her society wedding to her urbane rich jeweler, clearly a class enemy. Séverine strutting around town in those city clothes, wearing that gorgeous outsized diamond, throwing her wealth in the face of all those who had suffered during the war and not even realizing it. Séverine at the hotel bar, drunk and refusing his help as she caressed the Kommandant's face.

"These enemies are to be eliminated. Is that clear?" Pierre asked in an icy voice. He looked each man in the eye, his gaze resting a beat longer on the doubter and Luc.

The quiet in the room signified assent.

Chapter TWENTY-SIX

Like Séverine had done only a few days before, Paul approached the castle from the sidewalk opposite it. Like Séverine, his mind filled with images from long ago: he remembered taking tea with Séverine and the countess as a young boy, and attending Séverine's wedding reception on the lawn—and their near transgression in the cellar, but he chased the thoughts from his mind. He thought again about his father and Gisèle, but Georges hadn't told him anything he hadn't already guessed. He had always sensed something between them, some unspoken connection that was almost palpable when they were together, but he had ascribed it to their being old friends. It wasn't his business, and he didn't want to think about what their relationship had been—or was now for that matter. He was, though, moved that his father, normally so guarded with his emotions, so prudent and taciturn, had confided in him.

He clutched his well-worn doctor's bag as he headed up the walkway. His excuse, if anyone asked, was that Gisèle was ill, which was a distinct possibility, he thought, considering what she'd been through with Séverine over the last twenty-four hours. As he raised his hand to knock on the front door, questions and doubts assailed him. What was he doing here? How could Séverine have made such a fool of herself? How could she continue to be so obtuse? He had no worries about her conduct reflecting on him: as the town doctor, he was too well-known and respected to be tainted by what she'd done last night. He knew that most of the villagers would agree that you can't control the stupid actions of childhood friends.

And what she'd done was monumentally stupid. If she'd put a sign on herself saying "I am a collaborator," she couldn't have been more effective. So why am I helping her? he asked himself, although the answer was clear.

The countess answered his firm knock on the door in person.

"Not much sleep?" he asked, noting her drawn face.

Gisèle simply nodded and led him to the door of the library. "I don't have to tell you it's urgent. I am counting on you to protect her, Paul. You know how headstrong and foolish she can be." She stopped talking abruptly as if she'd already said too much.

He found Séverine standing with her back to him, gazing out the tall windows at the formal gardens. She turned at the sound of his footsteps. "Rescue mission, Doctor?" she said mockingly, the expression on her face defiant.

"Not funny, Séverine," Paul snapped. "You wouldn't by chance consider apologizing for what you've done, would you?" Séverine looked at him, a blank expression on her face. "No? That's what I thought. Well, I'll spare you the sermon. I know all about the scene in the bar, and I know about the coffin, so you don't have to fill me in."

She raised her hand to object.

"No," he said. "No time for that now. Let's be practical. I'm here to tell you that we've arranged to get you out of this town. In fifteen minutes a car is going to come to the castle and wait for you behind the stables to take you to Sainte-Eulalie. You'll stay there in the church and wait for me to come. It won't be until after my last consultation this afternoon—I can't raise any suspicions. Please pack your belongings and be ready.

"When I collect you from Sainte-Eulalie, I'll drive you to Limoges to take the train to Paris. The faster you get away, the better your chances are of survival. Is that clear?"

"Well, that was certainly succinct, Paul. Are you like that with your patients too?" Séverine asked.

"No. Generally, I'm gentler with my patients, but then none of them has ever been in the spot you are."

"And why am I in this spot, as you call it, Paul? Aren't you in a spot too? And why are you helping me? Out of guilt?"

Paul felt his self-righteousness deflate; he stared at the floor. Séverine always got it right when it came to him. Of course, guilt had compelled him. He'd behaved abominably toward Séverine, making love to her with abandon and desire, then abruptly turning off his emotions after the scene with Juliette. It was cruel.

And even though he loathed what she'd done afterwards, he saw it for what it had been: the furious and self-destructive act of a woman who had been hurt, and hurt, and then hurt some more. He knew that she was incapable of consorting with the enemy; her public act of collaboration was simply a public act of being Séverine.

And he had been the cause of it.

He raised his head and cautiously met her eye. He was aware that people were likely searching for Séverine even as they traded barbs here. He needed to get her away from the castle, away from the village, out of the region.

Séverine stood, unmoving, her arms folded across her chest.

"You're so irresponsible, Séverine," he exploded. "For God's sake, you've endangered yourself and all of us—do you even realize how serious this is?"

"Irresponsible? Look who's talking about irresponsibility, Paul."

For a long moment they glared at each other the way they had when they'd quarreled as children. And, as they had when they were children, each gradually and grudgingly gave ground now.

Séverine was the first to speak. "All right, Paul. You are irresponsible for making love to me and then telling me it was nothing to you. And I am irresponsible for the way I got my revenge. Are we even?"

"Never mind that right now," he said tensely. He scanned the terrace and the walkway; his ears were on alert for any unusual sounds. "I'll be in Sainte-Eulalie this afternoon. Until then, be prudent for once in your life."

He hurriedly picked up his doctor's bag and started for the door. But before he reached it, he turned around, walked back to her, and gently touched her arm. "We've both made mistakes, big ones. This isn't the time to talk about them. But we will. I can guarantee you that."

* * *

Huguette wasn't used to idleness. She always had a project, whether sewing or knitting or cooking, but today her knitting was going badly—she kept dropping stitches in the sweater she was making for Julien. Her mind was whirling. Juliette was shut up in her bedroom; Huguette had long had her suspicions, and now they had been confirmed.

Paul should have dealt with her problem, and long before now. But he hadn't. And why hadn't Paul done something for his wife? she asked herself bitterly. That, too, had suddenly become crystal clear. Paul was in love with Séverine. He was her soulmate, just as Georges was Gisèle's.

She found herself struggling to swallow, to breathe. The

truths she had refused to acknowledge, the emotions she had refused to give free rein were pressing in on her. She had been in denial, living in a world of illusions in which she had made a perfect marriage, had successfully climbed the social scale, had created an affectionate, close and loyal family, all of whom loved each other.

She closed her eyes as a wave of regret, fury, jealousy, and self-loathing poured over her, then she opened them again with a start as the doorbell rang.

Two young men she'd never seen before stood on the stoop. One, short, emaciated and in need of a haircut, was coughing badly. The other, tall, good-looking and affable, explained they were acquaintances of Paul's and wondered if he or his father could see his friend.

"I'm so sorry," said Huguette, regaining her composure. "You can wait if you like, or come back later, but they are both full up now with patients."

"That's all right. We'll be back later," the tall man replied. He turned to leave, and then turned to Huguette once more. "By the way," he said casually, "I've been told Séverine Sevanot is a friend of your family. I know she's in town, but would you know where she's staying? An old school friend would love to contact her."

Huguette kept her face carefully neutral. Even to her the words rang false. She lowered her head slightly, as if thinking, so that the two young men were unable to witness the multitude of contrary emotions that were crossing her mind and surely showing in her face. When she had composed herself, she answered impassively in her doctor's wife voice.

"Séverine?" she replied. "Oh, yes, we did have the pleasure of seeing her when she first arrived. She's staying at the castle, but I do recall that she often spends time in Sainte-Eulalie. Such a picturesque village, as you surely know. The Romanesque church is especially nice."

She closed the door and walked briskly to the kitchen. It was time to make lunch.

Chapter TWENTY-SEVEN

Sainte-Eulalie: March 1944

As Séverine entered the twelfth-century church, the late-afternoon sunlight streamed in through the stained-glass windows, illuminating the faces of the saints and the Virgin Mary. She crossed herself and genuflected before taking a place in a pew. She'd always found solace in churches, and this simple one, which inspired contemplation rather than awe, was her favorite.

She was grateful that this ancient church had been spared from the bombs and shelling so many places of worship had suffered in this war and the last. She remembered Paris's Église Saint-Gervais-et-Saint-Protais, another favorite of hers. Perhaps she would go there again when she returned to the city. It dated back to the seventh century, when fishermen and boatmen from the nearby banks of the Seine had worshipped there, and had grown to be a powerful church supported by the guilds. Then, on Good Friday 1918 a German artillery shell had landed on the roof, which had collapsed onto the congregation, killing ninety-one men, women and children. The church had been painstakingly rebuilt, but its haunting story of innocents dying in a sacred place had stayed with her, and each time she visited she had had to almost physically shake off the images of the rubble and dust and horror that came to mind.

War, she thought. Such a pointless, horrific endeavor, and yet people never seemed to learn anything from it. Some, like her husband, openly sided with the Vichy government. Others, like her sister and Luc and Paul, fought in their own ways against Vichy and the Occupation. She, like her parents and a great majority of people, simply wanted the war to be over and done with. Why had she never discussed that with her husband? Why had she turned a blind eye to anything but her own needs? The answer to that was clear: all she had wanted was to have a baby. Nothing else had counted.

And finally, in that one shocking moment, she had at last understood why her husband didn't want a child. That realization had brought her back to Sorignac, to her rapturous reunion with Paul, their declaration of love, his rejection...and her revenge. She shuddered. Even if taking vengeance on all men had been justified in her mind, how could she have gone so far as to drown her sorrows in a bar full of Germans, ending up literally in the lap of a Wehrmacht commander?

She had no way of knowing those soldiers had shot the town's beloved mayor, had burned his house down, were drinking the wine they had stolen during their rampage. But try to tell that to her accusers. People had always told her she was rash, and they were right.

She closed her eyes, blinking back tears as she bent her head. Paul would be here to collect her soon, and she felt an urgent need to wipe the slate clean. She must find a priest so she could confess.

Absorbed in her ruminations, Séverine didn't hear the footsteps on the cold stone floor. She didn't know whose hands touched her, whose strong arms pulled her from the pew. She saw the faces of the two men who seized her arms roughly and hustled her outside into a waiting car only fleetingly. She didn't see the face of the man in the driver's seat, only the shape of his head and the color of his hair, both of which she recognized.

The black Citroën Traction Avant picked up speed as Séverine kicked and tried to fight the two men on either side of her, but they gripped her arms tightly.

The car soon reached a clearing in the woods, where the driver and the muscular guards flung open the doors and jumped out, dragging Séverine with them. She felt the cold metal of a gun at her back as she was marched into the forest by the two rough guards.

"Leave her to me," the man with the gun suddenly ordered them. The noise of their leaving, the snapping and cracking of twigs of trees underfoot, gradually receded. Soon, the only sounds were the twittering of birds high in the trees.

Now she was alone with the man pressing the gun against her flesh. Abruptly, he halted, releasing the pressure of the weapon, and swiftly stepped in front of her.

"Justice will be done," Luc intoned. His face was expressionless as he raised his arm and aimed his pistol at her. Yet his arm was trembling and his voice was unnatural. She was close enough to see tears in his eyes as he whispered, "Run! Go on now—run."

Séverine held her head high and stayed where she was. "Come on, Luc. Put your gun down and we'll talk."

He wavered slightly but kept the weapon pointed at her.

She continued in a calm voice, "You gave me your carved rabbit all those years ago. I even took it with me as a good luck charm when the Germans invaded and we fled Paris. I loved that rabbit. I think it symbolized freedom for you, freedom from your father and freedom in general. The way you carved it—it looked like it was going to spring from its crouched position and take off."

307

She paused. "But I'm not like your rabbit. You see, I have no reason to run, nothing to run from. I won't defend myself, because there's nothing to defend. I do not deserve to be here, and you know it. I won't run."

She was silent for a moment as she looked him directly in the eyes and repeated firmly, "I won't run."

Luc hesitated for a second, and then anger and purpose replaced his absurd and useless urge to spare her. It wasn't his fault he had always loved her. These things happened. But even now, even as he threatened to take her life, she was defying him once again, as she always had and always would. He had given her this opportunity to get away and she had chosen to stand up to him, to prattle on about the rabbit that had gone back and forth between them. Why was she doing this? But then again, why did Séverine do anything she did? Who did she think she was, anyway?

Maybe she wasn't Gestapo, as they had labeled her. But the Party was right: she had fraternized with the enemy, betrayed her country. On top of that, she was a class enemy.

That's all there was to it.

Luc pulled the trigger.

* * *

The car wouldn't start and Paul cursed it. He was afraid to flood the engine and afraid someone—a patient or his mother or wife—would hear the choking noise and come to help him. He didn't need help. He needed to get out of there. One more try and it reluctantly chugged to life. Sainte-Eulalie was only a fifteen-minute drive. He was all right. He visualized Séverine as he drove away from the house and basked in the warmth he felt. To an outsider, it would seem incomprehensible, indeed outrageous, that he, a *résistant*, could forgive and even change his entire life for a woman some considered a collaborator. Yet that was exactly what he was planning to do. He didn't care what others thought or said. No one else knew her the way he did. She was ardent and passionate and made hasty moves that landed her in trouble. On top of that, she wouldn't listen to anyone, other than the countess and perhaps her sister. And of course, him. She had always listened to him and would listen to him now. He would fight all accusations against her and take on a lot of other battles as well. He was ready.

Sainte-Eulalie was calm as usual as he parked the car and got out. There was no sign of Séverine. She must be inside the church she so loved.

A feeling of unease came over him as he entered the empty sanctuary. He couldn't believe she would make light of their meeting and try to surprise him. It wasn't the moment to pull a prank.

He left the church and walked around the hamlet but still saw no trace of Séverine. He entered the cemetery, where they had made love only two days ago. The happy memory of their tender lovemaking was replaced by the memory of his rejection of her. He needed to talk to her about that, to explain. He had been a fool.

The cemetery was empty. Fighting down a wave of panic, he rushed back to the car and drove into the surrounding forest. Fear gripped him as he saw tire marks in a nearby clearing. He turned the engine off and got out. Instinct propelled him forward into the woods. Automatically he put himself in the place of someone who would want to do harm. Whoever had taken Séverine would have been in a hurry. She couldn't be far.

He found her only a few yards in. The bullet had gone straight to her heart; she'd tumbled to the ground, one arm flung to the side, the other close to her body. In a professional reflex, he bent down to take her pulse. As he touched her hand, he noticed the diamond ring she always wore was gone. The bastards. Not only did they kill, but they stole. He looked helplessly at her lithe figure, lightly caressed the face he knew so well. She looked defiant, even in death.

He had been on one knee, but in seconds he was lying beside her on the floor of the forest, gazing up at the green leaves and the blue sky above. He wanted to stay there forever.

Sorignac: 1945

Juliette and Huguette worked together to make a special cake for Julien's birthday. Although food supplies weren't abundant, they were a great improvement over the war years when flour, sugar, eggs and chocolate had been luxuries.

Restless, Julien started to follow his father to the clearing in the woods behind the house. Huguette stopped him.

"Leave your father alone. He'll be back soon," she said, enticing him with the offer of tasting the batter.

Paul meandered among the tall trees, his head down. His hair had turned entirely gray. He could almost see Séverine looking at him, then ordering him to get that lugubrious expression off his face. He expected her to pop out from behind a bush or tree and tap him on the shoulder. The echoes of their childish voices and the memory of their childhood games entered him like the thrust of a sword.

He approached their tree, touched its rough bark. With his finger he traced a line around the hole where he and Séverine had hidden their treasure as children. Immediately after her death he had searched the cavity to see if the heavy gold coin was there. It was, and there it remained, his only tangible memory of her. Now the tree was his pilgrimage, the place he went when he needed to be alone with her. He felt her presence; she was always in this place.

Huguette knew why he kept returning to the clearing. She too remembered Séverine and Paul playing their childish games, chasing each other around, in and out of her sight. Unlike Paul, she felt no sadness. Or guilt. She had done what she had to do.

On the other side of the village, a woman who had stopped by the shoe shop was admiring the diamond ring Luc's wife wore on her right hand. Many wondered how he could have afforded such an opulent jewel and where it came from. Most people had no idea. Some did. No one asked.

EPILOGUE

Marnes-la-Coquette: July 1994

Félix passed the rose bush, smiling as he thought of Kirk's enchantment with the lovingly cultivated little garden and the house. He was surprised that his mother, who could always sense his arrival, wasn't at the front door pretending to arrange the books on the shelves in the hall. Inside the house, which was always warm and welcoming and filled with bouquets of roses and the sound of music or the smell of pastry, all was still.

He knew that Caroline was dead even before he saw her, apparently asleep in her chair. He took her pulse to confirm the worst, then looked around the room as if it had betrayed him.

On the mantel among the familiar objects he noticed a new one, a white envelope marked *Félix*. Intrigued, he opened it and removed a folded sheet of paper covered with his mother's shaky but determined handwriting. He unfolded it, then scolded himself: he would read the contents later. But as he quickly scanned the message, certain words and phrases leaped out at him: "manuscript I wrote after the war," "he and I grew close," "the happy result of a magical moment I never regretted."

What manuscript? Who had become close with whom?

With his mother, there had always been so many mysteries, so many unanswered questions. When he was a young boy, he had considered himself lucky to be spared tales of the past. His mother had focused on the present, which had suited him just fine, and had filled everything around her with joy. But as he grew older he would from time to time ask her about his father, or her family, or the war, or how things were then. Her expression would become suddenly blank, and she would change the subject. At first he resented her silence; with the passage of time, he became indifferent—or so he told himself. He had always held on to the belief that someday she would tell him what she was hiding. And now, it seemed as if that was what she had done.

My darling Félix,

How odd to write a farewell note! But I realized that I might die before you ever knew anything about your past, and I wanted to be the one to tell you now, before it's too late. So whether I die in my sleep, which is my preference, or have to be carted off to hospital where I end my life in some ignominious way (let's hope not), I want to be assured that you will read this note I placed on the mantel. It will lead you to the manuscript I wrote after the war, when you were only four years old. In it, you'll find answers about questions you have surely asked yourself over the years.

You can thank your journalist friend, Kirk, for these revelations. As I spoke with him, I realized what a wall I had built around myself to forget the past and never speak of it. It was my way of blotting out the painful loss of my sister and Paul—but I know now that it was terribly unfair to you. I can only hope that you will forgive me.

You'll find the manuscript easily. It's in a box on the top shelf of my bedroom closet under a pile of sweaters. The key is in the first drawer of my dresser. I hid the key and the box all these years ago, predicting that you would never rummage in my affairs because I taught you to respect my privacy, and you always did.

What you read will, I hope, shed light on a period of time I steadfastly refused to discuss, so great was my hurt. My position was selfish, but it was the only way I could go forward.

I ended the manuscript with Séverine's death. But it was actually the beginning of another story, another chapter in my life. As you will learn when you read my tale—which, although fictional, is as close to the truth as I could come—Paul and Séverine and I had known each other since we were very little. Those two loved each other from the day they met, even though it took them quite a while to realize and acknowledge it.

I was the sister, the friend, the observer. I never had any romantic thoughts about Paul. But after Séverine's death, he and I grew close, united by our common grief and our childhood ties. We needed each other because we knew that we were the only people who had really known and understood Séverine. We consoled each other, laughed and cried together, remembered Séverine together. You were the happy result of a magical moment neither he nor I ever regretted.

Why didn't I tell you about Paul? Why was it so difficult? Because he was killed in an accident when you were two, and it was all too much for me. Losing my sister, losing the father of my child. … I constructed a new world and made up a story in which your father was someone I never really cared for and who had died in any case. I have few regrets in life, but this is one of them. Paul was a fine man, a wonderful, caring and reassuring doctor who was respected by all. Had he lived, I know he would have recognized you and you would have borne his name.

Now that you know who your father was, you can make inquiries about him and his life—if you wish to, of course. As for me, I hope my paintings will be a reminder of my life. Did you ever wonder why they were so colorful, so vivid? It was

314

because I wanted to create a beautiful world after the ugliness of war. I deliberately steered away from black and white, for it reminded me of the black and white judgments that condemned Séverine.

I leave you to mull over the tragedy of my sister's last days and to retain the one lesson that counts: revenge disguised as justice is not justice. Or, to put it more prosaically: Séverine's actions were imprudent and transgressive—but she did not deserve to die.

The letter continued but Félix put it down. He'd have plenty of time to read the rest and reflect upon it later. For the moment, he contented himself with taking in the cozy room, the sunshine that was now flowing in through the windows and warming it, the joyous colors of the flowers both inside and out. His mother had disciplined herself to keep her pain private. She had rebuilt her world, creating for the two of them a normal, joyful, positive life in a universe of her making.

And she had left him her story, the greatest gift of all.

AUTHOR'S NOTE AND ACKNOWLEDGMENTS

Although it uses historical facts, *Final Transgression* is a novel, a work of fiction. When I arrived in France in 1971, there were more than a few things I didn't know. One of them was the fact that I would marry a Frenchman and spend the rest of my life in France. Another was that I would need to learn about my adopted country – and there was a lot to learn. I knew, of course, about World War II (as seen from an American perspective) but I knew little about Vichy, the collaboration and the resistance and the daily life of the French under German Occupation. It is my hope that others who read this novel will learn something new about this period as well.

The book was based on a wartime story about the fate of a relative in my husband's family. Because I was so intrigued, I began reading about the southwest of France, where the events took place. I became aware of the vicious internecine wars between the French collaborators and *résistants*. The war was full of grey areas, as most wars are, but black and white judgments prevailed during the period called *l'épuration sauvage*, or the wild purge, that took place shortly before and after the end of the war, when more than 10,000 people in France are estimated to have been killed by their compatriots without trial. As soon as I immersed myself into the study of this relatively unknown aspect of the war, I knew I wanted to write about it, using historical facts about the place and period as the framework for an imaginary tale of love, betrayal, transgression and revenge.

My research consisted of reading scores of books on France covering the period before, during and immediately after the war. Some of those books are listed in the bibliography I have provided along with a glossary and a timeline. In addition to my reading, I traveled to the southwest of France, notably to the village of Oradour-sur-Glane, where, in 1994, for *Time Magazine*, I interviewed Jean-Marcel Darthout, one of the six survivors of the 1944 Nazi massacre of more than 600 villagers. Both the interview, in which Mr. Darthout recounted the events of that long-ago day, and my walks in the haunted streets of the martyred village then and on later visits were moving moments. A new town was built in 1946; the ruined village, classed as a historical monument, is open to the public. My research – the books I read, the places I visited, the people I interviewed – culminated in a vision of life before, during and after the Occupation, not only in Paris but in the provinces. The result was the imagined village that provides the setting for much of this book.

I would like to thank Samantha Chang and participants in her Parisian writing seminars – at both WICE and the American Library in Paris – for their careful reading and critiques of parts of the early draft. Special thanks go to my late friend, Janet Lizop, whose encouragement, editing skills, and knowledge of history spurred me on. I am only sorry that she did not live to see the book in print.

Many thanks to Linda Hervieux, Diane Johnson, Marilyn Kaye, Dorie Laurent, Tom Noble, Dana Pitts, Ron and Betty Rosbottom, Nancy Sayer, Lucy Sieger, Jan Tabet, Miriam Welty Trangsrud and Ward Welty for reading part or all of the manuscript and providing precious feedback. And thanks to John Pearce for other indispensable help.

My gratitude also goes to sons Benjamin and David Rochefort for their generous help on technical matters which remain a mystery to me and to other family members and friends too numerous to be named who encouraged me in this long endeavor. So many people were there for me along the way. I apologize if I have inadvertently left anyone out.

It goes without saying that this book could not have been written without the constant backing of my foremost reader, editor, historian and checker of historical facts, cook, husband and all-round supporter, Philippe.

GLOSSARY

Battle of Verdun (February 21, 1916 – December 18, 1916) – one of the longest and bloodiest battles of World War I, resulting in more than 700,000 dead

Boche – a pejorative French slang word for a German

Collaborationists – French citizens who sided with Marshal Pétain, the creator of the Vichy regime in France; the regime was nominally sovereign but was in reality controlled by the German authorities

Commune de Paris (1871) – a revolutionary government that ruled Paris for two months in 1871, culminating in a bloody repression called *La semaine sanglante* (the bloody week)

de Gaulle, Charles (1890 – 1971) – French General who, helped by Winston Churchill, created the Free French Government in London in WWII. The Gaullist government in exile became the legal government of France after its liberation

French Communist Party – a powerful party controlled by Moscow and paralyzed in the early days of the Occupation by the German–Soviet Pact, signed in 1939. After

Germany invaded the Soviet Union on June 22, 1941, the French Communist Party actively began a long and hard resistance

Gestapo – the police division of the Nazi Party, headed by Heinrich Himmler; it was responsible for the elimination of the political opponents and targets of the Nazi regime

Haussmannian buildings – Parisian buildings named after Baron Haussmann, the Prefect of Paris, who, between 1853 and 1870, carried out Napoleon III's orders to undertake a complete renovation of the city

La Coupole – famous Art Deco restaurant created in 1927 in Montparnasse where artists and writers gathered. Famous patrons included Pablo Picasso, Josephine Baker, Henry Miller, Henri Matisse, Amedeo Modigliani, Simone de Beauvoir and Jean-Paul Sartre

Maginot Line – a line of concrete fortifications named after French Defense Minister André Maginot and built between 1929 and 1938 on the borders of France to deter German invasions

Maquis – a general term meaning "hiding places outside towns"; in France, the term often referred to thick, dense woods in which *résistants*, called *maquisards,* hid during WWII

Milice – the paramilitary organization of 10,000 to 25,000 collaborators created by the Vichy government in 1943 to fight the Resistance alongside German troops. Merciless and greatly feared, a high proportion of its members were killed or sentenced to death after the war

Pétain, Philippe (Marshal) (1856 – 1951) – the most glorious general of the French Army in WWI and the idol of veterans. Constitutionally elected head of the government in June 1940, he created a new regime after the armistice (see *Vichy*, below)

Stavisky Affair/Feb. 6 riots (1934) – A political-financial scandal named after Alexandre Stavisky, an embezzler and crook protected by the moderate Radical-Socialist government. Stavisky's "suicide" in January 1934 was widely thought to have been a murder to keep him silent. *L'affaire Stavisky*, as it is known in French, resulted in the resignation of the French prime minister and violent anti-government riots

Stuka/Ju 87 – a German dive bomber and ground-attack aircraft whose sirens made a unique wailing sound to intimidate the enemy

Vichy – a spa town in the center of France, chosen as the capital of the collaborationist regime under Marshal Philippe Pétain because of its many hotels, which were used to house authorities

WC (water closet, toilet) – the name given to separate toilet rooms. An English term originally, the French pronunciation is a translation of the letters themselves: "doo-bluh-vay say"

TIMELINE OF
HISTORICAL EVENTS

February 6, 1934: Angered by the Stavisky Affair (see Glossary) and other political scandals, right-wing groups stage violent demonstrations against the government at the Place de la Concorde, with fifteen killed and thousands injured

August 23, 1939: The Soviet Union and Nazi Germany sign a pact of non-aggression and cooperation; the French Communist Party is outlawed, and its leader flees to Moscow

September 1939 – May 1940: The Phoney War, an eight-month period of relative calm between the declaration of war on Germany by France and the UK on September 3, 1939, and the German invasion of Belgium, Luxembourg and the North of France on May 10, 1940

June 10, 1940: The French government leaves Paris for Tours and Bordeaux; the city of Paris empties as thousands take to the roads in a mass exodus to flee the Germans

June 14, 1940: German forces occupy Paris, which had been declared an "open city" the previous day

June 18, 1940: From London, General Charles de Gaulle appeals to the French to continue the war against the Germans; meanwhile, Marshal Pétain asks for an armistice. Two-thirds of the country is now occupied by the Germans

End of 1940: Named "chief of state," Marshal Pétain sets up a new regime called Vichy that cooperates with Germany and makes laws excluding Communists, Jews and Freemasons from public office and business ownership. A system of rationing is organized, and citizens are issued coupons for everything from food to fuel

June 22, 1941: Germany invades the Soviet Union; the French Communist Party, no longer paralyzed by the 1939 pact, enters into resistance

December 11, 1941: Germany declares war on the USA. It is not effective until November 1942 with the invasion of French North Africa by US troops

February 1943: After the German defeat at Stalingrad and the liberation of Italy from Mussolini's Fascist regime, it becomes clear that the Allies will invade Europe, probably landing in France. The French Resistance splits into rival organizations

Spring 1944: The French Resistance is very active and significantly slows the movements of the German Army; numerous ambushes of German troops lead to massacres in retaliation

June 6, 1944: D-Day, the Allied invasion of Normandy, which begins the liberation of German-occupied France and later Europe

June 10, 1944: The SS Division das Reich encircles the village of Oradour-sur-Glane (35 miles from the fictional town of Sorignac, where the novel takes place), killing all but six of its 642 inhabitants. Men are rounded up into barns and sheds, where they are shot; women and children are locked in the church and burned alive

August 1944: A new French government led by Charles de Gaulle takes power, and the Vichy government takes refuge in Germany

May 8, 1945: VE Day, the end of the war in Europe

BIBLIOGRAPHY

Books in English

DUTOURD, Jean, *The Best Butter*. Simon & Schuster, New York, 1955, 247 pp. (novel)

FARMER, Sarah, *Martyred Village: Commemorating the 1944 Massacre at Oradour-sur-Glane*. University of California Press, 2000, 322 pp.

GILDEA, Robert, *Marianne in Chains: Daily Life in the Heart of France During German Occupation*. Picador, New York, 2002, 492 pp.

HORNE, Alistair, *The Price of Glory*. Verdun 1916, Penguin, London, 1990, 370 pp.

MASFRAND, Pierre & Guy Pauchou, *Oradour-sur-Glane. A Vision of Horror*. Official Publication, National Association of the Families of the Martyrs of Oradour-sur-Glane, 1992, 188 pp.

NÉMIROVSKY, Irène, *Suite française*. Vintage, New York, 2007, 416 pp. (novel)

OLSON, Lynne, *Madame Fourcade's Secret War*. Random House, New York, 2019, 464 pp.

PAXTON, Robert, *Vichy France. Old Guard and New Order 1940-1944.* Columbia University Press, New York, 1972, 478 pp.

RIDING, Alan, *And the Show Went On. Cultural Life in Nazi-Occupied Paris.* Alfred A. Knopf, New York, 2010, 400 pp.

ROSBOTTOM, Ronald, *When Paris Went Dark: The City of Light under German Occupation, 1940-1944.* Little, Brown & Co, New York, 2014, 448 pp.

ROSBOTTOM, Ronald, *Sudden Courage: Youth in France Confront the Germans, 1940-1945.* Custom House, New York, 2019, 320 pp.

SEBBA, Anne, *Les Parisiennes: How the Women of Paris Lived, Loved and Died under Nazi Occupation.* St. Martin's Press, New York, 2016, 435 pp.

VINEN, Richard, *The Unfree French: Life under the Occupation.* Penguin, London, 2006, 476 pp.

WEBER, Eugen, *The Hollow Years. France in the 1930s.* W. W. Norton, New York, 2014, 352 pp.

Books in French

AMOUROUX, Henri, *La Grande Histoire des Français sous l'Occupation. Un Printemps de mort et d'espoir Novembre 1943-6 Juin 1944 (T.7).* Laffont, Paris, 1985, 572 pp.

BERR, Hélène, *Journal 1942-1944.* Taillandier, Paris, 2008, 301 pp.

BOURDREL, Philippe, *L'Épuration sauvage.* Perrin, Paris, 2002, 561 pp.

FAUCON, Martial & Roger Ranoux, *Francs-Tireurs et partisans en Dordogne*. Le Lauze, Périgueux, 2006, 622 pp.

HEBRAS, Robert, *Oradour-sur-Glane. Le Drame heure par heure*. CMD, Saumur, 1992, 36 pp.

POUQUET, Jeanne, *Journal de l'Occupation en Périgord 1942-1945*. Ed. du Rocher, Paris, 2006, 252 pp.

SIEFRIDT, Françoise, *J'ai voulu porter l'étoile jaune*. Robert Laffont, Paris, 2010, 215 pp.

VERCORS, Jean Bruner, *Silence of the Sea/Le Silence de la Mer*. Bloomsbury Academic, London, 2019, 128 pp. (novel bilingual edition)

ABOUT THE AUTHOR

Harriet Welty Rochefort grew up in Iowa, traveled to France after graduating from college, and never left. She is the author of three nonfiction books about the French: *French Toast, French Fried* and *Joie de Vivre,* all published by St. Martin's Press. *Final Transgression* is her first work of fiction. Harriet lives with her French husband, Philippe, in Paris.

Her website is www.harrietweltyrochefort.com

Manufactured by Amazon.ca
Bolton, ON

18145324R00199